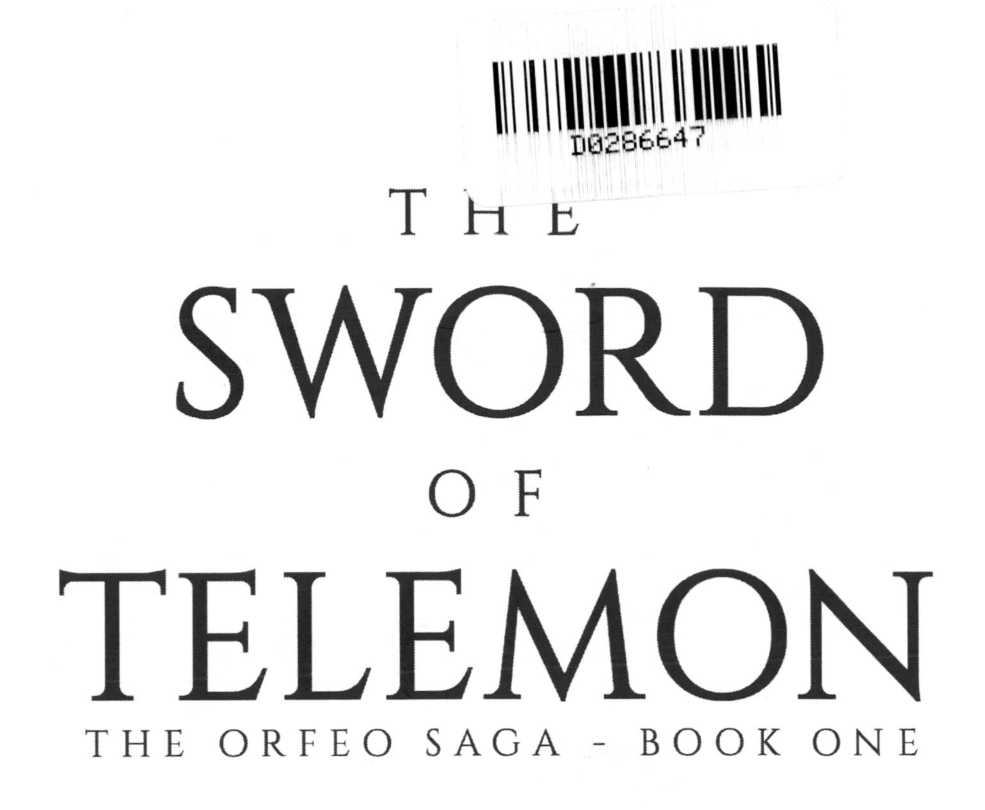


# THE SWORD OF TELEMON

THE ORFEO SAGA - BOOK ONE

MURRAY LEE EILAND JR

ISBN-13: 978-1517042226

ISBN-10: 1517042224

# Contents

# CHAPTER ONE

FAINT SOUNDS SEEMED TO MINGLE with the breeze, as they came first as distant whispers and then in wave-like gusts, now louder or softer, resounding along the valley walls and over the hilltops, carrying both a pleasant reminder of spring-awakened splendor and a sense of unease.

Subtly the day's stillness dissolved into disarray, as the restful rippling of the clear mountain stream now found counterpoint in the echoes of a great bronze bell, erupting in a voice of gentleness and power.

A sense of alarm arose, and faint cries of assembly carried from the valley, where men ran to join the commotion around the king's great tent.

Orfeo had been sitting on a flat rock overlooking the encampment when he recognized that something had gone wrong.

Raising himself more in disbelief than concern - as though his repose on the meadow and the bleating of his small goat flock made mockery of the frantic shouts below - he fastened his sandals and bounded from stone to stone toward the path and then raced in long loping strides down the hill.

The goats could look after themselves until he found them later.

When King Kiros summoned his people neither kinsmen nor retainers delayed, and now the mounting noise from below gave further spur for haste.

As he entered the encampment Orfeo heard first the clatter of swords in preparation for use before isolated words gave him a glimpse of what had happened.

"A raid," he heard repeated.

Someone must have seen danger approaching, and the image brought with it a vision of the Hannae from the north, galloping on their small, swift horses, bringing fire and pillage in their wake.

Once as a boy Orfeo had cowered in a thicket of juniper as the swordsmen had stood their ground against invaders and had finally driven them off.

Now he was ready to stand with the others, still a boy, perhaps, at sixteen summers, but able to wield a sword and hold his place in the line.

He ran toward his father's tent, dodging nimbly among the assembling warriors. The bell now sounded at close quarters and sent a chill of excitement through the crowd.

Standing on his platform before the great tent stood the king with raised arms.

Three armed men had pushed before him with weary movements, as if they had run a greater distance than the others and had already encountered the enemy.

"What news do you bring?" asked the king.

"We were too late," gasped the leader, Tyron, falling to his knees in shame and frustration.

"They reached the ship before us and sailed."

He was trying to catch his breath.

"They jeered at us as we reached the shore."

He held his weapon's hilt in smoldering rage.

"Then they are captive," said the king as if the admission robbed him of all inner peace. "My oldest son, Herron, and three companions were attacked today and seized by raiders."

Those in the crowd who had not already heard the news reacted both with shame and anger.

"It was a slave ship of Tyrian merchants," added Tyron.

"They landed several raiding parties, and they took captives among the men of Ikea to the south."

"Herron must be returned," said the king with a voice more focused upon a course of action.

"We must rescue or ransom my son from the slavers."

The assembled men shouted as a chorus in anger no less profound than their king's, while Orfeo stood in stunned silence as a new reality descended precipitously upon him.

His brother had been taken by raiders, and his father stood before the people and proclaimed that they must recover him.

There was talk of a council, and, after the king retired to his tent, messengers emerged at intervals to summon those who dwelt on the outskirts of the kingdom.

Orfeo wandered with conflicted thoughts to the tent he shared with his cousins, looking with confusion at his sword hanging on one of the outer poles.

There would be no immediate need for it, as the raiders were gone, and there would be a long preparation for any action they would take to recover Herron.

His cousins were still about the camp, speaking angrily of the outrage and apparently not immediately mindful that the king also had a second son nearly ten years younger than the first.

Yet Orfeo would likely be sought neither for aid nor counsel, as he had still not become a son again in his father's household, and the tribe looked upon him as curiously changed from his long sojourn in the kingdom of Pylos.

How strange it seemed for Herron, the brave and valorous warrior, to be sharing the same fate that the child hostage had once endured.

Orfeo stood silently just within the shadow of the tent and then, as if awakening from a frightful reverie, he bounded again toward the mountain, intent upon recovering his goats and finishing their feeding.

There was little chance that he would be missed.

Still Orfeo thought, as he climbed trail, of the great walled city of Pylos and how his life there had been one of both luxury and challenge. He remembered the warships of that city lined up in the bay of Megara, and the warriors of Pylos had been arrayed against the small tribe of Kiros, who as king had led his people in defense of their homeland.

It was another spring day much like this one, only it seemed part of the distant past.

Nearly ten years ago the captain of the ship of Pylos, Osric, had made his offer, and the king had retired to his tent and pondered.

There was talk about peace and an alliance and hostages. Orfeo still dimly remembered the words, although at the time he had not understood.

He had been brought before his father and told that he would be taken to Pylos by the invading army and that, because of this arrangement, there would be no battle and no dead men in the camp.

He was told that he would represent the Achians in Pylos and that his role was important as a guarantee of the peace.

But there was more to the story that he could see in his mother's eyes. She smiled through a veil of tears, and she seemed to tremble as she embraced him.

Was he five summers or six at the time?

He did not know his age for certain until he was in Pylos and there began to think in such terms as time and place and circumstance.

It was a new world, and he had loved much of it, but it had never seemed like home.

He had learned to read and write the strange script of the priests and the stiff, square signs of the traders.

He had been personal servant and companion to Nestor, son of the king of Pylos, who was two years older and just large enough to win at everything involving physical strength.

Besides, Orfeo was the servant, and he was expected to be neither brave nor clever.

Had not his own people surrendered him as hostage and abandoned him to the fates?

Orfeo reached the place where he had left his flock, and to his relief found they had strayed little from the patch of rich greenery.

Here in the solitude of the mountainside, the rush and commotion of the camp seemed an intrusion, and he sat back on the same rock from which he had been aroused, amused at himself for having run all the way back up the path.

Indeed, there was no reason for him to hurry, as his goats had virtually no other place to go, and slave traders were no threat to them.

The sun seemed to make the camp below dance in a magical array of flashes.

Even now swords were catching the light with their shining blades and accompanied the clamor of armor in signaling the outrage that had been committed against the tribe.

Yet in a curious way Orfeo felt less concerned than the others.

This rested on the idea that to him captivity in Pylos - where Herron would likely be sold in the slave market - was neither strange nor terrifying, and perhaps, as some of the people in the camp had said, Orfeo had become too much a boy of Pylos in his absence.

It had been eight or nine years before his escape, and even now he did not know just why he had climbed the unguarded wall of the villa and then slipped through the city gate at dusk.

Before his fifteenth year Orfeo had again managed to find his people, although at first his only guide was a vague knowledge of the direction in which he was to travel.

He had been taken aboard a merchant ship as a seaman, and he had sailed back and forth past his homeland several times before he had been able to determine that the land of King Kiros, the Achian, lay within the country some men called Minea and others Grecia.

By the time he reached home he was nearly sixteen, and then he came as a stranger, only dimly remembering a past he had sought with a determination that was neither reasoning nor resistible.

Orfeo, second son of Kiros, king of the wandering Achian peoples, had come home, and he stood like an enemy in the camp.

His mother looked without words and then wept, while the council seemed distressed and talked of reprisals from Pylos.

King Kiros had finally welcomed him home, but there was a reserve, a guardedness that left no room for a son who was not known to them and who was not heir to the throne.

Life had then slowly settled into an existence of moving from camp to camp in the summer and then remaining in the villages around Delphi in the winter.

He had at first lived in Kiros's tent, but things were not comfortable with Herron, who appeared to resent more than welcome the return of someone long forgotten.

It was as if Orfeo stood as a symbol of a shameful day all of them would have preferred to forget, and gradually he had come to understand how difficult his banishment had been for both his mother and father.

They had grieved long and bitterly over the fate that had taken a son, but it had been their duty to preserve their frail nation from a force that could have overcome all their defenses. The armies of Pylos had not been on Achian shores since that time, but they were still feared and respected on all sides of the great sea.

Orfeo knew only too well how futile any resistance would have been, and yet his stay in Pylos had taught him something else about life and living.

Again the clamor from below brought Orfeo from his reveries, and he realized that the sun was beginning its descent, and soon he must return the animals to camp.

It was always with regret that he walked down the path at the end of the day, as he enjoyed the solitude, and there were so many more complications below.

It was difficult enough for him to learn the customs of the tribe, but others seemed even more confused as to how to treat him.

He was, after all, a king's son; yet he chose not to live as a prince in the king's tent, but to dwell with cousins who owned goats and to spend days away from the interactions of the community.

This young Orfeo was a strange one, and perhaps he should not be completely trusted.

A mysterious air lingered about him, almost bewitching. He had a way with words and with song.

Perhaps it was something he had learned in Pylos, although his masters there had thought it to flow from his background under the skies.

Orfeo was both a poet and a minstrel, and it was said he could charm animals from the trees with his pipes and his soft, caressing voice.

"We've been looking for you."

On the trail Orfeo met his older cousin Euros, who seemed both worried and excited.

"The king has commanded that we march to Delphi for a great council. Messengers have summoned all the people, and we leave before dark."

Euros explained that the people had already started to pack, and as Orfeo neared camp he could see that many of the tents had already disappeared into great bundles of dark goathair cloth. All of the animals from the hills were being assembled together, and many had already been laden with things that needed to be carried.

Orfeo arrived at the tent of Euros just before others removed the stakes, and he managed to bundle his few possession into his winter cloak and then to bind everything together with a leather thong.

It seemed oddly comforting at moving time to have fewer possessions than anyone else; yet there was something humiliating in being a king's son who could carry his entire household in one pack.

Orfeo had taken part in a number of moves since his return from Pylos, but the experience always seemed both exciting and confusing, and he felt himself no natural part of it.

Everyone else seemed to know exactly what to do, and they went about their tasks as if all had been rehearsed, with roles assigned even to the children.

If someone were to tell him to do something, he always responded with no hesitation, but he had no way of anticipating the needs.

Perhaps he could be described as helpless in the midst of an activity everyone else had grown naturally to understand, although it was not clear that anyone else noticed.

They all seemed too busy with duties of their own.

The horsemen had already come to formation before the tent of Kiros, and they were now awaiting his appearance before they could begin the march.

Apparently there was a sense of urgency or need for haste, but few in the camp had any idea as to what had occupied the councils.

Shouts resounded among the men as they finally were directed to set off at a slow gallop. The rest of the tribe would follow, although now it was said that Kiros would ride ahead to meet Telemon at Delphi.

The legendary Telemon had been summoned from the northern marches, and he would lend his mighty sword and men at arms to any move Kiros might make to recover Herron.

Telemon the great warrior had led another part of the people in the north these many years, holding the Dorae at bay and securing the people of the south and their herds from the incursions of raiders.

Orfeo had never seen Telemon, but there was word of him from all the others.

His cousins had told stories of Telemon slaying a hundred Dorae warriors in one day, and once he had killed a lion with only a hunting knife.

Telemon was described as a giant and a man apart from others, a man of magical powers and fathomless strength. Rumor maintained that Zeus was his father when he had roamed the earth as a bull, and few expected Telemon to die as a mortal man.

The horse of Telemon was fabled in its own right, as was the long, gleaming sword that some said was a gift of Mars and could never be broken.

Telemon had been the champion of the people in their time of need, and it was said that if Telemon had been present in the bleak days of the invasion from Pylos, the humiliation would never have occurred, and a son would never have been taken as a hostage.

When the champion arrived from his northern outpost several days later there were reported to be bitter words from the tent of the king, but it was all the idle speculation of the camp's gossips.

No one knew what had happened, and few knew Telemon by more than reputation.

That he was without peer as a fighter no one doubted, but as to the rest he had spent little time among them.

By now more of the people had set out on their horses, with the baggage animals to follow and then the goatherds bringing up the rear.

Orfeo had not imagined the order to be otherwise, and he actually found the idea of a trek to Delphi as a relief from his endless days on the mountain.

It was not that he did not like his task, as he could conceivably have politely declined it and have spent the time idly about the camp, claiming his place as the king's younger son and bandying swords with the other young scions.

But it seemed more peaceful on the mountain, and even the loneliness seemed preferable to being among people to whom he would always be a stranger.

The road to Delphi was a twisting path through the mountains that provided both the pastures and streams of fresh water that the people needed in their moves between the green hills by the Western seas and the winter villages of Delphi and the inner mountains.

For the horsemen it would take no more than a day, while those bringing the herds would linger on the way for perhaps a week, slowly letting their animals browse through the meadows.

Orfeo and his cousins would be walking together, again sharing the same tent, but, as usual, staying at a distance during the daytime.

They camped the second night beneath a great boulder that overlooked the trail below, where they could see other campfires in the distance from other groups of the people who had traveled farther during the day.

In the morning Kiros and his closest advisers would meet before the crude temple at Delphi.

"So what happens now?" asked Euros, as they sat around the campfire.

"What if they don't get Herron back?"

"They'll find him again," said Orfeo, still not willing to look upon the event as changing his own place in the tribe.

Despite their distance, he respected Herron without particularly liking him, and he also had an understanding of that great world on the outside unseen by the others.

He suspected that Herron would still be alive, and there would be many ways of ensuring his safe return.

"Do you think Telemon will lead us to war?" asked Delf, the other cousin and the more precipitous of the two.

"Even the men of Pylos could not stand before his sword."

"And how would the mighty army of Telemon get to Pylos without a fleet or without a single warship, other than small fishing boats belonging to the tribe?" answered Orfeo, concealing a smile at the naiveté of his cousins.

Perhaps they understood the intricacies of the camp, but there was so much of the world of which they knew nothing.

"You doubt the strength of Telemon?" replied Delf in a rather annoyed voice.

Again there was an implication that Orfeo perhaps still held sympathies for the men of Pylos, who had not been the people to seize

Herron, although Pylos constituted the largest slave market on the northern shores of the Great Inland Sea, and it had been assumed by all that Herron would be taken there by the Tyrians who had seized him.

"I have no doubt," said Orfeo, aware that no amount of explaining would indicate to his cousins just what odds would face any assault upon Pylos.

What could they know of city walls, who had never seen a wall larger than that needed to contain their goats during the winter?

And what could the mightiest warrior do against the great army of Mir, general of all the forces of Pylos and trusted adviser to the king?

"But if they kill Herron, then you'll be the King's next son."

Euros apparently meant to cling to the subject.

"They will not kill Herron," Orfeo answered.

"And if they did, then the king would find another to be his heir."

The words had not been uttered aloud before, but Orfeo had always held the thought inside, aware that his father shared the same distrust of him that had infested the others.

Even Euros and Delf seemed relieved by the statement, as though they now need entertain no plots against the eventuality of his success.

"They'll probably already have made a decision by the time we arrive in Delphi," said Euros.

"Then they'll tell us to turn around again and march toward the western sea."

"There is really no reason for us to come to Delphi and even less for us to hurry," added Delf. "And it is just as well you are not there during the discussion."

This last was directed toward Orfeo.

"Why would that be?" the boy answered.

"Because there are people who say that if you had not come back, Herron would never have been taken." Euros answered.

"They needed another hostage."

"But the Tyrians took Herron," said Orfeo.

"And they probably had no knowledge of his rank among us."

"That's not the way some see it," muttered Delf.

"And that will be discussed in Delphi."

Orfeo slept poorly that night, as even a natural pessimism had not warned him that some of the tribe, perhaps his two cousins, would blame him for what had happened.

He awoke after troubled dreams just as the first rays of light filtered through the trees, and he found his left hand clasped over the blue markings on his left arm.

It was strange how long he had born the marks and yet how frequently they still returned to his mind.

It was the mark of a slave of Pylos, engraved in wedge-shaped numbers in a strange dye on his skin.

There was no washing and no scraping that had ever dimmed the color, and it was only another mark of his difference from the rest of his kinsmen. It was strange how it had come to him in the dream, although he could not remember what else had happened.

The mark loomed as an important personal scar in his mind.

The sensation persisted throughout the morning, but by the time Delf and Euros decided to stop for lunch by a small lethargic stream, thoughts had again returned to the plight of Herron and the succession of the king.

There was even more discomfort in that his cousins did not know how to relate to him now that his status may have improved because of Herron's disappearance or perhaps fallen greatly because he could be seen as responsible.

His place was thus more questionable than ever, although Kiros would probably find a more acceptable successor from among more distant kinsmen.

This would leave Orfeo a perpetual pariah, as - if he could not lay claim to the crown as his father's son - he would become no better than the lowliest slave.

# CHAPTER TWO

THE JOURNEY HAD TAKEN six days and nights, and by the morning of the seventh day the landscape suddenly seemed more rough and mountainous.

They were approaching Delphi, the last stragglers of a move that had seen a portable village virtually transplanted from one location to another.

Only a few lonely shepherds now remained in the clearing by the sea that had so recently been a bustling scene of life to the tribe, while now the sleepy groves of Delphi were not the solitary abode of priestesses, but a new locus of the village.

Sounds and smells sifted gently up the valley before the shrine as the tents came into view, and then all at once they were among the people again.

The animals were braying, and there was a brief flurry of welcoming that seemed to cross the clearing in a wave and then subside.

Another tributary had joined the stream, and the people were coming together again, but this time with a difference.

Already there were more tents than on any winter encampment Orfeo could remember, and space seemed to be set aside for more arrivals.

The tribe from all directions was gathering for a council, perhaps in preparation for war.

There were more horses, and the glint of armor and swords everywhere caught the sun like gleaming jewels.

Even the air seemed different this time, as though only a spark was needed to release a great accumulation of pent-up violence.

Not that there was any doubt as to how this would be supplied.

Almost from the first minutes Orfeo and his cousins spent in camp, they were beset by rumors about the approach of Telemon, who literally was expected with each gust of wind.

Word of Telemon the great hero was everywhere, and all spoke of his exploits with the sort of awe ordinarily reserved for the gods.

Indeed, once again Telemon would be their savior, if only he would make his appearance.

There was also much talk in camp about other events that had transpired during the last several days of meetings with the king and his advisers.

As Orfeo and Delf assembled their belongings at the outer edge of the camp, nearest to the pastures, they were told of strange messengers and portents from the east.

The mysterious Zurga had arrived on a great black horse, and in the evenings he appeared from the king's tent and walked silently among the Achians, speaking to no one, but keeping a grim smile that seemed to hide some unfathomable secret.

Zurga was not an Achian nor of a people known to the Achians, and rumors as to his origins usually were the sort one whispered rather than said aloud.

His physical appearance was not in itself imposing, if one could separate out those aspects that were anatomical and those that flowed from a personal force beneath.

An inner magnetism made this man of medium build appear to tower over others, and his slightness did not prevent him from moving about as if his sheer strength of will alone could impel submission.

Even the black garments, in themselves no novelty among warriors who wore black goat-hair capes of similar cut, seemed sinister, as no one could be sure of the material they were fashioned from.

They glistened like water at the same time they seemed capable of providing protection from a sword thrust.

Zurga was feared rather than liked, and yet he was known as a friend of the Achians and one to whom they had appealed for aid in the past.

He usually made his short visits during the winter encampments at Delphi, but now he had been away for a number of years, and this was the first time Orfeo had seen him stalk through the camp with his mixture of grand and furtive airs.

Perhaps most odd was the lack of an appropriate label for him.

In a sense he was like the priestesses, who were given automatic respect as a reward for their service to the gods, and yet he made no such claims for himself.

Some described him as a magician, although again he made no pretense of magic powers. Shaman was a word still used by the old believers for someone who had a special relationship to the powers of nature for the healing of illness or injury, and yet he had laughed at the term when it was used for him.

He never bothered to define himself, but he did not object to being called a Wanderer.

Clearly he had been about in the western world for years, and he often spoke of places known to others only vaguely by reputation.

Zurga appeared from the king's tent at dusk the day Orfeo and his cousins arrived, as though wearied or perhaps impatient with the interminable talk within.

He passed the tent just as Euros was placing the finishing touches on their encampment.

Delf had gone for water, and Orfeo was stacking small strips of wood for their fire that night.

At first he did not notice the presence of the stranger, or rather he noticed without looking up.

When he lifted his gaze to encounter the fiercely burning eyes of Zurga he recognized their source immediately, based upon talk with the others earlier in the afternoon.

Zurga watched him and had been watching him, and Euros had stopped his work within the tent to retreat in confusion, turning his eyes first to the figure in black and then back to Orfeo.

Even the camp seemed suddenly quieter.

"You are not of the Achians," said Zurga.

"I know you not."

"I am Orfeo, son of Kiros," Orfeo heard his voice speak in the formal cadences that set him apart from his cousins.

"You are not of the Achians," Zurga repeated.

"You are a man of the world beyond."

The voice sounded hollow and resonant, as if emerging from a cavern extending deep into the earth.

"I lived among the men of Pylos," said Orfeo.

"From my fifth year to my fifteenth I lived with Nestor, son of the king, and I was taught in his house.

Isocles was my teacher, and all I know of the world I learned from him."

"Ah........."

His manner suddenly mellowed, and Zurga approached almost within reach of Orfeo, dropping his voice to a softer tone. “I know Isocles well, and he is a man of great integrity and honesty.

I believe he may even have mentioned you to me.” He now sounded playful.

“Did he impart to you some of his wisdom?”

“Isocles taught me how little I knew and how helpless I will always be in the face of the gods.” Orfeo felt the eyes inspecting him for hidden flaws, but his own gaze was not averted, and he stood straight and proud before the black shape.

Zurga smiled and made as if to depart as stealthily as he had arrived. “Yes, this is better than I had hoped.

You have learned well your lessons from Isocles.

There is his mark about you, but we will speak of that more at a later time.”

He glanced with a disinterested contempt at the cowering Euros and then turned back to Orfeo. “Remember, you are a king’s son,” he said and then walked away without so much as a glance backward.

Delf returned with the water in time to see Zurga depart, and he breathlessly asked Euros what had prompted the attention, but the latter was now recovering his pride by turning scornfully on Orfeo with all the anger that had lain dormant as he crouched in the shadows.

“So you are not of the Achians.....as even an outsider knows.”

He shouted the words angrily, glancing after Zurga to confirm that he was out of earshot.

“You think you’re a mighty man of Pylos.”

“What business did the wanderer have with us?”

Delf asked apprehensively.

“Not with us, but with the boy of Pylos, who stands there thinking he is better than we are.”

Euros was now enraged, and the same ideas soon seemed to affect his brother.

“I am an Achian and your cousin,” said Orfeo, still standing as he had while talking with Zurga, but his heart was pounding, and he felt the same fears that had assailed him when he had originally stepped among his people after the escape and announced that he had returned.

“No cousin of mine consorts with Wanderers.” Delf almost spat the word.

“Even that unspeakable man could see that you were different,” said Euros.

"You even look like a man of Pylos," said Delf, who had never in his life seen a man of Pylos in other than a battle helmet and from a great distance.

"If you don't wish me to stay with you, I'll leave," said Orfeo.

"Go back to Pylos with your people," Euros answered.

Apparently all suspicions that the abduction of his brother would elevate the status of their cousin had been dispelled, as they had been in camp all day, and Orfeo had achieved no more notice than ever.

The visit of the Wanderer had also been humiliating to Euros, as it had caught him in a position where his fear had been visible to Orfeo, while the latter had received special attention for his being different.

It was, altogether, too much, and in his anger he could scarcely bear the presence of his cousin.

Better that the boy live by himself for a while, at least until the general rage at the atrocity from Pylos - if such it was - had died down.

Already Euros had felt that the rest of the village had somehow begun to treat him with more suspicion because of the strange creature that shared his tent.

Orfeo must live alone or with someone else who cared less about gossip.

The decision was made within minutes after Zurga departed, and then the anger seemed to subside as rapidly as it had arisen.

Perhaps even Euros felt ashamed that he had exploded so violently in a tribe where loyalty to one's kinsmen was reckoned not so much as a virtue but a way of life. His behavior had bordered on a kind of personal treason, and yet, at the same time, there were other issues connected with loyalty, and it was not at all clear which way the wind was blowing.

After all, Orfeo was still regarded with suspicion by much of the camp, and there could be nothing more damming about his background now than that he had spent most of his life, over ten years, in Pylos.

That these same people were not exactly those who only days before had committed a great breach of the peace did not seem to matter, as it was assumed Herron would end up at the slave market there.

Why not blame the men of Pylos, who maintained trading relations with the Tyrians?

Why also not blame Orfeo for this bleeding wound to their tribal identity?

There was certain guilt by association that both Euros and Delf perceived as soon as they arrived in the camp.

During the day, when Orfeo had been out of hearing, many others had asked pointed questions about him, and when he was around the tent, neighbors shunned the entire group.

There was enough talk to make the brothers fear for their own status in the community, particularly when it made a certain perverse sense that Orfeo might actually be implicated in the crime.

He was indeed a sort of outsider, and the actions of his ex-captors had removed his older brother from succession to the throne.

It looked suspicious that he should be in a position to benefit from the abduction; yet no one suspected that he would ever replace King Kiros.

Yes, it was best that Orfeo live alone for a while, and he assembled his meager belongings even before they were completely unpacked in their new surroundings.

The animals were all kept in a large enclosure at the edge of the encampment closest to the pastures, and Orfeo thought that perhaps he could find a place for himself beyond where the others slept.

He had no tent of his own, but the weather was not so severe now, and he would be able to keep warm wrapped in his cloak and the great woolen blanket his mother had given him from the king's tent.

At least in theory he could return there, which was by rights his home, but even before the kidnapping there had been tension between the family and the newly returned son who was so little a part of them that they had ceased to mourn his loss.

And Orfeo had lived with less luxury as well as more.

During the long travail of his escape he had often slept on the deck of a ship or the bare ground with nothing to keep him warm, although in Pylos he had lived in a great palace and had slept on a soft mat in an anteroom close to where Nestor slept. As he was always at the older boy's disposal, he had to sleep where he could hear his name called.

He had been warm, comfortable, and well fed.

Why, indeed, had he left all of that behind?

He wondered whether any of those he had known in Pylos would understand, and he was not even certain that he could have explained.

Isocles would know, if anyone did, and Orfeo allowed himself to think back upon the teacher who was perhaps more of a father to him than anyone else could ever be.

How strange that Zurga also knew him, and from the way the old Wanderer's face had brightened at the mention of his name, Orfeo knew that there existed a bond between these two wise men of the world.

Surely Zurga could not be all bad if he had been a friend of Isocles.

It was dark now, and Orfeo had settled into the place he had found where he could sleep without being disturbed. There was no need for a fire, although he would gather wood tomorrow, but he could not fall asleep when there was still such a clamor about the camp.

Even from his place on the outskirts Orfeo could hear talk of war and revenge and sacrifice.

No one knew what would issue forth from the king's tent or when the news would emerge, and everyone expected the arrival of Telemon.

What could have detained the great warrior of the north?

He was needed now as never before.

Sleep was slow in coming that night, as Orfeo thought of his banishment from the tent of his cousins. He knew that he could never go back, aware now for the first time how deeply their suspicions troubled their perception of him.

No, he could never trust them even after having shared a tent with them for nearly a year.

It was as if he had been a burden, and no sense of family loyalty had developed.

As soon as his presence had become inconvenient he had been exiled, and he knew that although neither cousin was evil or even bad, they were weak and unsure of their own places in the world.

His choices seemed day by day to shrink.

He felt he could not go back to the tent of his mother and father, as they had seemed relieved when he left, and now it was clear that the cousins had never made any kind of bond with him.

He did not know what he should do, but rather than ponder a question that had no answer, he made his thoughts turn to Isocles, whose many words of advice still lingered in the boy's consciousness.

He remembered the countless scenes in which Isocles sat as teacher for Nestor, with Orfeo at first just an onlooker and then a participant just as much as the king's son. Only Orfeo was a slave, and it would never do to show more understanding than Nestor.

So an understanding arose between Isocles and his eager pupil.

The great diplomat and scholar would ask a question to Nestor, and if he gave the wrong answer, Isocles would never ask Orfeo.

Instead there was a hidden signal of understanding that would flow between them, and Orfeo would recall the words. "Don't tell everything you know."

At first it sounded strange coming from a teacher intent upon communicating everything he knew, and then the reason became obvious, and the recognition of this deception seemed to form a cornerstone for the remainder of Orfeo's education.

Even though Isocles was an aristocrat of the city and an important man of affairs, his own ability to say everything that came into his mind was limited.

When his own grasp exceeded that of the king and others around him, he was not compelled to say so, nor was he obligated to place himself in open disagreement with the standards of the city.

Yet there was much of the creed of Pylos that Isocles obviously found not to his liking, which he communicated to his younger pupil in such a way that his older, slower pupil could not take offense.

Yes, Isocles was a man of rare insight, who knew the world and its ways, and Orfeo survived from day to day on his teachings. There was virtually no decision that was made without some inner reference to what Isocles had once said or done, even including the most recent decision to leave the tent of his cousins and live by himself.

It was a manner of weighing a number of complex factors and taking a reasoned course in accord with one's own nature.

To have done otherwise could have led to open conflict with the cousins, and by going before they commanded it, he had avoided the sort of harsh words that are never forgotten.

Something had been lost, but understanding had been gained.

Despite the pain it brought, Orfeo knew it was best he not depend upon an alliance with those who could never find it within themselves to trust him.

He could almost hear Isocles saying, "Put yourself in the other person's place and try to understand what he is thinking."

He had understood his cousins only too well.

Orfeo finally fell asleep with thoughts of Isocles, and perhaps these blended imperceptibly with the dreams that haunted his night.

In the morning he felt neither refreshed nor cheerful, although at first he could not sort out what thoughts had threatened his peace.

Perhaps he was not yet so far from the storm as he had thought.

# CHAPTER THREE

TELEMON HAD BEEN EAGERLY AWAITED with each passing day since the other Achian tribes had arrived, but this morning held about it a fresh aura that today would, indeed, see his appearance and with it the birth of a new hope.

The sky was a mixture of gray and black, with threatening clouds over the mountains and the hint of a great rain, but by mid-morning brilliant shafts of sunlight seemed to penetrate at irregular places, sending glowing lines across the horizon.

Orfeo had taken his sheep into the mountains, but he returned early in the afternoon after the thunder started, and the animals had become frightened.

The rumbling grew louder and closer, and just as he had returned the animals to their enclosure, it seemed to blend with the sounds of approaching horses, with hooves echoing through the valley and peals of thunder providing a salute to the hero as he returned to his people.

Telemon appeared with perhaps several dozen companions, striding first among them on a horse that would have seemed ordinary in every feature save for its great, brute size.

The man it bore also seemed undistinguished either in beauty or nobility, and at first glance Telemon was simply another warrior as he dismounted before the king's tent and strode proudly past the guards onto the platform. His armor was old and battered, and his fabled sword trailed like any other at this side, with no trace of precious stones or the intricate goldwork that embellished the weapons of some men in the camp. The boots were battered, and the cloak a dirty gray could have served to warm a shepherd on the hill.

Still something about the man compelled notice.

Perhaps it was only his size, which seemed somehow to grow as he left the giant horse behind, but there was more than bulk alone.

The movements themselves were awesome, as though each shift in position of every muscle was purposeful and absolutely implacable, with no room either for doubt or interruption.

Telemon moved like a predator, engraving his footprints so firmly on the ground that one would have imagined the dust to have assumed some permanent shape.

There was something like a coiled snake in his manner, as though notice were served to all that his appearance of ease and relaxation could instantly transform itself into a visage of terror and destruction.

All the anticipation of Telemon's arrival did not blunt the actual impact of his presence, and a hush descended on the camp as he rode among the tents, while the distant thunder seemed all the louder.

Of the armed men who had accompanied their leader, only one other followed into the king's tent, while the others took care of the animals and arranged their own tents near the great stone platform on which Kiros met with his councilors.

They too bore the stamp of Telemon in their austere dress and generally somber demeanor, but soon even this distance began to recede, as they became more a part of the camp.

Indeed, they were all known to the others, either as relatives or friends separated by a great distance in time, but all were of the people, the same tribe.

None of them, thought Orfeo, had ever lived in Pylos, and thus none were subjected to the suspicions greeting an outsider.

Delf and Euros were also in the camp when Telemon arrived, and they averted their eyes on passing Orfeo.

It was difficult to be sure, but the others seemed already to know about the rupture between the cousins, and Orfeo felt himself suddenly to have become more anonymous than ever in that he was treated as if he did not exist.

He walked the camp as a shadow, soliciting no greetings nor even curious looks.

In a sense the disappearance of his brother had made of him a non-person, and even the fact that there had obviously been no communication from his father or mother since the event made it seem all the more as though he were a man without a family, one who had been cast out.

He considered the possibility of visiting his mother and telling her of his grief, as, quite apart from the upheaval caused by the kidnapping, Orfeo was pained by the thought that harm should come to Herron.

But would it somehow be an embarrassment for the queen to receive her second son now, as though he had only come to remind her that he was all that remained.

The matter was complex and held possibilities from many sides, but Orfeo could not see a clear way in which he could act, and he resolved merely to hold his peace and exist as ever from day to day.

If he were a stranger in his own country, then so be it, but that was his fate and destiny, and he must not complain.

There was no other way open, as he had often realized that as an exile separate from his people he also could not be seen by them as a complete person.

Yet what if he attempted to construct an identity apart from the others?

Was it something a single person could do?

By evening Orfeo had arranged his new living quarters more comfortably, gathering firewood and assembling his belongings into an orderly but austere camp.

Just before dark he again had gone to the center of the encampment, where many of the tribe had gathered hoping to see Telemon when he appeared again, but there was no breaking up of the council, and instead great platters of food were taken inside.

The king and his advisers continued to deliberate, and by this time rumors were sweeping the camp.

One faction insisted that the men of Pylos were invading the country, as another contended that the Achians would go to war against Pylos. Orfeo still seemed lost in the storm, and he would have sought no other role than his anonymity, but something in the scene troubled him, and it was not until he was back at his small fire preparing for sleep that the source of his discomfort came consciously to mind.

The dreams last night had been more than vaguely disturbing, and now it seemed clear why he had avoided thinking of them all day.

They still seemed jumbled and confused, but certain details stood out, most prominently the idea of returning to Pylos as a hostage, only this time under a threat of death if he escaped.

The figure of Isocles emerged as if from the shadows, but in such a bloody, mutilated guise that he was at times unrecognizable and appeared only as a soldier.

Nestor of Pylos was seen with a distorted hate-filled face and sword, hacking and slashing at all around him, slaying friends and foes alike.

Through it all loomed a dark presence, both a spectator and motivating force, and only the eminence of Zurga could have towered so awesomely above the scene.

It was Zurga and the shimmering black cape that directed first one movement and then another, but it was unclear whether he was a force for good or evil or perhaps some intermediate modality of his own. Nevertheless, it was frightening, and the encounter of the night before with the Wanderer did not lessen Orfeo's suspicion that this was a man with whom one must always remain guarded and alert.

The feeling of some possible future threat was reinforced all the more by Zurga's appearance, this time in the flesh, standing quietly in the shadows and watching as though he had been there for some undetermined time.

He neither moved nor seemed to register that he had been seen.

"Do you wish merely to watch, or should I offer the wanderer a seat by my fire?"

Orfeo deliberately modulated his voice in the prim courtly manner of a gentlemen from Pylos, allowing the vowels to take a shape in his throat that had grown unaccustomed to such sounds since his escape.

"I see the world changes quickly these days," Zurga approached cautiously and seated himself on the other side of the fire, meticulously wrapping his cloak around him so that he seemed to consist of nothing more than a round, black object capped off by a head. "I recall your accommodations as having been somewhat more luxurious yesterday.

"Your visit was an ill omen," replied Orfeo.

"Or at least my cousins thought it so."

"Ahhhh......"

Zurga smiled with a mischievous warmth for the first time.

"Your teacher Isocles would have said that it is too soon to judge the nature of an omen, and that only after all events have run their course can one say which is good and which is ill."

"But all events will have run their course only after we are dead."

Orfeo was beginning to feel again the exhilaration of the verbal sophistries of the court.

With Nestor and Isocles and the other students there had been such a sparkling interplay of wit and imagination.

It was different food for the mind than quietly minding the sheep all day; yet both seemed important in molding his character.

"Exactly," the wanderer replied.

"And for that reason it would not be wise to judge merely after a day whether my visit last night was not a fortunate occurrence for you."

"Very well.

At least tonight there is no one to banish me from my own fire.

You are welcome."

Zurga meticulously removed pipe and leather pouch of leaf material from a fold of his cloak.

He began to speak of the weather and the camp and the food at the king's table.

At first there was no hint that he had been occupied there for the last days by a session of the council that seemed certain to become the longest within memory; but gradually he seemed to inch closer toward it, as though something related to the deliberations had some bearing on his conversation with Orfeo.

The latter, for his part, felt so many conflicting desires to ask questions that many times he resorted to the old device of biting his tongue, but the lessons with Isocles had been well learned.

He was holding his peace while the Wanderer inched closer to his objective.

"There's no question of going to war," finally Zurga leaped precipitously upon the subject and pronounced a judgment as though he had lead up to it through a torturous argument.

"The Achians are a brave and noble people......" He paused as if waiting for an answer, as Orfeo finally took the bait.

"But they could never....." Too late.

He realized that the wanderer had lured him into committing his thoughts.

"Yes, my friend, you are, of course, perfectly correct.

But no wonder you are not the favorite of your fellows. You know too much of the outside world, and the Achians resent being told that there are powers beyond their own."

"And they have never seen a city wall."

"But even those who have seen walled cities, at least from the outside like the hero Telemon......" His pronunciation of the word seemed strange in that he seemed to hold none of the great awe of the others.

"Even Telemon would throw himself in the face of certain destruction, and for what purpose?

There will be no recovering the luckless Herron through force of arms, and we are not even certain that the men of Pylos have him."

He shrugged in a bewildered, basically accepting grimace.

"And so I have told them all week.

They have not wished to hear it, but I have finally convinced them that there is no fighting Pylos, and the only possible way to get Herron back is through diplomacy.

The skill, I imagine, is one known to you through Isocles."

"Isocles often spoke the word and said it had to do with getting your own way without having to fight."

So many words of his old teacher came back to Orfeo as he spoke to the Wanderer in the same speech he had used with his teacher.

Isocles had also spoken of Wanderers, as though they constituted a force in the world that was connected neither to a nation nor a people. He had advised that one should remain silent and observe Wanderers, but tell them nothing.

"No doubt he spoke of it, but did he teach it?"

He smiled as if contemplating an absurdity. "Although I cannot imagine you need such skills for dealing with your sheep."

"Because the tool is not used every day, one must not give it away."

Orfeo was feeling the beginnings of anger, but he channeled it back toward the Wanderer.

"Well put, my boy. I am beginning to see in you traces of your master."

The wanderer's eyes seemed to constrict into slits so narrow that one could see nothing of his thoughts.

"But we have more important matters to discuss, and we must decide how we are going to bring your brother back from wherever he is without going to war."

Orfeo remained silent, merely gazing at the non-committal visage before him.

It was a test of his perseverance, perhaps, although he had long been practiced at keeping his thoughts to himself in Pylos. He would volunteer nothing.

Zurga narrowed his eye slits ever further, but when his scowl did not shake loose words he smiled.

"Has it occurred to you that you might play some part in recovering your brother?"

"It has occurred to me that all of us, the entire tribe, may have a part to play."

For some reason Orfeo found his heart pounding and his mind fondling stray thoughts from his dreams of the night before, but he maintained a steadiness.

"Come now, you needn't be so distant with me.

I'm making pleasant conversation about a subject important to both of us."

Zurga's voice was now warm and charming.

"No wonder they call you devious," answered Orfeo.

"Because with you appearances do not match realities."

"A strange thing to say, my young diplomat, but tell me, what do you have to lose by revealing to me what is really going on in your mind?"

"And you tell me, Wanderer, what benefit could follow from opening my thoughts to you?"

Zurga had now leaned back in a more relaxed posture and seemed to relish the exchange.

"Remember that you never know whether a happening is for good or ill until the entire course is run."

"I could take that as advice either way," answered Orfeo.

"Then I'll talk frankly with you, my fine friend, because truly I have little time for more parrying, much as I enjoy it."

Again the tone brought another aspect, this time one of somber business.

"Despite your current lowly estate, you are of more potential use to your tribesmen than you might imagine, as you are the only one among them who knows the ways of Pylos.

If they are to attempt to retrieve Herron by diplomacy, as I have suggested, then you are certain to be among the delegation."

"But you know Pylos as well as I...."

"Silence."

Again the scowl.

"Let me continue, and then I will leave you with your thoughts.

I am not of your people, and although I have aided your father against his enemies for several decades....and your father's father even before that ... I am still not completely trusted, as I have no roots here.

I am of all countries and of none, and even my coming and going are matters of my own choice.

I may not be seen again by the Achians for many years, and the bond that grows in such soil is never complete, but I can still be of use, perhaps with someone else who is an Achian."

"But they trust me even less than they trust you."

Orfeo could not contain his words.

"To them I am no better or worse than any other man of Pylos, which was their first thought when I returned, and it is still their notion. I am no longer the son of my mother or father but a stranger also of no country."

"Be that as it may, there is a stamp to your face and carriage that says Achian, and there is something about you that made you reject the world of Pylos. And, believe me, I know how difficult that must have been.

But you are an Achian, and someday all will know it as I know it."

Orfeo could not answer, but merely watched as the old man sprang lithely to his feet.

The thoughts were now swirling in such wild disarray that he could not organize an answer, but mumbled some disjointed reply.

Zurga nodded and turned with a last word.

"Think it over, my boy.

There is something about you that I like, and I think you might do well if you cast your lot to the winds of fortune.

When the call comes, do not hold back."

He was gone in a flicker from the campfire, and Orfeo was left alone with his demons.

The gloom that had remained at bay during the presence of another now descended in full force.

Orfeo was as deeply troubled as he had been at any time in his life.

In a sense talking with the Wanderer had been a strain, as he had felt himself resume many of the same defenses that had been such a part of his existence at Pylos.

There was also something about the Wanderer that inspired awe, although Isocles, without saying so directly, had obviously been skeptical that such men had understanding or powers greater than any other, but rather they so manipulated signs and events as to make them appear supernatural.

Certainly the other Achians thought of Zurga as being more than a man, while Orfeo's skepticism separated him all the more from their frame of reference. Still he would merely maintain his guard without making judgments.

There was no indication that Zurga could read his thoughts, nor at this point reason to believe that the Wanderer had evil designs.

That night Orfeo half expected the dreams to return, but he awoke in the morning feeling free and untroubled.

The sky was crystal clear, and the brisk breeze made him want to climb the mountain with the sheep, his father's sheep, and lie in the sun all day while they fed themselves.

Whatever Zurga had prattled about the night before now seemed insignificant before the realities of his life, and it was more than unlikely that the council would call for his help in retrieving Herron. To send an escaped hostage back to Pylos was in itself not a politic move, as how could the last two years be explained?

It was all too complex at the moment, although he knew that from his mountaintop he would dissect each possibility and come to understand the world about him.

Murray Lee Eiland Jr.

# CHAPTER FOUR

THE MESSENGER HAD OBVIOUSLY BEEN RUNNING, and his frantic look of frustration implied that he had long been searching for Orfeo and his flock.

He burst into the clearing breathlessly and began to declaim something about the council, but the words themselves did not seen important.

It was the message that Orfeo had been summoned, and for some reason there was no time to lose.

The flock was left, as someone else had been assigned to return them to the camp.

All haste was to be made down the hill so that the king would be kept waiting no longer.

Yet it was not clear from the message whether the subject was one of fortune or foreboding.

In any event, it could hardly be seen as unrelated to the talk with Zurga of the night before, although just what would result was impossible to foretell.

Orfeo ran with an easy loping stride, recalling as he did the long runs he had with Nestor of Pylos, sailing down the hills behind the city in great leaps that gave the illusion of flying, picking up speed as they soared faster and faster until neither could stop and only a delicate balance between falling and flying could be sustained until they reached the bottom of the hill.

It was a drunken, euphoric wildness that returned in snatches as Orfeo approached the camp, but he assumed all possible dignity as he approached the great platform of the king's tent.

He wore his shabby sandals and loose tunic, with the dull black cloak slung loosely about his shoulders, looking no more as though he belonged among the council than any other shepherd.

But the guards knew him, and with blank faces allowed him to pass, motioning him right to the main doorway and then pulling back the tapestry to allow him entry.

He walked blinking into the darkness and could almost feel the hush at his appearance.

Despite the daylight outside, the interior of the great tent was kept dark and oppressively hot, with the few torches contributing more smoke and heat than illumination.

Still there was a brilliance imparted by the vibrant reds and yellows of the tapestries hanging on the walls and the richly patterned rugs on the floor.

The state robes of Kiros were of similar velvet-like material, and he seemed to be embraced by rich crimson and indigo folds on his dais, overlooking the assemblage of notables and the stiffly seated Telemon, whose gaze competed with that of Zurga in its penetrating inspection of the newcomer.

The soldier and the wanderer occupied opposite corners of the room along the same side as the king's elevated platform, while the nobles were seated on the floor along the side near the entrance.

They were all obviously waiting for the king to speak.

"My son Orfeo, I have called you for several reasons and with grave misgivings to discuss the plans we have been making for recovering your brother from the Tyrians or the men of Pylos or whoever might have him now."

The voice was weary and sounded nothing like the vigorous warrior of old, but perhaps there was an added sadness because tragedy had involved his oldest son.

"The council and myself have been told by Zurga, and perhaps convinced by him, that the only way to bring Herron safely back is by persuasion, and that we should send delegates to Pylos who would most likely be able to accomplish that end.

Of course Zurga himself, who knows the ways of the world, must be included, which he has generously consented to do in our behalf.

At the same time we must give him fitting escort in Telemon and Orton, our two greatest warriors, who could protect him from harm. The last suggestion of Zurga, however, is still a question, and that involves your participation.

The council is divided and wishes to hear your voice."

Before Orfeo could answer another voice came from the nobles, and a small dark man arose whom Orfeo recognized as a kinsman to his mother.

"The issue of succession must be raised first," he seemed tense and worried, perhaps more about the fortunes of his family should both of Hermia's sons find an early death and the king be compelled to seek an heir from another younger wife. "If we have lost one heir to the throne, should we send the other off to risk his life with little chance of success?"

An angry muttering from the others quickly suggested where this idea stood, and at the same time seemed to seal the fate of Orfeo as an eventual successor to his father.

"What could such a boy do in the face of the might of Pylos?" said another noble.

"And what would they think when they discovered that he was an escaped hostage?" another voice added.

"His original state as a hostage need never be known."

Zurga now interrupted his silence and walked forth into the open space between the dais and the council.

"In the years since his return Orfeo has changed much, and there is more yet that I can do to change his appearance before he returns."

The wanderer seemed to refer to his own formidable powers.

"The question lies more around what he might be able to contribute merely as an observer who knows the ways of Pylos, of someone who knows the locations of the slave markets and the manner in which captives might be sold and distributed once they arrive in the city.

It is, after all, not a matter of admitting to the king of Pylos that his minions have unwittingly carried off another son of the Achian king and therefore are asking his release.

If they were ever to know Herron's true identity, the price would be high, if not impossible, and a treaty would doubtlessly follow that would be much to the disadvantage of the Achians."

"If we were to accept such a treaty from Pylos."

For the first time Orfeo heard the voice of Telemon, and it seemed to vibrate the air itself, originating deeper even than that of Zurga and inspiring the same awe as his appearance. But the Wanderer did not give way in the slightest.

"I'm afraid you would accept what was offered, and you will see the wisdom of that when you walk the streets of Pylos," said Zurga.

"There are limits to the courage and heroism of one man, and with all respect to your great skill and daring, I would not send you, my friend Telemon, against the entire army of a great city."

He held his arm imperiously extended as if to preclude the reply from Telemon that seemed on his lips.

"But we must have among us someone who can pass as a man of Pylos and circulate in those quarters of the city where we might find news of what has happened to the tall, fair Achian.

While I know the ways of the court well, I am obviously not one of their people, and I would be greeted there with the same suspicions as in your own camp.

But Orfeo could pass among them as one of them."

"And if the remaining heir were to be captured…." Again the first noble spoke, defending the position of his family.

"The succession will not be determined or discussed at this time," Kiros spoke firmly.

"I have every intention of remaining for many years among the living - should the gods be willing - and much can happen between now and then.

But we will make an attempt to recover Herron, and the suggestions of Zurga have been reluctantly accepted by me.

We will send a group of four, and we will pray for a favorable result."

The murmuring among the nobles indicated that the decision was not greeted without some misgivings, and Telemon allowed a downward movement of his right hand that unmistakably communicated his dissatisfaction.

But the matter had been settled, and there Orfeo stood, still without having uttered his first word and only now adjusting his eyes to the darkness so that he could read the faces around him.

There were looks of despair and hopelessness, with little show of confidence or pride.

The atmosphere stiffened Orfeo's resolve to speak with dignity and resolution should he be called upon, although he felt a trembling in his chest and a weakness in his knees as he took a deep breath and prepared himself.

"Do you have anything to say?" Kiros spoke with more than usual warmth to his son.

"Only that I will gladly do whatever is necessary to help return my brother to his people."

The words had been prepared, including the subtle meanings of "my" and "his." For the moment Orfeo had allowed another part of himself to speak in an unaccustomed voice, as though he were no longer a shepherd boy but a man of the council.

"Our friend Zurga tells us that you have been trained as a diplomat."

"Truly, father, I know Pylos from one end to the other, and if Herron is there, I will find him.

As for diplomacy, I will add any information I can to the wisdom of Zurga, whose advice I will follow every step of the way."

There was a rustling among the council, as though no one had expected the shepherd boy to know his mind let alone be able to express it in formal words that most could understand without being able to answer in kind.

Yet something deep inside was too wounded, hurt, perhaps even angry to allow him to give way to fear at this moment.

"I hope you will take your best clothes," chided the king, introducing a note of levity that brought a faint murmur of laughter, as, after all, Orfeo, despite his strong, confident voice, looked little better than an urchin.

"These are my worst clothes and my best, father.

I have none other."

Again it was bold talk to the king, and Orfeo could see that the words had awakened something in his father, who must have in some part of his consciousness recognized instantly that his second son had been left virtually as a beggar among the people whose respect he should have.

It was a rebuke the king had as much as asked for, and it had been accompanied by a short intake of air among the assembled councilors.

"My son, you shall have better before you go."

There was a note of sorrow.

"And your departure will be early tomorrow."

He turned to his minister.

"Send word to the Port of Megara to have a ship prepared."

He turned next toward a steward.

"They will be in Megara and ready to sail by evening." Now he turned again to Orfeo.

"You have done well, my son, to have returned from your captivity, and my heart has been proud of the ordeal you undertook in returning, despite the possibility that it may have compromised our treaty with Pylos.

But I know you have not been truly received as another Achian."

The old man sounded wearied and saddened.

"I was born an Achian and remain one," Orfeo said.

"Ahhhh....of course.

But perhaps this task will provide the opportunity to satisfy all doubts."

The message was deliberately vague, as a king at times must be.

As Orfeo emerged outside the tent into the bright afternoon, he knew there had been a hint to his mother's relatives that if he returned without Herron - after showing skill and determination to return him - then there would be time to speak of succession.

But of course it would ultimately only mean what the king wished it to mean. The audience had been short, and there had been such few words needed to decide his fate that each seemed all the more indelibly engraved upon his mind.

Still there were questions, particularly around Zurga's role and his suggestion that Orfeo's appearance itself could be changed to allow him to pass unrecognized among the people in his old home.

Indeed, it had been Zurga who, from the beginning, had argued that Orfeo be included, and the motives for this were not at all clear.

Isocles had often said that Wanderers should be dealt with only at times when there was nothing to be gained or lost, and then the only safe course was to observe from a distance.

The old teacher had been adamant.

Orfeo walked back through the camp, and already it seemed as though word had filtered to the outside that he had been chosen by Kiros for part in a dangerous mission.

Perhaps it was only his imagination, but he seemed to feel less of the suspicious, hostile glances that had always seemed to follow him about.

The others now appeared to watch with some comprehension that here walked a king's son, or one who was once a king's son.

Somehow it seemed easier to move with pride, although inwardly Orfeo knew nothing had really changed.

By the time he had returned to his own small encampment, he was again thinking about his mother, and now it was imperative that he visit her.

He again sorted through his meager possessions, choosing those that he would need on the journey.

The remainder could be taken with him when he visited her and left with the family retainers.

At least he should still have that right, as he had originally lived among them and had only voluntarily sought an exile among others of the tribe.

It was difficult to recall now why he had decided to live with his cousins, but it had initially been more comfortable for everyone.

The tent of Queen Hermia, which was, despite its name, actually the home of both king and queen, was located near the great royal tent of Kiros, which was more for state purposes than for use as living quarters.

In size the queen's tent was inferior, but the opulence of the interior far exceeded that of the council hall, with even richer carpets and tapestries, many from distant lands, in the hues of many suns.

There were fabrics from across the sea and draperies woven of threads intertwined with gold threads, while the serving women wore diaphanous, semi-transparent material that contrasted with the crude woolen garments of the villagers.

Here Orfeo had spent his childhood, and it was to this tent he had returned from captivity.

It was a scene Orfeo had seen increasingly less since his return, as the visits to his mother, now almost ritualistic in their formality, seemed to satisfy neither.

Yet there was still some need, apparently felt by both, to renew something of the past, to again reach an understanding and recognize that they were of the same blood.

Now, of course, with the mission to Pylos, there was no avoiding another confrontation.

Orfeo approached with a pounding heart, aware again of being merely a child in the world of men and women, but the feeling was mixed with a sense also of seeing farther in some ways than the adults around him.

He had, indeed, been taught by a great master, and there was no forgetting his exercises in logic and deduction.

They had seemed pointless at the time; yet there was something in those hundreds of hours with Isocles that had made him a different creature who was not truly an Achian, or a boy verging on manhood, or even his mother's son.

And Isocles had told him again and again, "Beware of good people who have wronged you, as they will wish to destroy any memory of their failure."

He knew it was the final reason why he had not been accepted back, as he had stood as living proof of his parents' inability to protect their own flesh and blood.

Perhaps they had done the right and responsible thing in sending him as a hostage, and yet that failure would always live within them and distort their reasoning into some inner suspicion that it was he who had been at fault.

He was, after all, the one who had failed.

The doorkeeper seemed surprised at Orfeo's approach, and a more careful look seemed required for his recognition, but he pushed aside the great tasseled draperies and allowed entry, announcing as he did so that Orfeo son of Kiros had arrived.

There was no one in the outer chamber at the time, but soon another of the family retainers appeared and motioned for Orfeo to follow.

At least here he had been expected, and news of the council's decision had obviously traveled quickly to the queen, as she needed no words from her son.

She reclined on a low platform in her private chamber amidst cushions and hanging folds of soft fabrics, with a great bronze incense burner on one side and a faintly glowing lamp hanging by a long chain from the top of the tent.

She was covered with a richly woven shawl that left her head free and allowed the flowing blonde hair to cover her shoulders, and in the dim light she seemed again like a beautiful slave girl rather than a queen and mother.

But when she spoke there was a weight to her words and sadness in her voice that prompted Orfeo to look for the tears that must have clouded her vision.

Again he was a source of grief to his mother, in his departure and return and now in his departure again.

The duties of a queen and mother so often seemed to run at cross-purposes.

"I'm glad you have come," she said, holding her head in the posture of stoic acceptance that had come from her renunciations.

"They have told me that again you will be going, and I have put together for you an assortment of new and elegant clothes."

So word of Orfeo's pointed comment had spread already to her tent.

"I wished only to take leave of you until we can rescue Herron and return him to his rightful place," said Orfeo.

"Pylos is not the end of the world, and I have survived the journey before."

"You have become stronger and more confident, my youngest son.

Nothing is too great for you, and nothing makes you feel fearful or sad."

The words brought a strange stirring from Orfeo.

"I have grown accustomed to fear and sadness," he replied, "but one cannot spend the day weeping about what cannot be changed."

"You will see as you grow older that many things can be changed, and many tragedies do not have to be, and that we are masters of at least some part of our fate.

But perhaps I surprise you by talking like something other than a mother.

I'm supposed to be solemn and tearful now that my only surviving son is again being placed up as a sacrifice.

And I am."

For the first time her grief was evident, and Orfeo felt an urge to take her hand and comfort her, but it had been so long since she had actually been his mother.

There was too much sadness in those years after he was taken to Pylos.

"I am sorry to leave you, my mother."

The words had scarcely emerged in their firm, manly tone when he too felt tearful and bowed his head with a swirling sensation of giddiness and grief.

"I have missed you and wished that you were again with us, but I knew that once you were part of us, there would be something.

They would send for you, or…." The queen stopped and simply watched him as he stared blankly at her.

She motioned for him to approach, and then she took his hand and gently pulled him onto the dais.

"We are Achians," she said in a new voice, "and it is a time of trouble for our nation."

All traces of tears were gone.

"We must not question our duty, and I know, my son, that you will do your best for your family and people.

You will risk even your life to rescue your brother, and there is no room for doubt or indecision."

Again she looked grieved.

"But that does not erase the feeling between a mother and her youngest.

I hope you do not feel wounded that I still treat you like my baby.

There is still too much….." She turned her head and seemed to concentrate before continuing.

"So sing for me," she said.

"The last memory I wish is for your singing, which I have allowed myself to hear only once since your return and which haunted me all the time you were away.

I wish nothing more than for you to sing."

The queen retreated once her request was made and took from under a velvet shawl the lyre he had used during his youth.

She arranged the shawl upon her face so that Orfeo could not see her expression, but he knew what was hidden, and the last shyness of his heart vanished, as he thought of his mother and father in those happy days before his exile, when he was still a carefree boy and son to a king.

The song blended the two feelings in a mixture of sadness and joy, reaching over the meadows where he tended the sheep and the great city where he had matured, echoing in the orange sunset on the battlements and the dawn on a mountain top, with the summer showers and rainbows and the pain of parting.

It was the song of his life, which Orfeo had held within him and which made even the listening maids weep with memories of their childhoods and children and parents and friends. The song was togetherness and solitude in one tone, blending all that had gone into one young life that stood on the threshold of a new and menacing ordeal, but there were promises too.

One never lost sight of the sunlight and the flowers and the nymphs in the woods, even if they were imaginary.

His last lines caused her to turn toward him.

"I have forgiven, and now you must forgive yourself."

The song ended.

# CHAPTER FIVE

THE DAWN SHOWED IN PATCHES through black, tortured clouds, as the four riders galloped relentlessly back over the same trail that Orfeo had traversed with his sheep just a few days before.

Then, as the light was beginning to achieve a steady dominance, they veered to the south toward Megara, where the Achians kept their boats and the traders of Tyre and Pylos often stopped to leave goods from across the sea and in turn to take on the richly colored fabrics and black cloaks woven by the Achian women.

The people here were a kindred tribe who lived always by the sea or on the sea, going their own ways until times of war when they reaffirmed their loyalty to Kiros and marched under his banner.

They made bronze swords and armor from the copper mines nearby, and these were bought not only by the Achians, but by other peoples bordering the great sea.

Even in Pylos itself and farther a Megaran blade was known for quality, and Megaran ships ventured both east and west, from Tyre to the very Pillars of Hercules.

The same path had been covered the night before by a messenger dispatched by Kiros to alert the seamen to prepare a vessel, and hopefully when the riders arrived at dusk they would be ready to sail.

There had been so much time lost in the council's deliberation that it seemed useless to hurry at this point, but Zurga was insistent that, if possible, they reach Pylos before the slave ship, which would probably have lingered to capture others to be sold there. If they had not sailed directly to Pylos, he hoped for a faint chance that Herron had not yet been sold, and thus they galloped their horses, and the stops were few.

Telemon rode first, followed by his companion Orton, while Orfeo struggled to maintain a steady lead over Zurga, who had a way of looking withered and ancient, but of moving with the grace of a dancer when the occasion demanded agility.

Orfeo had long been away from the saddle, but memories of his youth and his riding with Nestor of Pylos were summoned to propel him steadily onward, peering ahead through eyes narrowed to slits to avoid the dust of the trail.

There were no words exchanged or needed, but the glances from one set of eyes to another seemed to spell out a story that needed no other explanation.

Telemon was obviously displeased, and he was not a man to allow his feelings to go unnoticed.

It was difficult to tell whether he found the company of Orfeo or Zurga the most unbearable, as he could scarcely repress a scowl whenever his gaze fell upon either.

To the old warrior, wanderers - of whom he had encountered perhaps half a dozen - had always been objects of suspicion, to be avoided and handled with a bared blade when the least provocation arose.

Not that they were so common or had frequently crossed his path, but the folklore about their race was such that one could hardly remain neutral or unmoved by stories of their exploits.

To Telemon they were not comprehensible in terms of ordinary human motivation, and he was not certain he could freely disbelieve stories that they could not be killed like ordinary men.

With such a question of vulnerability they consequently posed a threat of the unknown, and Zurga was reputed to be among the most powerful of wanderers.

One could not sleep soundly in his company, and the same reservations were no doubt held by Orton.

Telemon's attitude toward Orfeo was perhaps more complex, and he probably could not have defined the mixture of feelings he experienced toward someone who was the son of his king and an effete, beardless youth of Pylos at the same time.

It was probably Orfeo's lack of military skills that Telemon found most craven, as the young man had brought a battered sword fit only for the practice field, and he almost certainly had no skill in using one.

He carried himself more like a scribe than a soldier, and while there may be explanations as to why some men became priests or scholars, none occurred to Telemon that did not at the same time imply a lack of integrity.

It was simply a matter of manliness.

If Orfeo were fit to be a king's son, then he must also be able to defend his position by force of arms if necessary.

On the contrary, not only was he obviously lacking in such ability, but it was not altogether clear that he even wished to acquire it.

His eyes saw Telemon as a coldly efficient brute, and the warrior perceived enough to read in Orfeo a lack of the unbounded admiration he felt from other men.

That the fault could be any quality of his own did not occur to Telemon.

By the same token Zurga was not entirely pleased with the assemblage, although he would not have contemplated changing its composition.

While he recognized the need for protection and saw Telemon as an ideal provider, he was at the same time even less admiring than Orfeo.

The difference was, however, one of subtlety, as the wanderer was not one to let his thoughts appear on the surface.

While Telemon might suspect that the personage beneath the glistening black cloak was not his friend, he could not hope to fathom the extent to which this was true.

Each found it expedient to have the other as a companion, and there was no point in openly voicing a mutual distrust or disrespect.

Zurga's intentions toward Orfeo were both more simple and complex, as his intended use of the boy - to make inquiries around the docks as to the whereabouts of a newly acquired slave - seemed to speak for itself.

Yet there was another purpose in bringing along a tall, awkward young man that would quite have escaped Telemon.

The Wanderer, indeed, saw something in Orfeo that promised complex accomplishments if allowed to mature properly, and he was particularly impressed by the boy's apparent flexibility in the face of obstacles that would have immobilized others less tenacious.

It had not been without benefit that Orfeo had studied under Isocles, although the Wanderer could not have known that this great master had seen the boy as his most brilliantly endowed pupil. Zurga also sensed the reserve that was capable of holding back feelings and of fencing with words.

There was more here than appeared on the surface, and the boy's resourcefulness labeled him as a natural survivor, whatever the disaster might be.

It was not unfavorable to be in the company of such people, even if one were a Wanderer with formidable enough resources of one's own.

Perhaps it was a Wanderer's talent to surround himself with such people who were most needed for the occasion.

Orton, if anything, was less disposed to charity than Telemon toward their two companions, as he so blindly worshiped his colleague that he picked up his feelings with a vigor that reinforced their strength.

Those that Telemon hated were doubly the enemies of Orton; yet he was a man more given to humor and enjoyment.

In stature he was only slightly the lesser of the warriors, and his shoulders were even broader, but he bore many more marks of battle than his captain, and great reddened scars showed on both arms and on several parts of his face.

His scowl was fierce and his smile almost laughable, coming from such a battered visage.

Orton now kept his brow furrowed in disapproval as he watched Zurga and Orfeo.

There was no telling what the council had in mind by sending such an unlikely company to bring about Herron's return.

Why did they not merely send the two champions to vanquish the fighting men of Pylos?

The stop for a short lunch had seen Orfeo and Zurga sharing cheese across a clearing from the warriors, who broke their own bread.

The sky was beginning to darken prematurely, and this brought some comment from Telemon, who voiced a general suspicion toward ships.

Zurga did not endear himself by adding that ships were made to endure all manner of weather so long as their occupants were unafraid.

Under other circumstances the exchange might have had a different outcome, or perhaps it would not have occurred at all, but the Wanderer's visage revealed to Orfeo that Zurga was taking at least some pleasure in mildly tweaking the warriors.

It was not at all clear just who was the most formidable, and for Orfeo, who felt helpless in such company, there was no recourse but neutrality.

He pretended to study a small bent twig with which he drew figures on the ground.

The afternoon was even more hurried than the morning, as the swirling black clouds created the illusion that the day was drawing to a close, and it had already been determined that the tides would be favorable for departure at sunset.

There was no time to delay, and Orfeo steeled his muscles against the fatigue that was gradually beginning to creep from one limb to the next in a numbing paralysis of will.

But Zurga still relentlessly brought up the rear, showing no signs of tiredness on his deeply wrinkled face.

At times he seemed to Orfeo like death himself tirelessly pursuing the riders, until the whole blended into a dreamlike distortion.

Zurga was the beast of hell wearing down his victims, who still frantically tried to cling to life as it sped by.

There was no choice but to strain every fiber to keep ahead, to strive and run and struggle to prevail.

The trees now seemed to whiz past and the group disappeared beneath them.

Orfeo clung to the reins and tried to think in terms other than time.

Finally the clouds were more than merely heavy with a storm, as the sun had dipped behind the mountains, and there was still no sign of Megara, but in the dying rays of daylight, there was a distant glimmering and a smell of the sea, and soon they came into view of the squat wooden buildings around the port.

A short and perilous pier jutted toward the sea from a rocky base, and the ships of the Megarans bobbed helplessly in the tide, looking anything like the proud ships of Pylos, but still able to meet the wind and waves on their own terms. A torch burned at one berth, and there were men still busied in loading provisions onto one of the ships.

At the approach of the horsemen through the settlement one of them detached himself from the group and sounded a greeting.

Telemon made an answer, and then fell into an animated discussion which Orfeo could scarcely hear, as the wind had now risen, and the words seemed submerged in the roaring of the sea.

Soon it became clear, however, that there was some question about setting sail at this time, as a great storm was threatening, but Telemon was adamant.

They had been instructed to leave as soon as possible, and a delay could possibly lessen their chances of success.

Telemon was now representing himself as fearing neither ships nor the sea, and he made his desire to debark so vehement that Zurga stepped forward to intercede.

The other man, who identified himself as Colin, Captain of their vessel, appeared hesitant to attempt reason with the great warrior whose fame had preceded him into all the Argive lands, but he addressed himself, somewhat reluctantly, to Zurga, who was not without reputation himself.

The Wanderer at least listened to the captain describe the seriousness of the weather, but he too seemed adamant, although it was not clear how much this was influenced by Telemon.

The latter stood without flickering a muscle and scowled, as though to talk of holding back now was cowardly.

The issue was soon settled, with Colin assuming a stoic lack of acceptance and motioning for his retainers to care for the horses.

The travelers followed him to the pier as the crew made its final preparations.

Zurga stood almost completely enwrapped in his black cloak, which seemed to grow or shrink in accord with its needs.

He glowered out over the waves and turned to Orfeo with a twinkle.

"Afraid?" he asked solemnly.

"Yes," answered Orfeo. "I'm afraid of the sea when it storms."

"Ahhhhhh........"

The Wanderer looked pleased at the answer, but appeared to chastise mockingly.

"That's not a good Achian to be afraid.

What will the warriors think?"

The reference seemed pointed at Telemon and Orton, who made no recognition of having heard.

"I'm more cautious and guarded when I'm afraid," said Orfeo. "It's saved my life more than once."

Telemon finally turned with a contemptuous scowl, as though goaded past endurance.

"And there'll also be a time when holding back will be the death of you, and it takes only once."

His manner did not seem to invite further comment, and he busied himself again talking with the captain.

"Are you a coward?"

Zurga asked, almost in jest and perhaps even mockingly of Telemon.

"I don't know," the boy answered.

"I don't really know what it means to be a coward or not."

"Said like a true pupil of Isocles," the Wanderer laughed.

Orfeo watched as the ropes for the sail were reattached and wound.

The crew, which numbered about a half dozen men aside from the captain, seemed apprehensive, but still ready to sail, and at Colin's command, they entered the boat, with Telemon striding forward just before the captain.

The boat was pitching heavily and rubbing against the moorings so that it seemed to settle as it was pushed free.

Then the full vigor of the sea began to take hold, as they gradually pulled away from the dock in the last light of a day that had begun at Delphi.

But it was here that the journey truly began, as the land of the Achians had once again receded from under the feet of Orfeo.

He was cold, afraid, and uncertain of the future, but life at the camp, whether in Delphi or the lands by the sea, had not promised much since his return.

He had a home neither with his parents nor kinsmen, and the strangers he now found in his company were no more nor less distant than those he had been born among.

Orfeo watched the land diminish in the distance and sang to himself.

Would he again see his home?

Indeed, where was home and who were his people?

# CHAPTER SIX

THE FULL FORCE OF THE STORM did not strike until just before the next dawn, as all through the night the ship had sailed beneath a sky of total darkness.

Orfeo slept below the deck on a straw mat that smelled of salt water, but he had kept warm in his woolen cloak, and there was a restful quality to the boat's motion once he became accustomed to the rhythm.

Even Telemon had at first looked clumsy and ill at ease in trying to move around the swaying ship, but soon he had mastered the art of leaning into the movement and balancing with the other foot.

He stood with the captain at the wheel and talked of war and old battles, while Orton had joined in with the crew and contributed his broad shoulders to helping with various tasks around the ship.

Zurga seemed to sleep not at all, and although he had stationed himself in one corner of the compartment occupied by Orfeo, his eyes always seemed to be open.

Finally when the storm broke there was no rest for anyone, as the waves suddenly seemed to take on a new pattern.

Instead of gradually lifting the ship to a crest and then allowing it to settle, they started to cross the deck, at first merely covering it with a surface of water that quickly receded, and then coming to submerge the entire surface for seconds at a time.

The sails were laboriously brought down, with the seamen struggling to keep a grip on the boat as much as to accomplish their tasks, and soon the movement became such that merely staying in one place, whether standing or sitting, required continual effort.

The wind screamed and beat upon them with a biting cold rain, while the darkness transmitted only the vaguest hint that somewhere above the clouds there was a moon.

The crew had weathered storms before, and Colin remained at the wheel with no visible signs of concern, but clearly Orton had lost much of his poise, and Telemon, the old warrior who had long flung his life in the teeth of fate, had summoned his composure for another test of endurance.

The boat creaked and seemed ready to burst at the seams, but somehow it remained intact from one upheaval to the next.

Orfeo clung to the mast in its extension below the deck, feeling his muscles begin to ache from the strain of perpetually grasping the wooden beam, but the alternative was to be buffeted about like a leaf in the wind.

He looped both arms around the great trunk and pressed his body securely upon it, but the storm seemed to grow ever more violent, as if there would be no relief.

Soon only Zurga and Orfeo remained below, and it had become clear that this was no ordinary storm in the history of the boat.

Most distressing was the accumulation of water in the hold, which now reached just below Orfeo's knees when the ship was on a level plane, and at other times it seemed to obey the flow of water outside the ship, rising and falling as miniature parodies of the sea.

The light was just sufficient to permit Orfeo a glance at Zurga, who clung to the other mast, but the wanderer's eyes betrayed no more fear than ever, and perhaps there was a trace of amusement. Surely the race of Wanderers was a different species from that of ordinary men, not even fearing death itself.

Orfeo knew the numbing terror of standing on the brink of nothingness, dependent only upon his own hands and arms to save himself from destruction.

It was then that the hatches above were closed so that there was now no light, but only the desperate turning and falling and clinging now in a lonely vacuum.

The sounds and the sensations more than made up for the lack of sight.

Above the deck others fared no better, as Colin had resorted to the expedient of having himself lashed to the wheel so that he would not be swept overboard as he tried to give the ship some small impetus in one direction rather than another, but essentially they were at the mercy of the elements.

One of the seamen, perhaps two, had already succumbed to the breaking waves, while Telemon and Orton clung stubbornly to any support that might save them from the angry waters.

No one had yet given voice to the fear or suspicion that this was no ordinary storm or that the ship was perhaps in real danger; but the realization traveled from face to face.

It was not clear whether the ship could survive much more of the incessant pounding, as it was already riding lower in the water, and the masts, even without sails, seemed unable to withstand another assault.

Then the rear mast splintered and disappeared over the side, trailing with it most of the railing from that part of the ship. Colin's stand at the wheel was miraculously undisturbed, but now there was a look of desperation about him that told a story to the others.

Orfeo had heard the great rending of wood above deck and, hearing nothing to the contrary from Zurga, feared that the ship was in the process of disintegration. His first thought was to make himself free of the confining hull, but plans beyond that included little more than the intention to cling to some floatable fragment of wood until the storm abated.

There was little time for any thoughts other than those directly related to survival.

The ship was twisting and turning so violently that water had somehow managed to find a way through the hatches or even the hull itself, and the level now extended to mid thigh.

Orfeo inched his way toward the ladder and slowly raised himself to where he could push against the hatch, but the sudden terror crossed his already shivering body that it was fastened, that there would be no escape from this trap of rising water.

They had been forgotten, and surely no one above deck would stop to think of them.

Indeed, the others might well have been swept overboard.

In his hopeless terror Orfeo was thrown from his perch on the ladder into the turbulent brine of the hold, but almost as a rebound he was again lifted into the air as the ship lurched forward.

Clawing at another perch, he found himself clinging to the base of the ladder and able to inch upward.

If he were to pound on the hatch cover someone might allow him to leave, he thought, but he realized that with the thunder of the waves there would be no hearing a feeble knocking from below.

At one point he cried out for Zurga, but the wanderer's voice, if he answered at all, seemed only to blend with the creaking of the ship's timbers.

If anything the pitching was becoming even more violent.

Then the boat seemed to stand upright, prow seemingly pointed straight down, and then the great crunch came, rending the air with sounds of splintering even before it was clear just which parts of the ship had not withstood the strain.

The water was now rising more rapidly in the hold, but somewhere there was a faint gray light.

It was a way out of the flooded prison, but it beckoned forward in the hold rather than above the ladder.

Orfeo scrambled toward it, blindly flailing his arms to propel himself through the water, only the ship now tilted so that he was hurled back and tumbled into a disorganized mass of arms and legs struggling to keep his head from being submerged.

Again he struggled toward the light, and this time he was able to leap and grab at a gaping hole in the deck, seeing as he did so in one brief field of vision as he swung that the whole front of the ship had disappeared, and water swirled where the first mast had been.

In another arching of his body he propelled his legs through the hole, almost immediately experiencing a sense of regret that he had left a relatively safe place for the unknown hazards of another.

The wind struck first, much more biting cold and overwhelmingly powerful than he had imagined.

He crouched against some protruding beams of wood for support and clung with all his remaining strength as the next wave crashed over the ship.

About him there was no trace of Telemon or Orton, and the entire crew had disappeared.

Clearly the ship was floundering and could remain afloat little longer, but what had happened to the crew?

Had they been swept off helplessly into the sea, or was there some other route to safety?

Then the image of Zurga came to mind.

The wanderer was still below, possibly drowned or still clinging to the shattered stump of mast.

There were only minutes remaining for him to be rescued, as the next great wave, or the one after, could send the boat to the bottom of the sea.

Inching toward the gaping hole in the deck, careful to keep from being swept over the side by wind or waves, Orfeo managed to look again over the torn edge.

He searched with his eyes where the wanderer had been but there was no trace.

Finally, the cloak caught a glimmer of light and revealed the wiry form clinging to a protruding rod far beneath Orfeo's perch.

The wanderer waved his hand, and it was only on sight that Orfeo realized that part of the background noise of the storm had been Zurga's voice screaming for rescue.

The Wanderer looked anything but panicked, but there was a gravity about his expression that left no doubt as to his concern.

Again the ship was wracked by a wave more furiously destructive than its fellows, and through a haze of driving rain Orfeo saw large chunks of wood torn from the floundering hulk that now supported them.

By this time his actions were not so much governed by thought, but by reflexes set into a determined pattern.

He must inch forward enough to grasp Zurga's hand and pull him from the floating coffin of the hold, but he was having trouble extending his arm far enough, and there was no rope to throw below.

He fell forward over the jagged opening and then, with another great lurching of the ship, he blindly extended his hand, not so much in expectation of success, but at least as a gesture of effort.

If they were going to die in the process, at least they would die with Orfeo's arm extended in readiness to receive the Wanderer's, as there was neither hope nor opportunity even to think clearly.

All thought had become confused in the noise and movements of swirling chaos.

The feel of something between his fingers other than water was a shock, and then it seemed to be draining away before he recovered his composure enough to clinch his fist upon it.

It was Zurga's shiny black cape, which he had somehow thrown as the proffered vehicle for escape, and now Orfeo braced himself to support the weight of another.

Zurga sprung upward with an incredible agility for one of his age and then implanted one bony hand upon the deck just as the boat listed to one side and aided him in depositing his body outside the hold.

He was free, and the two were now exposed to the angry, open sea, with only a sinking, disintegrating hulk to buoy them through what remained of the storm.

But there was still no letting up of the wind.

The two figures remaining on the deck appeared to expend their entire energies clinging to various protruding parts of the sinking ship, but at the same time Zurga appeared lost in activities of his own.

From his garments he removed a great belt-like band from around his chest and transferred it to Orfeo, managing either to shout instruction for its use or demonstrate with gestures how it should be fastened in place and then inflated through an air tube protruding from the front.

It was a device of utter strangeness to Orfeo, who noticed that the wanderer was wearing another belt of the same type.

It was clearly intended to keep a person afloat by such simple means that it seemed everyone going to sea should have one, but it did not answer the question as to what should be done when adrift in the water.

The answer must soon be forthcoming, as the ship was now more than half submerged and moved with such inertia that the last remnants of deck were rapidly succumbing to the crushing weight of the waves.

The end could come any second, but Zurga still held on as if he were awaiting a particular event.

Finally the greatest swell completely engulfed the remainder of the ship, and when the water subsided there was little left above the water line.

It was then that Zurga extended one end of the cloak and motioned for Orfeo to bind it around his waist.

With the next swell and the total disappearance of the ship the two were thus cast adrift, bound together by that curious garment of black that now seemed like no more than a thin rope between them.

Yet for some reason neither appeared to sink.

Both heads bobbed among the foam, and in a sense there was a greater stability even than on the doomed vessel, which had provided the sort of bulwark that could not bend sufficiently with the wind and waves.

Now the task was to await the storm's end, and almost as soon as that realization came to mind, the force of the swirling torrent of water seemed to diminish, and suddenly there was a brightness that cut through the clouds and blinding golden rays of hope.

Daylight had arrived, and somewhere calm and safety awaited.

Even the roar had diminished, the confusion of the maelstrom subsiding more precipitously than it had appeared.

"It's ending...." Orfeo could say little more as he turned himself toward the Wanderer.

"Did you ever think it wouldn't?"

The Wanderer seemed perfectly composed and no less dignified for his apparent helplessness in the water.

"Not the storm.....but I thought it would be the end of us."

"We'll survive," Zurga replied.

"Before this journey's over, we'll have more than this to worry about."

He seemed to regard Orfeo with a pleased countenance.

"That's not a very hopeful look at the future."

"Then perhaps the future is not all that hopeful," this time Zurga managed a wry laugh, as comfortably as if he had been seated by the fire in the Achian camp rather than adrift in the numbing waters of a turbulent sea.

Soon the mist had risen completely and the welcomed sight of land greeted them in the direction of the sun.

The breakers were suddenly both visible and audible, as if all during the storm they had lingered just off the coast where they could have landed.

Zurga and Orfeo continued to drift with the current until they seemed to be approaching no nearer to the beach, and then Zurga began to churn his arms in a motion that guided them toward shore.

Orfeo felt his confidence return as they were methodically propelled toward safety.

Only now did he begin to feel the fright that had accompanied this real threat to his life. He was surviving a situation that had at first seemed hopeless; yet the fear only now penetrated his consciousness as it was clear the danger was rapidly receding.

Murray Lee Eiland Jr.

# Chapter Seven

Zurga was the first to right himself and begin to walk toward the sandy beach.

"So we must find our incautious companions, Telemon and Orton," the Wanderer said as if the problem of dry clothes, warmth, and food were of no concern.

"I trust they will be somewhere close along the beach."

"You think they made it to shore without these?"

Orfeo was reminded of the bulging belt around his chest that had kept him afloat.

"I should think they would have done as well in the small boat," Zurga replied.

"I heard them shove overboard only a few minutes before we managed to climb out of the hold."

"You think they could have made it in the smaller boat?"

"You underestimate Colin," the wanderer continued.

"He's a fine seaman and has doubtless survived numerous wrecks just as I have survived.

He will have brought his passengers to safety."

"You sound unconcerned with danger, as though you have always lived and will continue to surmount all dangers."

"I will probably live longer than Telemon." There was a somber sound to his voice.

"At least I don't throw myself heedlessly in the path of any storm that could have been avoided merely by waiting slightly more than half a day."

"Then you must have known there would be a great storm."

"I knew, and Colin knew, and perhaps most of the crew knew as well, but it was clear that there was no arguing with Telemon.

The boat would have left anyway, with his wrath rather than his respect, and there was no point even in advising him to be cautious.

He would have all the more reason to distrust me in the future, particularly since I would have been proven right this time.

It would have been intolerable to him, and I imagined that we'd make it across anyway."

"No thanks to him," Orfeo said.

"I thought he was sent to guard those who were sent to get Herron back by diplomacy."

"Never forget that he gave no thought to either of us," said Zurga.

"He is not a bad man, but focused more on himself and his own needs than on the welfare of others."

Orfeo felt both an uncomfortable and admiring respect for the Wanderer's ability to see the weaknesses of his fellow man.

"The only question," said Zurga, "is whether to travel North or South along the beach, as we must make all haste to find Telemon.

Since he probably assumes we have drowned, he will likely set off for Pylos as soon as possible and there make our jobs more difficult."

"Then what's to prevent us from setting out on our own?"

Zurga seemed surprised by the suggestion, as though he had been accustomed to assessing all the possibilities.

"And why might we do that, my young friend?"

"In order to put me to my intended use as a spy along the waterfront," Orfeo answered.

"It would be far less conspicuous for us to arrive in two separate parties, and we would easily be able to locate Telemon once we were all in the city, provided, of course, that he actually did live through the storm."

"A true student of Isocles," the wanderer nodded his head as he straightened his garments and returned his cloak to its usual station.

"There may be wisdom in what you suggest, but there is a reason for us to travel escorted to two men at arms, since we will be moving forward from this point over land.

But I will keep the thought in mind to see whether it would have been a preferable course."

"And if I turn out to be right, then you'll distrust my advice all the more?"

Orfeo lifted his voice in a teasing jibe.

"Wanderers are not soldiers," Zurga smiled.

"In the meantime let's travel to the south.

The wind would have carried a small boat in that direction."

Orfeo managed to follow after the gaunt wanderer, but he became increasingly aware of a growing hunger and a great fatigue from the night and morning of fighting the storm.

His legs seemed unsteady, and there was a lightness about his thoughts that made him fearful that at any moment he would fall spiraling toward the sand.

As if aware of this discomfort, Zurga reached into a bag made of the same material as his resplendent cloak and withdrew a cheese-like substance which tasted of sweetness and salt at the same time and filled the mouth with a sensation of contentment.

Still they continued to walk, with Zurga methodically scanning the scene for traces of life.

The wanderer seemed so confident that Orfeo felt no real surprise when they came within sight of a small wooden boat.

Zurga quickened his pace and then stopped to look carefully at the last surviving piece of Colin's vessel.

"From the number of oars in their locks, I would think that most of the men reached safety, which means that our two companions are surely still among the living."

"Surely also they are just recently departed, as even the footprints near the water are deep and fresh," Orfeo added.

Zurga again appraised the boy with a curious gaze that seemed to convey some recognition that here was more than an ordinary youth of seventeen.

They set off after the tracks without further explanation until Zurga deviated away from the shore to a small hillock providing a good view of the beach remaining ahead of them.

"There go our friends," he pointed off the distance, and Orfeo at first had difficulty making out the shapes, but eventually he could distinguish eight stick-like figures walking away from them.

"Quickly," said Zurga, "Let's not be seen and reach the next village ahead of them."

"What village?"

Again Orfeo found it difficult to follow the wanderer's mind, but he suspected that there would be little benefit in asking, as the answer would come only when Zurga was willing.

This time their course turned inland away from the sea, and Zurga led as if he had traversed the same faint trails countless times.

They climbed for perhaps an hour, and then breathlessly pulled themselves to the top of a ridge that surveyed the water from both sides.

Looking back Orfeo could see the way in which they had come, and looking forward again there was the sea.

It was a jutting promontory of land they had crossed, thus saving a great distance by not walking the long way around.

If they descended as rapidly to the beach they would probably be ahead of their companions, and this is apparently what Zurga had in mind.

"I could tell we were on a small peninsula by the current and the tide," Zurga added, as if this in itself provided an explanation.

More likely he was trying to impress Orfeo that their advantage had not come about through a guess or accident.

"You're trying to beat them to the first village," Orfeo said.

"A likely surmise," Zurga replied confidently. "But perhaps the idea can best be understood if it were labeled as diplomacy."

"Telemon and Orton are our friends, not enemies."

"My naive child, diplomacy is for all the world, not just those we would seek to deceive.

And are you quite so certain that the two soldiers hold us dear? Did you see either of them thinking of our welfare during the storm?"

"They were fortunate enough to have survived themselves."

Orfeo followed with some difficulty, as the wanderer's strides increased in length and speed.

The old man seemed capable of expending enormous quantities of energy without tiring.

Finally they were again within sight of the shore, and Zurga, without venturing close enough to leave footprints of his own, satisfied himself that no one else had passed ahead of them.

He then indicated that they should proceed just enough inland to keep out of sight, and soon they began to see traces of civilization around them.

The trail broadened into a path, and, as they began to pass dwellings, this widened to a crude road.

Zurga did not deign to stop at any of the houses, but gave friendly waves to the villagers who watched their progress.

At last they entered the town, just at the point where the beach gave way to great boulders, and the sea encroached to form a small sheltered bay.

They had found a port certainly larger and busier than Megara, but still a far cry from the magnificence of Pylos.

Zurga seemed not at all abashed by the business around him, and he walked boldly past the outer fortifications into the heart of the town.

There was no stealth in his approach now.

Several armed men fell in beside them as they climbed to the highest part of town, where they found themselves directed to a small courtyard.

There the town master sat on an elevated chair that seemed a poor travesty of royal magnificence, yet was still more elegant than the court of Kiros.

"I am Zurga of Pergamos cast upon your shores by the chance of wind and tide," the wanderer began in a resounding, confident voice.

"I am traveling to Pylos with a message for the king, and I seek your assistance, for which I will gladly pay."

The light glistened upon his resplendent black cloak, and the others standing around the courtyard hushed as though expectant of some extraordinary transaction.

"Welcome, Zurga, to the port of Brina under the protection of Pylos.

I am Kyle, of the Lenites, who inhabit this coast.

We are honored by your presence, as we have heard many stories of one such as yourself who is reputed to work magic and to be a man of honor."

The master carefully inspected the newcomers as he spoke.

"Wanderer only," responded Zurga.

"Or some will have it more.

But I have also heard it widely said that the men of Brina are hospitable and honest.

I am pleased to be among you, with my companion Leos of the Achians.

I am also expecting two Achian warriors along with six Argive sailors, who were cast adrift from the same ship during the storm.

They should be close behind, and I wish you also to bid them welcome, as they travel with me and also have business with the king in Pylos."

Orfeo made no move to indicate surprise at the change in his name.

"Wanderers are welcome and boys in their company, be they Achian or not, but the issue is not so clear for Achian warriors, with whom we have not always enjoyed pleasant relations in the past."

Kyle did not seem menacing so much as cautious.

"Then the names of my companions may prove further cause for anxiety, as I am accompanied by no less than Telemon and Orton, the two greatest champions of their people."

"Ahhh……"

Kyle drew back perceptibly, and the retainers reacted with immediate interest and concern.

"But they come in peace, wishing no harm to anyone, and surely even a great warrior needs permission of the master of Brina to pass inland across country to Pylos."

Orfeo looked in mild amusement as the Wanderer's facile tongue prepared the way for others so much more effectively than Telemon himself could have secured a welcome.

Clearly there was good reason to have come ahead; yet that was not all Zurga had in mind for the day.

Indeed, after he had successfully calmed the fears of Kyle and his men, with a subtle blend of reassurance and flattery, he also secured for Orfeo a new set of clothing, which gave him the appearance of a young gentleman.

The new tunic was finely woven of white wool, with elegant embroidery in black along the edges.

The sandals were the finest Orfeo had worn since his days in Pylos, and even the cloak was an improvement over the garments he had lost to the sea.

By the time Telemon and Orton arrived, the wanderer and Orfeo had successfully installed themselves in elegance among the retainers of Kyle, feasting on fruits and freshly roasted meat.

The sky was already beginning to darken as a chorus of shouting had arisen down in the village and a great cluster of men appeared amidst shouting and the clamor of arms.

Telemon did not customarily arrive without fanfare, and he had, as was his custom, loudly announced his name upon his arrival. The armed men of Brina, expecting his arrival, had responded with no overt hostility, but still they found it necessary to accompany him to the master's reception yard, as they were not so reassured by Telemon's haughty, militant bearing as to assume his peaceful intent.

"I am Telemon the Achian on business to the court of Pylos," he intoned imperiously in the direction of Kyle.

Apparently he did not notice the figures of Zurga and Orfeo seated prominently among the retainers.

Orton stood proudly at his side, while the sailors of Colin stood ill at east in the background.

Kyle seemed at first rather annoyed at the demanding tone, but after noticing the undoubted determination of the warrior, and perhaps with a memory of Telemon's reputation that had spread far beyond his own land, the master of the city turned deferentially to Zurga.

"Our friend Zurga has made us aware of your arrival and bids that we welcome you as friends." He clapped his hands together and bade that a small table be brought into the courtyard and set with food for the travelers.

Almost before he knew what had happened, Telemon was invited to be seated for a feast.

Obviously the warrior had been startled at the name of Zurga, and he was even more surprised to see his two companions ensconced in such comfort, but he too was not without diplomatic skills.

The surprise was fleeting across his face, and within a few silent seconds he was able to compose a reply.

"Ah, there you are.

You two are hard to keep track of, but at least you've saved us the trouble of looking for you."

There was not a word about their having survived, nor any wonder that they should have found safety in Brina first. Even less was there any overt recognition that the Wanderer's presence had made the way easier in dealing with the men of this town, yet surely these facts were not lost on the old warrior.

He nodded with inner appreciation of how he had been made to appear a blunderer, and he merely stored away a reminder that his two companions had something about them that bore watching.

At least the Wanderer was potentially dangerous, if the same could not be said of the king's citified son.

Kyle proved most helpful later when arrangements were being made for the overland journey to Pylos, as none of them now wished to continue by sail.

Now it seemed just as easy to travel five days by land, particularly as another great storm threatened.

Arrangements were made for Colin and his companions to return to Megara on a Lenite ship. For a ship to Pylos, however, the companions would be required to wait three days, and Telemon was too eager to get moving again.

He insisted that they make the rest of the trip overland, and horses and provisions were readied for the four companions to resume their travels in the morning.

Meanwhile the Lenites provided a most gracious hospitality, and the warriors drank far into the night while Zurga conferred with Kyle.

Orfeo found himself incredibly worn by events of the last day, as he continued to relive the experience of leaving the ill-fated ship.

It now seemed like the distant past, in some ways like little more than a violent swim, although one brave sailing man had perished.

Still the warriors seemed unperturbed, and if Zurga let the matter disturb his sleep, there was no evidence on the surface.

Perhaps it was merely the lifestyle of those people who traveled about in the world partaking of its intricacies and intrigues.

Orfeo was not sure he was cut out for such adventure.

# Chapter Eight

The road from Brina to Pylos climbed sharply from the sea into the mountains overlooking the town and then plunged defiantly into a series of rocky ridges and ravines that turned the landscape into a barren wasteland with only a few scattered villages.

They crossed several small valleys populated with isolated farms, but the entire first day's journey did little to relieve the monotony of the landscape, and they seemed just as far from their destination as at daybreak.

They had ridden at a pace comfortable for the horses, as there would not likely be replacements until they reached Pylos, and they were not pressed now by frantic haste.

Kyle had warned them that morning about brigands in the mountains, but they had seen not the remotest trace of danger.

The horses seemed able to continue even after the sun descended, but finally Telemon called a halt to the day's journey and indicated that they were to make their camp beneath a great rocky overhang that shielded them from the wind and prying eyes that might intrude from the west.

Orton built a low fire, and the four travelers shared a meal of fruits and cheeses from Brina.

Orton had also procured several skins of wine, which he generously offered even to Orfeo and Zurga, toward whom he was showing increasingly more trust.

They began to talk stiffly, at first, as though their throats were still clogged with dust of the trail, but before they drifted off to sleep there was a growing feeling that indeed they shared a common purpose if not a common approach to life.

Telemon particularly seemed to bear more respect for Zurga, and he cautiously approached the question of how the latter two had survived destruction of the ship.

Zurga, with his eyes twinkling in reflected light from the fire, was slyly evasive, lightly calling attention to folktales about the special powers of Wanderers.

"Can you walk on the waters?"

Telemon asked skeptically.

"Only if I must," Zurga replied, at least secure in his knowledge that he could not be called upon to do so now.

Orton apparently believed in Zurga's powers, at least more than Telemon, as he seemed to think it not a fit subject to joke about.

There was something both more serious and more lighthearted about him, as he had become neither such a grim killer nor a lusty liver as his friend.

Both, however, treated Orfeo as no more than a boy, which only Zurga seemed reluctant to accept.

Telemon particularly began to chide Orfeo as to how he had survived the storm, but Zurga did not allow a reply, volunteering himself that he had been greatly aided by the boy.

This was received skeptically, but with the reservation from Telemon and Orton that, like other claims of the Wanderer, it just might be true.

The next morning was overcast and gloomy, like the sky before they had set out on the ships from Megara.

The horses seemed well rested, however, and they began making good time across the wide valley that opened up before a range of hills that promised to be much more formidable than those they had crossed the day before.

The tops were hidden by clouds, but when they started upward again sometime after their noon rest, the road seemed well kept and easily passable. It was perhaps this evidence of heavy traffic that made Telemon cautious, as it would be the likely place for bandits.

The great warrior decreed that he would take the lead, with Orton riding enough in the rear so that all of them being caught in an ambush together would be less likely.

Still, even early in the climb, Orfeo could see many places where a surprise attack could have been launched; yet there was no sign either of trouble or of other travelers today.

Perhaps Kyle had exaggerated.

They reached the top of one ridge sometime near the middle of the afternoon, and Telemon expressed a hope that by evening they would again be out of the mountains.

But this was soon dispelled when they again started uphill, winding around blind turns without any expectation as to what lay ahead.

The danger presented itself without warning and so unobtrusively that only Telemon reacted with a clear comprehension that they had been attacked.

They had ridden up a narrow defile with sheer granite walls and a chill, damp wind that seemed to have come from a great cavern.

Only a slice of sky was visible above the steeply sloping sides, but the trail seemed to lead toward the top where they could again feel safer from any unseen enemy.

Perhaps they had begun to ride faster from some unconscious fear of such places; yet even when the three forward riders rounded a turn and saw the way blocked by a boulder, there seemed to be no possible reaction that could save them from further danger.

Then a great rumbling noise arose from the rear just as Orton galloped around the bend, and the cloud of dust at his heels announced that the trail behind him had been closed by a rockslide.

They were trapped in a small prison of sheer stone with no apparent escape, still contemplating a response when the armed men leaped upon them from a ledge perhaps ten feet off the ground, but which had been invisible until the onslaught.

Telemon, of course, had already drawn his sword before the first sight of an enemy, and there was something so reflexive in the great, sweeping motion of his arm that the first body seemed hacked to an amorphous mass before it had completed the arc of its jump.

Orton was less ready with his weapon, and he found himself grappling with two men dressed in shaggy dark tunics, while other invaders seemed to swarm about them.

Orfeo had scarcely time to think, as he was tumbled rudely from his horse.

In falling he caught sight of a fiery sphere that Zurga swung on a thin chain, making great swirls through the air as it descended first upon one and then another, but even he was sorely pressed, and the situation appeared hopeless.

Almost with realizing what he was about, by some preconscious instinct for survival, Orfeo sought out routes of escape, spying with a quick glance the one rent in the rock that must - although he could not tell how - lead to the ledge that had held the armed men.

If he could only slip aside as the men fought, hoping they would continue to ignore him, he could possibly pull himself above the turmoil and climb to safety.

Surely he would be no help below, and now he was aware that over ten men had taken part in the attack.

He sprang with clear purpose toward the other side of the gorge and slipped deftly into the cleft in the rock that led upwards.

He arched his back so that his feet held on one side, while his body provided a counter weight, and even though there was no place for his hands to assist, he was able to inch his way upwards, stretching each muscle for maximum speed and agility, aware - now that he was hidden from view - of the noise from the fighting below.

Then he was on the ledge and seeking out further escape with his eyes until the two figures intruded upon his awareness.

Two more of the invaders still stood above, both with bows strung and awaiting what would present itself below as a clear shot.

So rapt in their duty were these two that they both remained unaware of Orfeo's approach from the rear, and they were toppled forward with a rush that almost destroyed his own balance and sent him back to the scene of carnage from which he had emerged.

But there was still no holding back, and he began to ascend the first likely route that presented itself, feeling himself rise above the noise, or was the noise dying out?

Had the great Achian hero fallen with his companion, and had the wanderer Zurga finally laid down his fiery orb?

The mace of fire still was reflected on the walls below.

Perhaps all was no yet lost.

Better that he made greater haste in escaping.

Another twenty feet above the first ledge Orfeo found another, wide enough for five men to stand, but not promising of a comfortable bed.

It was here that the holds for his hands and feet disappeared, and it was clear he could go no farther.

At the same time he seemed well hidden enough, and there was always the possibility that he could climb down at a later time if the bandits departed after despoiling his friends.

He settled himself upon the ledge, prepared either to wait or defend himself with the short sword he had carried from home.

He would certainly not be removed from his perch without taking at least one enemy with him; yet there was a possibility he would not be noticed.

Soon the clamor died completely, and for a while there was complete silence.

Then voices broke the air, although as yet they were too quiet to be understood and strangely disquieting.

Something was dreadfully wrong, but he could not determine what until the voice of Telemon resounded along the walls in a great echoing cry.

The next thing he heard was his own name, shouted both angrily and expectantly.

They were still alive and calling to him.

By some great feat of arms, the bandits had been defeated, and at least Telemon still lived.

Orfeo crept down to the first ledge and, seeing no one about, cautiously peered over the top.

Below all three sets of eyes returned his stare, while about them the bodies of bandits lay piled in disarray.

The visages turned upward were not, however, startlingly more friendly.

Obviously he would contend with considerable anger below.

When Orfeo descended the remaining distance and stood face to face with the old warrior, he felt a massive anger beat at him, as though he had been guilty of an unpardonable breech of decorum.

"If you were a warrior, or even a man, I'd kill you for that," Telemon allowed no trace of respect.

"But we'll talk more of it when we reach camp this night.

There will be more said later about your cowardice in the face of danger, and the memory will linger long with me and with our people.

You are truly a man of Pylos rather than an Achian."

Even Zurga, who himself was not a warrior nor thought like one, seemed angry, as the four continued up the defile until the sky opened above them, and they could see a long gently sloping trail to the fertile plains below.

Still they pressed onward, as the danger had not disappeared.

They had survived one attack by bandits, but there was no guarantee they would not be set upon by another group.

Before dark they found a suitable place on an embankment overlooking a stream.

There they made camp and consumed their rations of the day, still silent, as if awaiting the ordeal that Orfeo had unwittingly brought upon himself.

"Explain your cowardly actions."

Telemon brought the matter into the open with a contemptuous voice.

"I am waiting to see what this young man of letters can do with his silvery tongue to defend himself."

He sat on a large rock by the campfire, while the silent Orton sat on Orfeo's other side, radiating the same disgust.

"You say I was a coward," Orfeo began, fighting a tightness in his throat that had threatened to choke his breath as it increased during the day.

"If being a coward means that I was afraid, then it is true.

I was afraid.

If being a coward means that I sought to run and save my life, then it is true.

I wanted to survive."

"It's your kind that spoils an army," Telemon interrupted angrily.

"When safety lies in standing together, when the only security a man knows is that the territory just behind him and to either side of him is held by a friend, then to think of oneself is to bring destruction to all."

He drew his great weapon as if the dramatize the point. "Only we have a calf who bolts when danger strikes and leaves his companions without a guard on one flank."

His rage only increased as he spoke, and Orton silently seemed to mirror these feelings.

"But I thought we were all dead," Orfeo now blurted out the words, both in fright and in a desperate effort to defend himself.

"There were so many of them, and they were on us before we had any means of defending ourselves."

"Did you expect them to write their intentions on a sheepskin and give us time to arm and prepare a position?"

Orton now interrupted caustically.

"They were bandits, and we had been told to expect them.

Did you give no thought to what you would do in case of an attack?"

Telemon glared fiercely.

"But better that one survive than all die," Orfeo answered.

"And do you think for a moment that they would have let you live?

Could you imagine that once we had been killed, none of them would remember that our number was four instead of three and that the younger of us had slipped into a cleft in the rock."

"I may or may not have escaped."

Already Orfeo had been aware that his passage upward along the rock had been limited.

"I would not have escaped," he added solemnly.

"I did wrong to think only of myself, or rather to take the short view.

The chances of all of us would have been better had I fought with the rest of you."

Orfeo now felt completely beaten and submissive, as though a great error had been confessed, and he was dependent upon forgiveness in order to retain any place with his companions."

"But then if you had stayed in the gorge with the rest of us, you would not have been able to topple the archers," said Zurga.

"And then at least one of us would surely have fallen."

Orton and Telemon looked startled and displeased.

"Ahhhh....yes.

The archers were above us."

Telemon appeared reluctant to concede the smallest point. "And it serves you well that you did not mention them in your defense."

He looked at Orfeo with more compassion and swung his sword almost gently so that it rested on the boy's shoulder.

"Look, my boy, you are a defenseless whelp and of no help to the rest of us when we are attacked.

But there is still something about you that is not all bad.

It's just that you have never learned to be a soldier.

You have never acquired the art of saving your life by means other than your wits, and, believe me, there are limits to that."

The old warrior now had softened his tone, while Orfeo tried to accept the words with his full concentration. They were not, indeed, the wisdom he had been taught by Isocles, and perhaps they stood at opposite poles to the image of behavior preached by his great master.

But even with his skepticism there was something he could learn.

The master had emphasized that everyone has his message to deliver.

"Even the Wanderer knows how to fight," Orton had also cooled his anger, but he apparently had gained a further respect for Zurga from the latter's skill at wielding his mace of fire.

The respect probably extended to the germ of a reluctance to face this weapon, as it had bestowed destruction as lavishly as the sword of Telemon.

"You must learn," the Wanderer said solemnly.

"I've heard that those who live by the sword die by the sword, but I have not convinced myself that this death comes about any sooner because of an ability to use a weapon."

He ran his hand along the blade of Telemon's great shaft of metal.

"After all, it's merely another technique, and you can always choose when and where to use it."

"I'll learn," Orfeo heard himself say.

"I will learn to defend myself."

"A fortunate decision," Zurga added with a trace of a smile.

"Of course it catches me by surprise, but I just happen to have brought the weapon of one of those unfortunates we left back at the gorge."

He swung the cloak aside to reveal an extra scabbard at this belt.

"It's yours to carry from now on."

"And the burden of defending the group is also yours to carry," Telemon still remained austerely distant.

"The next time you turn you back on your friends will be the last if I'm in your company."

Orfeo drew the sword and swung the blade awkwardly above his head.

It was longer and heavier than the short sword he had brought with him.

How strange that, after all these years, his life had finally devolved upon the sort of barbarity that Isocles had always cautioned against.

The conversation between Orton and Telemon took a turn toward other matters, as they reminisced about old battles and other bouts with armies and brigands.

Zurga seemed to amuse himself with his own thoughts, and Orfeo lounged sleeplessly by his new weapon.

Thoughts of the day would not relinquish their hold, and he lay tossing about long after the others had drifted into the sleep of a warrior who could awaken and be instantly ready to defend himself.

The aura of readiness was suddenly more visible to Orfeo, as though the day had provided a lesson in survival that was every bit as real as the shipwreck.

The world was dangerous, and one had to keep his head in all situations.

But there were times when coping with these dangers could not be done alone, but only with the cooperation of others.

There was also the possibility, held as a truth by his companions, that Orfeo would be better off with a skill at weapons.

If only he could see his old teacher Isocles when they arrived at Pylos he could clarify his new feelings.

Of course there were many obstacles to seeing the old man again, not the least being his status as an escaped hostage.

# CHAPTER NINE

By the next morning all overt signs of anger toward Orfeo had disappeared, but it was clear that he was even more isolated from the warriors, and even the Wanderer kept more distance than before.

They rode more slowly now, as the horses had begin to show signs of overuse, and if they were to become exhausted at this point there would be no easy replacements.

They were now passing through small farming villages, where the peasants spoke a dialect of Pylos and reminded Orfeo of the countryfolk who lived around the great city, but they were still told that another two days journey lay before them.

There were also local village masters who took a great interest in any business destined for the court at Pylos, and Zurga expressed clearly his belief that word of their impending arrival had sped far ahead of the travelers. If they were thought to be important, they would be welcomed into the city by functionaries who would know their exact descriptions.

Partially to keep the spies at a distance Zurga also cautioned them to make their stops for meals between villages, and Telemon accepted the wisdom of this evasion.

For the mid-day meal the company stopped on a broad platform of rock that was enough raised above the flat valley to permit at least a view over the road they had traversed and a short distance of what they were to cover.

Here Telemon ate greedily and then sat back with a contented but rather caustic smirk.

"It's time for the first lesson in swordsmanship," he said with a good natured shrug.

"Cut two stout branches from the tree," he gestured to Orton, and then he arose to help with the task.

"Remember," Zurga also seemed to enjoy the prospect, "the same principles that apply to diplomacy apply to war."

"Wrong," Telemon thundered, looking at the wanderer with a full awareness that he had been baited.

"Don't listen to that scabrous old bag of tricks.

The first need of a warrior is strength and agility."

"And how about cleverness?" replied Zurga.

"A game for courtiers," said Telemon, whom Orfeo increasingly was beginning to appreciate as capable of his own form of diplomacy.

The old warrior selected staves slightly longer and considerably thicker than his sword, and he began to swing his weapon in a graceful semicircle as if cutting down invisible enemies.

He instructed Orfeo as to the rules, which did not permit direct blows to the head, and he indicated that neither of them should strike to maim.

Orton smiled as if this would apply, of course, to only one of the contestants, as Orfeo could not be expected to deliver a blow one way or the other.

"Are you afraid?"

Telemon spoke as he removed his breastplate of armor, revealing massive shoulders that seemed to belong to a much younger man.

While Orton was visibly scarred about the face and arms, however, the great champion had only the remains of a gash on his left shoulder.

"Of course I'm afraid, Orfeo replied.

"Then you're wise in at least one respect," said Telemon.

"Never underestimate your enemy.

Pay him the respect of fear until you've killed him."

He gestured toward Orton as he picked up his own shield.

"Lend the pup your shield, and we'll go a short round."

Orfeo adjusted the awkward leather and bronze implement onto his left arm, and then swung the staff with his right.

He had often seen his cousins practice their skills at arms, but he had chosen to remain as a spectator.

Now that he was to enter the ring there were feelings of fear and an unreasoning guilt that he was not keeping faith with his teacher.

A scholar, whether a teacher at court or a shepherd for his father's sheep, does not bear arms.

He watched Telemon approach with his cold, killer's precision.

"Hold your shield high enough to deflect my blows, and watch every move of the staff."

The warning was scarcely delivered when the warrior's weapon descended with a great thudding sound on the shield, which Orfeo raised just in time to protect his body, and then Telemon twisted so that a backhand blow approached from Orfeo's right side, causing him to bring the shield across his body so quickly that he nearly lost his balance.

Before he could properly right himself the next thrust came from directly above, but the shield, in rising above Orfeo's head, exposed his midsection so completely that Telemon, evading the shield with a deft change of direction, planted the staff squarely upon Orfeo's ribs.

He sprawled helplessly to the ground, dropping the staff and landing painfully on the shield.

Telemon stood above him as though another thrust could at any minute sever his head, but instead he backed away and began to explain what had gone wrong with Orfeo's strategy.

"Your biggest mistake was in allowing me to do all the attacking," he said.

"There wasn't a single thrust in my direction, so that eventually, if all you could do was parry, I was bound to break your defense."

The warrior continued to re-enact the encounter, as though once surprised by Telemon's onslaught, the boy could have done anything else.

"You weren't thinking," said Zurga.

"You were letting him set the rules and simply falling into his game."

"Don't listen to him," Telemon replied.

"Ask him if he wants to joust with me, and then we can see whether all his thoughts could save him from, sore ribs."

"Attack the problem logically," Zurga repeated, deftly sidestepping the mocking challenge, although there was obviously no malice between the two now.

"Am I to follow two masters?" asked Orfeo.

"Follow your own inclinations," Zurga responded.

"Defend yourself."

Telemon spoke again and approached, with Orfeo drawing his shield up again to fend off the blows, only this time he responded to a sudden impulse to strike out first, thus preventing the warrior from so quickly gaining the upper hand. His first blow was, in fact, premature, and Telemon merely backstepped slightly and then launched his counterthrust toward Orfeo's left shoulder. This time the parry did not seem so engrossing, and he was able to avert the blow while at the same time striking out again on his own.

The blow was deflected outward by Telemon's shield, which seemed so powerfully wielded as to constitute a weapon.

Orfeo could see the entirety of Telemon's body open up as a target while the shield thrust outward, but his staff was not in position where he could use it, and suddenly he was aware that Telemon's weapon was winging its way confidently again toward the sore spot on his ribs.

His retreat was hasty, and he turned with all possible agility to avoid the shaft, narrowly missing it and then striking out for that part of his adversary that had momentarily been vulnerable.

Unfortunately it was again covered by the shield, and the force was harmlessly dissipated.

By this time Telemon had freed his own staff from Orfeo's shield and had propelled it in a low loop toward his waist, dropping its target just short of the mark onto his calf, where the force lifted Orfeo's right foot off the ground and again sent him helplessly off his feet.

This time there had been several exchanges before the blow landed, but there had similarly been no threat toward Telemon, who stood laughing at the plight of his young pupil.

"The second time you have shown improvement," he said, "but you still would be dead."

"Use your head instead of trying to beat him at his own game," Zurga intoned again, and this time both Orton and Telemon laughed derisively.

While the men bantered among themselves and Orfeo massaged his sore muscles, he found himself breaking the exchange down into its components, desperately trying to derive essences, to define priorities, to establish a series of limited goals that could lead to his successful defense, but all the preachings of Isocles seemed useless beside overwhelming skill at arms and brute force.

Then he again noticed the scar, only this time it seemed to be in two parts, as though the wound had been inflicted twice.

Perhaps there was a clue.

If Telemon had ever been bested in a fight, then it had involved something faulty in the defense of his left shoulder, but this seemed an unlikely place to be able to strike, as it was heavily guarded by the shield.

Then, however, it came to mind that even in their last exchange, as Telemon had used his shield to attack aggressively and force Orfeo's staff to one side, this part had been exposed.

It happened with that fierce thrust of the shield, and the body had lain vulnerable before a staff that was elsewhere.

Orfeo still sat on the ground, now moaning about this painful calf and all the while reconstructing, backwards, a series of events that could lead to Telemon's great push of the shield coming at a time when Orfeo's staff would be able to take advantage of the opening.

It must come after a feint in which the staff was brought toward the left side, then dropped to avoid the shield, and then thrust again quickly toward the shoulder, only there was no time for blundering.

It was a matter of urgent timing, and he could make no mistake or his own defensive lapse would be exploited.

"Get up and fight like a man, only this time be aware of the possibility that I can also strike from below." Telemon was warming to his task and appeared to enjoy the sport.

"He's stronger and quicker than you," added Zurga.

"Watch for the right opening."

Orfeo's attack this time came before his teacher was fully ready, and Telemon retreated for an instant in order properly to attach his shield.

The first effort to get Telemon to rush with his shield failed simply because the old warrior had more tricks and this time parried with another stratagem.

He simply backhanded with his own staff and then charged heedlessly forward, arching the weapon above his head so that it descended harshly upon the tip of Orfeo's shield, glancing onto his head as it did so and forcing the edge of his shield roughly against the bridge of his nose.

They sprang apart with Telemon in fine form and the boy somewhat dizzied by the encounter, but still ready to fight.

Now, however, he could only block the series of blows that began to rain in, and soon a shaft of pain shot from his shoulder to his knees.

Telemon's staff had found its way onto an unguarded right shoulder, and again Orfeo had fallen victim to the mighty warrior who was teaching not so much by direction as by example.

"Keep your shield higher," he said, "but be prepared to move it as quickly and deftly as your sword."

Orfeo again looked at his mentor, only his eyes could not avoid the scar.

Somehow his entire attention seemed to rivet itself upon this damaged strip of flesh that held a key, only he knew that even in this recognition he must not allow Telemon to guess his thoughts.

There must be a manner in which Orfeo could get that shield to lunge forward while his own staff lingered in readiness to strike the instant's target.

The way must be found.

"I've killed you three times already," Telemon chided playfully, and you still haven't learned to defend yourself.

"The last time he showed promise," Orton added, implying a certain awareness that perhaps Orfeo would be able to acquire the necessary skills.

"Remember, you can never beat a champion at his own game," Zurga too was chuckling, although there was a deadly seriousness even about his humor.

Orfeo mounted the shield and gripped the staff firmly, advancing without fear toward the man who had slain many hundreds on the field.

Although he could now only suffer a bruise at worst, a certain inexplicable honor seemed to rest on finding a way of dealing with this new and threatening force that had been intruded into his life.

He was being roundly humiliated before three people who expected merely that he would be repeatedly defeated at the hands of a great champion, only there was something in Orfeo that would not submit to the natural order or the justice of suffering defeat at any hands when he still had all his resources to defend himself.

The next encounter must break the chain.

"This time will be different," Orfeo announced with a voice that seemed calm above an inner storm.

"You mean I'll tumble you from the left rather than the right?"

Telemon seemed to dance tantalizingly out of reach, lowering his shield as though he were daring the boy to charge.

"He means to topple you this time," Orton added playfully.

"Very well, you may charge first and strike hard with your first blow, my friend, because Telemon does not submit even in jest."

The words carried a flicker of hope, although Orfeo did not stop to dissect his awareness that his words had prompted Telemon into just the sort of heedless countercharge with his shield he had hoped to provoke before.

Orfeo's staff sailed harmlessly toward the shield, which moved in its practiced pattern to block the force, and then it lunged forward, carrying with it the body of the great warrior and some aura of what a meeting with this force on the battlefield might mean.

The opening was there, Orfeo's staff was poised, and then it was in blind descent, suddenly with all the force of his arm and wrist and shoulder and body, even his fingers, concentrated only on speed and strength, as if the staff were to cleave a rock or fell a tree.

The sound of its impact reached his ears before any awareness of whether it had found its mark, and suddenly Orfeo had swung to an instinctive stance of self-protection, bringing his own shield to fend off a blow that never landed.

The encampment was suddenly quiet, as Orton watched with stunned disbelief, and even Zurga appeared at a loss to explain what had transpired.

The wrong body was on the ground.

For some reason Orfeo still stood and Telemon was only now lifting his head and cradling the scar on his shoulder which even betrayed a faint trace of blood.

The lesson for the day had ended quite as suddenly as it had begun, as the great Achian slowly resumed his footing and stood facing his assailant, still surrounded by the silence of his companions.

"You will someday be a great swordsman, my boy, but you have much to learn.

It will be my honor to teach you and perhaps to learn something myself."

Still the others said nothing, as they all gathered together in a circle to finish the last scraps of the noon meal.

There was no more talk about the event until they had traveled the rest of the day and sat around a small campfire later in the evening, resting from the journey.

As they were now among many scattered farming villages, less exposed to bandit raids, they had decided that a campfire would be permissible, and the four now talked with a new closeness that had been wordlessly born of the encounter between a boy and the greatest swordsman of the age.

Clearly, in a matter of time, the conversation must return to that one vital point that had left them all stunned in varying degrees.

"You got me just where the other two did," said Telemon.

"The first time I was no older than you, and a Hannae warrior drove a lance home just as my shield dropped.

But I was not incapacitated.

I killed him in the next exchange and continued to fight the rest of the day."

"I well remember the second," said Orton.

"I stood watching helplessly as you were beset by Thracian pirates."

"It was a fair exchange," Telemon added.

"One of them merely landed a lucky blow, and there I was, disarmed and helpless, and would have been dead if the man had not fallen in his own enthusiasm and given me a chance to crush his head with a mace.

It was luck that I survived, but then it's luck for all of us, great and small alike. We're all here at the tolerance of the gods and could be taken at the snap of a finger."

"Ahhhhhh, but was it luck today?" Zurga interjected.

"I had the distinct impression that our Orfeo saw scars and heeded well the message that you have a careless way of dropping your shield too low at times, which is perhaps your only weakness.

And then he made certain that you would do just that when he was ready to take advantage of it."

"He would have been dead after the first exchange," Orton apparently found it necessary to defend his friend, although even in this there was a new respect for Orfeo.

"But it's something I must correct," said Telemon.

"As a warrior I know that there are always ways in which I am vulnerable, and my survival depends upon learning to overcome them."

"You must admit, though, that it was not skill, but cunning that won the day," Zurga referred back to his own directions.

"Yes, of course, but then it has not always seemed so expedient for me to appear overly clever."

Telemon had let himself slip into a relaxed camaraderie with the Wanderer.

"If one walks the world as an allegedly invincible swordsman, one's enemies would grow all the more cautious unless there were some appearance of weakness."

"You mean you pretend to be rash and incautious?"

Orfeo sounded incredulous.

"Does that surprise the little fox who pretends so much himself?"

Telemon retorted bluntly but with a smile.

"Then why the sword?"

The words came out before Orfeo had stopped to consider.

"Because neither force nor tact alone are enough for survival in this world, and one must get by in any way he can."

Telemon spoke somberly.

"If one area is neglected, the highest accomplishment in another amounts to nothing if you're dead."

He gestured toward Zurga.

"Your Wanderer friend there will be the first to tell you.

He's as dangerously slick with words as any man alive, but he can also defend himself with arms when the need arises.

After all, one does not reason with a charging boar."

Telemon and Zurga talked long into the night, with Orton resting in obvious pleasure that the previous ill feelings in the band had been dispelled.

Orfeo was not exactly comfortable, as his body still bore the lumps of his beating during the day, and he limped on the leg that Telemon had chosen for the one great sweep of the staff, but the rewards of the battle had been more than worth the small suffering.

He was now one of them, a respected, although perhaps insignificant, part of a great undertaking to recover his kidnapped brother.

At his side he was proud to know that great Telemon rode, flanked by another warrior who would stand as a giant in his own right.

Then there was Zurga, whose reputation was no less awesome, a wanderer with powers that seemed unobtrusive yet were capable of meeting many diverse threats.

Among this company Orfeo was now a proud member, committed to his task and to the burden of being worthy of them.

Things had changed this day and would not again be the same.

# Chapter Ten

The next morning they were back on horseback headed toward their goal, and now the countryside definitely took on a flavor familiar to Orfeo from his previous stay in the lands of Pylos. The road was better tended, and they had traversed enough distance at noon so that they were within reach of the city by nightfall, but Zurga thought better to make another camp for the night and enter with the sun the next day.

That way they could do their business with as little time as possible in the city, perhaps even concluding the ransom of Herron before the day ended.

Success would depend in large measure upon completing the transaction before anyone suspected that this personage was of greater than usual importance to the king of the Achians.

The campfire that night was less boisterous than before.

Telemon had fallen into an ill humor when he began to contemplate spending time behind walls, and he kept repeating his intention of being again in the open countryside by the time night fell.

As he had always distrusted fortifications and had viewed walls more as prisons than protection, he was anxious at the thought of being confined, perhaps coming closer to showing fear about this than to anything else he could imagine.

Orton had once as a youth served as a mercenary for the Tyrian merchants in the east, however, and part of this had been as a palace guard. He tried to reassure his friend as to the safety of walls, but to no avail.

They talked gloomily among themselves.

Zurga used the time well, however, to instruct Orfeo as to how he might best make inquiries at the docks and around the slave-markets, although the question of his own markings appeared to cloud the picture.

Slaves of Pylos were customarily given a mark on each wrist indicating they were bondsmen of a given master, but as a hostage Orfeo had also been marked, in this case on his upper arm.

Ordinarily this did not show beneath the sleeves of his tunic, particularly when he wore a cloak, but in the sun of Pylos men wore sleeveless garments, and if Orfeo were to appear as one of them, he too must go about so clad.

There was also the question as to what would happen should his earlier status as a hostage somehow be exposed.

While there was little likelihood that the small dainty houseflower of the hostage years would be readily recognized as the tall, man-like boy of today, there was still the mark.

Zurga appeared surprised when it was called to his attention, and he addressed himself to a solution.

First he sorted through a collection of small vials and packets drawn from various compartments of his cloak.

It seemed incredible that any of this had survived the rough usage to which the garment was subjected in the shipwreck, but there was apparently no damage.

As the wanderer continued to talk of other subjects related to life in Pylos, he boiled a flask of water over the fire and slowly began adding small amounts of the mysterious substances arrayed before him, allowing the water to take on progressively changing colorations.

Finally, however, the moisture seemed to be diminishing, and only a green tarry residue remained in the flask.

When this cooled it was applied as a salve to the marks on Orfeo's arm and covered with strips of cloth.

Orfeo assumed it was meant to mimic a bandage, and the substance so concocted would convince anyone of its medicinal nature.

Zurga continued his commentary as though nothing else important occupied his mind.

"The court at Pylos has no doubt heard that there are four of us headed for an audience with the king, and certainly they know the names of both myself and Telemon.

As for you and Orton there is little likelihood they have more than a vague description.

Probably you would be assumed to be a servant, and if you were to go about certain tasks as soon as we enter the city, they would waste no further time in watching you.

After all, the court of Pylos has important matters on its mind, and the goings about the city of an insignificant Achian boy would be little observed in a great port where strangers from all over the world congregate."

"Then you think I ought to dress as a man of Pylos?"

"That's another matter to be arranged as soon as we are in the city and you feel safely anonymous.

You can emerge merely as another citizen who has some interest in the new slaves that have just arrived in the city.

You are fair for a man of Pylos, but properly dressed no one will question your presence."

Telemon, who had overheard most of the conversation, quickly interjected an agreement, and the four turned to planning in detail what they would do on the next day when they entered the great metropolis.

Telemon and Zurga would proceed to the palace, while Orfeo busied himself caring for the horses and hopefully eluded observation so that he could make inquiries at the docks.

Orton would linger about the city in case of trouble, providing some sort of protection for Orfeo and at the same time mapping out a route by which they could leave hastily in case of trouble.

At least during the first part of their stay behind walls, all went according to the hastily drawn plans.

The next morning they paid more attention to dress than during other parts of the journey, taking the trouble to make a suitable appearance as befitted emissaries from the King of Achia.

They then proceeded leisurely toward the city, finding the great walls massive and awesome as they blended with the stone cliffs overlooking the harbor.

Telemon kept an outward appearance of supreme disdain, but clearly this was not the battleground of his choosing, and as they approached closer to the towering structures of masonry, the mantle of leadership seemed to slip more firmly into the grasp of Zurga.

This was, if anything, a realm more familiar to the Wanderer than the crude camp of the Achians, and he looked resplendent in his glistening black cloak as he responded to the challenge at the city gates, explaining that they had come on an official mission to speak with the king. Obviously they had been expected, and the head gatekeeper appeared to waver not the least as he granted passage.

He added a suggestion that they stay at a certain inn, which he gave directions for finding, and Zurga rather imperiously, within hearing of the guards, ordered Orfeo and Orton to proceed there to make arrangements.

Then, just before setting off toward the palace he turned to Orfeo and spoke brusquely.

"Boy," he sounded haughty and distant.

"Take the bandage off your arm so that the city folk will not see that you have just come from the country."

The guards laughed coarsely as Orfeo blushed, but he did not move, fighting an instant's suspicion that he was being betrayed.

But no recourse presented itself, and he felt his pulse quicken when the command was voiced a second time.

With a quivering hand he slowly began to remove the binding, and then it was off.

He expected to be seized and carried off as an escaped hostage, but there was nothing.

Where the bandage had been, all traces of markings had disappeared, although he had been told originally that no known substance could remove the emblem engraved into his flesh.

It was Zurga's idea of a jest to have arranged it thus, and he flashed a sinister smile as he rode off with Telemon.

The gatekeepers had returned to their own duties, now ignoring the awkward boy.

Orton handed him the reins to his own horse, and the two set off to find the inn, Orfeo now finding himself playing the role of an ignorant serving boy.

The major business of the day was in the hands of Zurga.

Finding the inn, of course, was not so easy, and Orton had to ask directions several times before they located the large, poorly kept building with an enclosed courtyard full of straw and extensive stables to accommodate travelers from distant lands.

Pylos was a crossroads for many types of trade, and horse caravans converged here, allowing the exchange of goods with seafaring traders of Tyre and Kalamatta.

Orfeo found himself besieged with and almost overwhelmed by both the familiar and strange sights and smells of the great city that had once been his home.

What he experienced in returning, with the reawakening of memories, was obviously greater than for Orton, who had never been there.

At least the soldier seemed to view everything through defensive eyes, looking for routes of escape and access to the walls or harbor, for outposts of sentries.

While Orton bargained with the innkeeper, Orfeo stabled the horses, transferred the belongings of each traveler to a safe place in the room assigned to them.

Orton made a great commotion, probably so that Orfeo would be noticed less, and then he suddenly sent the boy off on an obscure errand to buy clothing.

At last Orfeo was on his own, and the task before him was simply to outfit himself so that he could pass among the people of Pylos as one of them.

The bazaar was doubtlessly in the same place it reputedly occupied for hundreds of years, and Orfeo set out at a brisk pace.

As he walked there was a new feeling that slowly began to penetrate his veil of fear and foreboding.

In a sense he had returned to what had been a true home for him with a greater meaning than the Achian camp had ever held.

He was home, among the people he had lived beside all those years, and here he had been a hostage, but his role had been clearly defined and accepted.

There were other hostages, and they had certain prerogatives and rights about the city, particularly those under royal protection. Back with the Achians, in the camp of his birth, it had never been such.

Orfeo had been alone, one of a kind, out of step and out of place.

Here he had belonged, and there was a confidence now in his step he had lacked without knowing it.

The sounds of the city's speech swirled about him, and he found himself speaking to a shopkeeper in the bazaar with an accent he knew sounded properly native and perhaps even elegant.

He had been taught well by Isocles, who had pointed out all the subtleties by which men of various classes could be identified by small characteristics of their pronunciation.

Orfeo bought himself a smart tan tunic, and he replaced his black Achian cloak with a short, soft leather garment that extended in back no farther than his waist.

Young men of good family wore such clothing around town, and Orfeo had gone so clad in the days just before his escape.

He changed in a small covered alcove behind a clothing shop, folding his old tunic into a woven bag that he carried slung over one shoulder, Now for the shoes, and he was feeling the elation of being in a great port, where the winds converged from many directions, and adventure seemed to permeate the very stones.

He wondered why he had ever voluntarily run away to the home of his people.

Indeed, were they really his people?

The docks had not changed.

Great sea-going vessels were secured to the piers, and the activity was every bit as frantic as in the bazaar, although in a more open setting.

Blacks from the lower continent and short, swarthy men from Tyre and the West sweated in the sun, while the great merchants looked on with the same imperturbable security.

Orfeo looked toward the mountain and saw the outline of the great palace etched against the stone wall.

Zurga and Telemon were no doubt being received there, almost certainly by people Orfeo had known, if not by Nestor and even the king himself.

Orfeo moved at ease among the dockworkers and travelers and assorted drifters who worked or idled about the boisterous hub of the city.

He stopped where a group of young men had gathered around an old sailor with an exotically colored bird who was alleged to talk.

Finally, after rather harsh prodding, the beast blurted out a few obscenities in a language all knew, and the old man collected a small wager he had made with one of the boys.

How strange that among these people of roughly his own age Orfeo did not recognize any faces, but it had been a long time.

He was addressed by one of them, who commented about the bird, and as if by accident he found himself walking along the wharf talking with a boy named Karl.

The trade had been brisk this year, with more and more boats from the west.

Suddenly Karl stopped with a scowl.

“Well, this is as far as we can go anymore.

I almost forgot myself and risked abduction by our gracious guests.”

The last word was curiously inflected.

Orfeo looked up to see, standing before them, a squadron of a dozen guards blocking off one entire portion of the wharf, and beyond there were ships of a peculiar and distinctly military appearance.

Some seemed both ominous and unique, and both ships and men at a glance were not men of Pylos.

“Who are they?” Orfeo asked, thinking after the words that he may have been unwise to ask such a blatant question about people everyone in the city must know about.

“Oh.......fine sense of humor,” replied Karl.

“But ignoring them won’t make them go away, and of course there are rumors of worse.”

He spoke in a hushed, fearful voice.

"I've been away from the city for a long time," Orfeo answered.

"I know little of these men or rumors."

"It may be just as well," Karl said.

"At first there was a lot of talk when the Kalamattans arrived or were welcomed here by Prince Nestor himself, as though we had never been enemies, but then when the strange boats came, and with the Therans going and coming between the boats and the palace….."

He was visibly squeamish.

"It's something most people don't talk about anymore, only everyone knows that things aren't right and haven't been right for a long time."

"The Therans?"

The name seemed to register distantly, as though it was a word unremembered since its emergence from the mouth of Isocles, who had taught of the strange island to the south from which no man returned.

The Therans were the cursed race of the Devil, some said, the land of darkness and evil, and now there was talk that some of these people held great power here in Pylos. It was difficult to comprehend.

"The Therans," said Karl gently.

"And rumors of wars and invasions and ransoms and tribute.

Only there's no way of knowing what to believe, and it can't all be true because it's so contradictory."

Orfeo continued to elicit one explanation after another, although by this time the information was so contrary to expectations that he did not know how much he should believe.

For one thing there was talk that Kalamatta had become ambitious to conquer and enslave its neighbors, and apparently all the towns along the south coast for hundreds of miles had fallen.

But at the same time there was talk that the Therans had completely taken over the governing of Kalamatta and that this nation now owed homage to the Theran king, Sargon the Fourth, whose very name had previously been whispered as a mysterious and foreboding messenger of doom. When Orfeo had been in the court of Pylos, the very existence of Sargon and his nation was known mostly through gossip, and no one had ever knowingly seen a Theran.

Karl seemed to know little else, or he may merely have been unwilling to talk about these creatures who could just as well have walked from a legend into the real world.

So the strange boats in the harbor belonged to Therans, as if this were an explanation for strange events.

Karl went about his business, and Orfeo again walked down the wharf in the direction of the strange boats.

Again he saw the guards, but this time he took a closer look at the ships, which differed from Achian vessels in size and means of locomotion.

There were sails, but these relatively small expanses of cloth obviously were not so important as the oarsmen, who were no doubt galley slaves as in the great Tyrian ships.

Only on these enormous boats, which appeared larger as Orfeo began to notice details, there were three rows of long oars extending from each side.

The prows were long and pointed, as if they constituted giant battering rams, and portholes along the top made no secret of the fact that archers could effectively turn these ships into formidable instruments of war.

Nothing afloat that Orfeo had ever seen could stand against such a machine, and this realization made him shudder with anticipation.

Obviously there were strange things afoot in Pylos, and somehow his brother Herron had become caught up in them.

Even now he could be languishing in one of those ships, chained to an oar.

In such a case it was difficult to imagine how even the great Telemon could prevail against such awesome might.

Orfeo continued to wander along the docks, at times overhearing snatches of conversation, often joining in to converse with others.

When the sun reached its highpoint he purchased some white cheese of Pylos from a vendor and against tasted the soft white bread he had not known in the years since his escape.

There was a feeling again like a return to an old home; yet he kept about his business, learning much that was baffling and disturbing.

Apparently the seizure of slaves by a Tyrian merchant ship was now a common occurrence, as they had been commission by the king of Pylos himself to bring men for the Kalamattans and Therans, who reportedly were paying good prices for muscle to man their boats.

But hundred, perhaps thousands of hostages had passed through the port within the last several months, and everyone knew that all could not be destined for the galleys.

There were rumors of slaves being taken to Kalamatta and even to Thera, although, of course, no one knew anything about this for certain.

No one knew even that Thera existed, save that some said it was a great island lying to the south and that outsiders had for centuries not been allowed.

It was something even Isocles had known little about.

Obviously the matter of locating a captive was not going to be so simple as it had seemed, and Orfeo returned to the inn disheartened, although he half expected Telemon and Zurga to arrive from the palace with good news.

Telemon had said that he would not spend the night within walls, and perhaps he had wrought a miracle of persuasion.

When Orfeo arrived at their quarters, even Orton was gone, but apparently he had only set out to find the others, and soon all of them arrived, with expressions that immediately conveyed a lack of success.

At Zurga's request, Orfeo quickly contributed what he had learned, and the others appeared not at all surprised.

"It's indeed a grave situation," said Zurga.

"There was talk around the court of Therans, although we were not today admitted to a formal audience."

He grimaced as though contemptuous of this blatant breech of protocol that was supposed to remind barbarians that they waited until the king of Pylos wished to see them.

"We presented our request to a petty magistrate, and he told us to come back and then possibly we can see the king."

"And in the meantime, you expect us to sit here in this prison like slaves, while someone else holds the key."

Telemon was obviously irritable and perhaps at some level frightened.

"I'm staying here for the night, and I'm certain Orfeo won't hesitate to stay."

Zurga spoke with a certain petulance himself, as the day had gone poorly.

"Our friend Orton is not afraid of walls...."

"Who's afraid?"

Telemon was now angry enough to remain.

"It's just that I like to pick my battlefields."

"Well, hopefully there'll be no fighting tonight."

Zurga was reassuring, but Orfeo knew his moods well enough now to realize that he was not happy.

In the evening, after the innkeeper had served great portions of beef and bread, Zurga went by himself into the darkness, indicating casually that he had business of his own.

Telemon and Orton by this time had consumed enough ale to relax them, and they traded stories of battles away from their homeland.

Orton was careful to include much talk of his adventures in cities, illustrating how the appearance of vulnerability is only an illusion.

The walls and streets could be used to tactical advantage, and a master warrior like Telemon could soon master a whole new realm of combat.

Orfeo was still awake when Zurga reappeared, as there had been too much excitement during the day to allow him to sleep now.

Zurga appeared surprised, but then he motioned for the boy to join him in a far corner away from the small fire.

"Tomorrow you'll be going to court with us, as the magistrate specially requested that all four of us be there."

Zurga smiled sardonically.

"But I believe it to be just a formality to show is that they know of our coming and our number.

A little disguise, and no one will know you, and of course you'll expose your arms."

"How.....?"

Orfeo began the question.

"Don't ask how a deed is accomplished.

Just be grateful that it is done."

"But Isocles taught me always to ask the how, and now that I'm in his home city..."

Orfeo was taunting the Wanderer, who also was more than casually concerned with the whys.

"If Isocles is such a great man, then let me return the markings on you arm, and you ask him for the same favor."

"Very well, if the wanderer cannot give me the how, I'll find it for myself."

"You'll need all the luck you have just to live through the next several weeks.

Waste none of it in seeking explanations that are beyond you."

Now Zurga smiled, which was the equivalent to a laugh from anyone else.

“So tomorrow I’ll again be in court with the king and my friend Nestor?”

“And, fortunately for you, your friends Orton and Telemon will also be there, not to mention myself.”

“Do you think we might get word of Herron?”

“Not likely,” said Zurga.

“From what you learned today, and what I heard on my walk this evening, we are as far from finding Herron as when we began.

Perhaps, however, we are finding much that will serve us well at a later time.

# CHAPTER ELEVEN

"A NIGHT SPENT BEHIND WALLS AND STILL ALIVE?" Orton was at least in good spirits as the four shared fruit and cheese at the inn the next morning. Telemon acknowledged that the experience had not been fatal, but still made it clear that he wished to have everything finished today so that by evening they would be safely away from this accursed place with its teeming multitude.

"If you think this is a city, you should hope that our travels do not take us to Kalamatta," added Zurga.

"Or Tyre," said Orton.

"We're not even safely out of this one yet, and already you're planning more mischief," Telemon tried to sound surly, but even he was cheerful enough, if not exactly optimistic about their prospects for the day.

"As I see it," Orton began, "there doesn't seem to be much to worry about today.

They've heard our request, and obviously see us as occupying a rather low priority.

Likely they will make some sort of search for Herron, and, if they find him, they will probably allow our ransom, which is more than his worth as a slave.

If he is not in Pylos, then we will be refused."

"In all this clamor, how would they know whether he was here or not?"

Telemon still had not abandoned the notion that the city was impossibly complex.

"You can be sure that if he were brought here as a slave, he has been entered in the records and accounted for and even taxed," said Orfeo.

"But maybe things are different when captives are brought to the Therans."

"That is something else to reckon with," said Zurga.

"And if we were to find that Herron mans the oars of one of those ships our friend Orfeo has described, then we are in trouble."

"It means that we ransom him from Therans," said Orton.

"Not so easy as it sounds," said Zurga, sitting back and running a long, bony index finger along his beard.

"Once one enters the service of Thera there is no return, and I might say even that once a man sees the inside of one of their ships, he is not likely again to come ashore anyplace other than on Thera itself."

"So you know something of these strange creatures," said Telemon.

"I know enough to be apprehensive." Zurga spoke with no trace of doubt.

"If Herron is on one of those ships, he will not be ransomed."

"Then we take him by stealth and force of arms," said Telemon.

"And Therans will feel my sword for the first time."

"Again not so simple a matter," added the wanderer in measured tones.

"They are not quite like other men in their habits."

"Do they bleed and die?"

The old warrior asked.

"Ah yes, their blood is red, but there are many differences which we will deal with when the time comes."

Zurga's tone was ominous, and Orfeo shuddered to think that even the Wanderer felt an obvious and fearful respect for these strange men from the land of Thera.

Orfeo listened with a growing unease as Zurga outlined their plan for the day.

Although trouble was not likely, there was also discussion as to how they should best leave the city quickly should trouble arise.

A disguise was arranged whereby Zurga applied several lines of dark pigment around Orfeo's eyes and mouth, and suddenly he appeared older, as though a complete transformation had taken place.

As a precaution they packed their belongings and took the horses along, planning to leave them before the palace so that a rapid departure could be made if necessary.

This last was Telemon's idea, although, strangely, Zurga did not complain.

As they approached the great hall atop the hill where Orfeo had lived so many years, a mass of familiar objects intruded to carry with them a wave of nostalgia for a bygone era, but there was as much that seemed new and unexplainable.

Everywhere there were armed men, and several times they saw litter cars borne by slaves, completely hiding the occupants behind curtains.

Orfeo assumed, without reason, that they contained the dread Therans, and the quiet that descended as these vehicles came into view confirmed his suspicions.

At the gate all four were admitted as if expected, and with few preliminaries they were admitted to the back of the great hall, where they were to await their turn in presenting a petition to the king.

No words passed between them as they adjusted to the subdued light and echoing vastness of the audience room.

Orfeo well know the scene; yet he immediately noted differences.

The king sat on his throne, as before, and he appeared to have aged little, but Nestor was now grown into a man and sat on a great chair slightly lower to the right.

The ministers had their usual places, and there were some familiar faces and some that were not.

The greatest change, however, was in the gallery of about twenty chairs to the left of the king, which had traditionally been reserved for representatives of various noble families.

Now they were occupied by armed men, who looked like those he had seen at the docks.

Sitting, nearly obscured by the warriors, were about half a dozen short figures whose countenance seemed colored by their pale green robes.

Orfeo's heart seemed to jump in momentary fright.

Even without asking Zurga he knew they were Therans, sitting as if in attendance upon the king's decisions.

Only it was not at all clear who held the upper hand.

Another surge of feelings came as Orfeo turned his gaze across to the advisers who stood in front of the king.

Even from the back, he recognized his old teacher Isocles, who was now stooped and gray, but still obviously alert to all around him.

The court pages were all new, of course, and Orfeo recalled his service in that office, calling before the king various petitioners.

Business was proceeding as before as the king, in a voice muffled from boredom, granted a dissolution of a marriage, conferred property rights on an heir, and settled ownership of a well.

Now Telemon the Achian was called, and the four stepped forward to take their places before the broad stone steps leading up to the throne.

As he approached closer, Orfeo could see how so many other things had changed.

King Linaeus showed none of his jovial self, and Nestor watched with a look of cold annoyance, as though he had grown to be a hard, rigid man.

The soldiers appeared imperiously unconcerned by the trivialities before them, while the Therans provided a disquieting flavor.

As Orfeo moved closer to the king he experienced a clammy sensation, as though suddenly he were in the presence of an evil so pervasive and subtle that he would be powerless against its influence.

The men of Thera showed the same basic features as men of other origin; yet the sallow complexions, the long straight noses with prominent nostrils, the eyes with lazy snake lids that appeared to droop down over the eye itself, but which gave an appearance of greater rather than diminished alertness, all conspired to lend a peculiar aura of danger.

Yet it was not the fear one would feel in the face of a great warrior, as no evidence of physical strength or valor was manifest.

There was instead a promise of stealth and compromise, as though any violence would come by some poisonous form of food, air, water, or even thoughts themselves.

The Therans sat without moving so that it was difficult to assess their bulk, but there was little question as to their intent.

"A representative from Kiros the Achian has presented a request to ransom a captive he believes to have been seized by a Tyrian boat that may have brought its captive to Pylos."

One of the minor court ministers began by introducing the case, and he gave enough background so that the others could understand what issues were involved.

"Would the four plaintiffs please identify themselves," a scribe, who apparently was taking notes, made the request.

At Telemon's announcement of his name there was a murmur, as though his reputation indeed was well known, but at Zurga's announcement there was an even greater ripple of excitement, as though this was a true surprise.

Even Isocles, who had previously not stirred himself turned around and looked with a pleased countenance.

The introductions of Orton and Orfeo, under assumed names, were made while the company was still distracted with the thought of having two distinguished visitors.

"Welcome to Pylos," spoke Isocles, obviously directing his words to Zurga.

"It has been many years since I last met the master Zurga, and I believe that he arrives at an opportune moment."

There was something about his words that appeared to make others uncomfortable.

"I'm pleased to be in the service of King Kiros," answered Zurga, correcting the slight by which the title had previously been omitted.

Obviously to men of Pylos the Achians did not merit a king. "And I am pleased to be among my friends in Pylos again.

May I pay my respects personally to King Linaeus, whom I also have not seen in many years.

"But we remember you, Wanderer," the king answered with a mixture of fondness and regret.

"You have frequented our port rarely as of later years, but then I do not know whether we are fortunate or poorer from your neglect."

"I am flattered that you bear me in mind at all," Zurga responded, now stepping in front of the other three.

"But perhaps this time our business will be pleasant without qualification and a source only of fond memories."

Orfeo listened as Zurga presented the king with a small gemstone, which was carried to him by one of the pages.

As Zurga was describing how the gift could forecast weather by becoming itself clouded and opaque before a rain, Orfeo's gaze fell upon the Therans, who had altered drastically in countenance.

Although there still had been no movement, the faces were uniformly transformed by looks of hatred and rage.

They too appeared at least to know of the Wanderer, and there was obviously no love between them.

Whatever else became of the petition, this day would not end well.

"To business first," directed the king, indicating that one of the ministers should reply to the original petition.

"I deeply regret reporting to your majesty and to the men of Achia that we have made a thorough search of our records to no avail.

There is simply no mention of such a captive coming through this port, and we must conclude that he never reached our city."

"Or that he was sold to the Therans," Isocles's voice had lost none of its clarity or daring, and he was suddenly standing beside the minister, obviously intent upon some kind of confrontation."

"Back to your seat, old friend," Nestor was to first to respond, and he seemed more worried than angry.

"You are out of order," the chief minister began a chastisement.

"I will not be silenced again by any of you, including this gallery of silent intruders into our affairs, who have brought a dark cloud over our city."

A gasp arose from many sources, as the old teacher began his complaint.

"I have watched in relative silence these many months as our institutions and our freedom have been eaten away by this cancer, but the time has come for us to refuse further inroads, for us to expel the curse and again hold up our heads."

"My friend, I beg of you to be silent."

The king had risen and stood looking in horror toward Nestor, who had turned ashen.

The audience was in a tumult, with many slipping as quietly as possible to the exits.

Orfeo watched Orton and Telemon appraising the layout through their professional eyes, but it was Zurga who, stepping back among the others, unobtrusively slipped a sheathed sword from under his tunic to Orfeo.

"Watch for changes," he whispered, exchanging looks with Orton and Telemon.

Again the hall became unnaturally quiet.

"In all respect to your majesty," Isocles continued, "I feel that I can remain silent no longer.

If I cannot be heard at court, I will schedule a great city meeting in the amphitheater, and I will tell the citizens that our liberties are being taken away.

I know the fate of Kalamatta, and I will not see the same happen here."

Isocles was again ordered to remain quiet by the king, but now Orfeo saw one of the Therans rise solemnly, and a low, hissing sound issued from thin sneering lips.

He moved only enough to enunciate the words, and his straight black hair remained in place.

"I, Bayan, am here only as an adviser," he stated.

"While I do not seek to influence your actions, I must state that I believe the four Achians are spies and that talk of a captive is only a pretext.

They must be detained for questioning." He appeared to address his own guard of soldiers rather than the king.

"So far as this man is concerned," he pointed to Isocles, "I would also suggest that he be permanently removed.

He has long been a thorn in the side of efficient government, and the time has come to pluck him out."

"Not while I am the king," Linaeus's words were almost inaudible in the general clamor, as the Kalamattans actually began to advance, at first toward the Achians, and then they were distracted by Isocles, who apparently had suddenly realized his blunder and had turned to flee the hall.

From that point Orfeo had before him only the immediate field of his vision, and everything seemed to happen at once.

The captain of the guard struck out at Isocles just before Telemon's sword separated his head from the remainder of his body, and now all the Achians followed Telemon in a frantic charge at the Therans, whose guards fell like trees before the hurricane of Achian wrath. Telemon's sword swung broadly in great arcs, clearing the path in front of him, and then cleaving the skull of Bayan, who had lost his immobility and had turned to flee, but the Therans had no exit and had, indeed, occupied a corner of the hall.

The slaughter was incredibly quick, and Orfeo found his own blade wet for the first time with human blood, finding flesh beneath the green robes, and then he turned to stave off the expected charge of the Kalamattans, but they obviously had found a sudden distaste for violence, as though they had no great interest in saving the Therans.

Their efforts, once the cream of their number had been decimated by Achian swords and Zurga's great swirling mace of fire, were halfhearted and inept.

By this time the guards of King Linaeus streamed in from several entryways, but they were obviously uncertain as to a course of action, and perhaps there were none who wanted to stand in front of the mighty Telemon.

They hastily formed a line across the hall at about the point where the Achians had stood in presenting their complaint, but when the Achians, fresh from their slaughter of Therans turned toward the exit, the guards made only a slight resistance.

In one brief interval between the charge back up the hall and the collapse of resistance from the men of Pylos, Orfeo turned once to his right, and there was the dying Isocles staring at him as though transfixed by a vision, obviously now having recognized his pupil and looking through the eyes of one who had learned caution much too late and was paying a price with his life.

"It's you," the words seemed labored, as though breath was rapidly failing.

"You're the one now, and you must carry on my work.

You're the last hope."

And amidst this turmoil the old teacher bowed his head in death, overcome not by the logic he had taught and lived by, but destroyed by the very heedless force he had sought to oppose.

Orfeo was running, still wielding the sword, and then suddenly they were outside the palace, racing across the courtyard, hurrying through the untended gate, running down the streets where the townspeople were even unaware that there had been a commotion at the palace, and then all at once the bells began to ring, and the great horn sounded.

Still there was no explanation, although Orfeo knew that when the gatekeepers registered the alarm, the great city would slowly be closed.

Already they were back to the horses, and there was no more time to bother with the amenities of leaving in good order.

Telemon, Orton, Orfeo, and Zurga rode breathlessly through the narrow streets toward the great gate, and already one massive door was in place and perhaps a dozen guards stopped in their work to scurry toward their waiting weapons as the Achians sped by.

Telemon and Orton each felled a man who sought to impede them, and suddenly they were galloping down the road away from the city, free of its gates and walls, once more into the open country where they at least stood a chance of ultimate escape.

The whole chain of events from the words of Bayan, setting into motion the guards, had seemed so sudden, as if time itself raced to catch up with them and record their deeds in terms of seconds and minutes, but they still did not stop, aware that there could be pursuit.

Only now did Orfeo allow the grip on his sword to relax, and he managed to slip the blade through his belt so that he could devote his hands to riding.

His coat from the marketplace had been lost in the haste, and he now carried visions that burned to the very center of his consciousness.

He reviewed the scene of Isocles, his beloved teacher, cut down before his eyes, while his strange words echoed in his mind.

What had they meant?

There was also a feel of the sword on human flesh and the sensation of a man, a Theran, dying beneath the sword of someone who had been a pupil of Isocles.

Yet the teacher had died from his lack of skill at arms, and now Orfeo lived.

Had the teacher been wrong?

Was Telemon's way the only course a man could take in this life?

Still they rode, feeling the horses tire and slowly feeling more secure that no effective pursuit had been mounted.

They had outrun even word that they should be apprehended, and finally, toward nightfall, they stopped at a village, hastily arranged a trade of horses, and after a few words between Zurga and Telemon, were off riding again through the night.

There was a bright moon in a clear sky, and they covered a great stretch of territory, heading north as Zurga had suggested into the lands of the Marshae, where the king, Praxis, was well known to the Wanderer and promised a friendly reception.

There they would be safe from whatever pursuers Pylos could send.

But what of the Therans?

Now Orfeo's mind was beginning to sort out events as his body adjusted to the monotonous pounding of the horse's hooves.

There had actually been something exhilarating about the collapse of the Therans beneath Telemon's mighty sword.

That was what the Achians had meant when they referred to him as a great leader.

Even though their attack had been unplanned, each of them had somehow become an instrument of Telemon's will, charging along with him, following his impulse and buoyed up by his strength and determination, and then he had led the retreat from the hall.

It was not so much Telemon's leading the way, but all turning with him, when the Therans lay shattered and bleeding, and proceeding with the most logical, efficient means of absenting themselves from the hall and escaping from the town.

There was no time for decisions or indecisions, but simply a matter of accomplishing an objective. Indeed, Telemon was a great warrior and champion, but he wielded more than himself, directing the activities of those around him as though they were extensions of his will.

Again the image of Isocles returned, and throughout the night as the four fugitives rode, visions of his teacher flickered across Orfeo's mind.

Force of arms was the key, the idea Isocles had rejected; yet he had fallen because of his lack of skill.

His world had ultimately been governed by laws other than logic.

Isocles had over and over again defined force out of existence, arguing that a man was most likely to be killed by a sword if he carried one.

But he had fallen beneath the weapon of a lesser man, and had he been able to defend himself he might still be alive.

Clearly there was a flaw to his thinking, and the realization to Orfeo was both shattering and liberating.

His whole mental world had seemed to be a gift from Isocles, and now there were parts that did not fit together, something, perhaps the first, that must be rejected by the same inexorable rules Isocles had taught.

Dawn found the four still riding across rockier terrain.

Now there seemed to be fewer signs of farming, and the villages were more scattered, Zurga indicated that they should again change horses, and this was arranged at a village they reached just when the sun had completely established its hold upon the horizon. They had a breakfast of milk and fruit, and then rode off at a slower gallop, turning off the road a few miles from town and leading the horses into an area sheltered from view by a great outcropping of rocks.

There they almost wordlessly arranged their few pieces of bedding and slept as the heat of the day grew about them, and finally as the sun began its descent Zurga awakened the others and directed that they move forward toward the kingdom of Praxis.

There was no way of gauging the zealousness of the pursuit, but there was no use taking chances.

The Therans, if they still maintained their influence in Pylos, would allow no one of the four to be spared.

Zurga spoke for a few minutes with Telemon as to what the other Therans on the boats were likely to do.

Soon they were off again, riding with a relentless precision, allowing the horses to set a pace between them to reduce the likelihood of their tiring too soon. The country was sparsely settled now, and perhaps there would be difficulty in replacing the animals should they prove too frail for the task.

Just before dusk the road veered into sight of the sea again, and Zurga halted the procession so that he could scan the horizon through a small black tube he had withdrawn from one of the seemingly bottomless compartments of his cloak.

Apparently there was no sign of ships, but the possibility that they could be pursued by sea brought a new weight of dread to the fugitives.

Surely the Theran vessels did not depend upon the wind, and even now they could be speeding their ranks of galley slaves to head off any escape to the north. Herron himself could be one of the oarsmen.

By nightfall the group was again ready for a rest, and as the sky had clouded over, the moon provided little light.

There had as yet been no sign of pursuit, nor had they any reason to believe that the villagers in this region knew of the incident at Pylos.

They were already close enough to the limits of the kingdom so that allegiance to a central authority was tenuous at best, and except during times of war the power of Pylos was little felt here.

"How does it feel to be a hunted man?"

Zurga spoke to Telemon with an ironic, mocking tone.

"It's an unaccustomed role, I must say." Telemon answered with no trace of humor.

"Most of my fighting has been in defense of my own soil and people, but this takes some getting used to."

"And some planning," the Wanderer wrapped himself in the great cloak as if preparing for sleep.

"Already, in only a few short weeks of our journey, we have incurred the wrath of Thera, which is a curse never forgotten."

"All things are forgotten," Orton answered.

"There is no arm so long as to repay all injuries."

"None but Thera," Zurga replied.

"But then you have much to learn on that score, and I do not wish to burden you with more dread than you need at this point."

"You make us all shudder," said Orfeo.

"And shudder you should, if it would help," the Wanderer said. "But I'm afraid that we have unleashed a power far more malignant and unforgiving than any we have known, and I, for one, am overcome by a heavy sense of pessimism and apprehension."

He held up his hand as if to preclude further comment.

"But take no notice of my ravings now.

We need not consider the fate of nations when we are still ourselves in danger within the next several days, and even when we reach Praxis, who knows what the Therans have been up to there."

He slumped back and closed his eyes, as if instantly out of touch with the others.

At such times Zurga appeared to sleep soundly, but Orfeo never surrendered the suspicion that even in sleep Zurga maintained more alertness than other men.

Telemon started to gather a few dead branches for a fire, and without describing his thoughts, arranged it against the rock so that it could not be seen from any distance.

He then sat back sullenly and removed his sword from its sheath, beginning a methodical process of cleaning off the encrusted blood.

Orfeo and Orton followed suit, with Telemon, as if exasperated, instructing Orfeo as to the proper method so that the blade would not be dulled.

Then he began to use a rough, metal rasp to further sharpen it.

"It looks as though I'll have plenty more use for this."

He worked intently.

"Do you believe what Zurga says about the Therans?"

Orfeo glanced cautiously toward the Wanderer, but apparently decided to talk anyway.

"Who knows what to believe, but they were the slimiest bunch I've ever dealt with."

Telemon recounted the scene with no trace of remorse.

"They bleed and die like anyone else, but they send shivers up your spine in doing so, as though they still have the upper hand, like maybe they're all part of one giant beast that can afford to loose several appendages, knowing that eventually it will triumph through sheer bulk and determination."

"It was creepy all right," said Orton.

"But they're not masters of the world, not yet anyway," Telemon inspected his blade.

"And it makes little difference what happens in Pylos and Kalamatta.

Our task is to recover Herron and return to the safety of our own lands."

"The way Zurga talks, no lands are safe from the Therans."

Orfeo interrupted for the first time.

"What does he or anyone else know about it," Orton replied.

"He seems to know a great deal, doesn't he?"

Telemon turned to study the sleeping form.

"He's quite a spook, that one, but perhaps worth his keep.

I have an idea he knows more than he's told us so far."

The fire flickered and slowly began to die.

Orfeo felt himself approach sleep reluctantly, but with the fatigue of the long ride inexorably overcoming all resistance.

At last he was oblivious to all his surroundings, but still allowing disorganized and fearful impulses to flicker across his mind.

There were dreams of Isocles and the Therans, and thoughts as to what sort of man he was becoming.

While he was no longer an Achian, he could also not see himself as a man of Pylos.

Indeed, his life was probably forfeit in that city, as he had committed a great crime within view of the king and court.

Somewhere in that great void out there, Herron waited.

No doubt he had somehow fallen into the hands of those green-robed creatures of slime.

But how to achieve a rescue?

All seemed dark and hopeless, and, as he awoke at intervals during the night, the moonless sky echoed the complete and endless void of his hopes.

# CHAPTER TWELVE

By morning of the third day since their escape, the travelers noted that the character of the villages had changed again, and the natives spoke with another accent, adorning themselves with garments of a different cut and drabber colors than the heavy woolen garments of the Achians.

These were the Marshae, from the land of Lakonia, whose king Praxis was known over a wide area as a brave and learned man, although his city was much smaller and less grand than Pylos.

While the Marshae lived close to the sea, and their fishermen brought back an abundant catch, they had not taken to the seas as had their neighbors, instead carrying out their trade overland in finely worked objects of precious metals and fabrics of intricate gold brocade.

The Marshae were relatively peaceful, having avoided wars of expansion among their less advanced kinsmen to the north, but both peoples stood as a barrier against the barbarians on the other side of the great mountains, and, if attacked, they well knew the principles of survival.

Not even the power of Pylos awed the Marshae, whose merchants had a reputation for honesty and subtlety.

Zurga had spent many delightful weeks during his travels here, and even Telemon was making no complaints about the prospect of spending time within the walls of a city.

It was not until the fourth day of travel that Orton finally caught a glimpse of the towers, which occupied a rocky bluff above a small harbor.

The villagers had all been exceedingly friendly on the way, and the reception at Lakonia was almost too good to be believed.

A gatekeeper recognized Zurga immediately and passed the entire group without question, and then they ascended slowly through the narrow streets toward the palace, which made up in elegance what it lacked in sheer size.

Everywhere there were great carved beams of oak, with black bronze fittings of pleasing complexity.

The buildings were orderly and well kept, and even the crisp, chill of the air echoed the general cleanliness of the city.

People went about their tasks in good humor, and all about them the travelers were greeted as though some special event had presaged their arrival.

News of Zurga's return, in particular, had apparently spread faster than the four had moved, and when they arrived at the palace, a chamberlain was already waiting with word that they would be received immediately by King Praxis.

The hall was built along the same general lines as that at Pylos, although the differences quickly spoke of the reasons why Marshae and men of Pylos were not of the same nation.

Perhaps the first feature that Orfeo noticed was the size, which was far inferior to that of Pylos, but there was a more intimate atmosphere, as one could look directly at the king and see him as an individual rather than a distant symbol of power. Praxis stood bareheaded with his feet wide apart, relaxed and warm, receiving his guests as if it were a genuine pleasure to do so, and allowing his words to emerge without pretense or pomp.

"The same fortunate wind that brings back my old friend has also taken away our enemies," he said.

"Welcome again to Lakonia, and enjoy our hospitality, my friend Zurga.

May your companions also receive my affection and trust."

"When all else changes in the world, and threats fall upon other lands, at least there is one civilized place left for our retreat," Zurga answered.

"We arrive in haste, my friend Praxis, although I trust that we will attract no new trouble in your direction."

Zurga had approached the king, and, after a deferential embrace, turned to introduce his companions.

The name of Telemon brought an appreciative gasp from the retainers, and Praxis studied the craggy face carefully, finally commenting in puzzlement.

"Is it Zurga or Telemon, or perhaps just the wind, who has driven away our detested visitors from the mouth of the harbor. It was just in the hour of your coming that the hateful Theran ships disappeared for the first time in months.

I was hoping you could tell me why."

Praxis appeared to speak his mind openly, as if the arts of politics were unknown in his court.

Orfeo listened while the two compared stories, feeling a certain hopelessness as more deeds of the Therans were recounted.

Apparently they had first appeared at Lakonia about three months before, in the wake of news of the preceding year that they had heavily infested Kalamatta and were strongly influencing the course of policy in Pylos.

At Lakonia, however, they had stopped only at threats, sending one great galley to the dock, requesting an audience with the king, and then demanding a series of concessions by which the independence of the city would be surrendered in return for protection against invasion.

The threat was never completely spelled out, however, as Praxis had refused the agreement, but the galley had never really left.

Indeed, it had anchored itself outside the harbor, visible only as a speck on the horizon, but it was ostensibly acting as a guard or a census taker.

No ships were disturbed either in coming or going, but the great vessel at times grew nearer and farther.

Periodically it seemed to be relieved by another ship, and at one time there were three, but there had always been a presence until this day, just before the travelers arrived

The townspeople had grown frantic with curiosity as to what would happen, and preparations for war had been made, but there was no evidence of outward hostility from the Therans, and on the surface their offer had been generous enough.

They promised protection merely for the right to set certain policies and to use the port for their own ships.

The king would remain, but would take on Theran advisers.

Perhaps it was just in this way that the Therans had seized the real power in Kalamatta and had attempted to do so in Pylos, and possibly the real power there had been exercised by them.

Zurga described to the king what the four had seen in Pylos, and he too seemed not to be holding back, but spoke directly.

His warning was firm.

"Much as I would like to take credit for driving away this threat, my companions and I cannot say we were responsible, except perhaps as an indirect result of what happened at Pylos.

I will say that the danger has not passed, and that, if anything, this whole part of the world is in greater danger than I had imagined.

While the Therans have been content for centuries to inhabit their own land, for some reason they now seek to extend their dominance into other lands as well.

There is no question that their conquest, whether by stealth or force of arms, would mean the destruction of our lives and nations, and we must resist at all costs.

At the same time I know much of Theran power, and I cannot pretend that the road to independence will be easy.

They are far more dangerous than you imagine, and I dare say that the one galley observing your commerce could have wrought great destruction if it had so desired.

The city itself could have been threatened."

He turned as if to make his words distinct to all within the hall.

"There is no choice but to resist the Therans at all costs.

The life of a Theran slave is no life in terms of what you have grown accustomed to, and, if they prevail, all is lost."

"Your warning will be heeded, and we have already assumed nearly as much from the rumors brought back by our merchants as to conditions in Kalamatta.

But we will speak more of serious matters later."

Praxis seemed to strive for an atmosphere of festivity, although one could hardly miss the gravity beneath his smile.

"Let us celebrate the arrival of friends and allies, and let us have a great feast and entertainment."

He motioned toward the attendants, who obviously had already prepared for his command.

As Orfeo watched, a steady procession of serving men began to change the complexion of the hall, decorating the great oak table with flowers and then arranging platters heaped with delicacies.

Fresh garments of a white, soft material, edged in crimson, were brought for the visitors, who were provided with bowls of hot water to wash off the dust of the journey.

Orfeo found himself the object of an attention more flattering and comfortable than he had ever known.

The Marshae had a reputation for having cultivated the gracious arts of living, and surely this seemed true in their ability to make a guest feel welcome.

A cup of wine seemed to materialize from nowhere, and suddenly Orfeo was sitting at the table with his companions and the king and chief nobles.

The queen and infant prince were introduced, and the nobles paid their respects first to Zurga, then to the hero Telemon, of whom they had apparently heard great things, and finally to Orton and Orfeo.

There was no talk of the Therans or any other unpleasantness, and the entertainments and drinking continued long into the night.

The memory of being led to a small room in the palace was only a blur, as Orfeo had liberally taken of the wine as he relaxed, allowing himself to become aware of just how much tension he had labored under since the boat had carried them away from the land of Achia toward the court of Pylos.

The time was so short when he thought of it, yet so much had happened, and he was beginning to feel like a creature of another sort, even more cut off by experience from his people.

He followed one cup with another until finally he looked about him at the massive carved beams over his head and realized that he had retired for the night, and the next morning the cares would again descend.

Someplace off in the distance he could hear the great bull voice of Telemon singing in merriment with the clamor of music, but for him there was only sleep.

Sunlight streamed through the window, lighting up a bright rectangle around his pallet on the floor, and Orfeo looked around to see that he was alone, but that his small room communicated through a broad door with a larger chamber.

He leapt to his feet, stumbling with the awareness of a headache, and walked into the other room, observing Telemon apparently asleep on a narrow cushion.

The old warrior opened one eye, however, just as Orfeo was about to leave.

"I thought I heard someone stirring," he said. "Are you ready to start killing Therans today? Telemon slowly brought his head and shoulders erect, glaring with a mellow scowl.

At times his sense of humor lacked delicacy.

"Go back to sleep," said Orfeo.

"I'll take care of them.

"Ahhh…I know it's time to get up now."

Telemon laughed sourly.

"When a boy offers to defend me against my enemies, it's time I'm up and about."

He looked around peevishly.

"Orton," he shouted.

"Where have they put you?"

"I'm safe," the other appeared at the doorway looking somewhat worse for the night's festivities.

"That was a hard feast," he said, "and I'm starved for another."

"There won't be another until there's something to celebrate, and I can't see that coming while those green lizards are out there waiting for us to turn our backs."

Telemon was lacing his boots.

"What about that other devil, the one on our side?

Where has he gone?"

Zurga had disappeared earlier, as he seemed to be in none of the adjoining rooms, and Orfeo walked hesitantly down the hall in search of him.

He was greeted by a guard, who immediately ordered that food be brought to the travelers, and then he explained that Zurga had been given lodgings in the king's personal wing of the building.

The three slowly organized themselves around the food, and Telemon began to talk about their narrow escape from the walls of Pylos, explaining that for some reason he did not have the same feeling about this city and that he would probably survive his tenure here.

Just as he was suggesting ways they might spend their morning, Zurga returned, looking smug and, as usual, in possession of more vital facts than the others.

"I can't say that we've decided everything yet," he began in manner apparently intended to mildly annoy Telemon, "but King Praxis and I have discussed the various courses open to us, and we have received a most pertinent message from one of the king's agents just returned, having left Pylos twelve hours after we did."

He seemed to require prodding.

"Fortunately he confirmed our stories and observed one other event that may be most significant for us.

The Therans apparently have completely abandoned the city, having sailed all of their warships from the harbor within an hour after their leaders were cut down by us in the palace.

Word was allegedly left, however, and I don't know in what form, that the Therans expect to return shortly as conquerors.

At such a time they vowed a total destruction of the city's populace for the unforgivable crime of taking arms against a Theran…."

"Taking arms," Telemon interrupted.

"We did more than merely take up arms."

"Even drawing a weapon in the presence of a Theran is an offense punishable by death, and no doubt our punishments will be adjusted accordingly to include a most terrifying, painful destruction."

He appeared to consider the matter as mildly amusing."

"Wait until they find what I have in store for them," Telemon muttered.

"I don't take kindly to threats."

"Be that as it may," Zurga could not resist a chiding tone, as though he had some doubts about Telemon's abilities to make good on his boasts, but he would not say so openly.

"The new information may well affect our plans, as we have not been sent here to fight Therans, but to recover Herron who, quite likely, has been in Kalamatta these last weeks or who has just returned to that city in the galley of a Theran warship."

"And if he is to be rescued, then we should do it before any invasion of Pylos, as he will be in great danger during the fighting."

Orton appeared worried.

"With your first suggestion I agree," Zurga continued calmly, "but again I must correct your assumption about the Theran warships.

If they attack Pylos, with its current defenses, they will overwhelm the city with surprisingly little effort, most certainly without loss of a ship.

The Therans only move when they see their success as absolutely certain, and they would see the loss of a single boat as intolerable.

You have not yet grasped the gravity of the threat they pose.

The fact that many fell beneath our swords with apparent ease has given a distorted impression.

They will not again fall so lightly, and, I fear, the consequences of our act will reverberate over a wide area and for many years."

"I'm becoming impatient with your talk about these devils as though they were gods."

Telemon showed his annoyance.

"Let's get on with the planning, or would you have us surrender our lives on the spot and allow them to lead us to our execution?"

"If that would allay their wrath, then I would seriously consider it, but it involves matters well beyond your ability to comprehend at this point."

The Wanderer now seemed to be reasoning with a child.

"You want plans, then we'll make plans.

Provided that we still wish to attempt a rescue, then we must journey to Kalamatta.

The problems we will face there defy your ability to imagine, but at least we will probably be within reach of Herron.

Our only chance of success depends upon the possibility of turmoil and confusion that will accompany preparations for the war."

"So we go to Kalamatta?" Orton sounded pessimistic.

"We just slaughtered an important contingent of Therans in Pylos, but shortly after our escape, we show up right at their stronghold.

Somehow it seems that we'll be walking into the lion's jaws again." The objection seemed based not so much on fear as caution.

"Of course we go carefully disguised," Zurga interjected.

"I haven't lost my senses to the point where I would appear among the Therans as Zurga of Melitis, by which identity I have long been known to them, but there are many ways in which appearances and manner may be convincingly changed, and I daresay the same is true of Telemon and Orton.

Orfeo presents no problem at all.

"Our mistake was in letting a Wanderer take part in this," Telemon neither meant the words nor did he reject Zurga's suggestions, but he was clearly exasperated with the idea of assuming a new role.

"I suppose you'll have me travel to Kalamatta as a seller of ladies ear rings and bracelets."

"As fine an idea as I've heard today," the Wanderer answered.

"Since merchants are continually entering and leaving the city of Kalamatta, how better could the four of us enter unsuspected than as merchants of Lakonia."

"And I suppose you'll have me selling fine broadcloth, with my soldier's hands and scarred face?"

Orton was mirthful.

"Orfeo should pose as a soldier, guarding the merchants," chided Telemon.

"No one could see through that disguise."

"He did his part in Pylos, and you can be sure that before we leave, he'll be more of a swordsman than he is now, as the three of you will have little to do but practice with your weapons," added Zurga.

"Are you saying that I didn't carry my part in Pylos?" Orfeo addressed Telemon with a sense of wounded dignity.

"Ahhhh, my boy, you were strong and courageous, and I have only been anxious to continue your education."

"I should think we must all be respectful of the only man who ever felled the great Telemon and lived to tell about it," said Orton.

"Enough of play," Zurga's voice was heavy with concern.

"So we have decided to set off for Kalamatta as soon as we can prepare suitable disguises?"

He paused as if waiting for objections.

"Then it remains only that I make arrangements with King Praxis and find when the next group of merchants is traveling to our destination.

Then we must prepare ourselves carefully, schooling our speech so as not to betray another background, learning the essentials of our new trades, and acquiring skills necessary for survival in a strange land."

He lowered his voice ominously.

"For I trust that none of you have ever faced a danger more severe than what we are challenging, and I am not at all confident we will return alive to Achia."

Even Telemon suppressed his usual rejoinder as Zurga left, and the three maintained an awkward silence.

All sense of having escaped from danger seemed hollow and meaningless, as they knew that greater hazards lay ahead.

# CHAPTER THIRTEEN

THE DAYS AT LAKONIA stretched into weeks and were so restful and filled with the warmth of good companionship that Orfeo could for days at a time nearly forget about all threats the future promised.

It was here that his eighteenth birthday was passed amidst a celebration of the hour by the travelers and their new friends at the court, with King Praxis himself sending a gift of finely worked leather sandals, while Telemon had fashioned a new sword with Orfeo's name engraved on the hilt.

The weapon came into almost immediate use as Orfeo worked hard to practice his skill, and Telemon, bemoaning solemnly that Orfeo had long passed the time in his youth when such abilities should have been acquired, made it clear that this could be a last chance.

Survival could possibly depend upon how well he assimilated the lessons of the next weeks, and always the specter of Isocles stood before Orfeo as a warning.

In times of trouble guile alone was not enough.

"I swear that you have grown bigger both in height and bulk since we left," Telemon said with a smile.

"You no longer let your shoulders droop, but you stand taller and prouder."

"Despite the danger, I feel alive, and I like traveling.

I am learning about the world, and I especially like being safe behind city walls."

That was not entirely true, but a give and take had grown up between the boy and the warrior which allowed each to verbally toy with the other.

"It's not everyone I would let address me with such lack of respect," said the warrior.

"You're just trying to be agreeable because you fear I may be king someday."

"When I first saw you in your father's tent, I could never have imagined you as king, but now I'm not so sure.

You have much more subtlety about you than I had imagined."

"And you have much more subtlety about you than you allow to show," the boy answered.

Zurga remained quietly out of sight as the warriors tutored their young pupil, but all the while he was conferring with a succession of merchants and diplomats, including many agents that Praxis used as spies in distant lands.

The survival of his city had never been left to chance, but was dependent upon his reading the course of events in his world, and thus Praxis made himself better informed than any other monarch whose lands bordered the inland sea.

Zurga made good use of this information, painstakingly constructing a scheme by which he and his three companions could pass undetected within the walls of Kalamatta.

Much depended upon the plans of Lakonian merchants, who sold both fruits and jewelry to the Kalamattans.

The first cargo was usually taken directly by boat to the great metropolis of the west, and as summer neared its end, and the trees were laden with a dozen varieties of enticements, the boats would soon begin their rounds.

The jewelry and fine fabrics were traded by another class of merchants, whose traditions were rigid around the issue of travel.

They moved overland, first east and then south, taking perhaps three times as long. But avoiding the perils of the sea and delivering their costly commodities in more assured safety.

Clearly the travelers, in attempting to evade detection, should split up, with some traveling by sea and others by land, and Zurga soon worked out a plan.

Orton and Orfeo, being the most nondescript and least recognizable members of the group, could probably travel together in safety, particularly if they were in the company of a caravan of about a dozen merchants and twice that number of escorts, who were made up of Lakonians and mercenary guards from the lands traversed during the trip.

Long before they arrived at Kalamatta, they would be met by a delegation of soldiers from that city, who would travel along for security, which referred more to the internal security of the nation than the safety of merchants.

The Kalamattans, as a prosperous trading people, had long carried on relations with many distant lands, but they were traditionally cautious, and their concern with safety had apparently multiplied since their investiture by the Therans.

During the trip both Orton and Orfeo were to represent themselves as merchants of silver goods, and both set about the task of learning these items from several of the king's trusted agents, who would also be present on the journey.

Orton grumbled about this task, but caught on surprisingly quickly, and Orfeo found himself intrigued by these elegant trinkets that the women of Lakonia so ingeniously designed.

Telemon and Zurga had decided to travel by sea, but it appeared most advisable for both to go on separate boats, at a separate point in time.

As Telemon, without indicating that he was at all afraid, did not seem anxious to arrive first in a strange metropolis, feeling as he did about being within walls. Zurga planned to leave first, hoping to prepare a place where they could meet in safety.

As soon as the dates were set, the four seemed busier than ever with learning what amounted to new ways of life.

Only Zurga stood supremely confident, as though the task of assuming a new identity was a relatively simple matter.

His explanation to Orfeo seemed to open more questions than it answered.

"You look upon me now as Zurga of Melitis, a Wanderer, and some say an evil charlatan, but you have no way of seeing all that I have ever been or will be."

Zurga spoke in the calmly measured tone of mystery that he used to annoy the warriors and tease Orfeo's curiosity.

Clearly he was implying that he had appeared in many diverse roles in the past, and his current identity was no more than a convenient skin of the moment.

While he was not about to divulge the really fascinating details, his message was, in effect, that he was many men, while the others were limited to only being themselves, and this gave him an additional aura of potency.

Orfeo, however, was no longer so uncritical in what he accepted.

"Isocles once said that the successful Wanderer is a good showman, combining the skills of an actor and a merchant."

The boy matched his companion jab for jab.

"So while you may have taken on many appearances in your long life, until you can be more than one place at a time, you shall still remain only one man to me."

"Give a lad a sword, and soon he'll be swaggering about like a warrior, knowing all and telling all he knows."

Zurga lounged grandly on a great cushion of fur, daintily feeding himself fruit from the orchards of Lakonia.

"But he should never forget to fear Wanderers most of all. A sword is, after all, not much of a weapon against cunning."

"If words alone could win the world, then Wanderers would rule," Orfeo answered.

"At least Telemon is trying his best to teach me to be a swordsman, while you do little to teach me how better to meet the demands of the world."

Orfeo remained aware that Zurga was more than a helpless wielder of ideas, but he seemed concerned with hiding his knowledge from the boy.

The gaunt old figure had been more than a useless member when they had been attacked by bandits, and in the great charge against the Therans in Pylos, he had wielded with devastating effect his great flaming sphere.

"Your tongue wields its own blade, my young friend, but then you enter upon the stage of the world with greater advantages than attended even my own launching."

"You must be referring to my good fortune in having Telemon and Isocles as teachers, each supreme in his field." Orfeo had guessed the implication and had blocked Zurga's next move.

"Not at all, lad."

Zurga now took on a more serious tone.

"Your fortune consists of having me as a teacher, but you will not realize what I have taught you until after I am gone."

"If your boast is true," Orfeo answered, "then let us begin our lessons.

I am eager to learn, for example, of the flaming orb with which you smite your enemies."

"Always going too fast," Zurga laughed.

"No, for that you must be initiated in other arts and understand principles that would now be incomprehensible to you.

But let us start with more simple matters."

"Like the manner in which you removed the markings from my arm."

"Ahh, that too must wait.

Surely you must be satisfied with less."

"Perhaps I must be satisfied that I become a warrior like Telemon, as he does not hold back his secrets, but seeks that I practice and learn everything he knows."

"What a formidable creature you will be, trained in the logic of Isocles, the swordsmanship of Telemon, and, perhaps, my wisdom."

Zurga was now preparing his pipe as though it involved his full attention and Orfeo was of some peripheral interest.

"I may not need your wisdom by the time you're ready to teach it to me."

"Make no mistake, my young friend, you will need it, and you will need much more than any of us can teach you.

The world around us is changing, and when the Therans come, there will be no time for the sort of leisurely life your people have led for centuries.

The stakes will be higher, and your survival is not at all assured."

He spoke with a nonchalance implying only a distant interest. "You, unfortunately, have been more or less singled out in this conflict.

Whether you know it or not, your role will be an important one, if you live.

You will have resources beyond those of most men, and you must throw your life into the effort to preserve this world of virtue and vice that surrounds us.

You have no choice, but the time and circumstance have chosen you."

Now the words came slowly and with oppressive weight.

"I will teach you my secrets as the occasion arises, and I only hope it will make a difference.

If the advance of the Therans is even slowed, a great feat will have been accomplished."

The conversation had a deep impact on Orfeo, and never again did he address the wanderer with quite such irreverence.

Without understanding the details, the message had penetrated that the times were crucial for the world about the inland sea, and the Therans represented a threat of incalculably greater magnitude than anything faced before.

The task of acquiring skill as a swordsman was approached with even greater vigor, and Telemon was pleased with the manner in which his pupil responded.

Even the old warrior had much to say that influenced Orfeo's thinking, and he took in one piece of information after another, organizing each into his own version of a coherent picture.

Particularly after Zurga sailed for Kalamatta in a ship full of apricots, Orfeo felt more dependent upon the tutoring of Telemon, who taught by his own example of informed courage.

"Remember, it's not recklessness that wins," he would say, as Orfeo would again have exposed some weakness in his zeal to bring an encounter to an end.

"You're taking chances, my boy, and however you may wish to make things appear, you must play it safe on all occasions when there is an alternative.

You have but one life to lose."

For Telemon swordsmanship, or rather the ability to survive under conditions of combat, had taken on a mystique of its own, with a philosophy suited to its requirements.

Just as Isocles had surveyed the world through eyes of reason, Telemon saw everything in terms of its defensive or offensive potentialities, while every element relating to his resources, his mind, body, and weapons, was carefully scrutinized.

He paid attention to the amount he ate, drank, slept, or remained motionless.

Not that he never indulged to excess, but it was always with a conscious permission, as if he were keeping track of everything, and he would allow only certain deviations at well chosen times.

By the same token his approach to other people was as calculating as that of any politician, and as he passed the time of day in apparent idleness with strangers, he was at the same time subtly mining for their weaknesses.

By the time the great warrior was ready to set out on his journey, which was to be slowed by many stops in other ports while the merchants sold their elaborate textiles, Orfeo had absorbed something of his attitude toward life.

Indeed, the role of soldier was every bit as complex as any other, and more seemed to rest on one cast of the die.

Mistakes could easily be fatal.

Finally the day also came when Orton and Orfeo arose early and mounted their steeds as part of a lengthy caravan, first riding east, around an outcropping of the inland sea, and then south toward Kalamatta.

Now Orfeo was a merchant, and he comported himself as such, finding also that here was another complete way of life that demanded total commitment for success.

He was now a dealer in silver wares, and at the few cities in the route of the caravan, he plied his trade with diligence and an eager eye to learn.

In Kalamatta he must be expert.

Orton was perhaps not so entertained, as he had for too many years held the soldier's disdain for the peddler, but he spent more time with Orfeo, obviously missing Telemon's trusted ear as well as his company.

Soon he was confiding his life's story to Orfeo, who found new complexities in what had at first seemed such a straightforward soldier.

Orton had grown up as an Achian shepherd in a band to the east of Kiros's territories, although the king's nominal rule was recognized even there.

In these marches, however, the Hannae were more of a threat, and the men had born arms more often, depending for their survival on constant vigilance and frequent violent encounters.

Orton's father had particularly emphasized that his son be proficient with the sword, and when a family feud erupted within the camp itself, his skill had resulted in the death of a kinsman.

The feud now deepened with the element of blood, and sides were chosen within the village. To avert a general slaughter, the chieftain banished Orton, who had no other course than to wander abroad, a man without a people.

He had worked as a mercenary first for the Dardanos, a group related to the Achians and held in check by their power, and then had wandered along the eastern shores of the great inland sea, finally taking up service with the Princes of Tyre as a hired sword.

He rose to the royal guard and commanded a squadron, but when he heard that his homeland was sorely threatened by a fresh, resurgent army of Hannae, he had abandoned his post and ridden in haste toward home.

Fortunately the great battle had taken place before Orton met with any of his kinsmen, and he had fought heroically at the mighty Telemon's side.

There was no question about his again returning to exile, and the bitterness around his departure had subsided.

Yet he could not return to the old life, and in some unalterable manner he had defined his existence.

He was a professional soldier, perhaps with Telemon the only other among the Achians who was that and nothing else.

He traveled with Telemon, and an ever changing assortment of others, who always held the option of returning to their home village and living as an ordinary man with a wife and family.

Orton, like his companion, bore no badge or insignia, except perhaps his very face, but he was clearly and inescapably a soldier, and he would continue to be until he died.

Not that his role was all so bleak and lonely.

He traveled much, and he was always welcomed among his widely scattered people.

He and Telemon taught the arts of war, aiding their kinsmen in the manufacture of weapons and the maintenance of arsenals, and, of course, they were the only full time force that specifically did the bidding of the king.

There was always food, even when the villages shared a common scarcity, and money was always moderately plentiful.

Women too were attentive to the wishes of heroes, and from all sides they met admiring and appreciative looks.

Orton also told much of Telemon, during those long evenings by the campfire.

As the caravan stopped at dusk, there was always time to kill left over in the evening before they were tired enough to sleep, and Orton, after first ascertaining that he could not be overheard, would expound upon the adventures of his friend. Actually he spoke more of qualities rather than individual exploits, and Orfeo came to see the elements necessary to be a good fighting man.

Essentially it was a matter of discipline, requiring total commitment to a life-style and a complete immersion in the instincts necessary for survival.

Telemon reacted so quickly that he could eradicate danger before others had even sensed its presence, He was able to concentrate so thoroughly on the task at hand, that few details escaped his scrutiny.

Orfeo's respect for the hero increased the more Orton spoke.

The overland route to Kalamatta was more than simply a pathway through the wilderness, as the merchants visited a number of smaller towns along the way, giving Orfeo a chance to perfect his mannerisms as a trader of silver.

The journey was also not without danger, as wild bandits at times harassed the highways, and here the customs were particularly harsh.

While the freebooters who occupied the central plateau of the lands of Pylos were men of the same blood and backgrounds as the more placid villagers, and thus open to more or less negotiation, the coastal lands were traversed by roving groups of barbarians from the east, who looked upon all aspects of the city culture as alien and hostile.

They slew without mercy and destroyed what they did not need.

Spies were also an ever present danger, despite all efforts of Praxis to assure the loyalty of his merchants.

Indeed, the caravan picked up new members from many villages, as it was customary for smaller traders always to travel in larger companies.

Surely at some time before their arrival in Kalamatta a spy could well join their number.

As a precaution, Orfeo and Orton began progressively to keep less company with each other so that the newcomers would not tend to identify them together.

Particularly after they crossed the frontier of Kalamatta and were joined at the same time by several suspicious rogues of no discernable business, they took up their quarters on opposite sides of the camp, at the same time maintaining a watch over the other's safety.

As they approached within about two days journey of the city, a new danger intruded, as Kalamattan patrols appeared regularly throughout the day.

Usually at some time during the morning and again in the afternoon, the caravan was stopped, and certain members were selected, apparently at random, for questioning.

It was not clear exactly what the security guards were seeking, nor did there seem to be any particular reason for their search through many bales of merchandise. The whole atmosphere of the caravan changed, however, and now men seemed more ill at ease and kept more to themselves.

There were rumors floating about of a great oppression within Kalamatta, where the townspeople were now frightened to voice the slightest criticism of the king.

Discussion of anything concerning the Therans was forbidden, and some of the reason for this fear soon became apparent.

On the day before they were to reach Kalamatta, after having passed through villages in which the peasants worked grimly and humorlessly, ignoring travelers as though they had been instructed to talk with no one, the caravan was stopped by a troop of guards far more sinister than those that had come before.

Perhaps fifty heavily armed Kalamattans were led by a small figure who at first seemed to be one of them, but Orfeo noticed differences that lead to an inevitable conclusion.

The figure did not appear at all like the robed dignitaries the travelers had attacked successfully at Pylos, but he was, nevertheless, a Theran.

Indeed, while he was physically small, he carried a vicious looking metal bow that appeared far more lethal than anything Orfeo saw among the Kalamattans, and hanging from his saddle there was a barbed mace that seemed designed not merely to inflict mayhem, but to do so in a particularly painful manner.

At first the merchants and travelers were assembled in a line beside their beasts, and then the captain dismounted and inspected each thoroughly, as though looking for escaped prisoners who for some inexplicable reason would be returning to a prison city.

Then the Theran inspected the company from his horse, and Orfeo could feel around him the terror felt by both his Kalamattan escorts and the traders. There was something so coldly evil on his face and in his bearing, as though he saw the entire world as surviving only to bring benefit to him.

Otherwise they would all be dead men.

"I like not the looks of this man," The Theran hissed the words with a lisping accent, pointing to one of the travelers who stood a few feet from Orfeo.

As though they needed no further explanation, the Kalamattans seized him and carried him before the company, and at another gesture the man was disemboweled and trodden beneath the captain's horse. It was over in a brief moment, as though the Kalamattans enacted commands without the slightest thought of hesitation.

"Warn them."

This time the Theran appeared to smile without humor.

"You will tomorrow pass through the inspection point at the gate of Kalamatta," the captain said. "Those of you on legitimate business will not be detained, but spies, traitors, and idlers will be seized and executed.

There will be no treachery in our city, and enemies are dealt with simply and expediently."

He gestured toward the mutilated body.

"Take heed," he laughed and motioned his troop to follow.

The Theran appeared bored and indifferent.

"Perhaps we've crossed the river to Hell," Orton sought out Orfeo during the evening meal and spoke in a low voice.

"But there's no turning back at this point," came the answer.

"Perhaps...."

Orton was visibly disturbed.

"I'll feel better when we find Zurga and Telemon."

He quickly looked around to make certain that no one had heard the names.

Sometime in the middle of the next afternoon they crossed the great drawbridge spanning the moat and were within the large gateyard standing before the inner wall.

On all sides armed men looked down from above, but the guards found nothing that aroused overt suspicion, and, traveling separately, Orfeo and Orton found themselves within the greatest city of the West, a metropolis rivaling Tyre herself at the other end of the inland sea. Suddenly Pylos seemed small and provincial, as Orfeo caught the rhythms of a vastly more complex way of life.

There were problems to be faced here that he could only imagine.

# CHAPTER FOURTEEN

THE FIRST TASK WAS TO ARRANGE lodgings at an inn, and this proved to be easier than expected and at the same time more disquieting. The agent processing foreign merchants suggested a certain establishment with a forcefulness that implied obedience.

They made their way to the Boar's Tusk, which they found to be peopled by other merchants. Clearly the authorities left nothing to chance, concentrating foreigners into one small segment of the city so that they could be better watched, and perhaps also so that they would have less contact with the local citizens.

Further restrictions appeared as they registered for their rooms, with the Master of the Inn requiring that they show the small leather strips they had been given at the gate, each labeled with a number and a seal.

Certainly a strange and ominous order had been imposed upon the city.

Actually the new system was likely to make their second task easier, as Zurga and Telemon were likely also to be lodged nearby.

Indeed Telemon appeared the next morning, having himself been watching the arrival of strangers, and he presented himself in even a more peculiar disguise than on his departure.

He was now an armorer, or rather a blacksmith who specialized in the machinery of war, but his appearance was radically changed.

The long black hair and fierce beard had vanished, while his stiff sandals, that laced to the knee, had been altered to give him a sort of perpetual limp that he found quite natural and even, after a while, comfortable.

He still bore his sword, but the scabbard was not nearly so ornate, and his simple tunic suggested more a tradesman than a warrior.

Strangely, though, it was Orfeo who recognized him first, as Orton had never seen his friend shaven.

Zurga too made first contact, as though he had merely been waiting for the others to assemble.

He simply appeared without explanation, saying that his room was not watched and, if approached by solitary men, they could meet there unnoticed.

His hair had been bleached and reddened, and his whole complexion appeared to match, suggesting more an origin among the barbarians who now menaced the civilized world from the north.

The robe was the same, but it had been turned and fashioned into a more ornate garment suggestive of a physician, and Zurga's goods of trade, herbs and medicines, ideally fit his talents.

He seemed to feel secure in the new surroundings, which was true for none of the rest, but at the same time he appeared disconsolate and depressed.

His news was gloomy and filled the travelers with foreboding.

"The Therans are masters here," he said, "and the entire city and nation lives under a tyranny that every day increases its grip.

The populace is slowly falling to the level of slaves, and yet it occurs so subtly that they are unaware.

But even darker are the rumors of a great invasion toward the west.

Even now the warships are being loaded with provisions, and soldiers are arriving from the provinces.

A great Theran barracks holds thousands of their soldiers, and the Kalamattans cooperate in full force, ignoring the fact that their own freedom becomes all the more fully lost as they aid their masters."

"How did the Therans gain command here?"

Asked Telemon.

"The same way they will gain control in Pylos and eventually in Tyre too, if they are not stopped," Zurga answered.

"But that seems to run well ahead of their immediate goal.

The Theran galleys are manned by slaves at the oars, and no doubt many are Achians.

If Herron still lives, he is likely chained below the deck of a warship."

His words turned caustic.

"It lies with us merely to rescue him from his captors, as all thought of ransom must be abandoned.

The Therans do not bargain, but only seize and command."

Indeed the picture appeared hopeless, as the prospect of forcibly freeing Herron loomed as virtually impossible.

Even Telemon uttered no rash words, and Orfeo could not in his most extravagant imaginings conceive a plan.

It was decided, nevertheless, that they at least explore the matter further, and Orfeo was chosen to make what inquiries he could around the docks, trying to get as close as possible to the Therans.

Telemon and Orton, deciding to go separate ways in order to avoid suspicion, had no specific tasks, but seemed interested in learning as much as possible about the Therans.

Zurga, surprisingly, did not even wish to venture forth upon the streets.

There was something about the place that disturbed him more than anything he had previously encountered, and he spoke of doing his business in the evenings when he would not likely be noticed.

Possibly it was the Therans that worried him, as he mentioned several times how plentiful they were within the city.

The next day Orfeo went to the market with some of the other silver merchants who had accompanied him on the caravan, and he busied himself in disposing of his goods. Until the middle of the afternoon, he kept his attention strictly turned to business, but the lure of the docks eventually overpowered his caution, and he set out to see what he could find of Herron and the Theran ships.

It was just as he was leaving the silver market that he was caught in an incident that was initially disquieting and then profoundly moving.

Without warning armed men had suddenly materialized around the stalls, and everyone was cautioned to kneel, as a royal visitor was soon to pass.

As Orfeo had averted his eyes groundward, there had suddenly appeared just on the periphery of his vision a troop of armed Therans, and then an elegant litter car that gleamed with gold and precious stones.

Orfeo froze where he was stationed, and then he was aware of figures walking among the stalls, looking at the silver pieces and exchanging comments in a tongue barely recognizable to him, but the gay, feminine voices were not unlike those of his mother and her attendant ladies.

As they had passed perhaps twenty feet from him, possibly he could just lift his eyes enough to see what was happening. Apparently they were buying jewelry at one of the shops, and the Theran men-at-arms hovered as though the women were of great rank. He could just see the bottoms of their flowing, long gowns, and then they turned in his direction, with an older woman letting her gaze fall directly into Orfeo's eyes and making no move to have him chastised for his insolence.

He continued to watch, marveling at her grace and beauty even though she must be a mother, and then he was aware that she too was a Theran, only of a subtly different quality.

Her skin was radiantly white and soft, and her hair a sunstreaked mixture that was only slightly darker than Orfeo's own.

The set of the nose and mouth, with wide and inquisitive eyes, were vaguely reminiscent of the emissaries at Pylos, but they resembled only slightly the short, thickly-built soldiers.

And then the princess came into view, and Zaide was a radiant creature who had inspired poets and singers before she was into her teens.

Already a legend among her people, she was aloof and superior, rightfully arrogant and presiding over the very stones at her feet.

Her hair was dark, as were most Therans, but the features were chiseled in ivory, tipped with the rose of a summer dawn, and sparkling with an inner glow and life that seemed to threaten the serenity of the royal trappings around her.

Princess Zaide, the name echoed as if whispered on a hundred lips, and it came to Orfeo as he gazed in rapt attention, not daring to move, but fearful that his eyes would be diverted from their feast.

She was a goddess, the earthly personification of the images that the people had worshiped at Delphi.

She was Aphrodite and Diana and Juno.

If she saw Orfeo, no sign of recognition registered, and she proceeded grandly to the next stall, imperiously surveying its wares, and then returning to the little car.

The entire party, including the soldiers, had disappeared before Orfeo again became conscious of his immediate surroundings.

First the sounds penetrated, and then a bright light.

He was looking toward the sun, or was it merely drawing his gaze through his rapt attention to something that had vanished.

He thought of where he was and where he had come from, not knowing for the moment if anyplace was home, but feeling a great longing for warmth and closeness and belonging.

Here was a woman he wanted to be near, and with this desire he wanted all the other comforts of a home and a full life.

Then he was walking toward the waterfront, telling himself that he was behaving like a silly child.

A Theran princess was by very definition an object of evil and villainy, and clearly she was merely a part of the conqueror's train.

All the more reason why her beauty should be despised and rejected, as it was no more than another weapon of the enemy.

Still there was something in Orfeo that reacted at a level beneath or beyond reason, and a curious longing had been provoked.

He not only found himself wanting this princess, or wanting something about her, but obsessed with the desire for the closeness and intimacy that he had been exiled from when he first was sent to Pylos as a hostage. It was as if he desperately wished to return to some secure part of his childhood that was now only a dimly remembered dream.

Sight of the great harbor at Kalamatta served to return Orfeo to the real world, and he was virtually overwhelmed by the immensity of the docks and the great number of ships.

Certainly this was the commercial hub of the world, and about him moved men of all nations and customs, including some whose origins he could only guess.

As at Pylos, the Therans had appropriated a large area to themselves, with armed guards keeping outsiders from straying too near, and here the great galleys looked even more ominous.

There were a dozen great ships with five rows of oars, and their sheer bulk made believable the rumors as to how they had crushed the navy in scant minutes.

The prows of these great dragons of the sea were shaped into massive battering rams, which protruded on several levels so that any size ship could be impaled.

Surely the combined force of the oarsmen could outstrip the speed of the fastest sailing vessel.

One of these galleys appeared even larger than the others, and the sides shown as though gilded with some rare metal.

Perhaps it was a flagship or the vessel that carried such royalty as the princess Zaide.

There were also about thirty smaller vessels, with two or three ranks of oars, and these seemed clearly superior to anything Orfeo had seen before.

Orfeo wandered about the wharves and among the stalls set up by merchants, at times feeling overwhelmed and lost.

As no ready access to the Therans presented itself, indeed, no method of coming within fifty yards of the ships, Orfeo began merely by absorbing what he overheard in passing conversations.

Soon, however, he ran across a group of fruit sellers from Lakonia who had obviously sailed since the four had set out.

Orfeo addressed them, and he was received as a friend in that his reception from King Praxis was known.

Such was the spirit of the citizens of Lakonia that they had some understanding of the affairs of state, and yet they were most trustworthy.

They loved their homes with a passionate loyalty, and treason was virtually unknown among them.

Incredibly enough the merchants had just concluded an arrangement with a Kalamattan, in the employ of the Therans, to deliver virtually their whole shipment of fruit to the barracks surrounding the warships.

As labor would be in short supply, Orfeo was invited to help, which he promptly accepted.

Soon he found himself laden with sacks of fruit, wending his way through the crowd as part of a line of bearers.

The area was too crowded for pack animals, and the carrying at this point was all done by human beasts of burden.

From a shorter distance the Theran ships seemed even more awesome.

Orfeo could easily imagine the terror felt by the crew of smaller vessels being overtaken by such monsters, and his thoughts were all the more heavy as he thought of this power spreading throughout the great sea.

Surely nothing could stand before such brute force.

The fleet of Pylos would be swept aside like so much driftwood.

Just before a party of about a dozen bearers entered the Theran compound, one of the Lakonians had jokingly said that they should not linger overly long for fear of ending up in the galleys.

The warning seemed without humor as they began to see large clusters of chained men, who were obviously at other times bound to the oars and made to sweat for their bread. The men were a motley assortment, with blacks from the far lands on the other side of the great inland sea and short, yellowish natives of the East.

With a sinking heart Orfeo heard a familiar sound of Achian song, looking in vain for the singer, aware that other Achians stood among the slaves.

None of the faces were familiar, but clearly the slave raiders had struck hard among peoples of the coastal lands and the islands.

Herron must be somewhere among these luckless men, trapped in an existence remote from his upbringing.

Again the fruit sellers passed through the line of armed men guarding the Theran compound, only this time they were more thoroughly scrutinized.

They were counted, lest a slave be among them, and then released.

How oppressive the atmosphere had seemed, and except for the abortive snippet of song there had been no trace of happiness or laughter.

By this time the last vestiges of light were disappearing, and Orfeo started back toward his room.

He impatiently ate in the large common hall of the inn, and then he proceeded to Zurga's quarters, carefully observing that he was not being followed. The wanderer was despondent and grim when Orfeo repeated to him what he had seen, but he responded with more interest when Orfeo told of the Princess Zaide.

Orfeo realized that she had nothing to do with their business in Kalamatta, but he felt compelled to talk of her, as though it would bring some obscure sort of contact between them.

"I have heard of the princess," Zurga said.

"She must be nearly your age now, possibly a year or two younger.

Her father is brother to the king, and she herself stands in the line of royal succession."

He seemed to dismiss the subject with a gruff gesture.

"Tell me of her and the Therans," Orfeo was curious.

"They all seem of different races, yet with some features the same.

But the soldiers are short and muscular, the diplomats were dark and snake-like.

The princess and her attendants are taller, lighter, and beautiful.

They are somewhat alike, yet each seems born to his role."

"That's closer to the mark than I would have expected from you," said Zurga, "but what makes you think I have the answers?"

"Don't tease me, graybeard," said Orfeo.

"If you want me to report my observations to you and be your eyes in this world, then you'll tell me what you know."

"Ah.....true."

Zurga now smiled and sat back contemplatively.

"Of course I can tell you only legend, as the events are lost in antiquity, but there are stories about the island of Thera, which was then known by another name.

Perhaps a thousand years ago the land was inhabited by a tall, fair, and vigorous people, whose science and knowledge far surpassed that of the lands around the inland sea.

These people were benevolent to others and limited their nation only to the island."

"Ultimately," Zurga continued, "they were invaded and conquered by another people from the west, who poured over the land like a plague of locusts, greatly outnumbering the defenders, although even so the contest was close.

Finally the invaders installed themselves as rulers, but with a curious deference to the conquered.

The original royal family was forced to marry exclusively within the royalty of the newcomers, which produced a completely different people from which the current upper class has sprung.

As the invaders were short and stout, the new offspring of these unions are taller and fairer.

The ruling and magistrate class derive from these unions, while the soldiers are a pure line from the invaders.

The priestly class was allowed to remain intact, as the invaders adapted the old religion, which is based around the god Vulcan, whom they believe resides in the great volcano at the center of their island.

Two hundred priestly families survive and claim a pure lineage for a thousand years.

They intercede between Vulcan and the Therans.

The remainder of the original inhabitants have died out or live in scattered and hunted bands in the hills. Of that there is more rumor than fact."

The wanderer looked at his listener with a twinkle, as if daring Orfeo to doubt a word of the story.

"Now are you satisfied that you have enough information on which to base your observations?"

Zurga laughed and helped himself to a great pipe of a noxious-smelling compound.

"I only wonder what other data you have omitted," answered Orfeo, "and marvel that you have said so much."

"I have an idea that the Therans are going to be around for a long time," the wanderer answered, "and we had better all get to know them.

For some reason they have apparently only recently embarked upon a scheme for conquering the remainder of the world.

If they are no more generous than they were after they overran their current homeland, then we will all suffer enslavement.

I cannot exaggerate the dire peril that faces our world.

"How came you to know of Thera?" asked Orfeo.

"As I came to know of the rest of the world," Zurga answered.

"By keeping my eyes and ears open."

After convincing himself that he would get no more from the wanderer, Orfeo returned to his room, finding Orton there waiting stealthily in the hallway.

The warrior looked worried and perhaps even frightened, but he merely asked whether any progress had been made, indicating that travel throughout the city was difficult for him, as he had been stopped for questioning several times.

There were spies everywhere, and the Therans had apparently cautioned the Kalamattans that any trouble would bring forward instant and violent reprisals against the citizenry.

The city was thus kept quiet under threat of punishment.

Orton spoke also of Telemon and his attempts to find some trace of Herron, but the warrior was apparently being particularly cautious, walking only with the aid of a crutch. He also had been questioned several times, but so far no great threat had arisen.

Perhaps what bothered the warriors most was the wealth of rumor that flew about the city.

No one knew just what was supposed to happen, but all spoke of a great invasion that would soon be launched and of great movements of soldiers.

The future looked bleak indeed.

# Chapter Fifteen

Unfortunately Orfeo had no legitimate business at the docks. Today his dealings in jewelry in the marketplace were concluded early, and he went looking for another excuse to get near the Theran compound. He wandered about the wharves and warehouses, marveling again at the immensity of the city's commerce, but nowhere could he find the Lakonian fruit merchants, and no other access presented itself. There was much talk of war, however, and Orfeo on several occasions found himself talking with others near his own age.

Apparently the people of the city lived in terror of Theran wrath, and the specter of their naval defeat still loomed with powerful effect.

Several times during the day Orfeo heard the story of how the great Theran vessels had crushed the Kalamattan vessels with such ease, and there was talk that after certain unfortunate incidents recently in Pylos - the details of which were only whispered - the Therans intended to bludgeon this fine city to a bloody pulp.

Wasteland would spring up where people had once flourished, and the Kalamattans did not doubt that it could be done.

Indeed, they had been impressed into Theran service to act as the shock troops.

The Therans were not overwhelmingly numerous, but their ferocity was legendary, and a troop of ten could be counted on to defeat a hundred ordinary warriors.

High among the list of awesome weapons were the catapults that accurately shot great stones at enemy ships and sunk them within minutes.

There were also metal arrows shot from vicious reinforced bows, darts with exotically poisoned tips, and great battering rams on enormous ships.

No man dreamed, indeed, that he had seen even a fraction of the potential arsenal, and worse was rumored.

There was talk of deadly projectiles and impregnable armor.

Orfeo greatly increased his fund of information during the day without getting any closer to the Therans.

It was as he began his journey back to his room that his brain was jolted into activity, and he was not at first even aware of what was amiss.

Then his attention focused upon an old man he had seen several times earlier in the day prowling around the docks, and now it was apparent that he too had been merely seeking information much as had Orfeo.

A number of factors emerged in a jumble.

The man hobbled on a crutch, which immediately reminded Orfeo of Telemon's similar device.

Both limbs looked sound, and certainly the man was not visibly infirm.

Then a peculiar aspect about his face awoke some distant memory.

The man looked like someone he had once known, perhaps in Pylos. It was Leilon, the wanderer who occasionally visited Isocles.

This man looked incredibly like him, and yet at the same time he looked like Zurga.

He and Leilon and Zurga must all be Wanderers and all of the same people, which in itself brought up many questions. Orfeo was following the man before any clear plan had been reached, and he began to take care to keep from being too obvious.

So there was another wanderer looking for information, and he too had lightened his hair and changed his features.

The man was now walking faster, as though the limp were miraculously better.

Finally they reached a shabby building near the city wall, and the man disappeared up a narrow flight of steps.

Orfeo lingered unobtrusively outside to make sure that this was not simply a temporary stop, and he left the area by walking around that block of buildings to see whether the man could have left by another staircase.

Yet no visible means of escape presented itself, and Orfeo now hurried back to Zurga's lodgings.

The Wanderer would have some further explaining to do.

"I'm afraid you have made a mistake," Zurga answered after the story had hastily emerged.

"Not only did you expose yourself, but you have led them directly to me."

He appeared solemn, but not particularly worried.

"But he was not aware...."

"Go to the window and look out through the corner of the slats," Zurga directed.

"You will probably see a young girl in her mid teens, who will appear older if she has a deep red shawl about her. I suspect she will be standing by the gate across the courtyard, covertly watching the windows to see if you will throw one open when you return.

Then she will know exactly where you are staying."

"There is a woman standing just where you indicated, only she has no shawl, or rather there's a thick red sash about her waist.

She has blondish hair, fair skin, and wears the same sort of sandals as traders from the east.

She is pretending to be interested in fruit sold by a peddler, but she prolongs the conversation."

He looked into a broad smile of the Wanderer's with annoyance.

"What does this mean?

Are you playing games with me?"

"No games." Zurga laughed with real mirth for perhaps the first time since they had arrived in Kalamatta.

"Only you have a great deal to learn, pup, and this will be a valuable lesson.

You are to walk down the stairs and approach the girl, greet her by the name Clarice, and tell her that your master wishes to see Nadahr at his earliest convenience.

Hand her this strip of leather and somehow make her feel as though you have the upper hand.

She would be quite abashed to think that you had been aware of her surveillance, as she is well trained.

Then return to me, and we will discuss your mistakes.

Orfeo followed instructions, emerging in the courtyard without a glance toward the girl, who appeared not to see him at all.

When he approached her directly, however, she looked up with a startled expression, and the response to her name was electric, although she brought herself quickly under control.

Orfeo delivered his message as if she had stupidly fallen into his well-laid trap, and, with her composure somewhat shaken, she indicated that she would carry his message with no guarantee that she knew who it was intended for, whether he would receive it, or if he would act upon it. As Orfeo turned to leave he glanced covertly at the window, but then surmised that Zurga had no reason to be watching.

After all, he knew exactly what would happen.

"So you found yourself a Wanderer today and thought you had followed him to his lair," Zurga began derisively.

"Let me tell you that you do not follow a Wanderer without his knowing of it, and when you are so confident you have the upper hand, you are always easier to follow yourself."

He again assumed his voice of total control.

"Fortunately, I knew that Nadahr was likely to be in this area, and your description matched.

I also know that he would always have Clarice handy, and I know fairly well how she would operate.

He has traveled with her since she was a small girl and was abandoned by nomadic Dorae in the north.

Her people and yours are related, and the two of you have much in common from your training.

But I fear she was ahead of you this time."

The embarrassment flushed red across his cheeks, and Orfeo thought both of how much more careful he must be in the future and how fortunate he had been that this mistake was not fatal.

In a city as dangerous as Kalamatta, one slip could destroy their purpose and jeopardize the safety of others.

Then it occurred to Orfeo that Zurga's chastisement had deterred him from pressing forward with questions, and again he began his efforts to drag forth more information.

"Why is it that Wanderers have a family resemblance, as you, Nadahr, and Leilon could all be brothers in appearance and even in age?"

"A good question and a quick observation.

Yet we are not exactly brothers."

He appeared to ponder.

"I will not do you the disservice of telling an untruth, but at the same time it is best at this point not to tell the whole story.

Perhaps you should make surmises of your own."

"In the first place," Orfeo broke in, "while everyone else is identifiable with a place of origin, no Wanderer I have ever seen is likely to be from where he says, as I have heard you identify yourself as

Zurga of Melitis, Tyre, and Pergamum, and surely even you could not have been born in three places at once.

"I also find that strange," mocked Zurga.

"It also seems as though Wanderers not only know each other well, even to small details of their habits, but they also avail themselves of the same devices.

For example, I have heard rumors that when attacked by bandits, Leilon also fought with a flaming orb."

"Meddle not too deeply into the affairs of Wanderers," Zurga warned with a smile.

"Then tell me...."

Orfeo felt an excitement, as though his curiosity drove him ever forward.

"You'll be told all you need to know, and that which does not concern you I will withhold."

Zurga raised his voice to a bellow.

"Now mind your own behavior.

You have much to learn."

Orfeo sat back to share a simple meal with the Wanderer, sorting out events and impressions as best he could.

Obviously he had annoyed Zurga by his questioning, and this could only have come about if he had strayed too close to matters of deepest secrecy.

Very well, he would not push harder now, but he would keep his eyes open.

In the meantime he was to keep a lookout in the courtyard for Nadahr, and when the other finally did appear it was in an entirely different guise, without the crutch.

He now comported himself much as an eastern merchant, with a felted hat of a high conical shape and a striped robe, but Orfeo's sharpened perceptions were not deceived. He obeyed Zurga and ran down the steps, addressing the visitor softly by name, which brought no visible response.

He then indicated that Clarice also should come, and at that the girl emerged from the shadows close by, this time attired as a porter and entirely unrecognizable.

Perhaps they were merely demonstrating that they too could be deceptive.

As they approached Zurga's room, Orfeo sensed a peculiar wariness from Nadahr, as though he was alert at a profound level to the possibility of foul play.

Both hands were hidden in his robe, and he seemed to survey everything with his keen gaze.

When he saw Zurga, however, he smiled warmly, and the two clasped hands in greeting.

Soon Clarice and Orfeo were told that they could best occupy themselves elsewhere, while important matters were discussed, and Orfeo found himself leading the girl, who now appeared as a male, along the passageway to his own room.

Perhaps he could find out much from her.

Indeed Clarice seemed to have mastered the art of apparent openness, while she actually revealed little.

As Zurga had suggested, she had been born among the nomadic Dorae, who were related by strong blood ties to the Achians of King Kiros.

But little of her childhood remained a conscious memory, and she spoke about her years since Nadahr had taken her into his service.

At first she seemed aloof and superior, but she began to relax with Orfeo, as though he was a person more of her own kind than anyone else within a month's sea journey.

There was something also of a nostalgia that gripped Orfeo, and he was reminded of many scenes at home, around the great fires in the summer encampments and the feast days at Delphi.

When he thought of living among his people, so often the images were of events experienced before his stay as a hostage in Pylos.

Somehow that had killed something in him, or rather instilled a suspicious nature.

This Dorae girl had no doubt felt the same sort of isolation, but of this she did not speak.

There must also have been some reason why she was not still of her people.

"How long have you served Zurga?" she asked.

"I'm not exactly in his service," Orfeo answered, but then realized that in some respects this was so.

For an instant he even caught a hope that in the days ahead, if any of them survived their ordeal, perhaps he would serve Zurga instead of returning to his people.

In this there seemed to be a future.

"Then how does he trust you to be about him and know his secrets?"

There seemed to be no guile in her questions, and Orfeo felt that he could share with her a small part of his life.

"Zurga shares much with me, but there is also much he keeps to himself."

He watched her expression.

"Perhaps I know as little as you," she answered.

"Do you know what land the wanderers come from?" he asked.

"From all lands, I would imagine."

From her perplexed frown he knew that the question had never occurred to her, and before his eyes her expression underwent a transformation.

"You mean they are all from the same place?"

"I don't know, but I find it amusing to think about."

Orfeo decided to limit their speculations at that point.

They talked throughout the early evening hours, by candlelight, with Orfeo spreading before them an assortment of cheese and fruits he had obtained at the marketplace. The breeze seemed so peaceful, and the streets outside seemed to show a gentle repose, yet there were constantly sounds of armed men marching, with swords and shields, and armor plates rubbing together as a necessary accompaniment of peace.

The Kalamattans were frightened and stood on the brink of a slavery more abject than any they had ever witnessed, The streets were calm and serene, patrolled by soldiers.

Yet who could wonder that the average citizen could not comprehend these new and strange events.

Finally, when Clarice and Orfeo returned to Zurga's room, the two Wanderers were sitting wordlessly in opposite corners of the room, obviously done with their talk and not pleased with the outcome.

Zurga began to talk with Clarice, inquiring politely as to how she enjoyed her tasks with such a harsh master as Nadahr.

The other wanderer took the same tack with Orfeo, hinting that he would make far better use of the boy, and then he suddenly turned serious.

"How did you know what I am?" he asked.

"I could see from your first glance that you knew me to be a Wanderer."

"We apprentices do not tell our secrets, do we Clarice?"

He caught the laughter in her eyes.

"And we thank you for having allowed us the time to discuss the state of the world and to make our plans for dealing with it."

"Ahh....my servant has grown too grand for his clothing."

Zurga chided affectionately.

"But there is much yet that he does not know."

Soon Nadahr and Clarice departed, and Zurga lost what little spark of enthusiasm he had shown to his visitors.

"Leave me, boy....." he seemed weary.

"The curse of darkness slowly descends upon us, and the world that we have known is slowly dying, but there is now nothing to do but sleep and contemplate a rash, useless rebellion against fate."

He waved away any protest.

In his own small room later during the night, Orfeo listened to the clanking of armor and pondered what Zurga had said and, even more important, the way his feelings of impending doom were even penetrating his usually composed facade.

There was so much to think about, and the image of Princess Zaide returned to his mind.

He allowed himself to fantasize just for a moment what it would be like to be the beloved of such a sublime creature.

Clarice also seemed so warm and appealing, and yet there was a distance of another sort about her.

Home seemed farther away than ever and more remote as a concept.

Again he reminded himself that home must be where he happened to be sleeping at the time.

If Herron were not found he would have even less place along his people, as he would then have to be destroyed to make way for someone else to take the throne.

# Chapter Sixteen

Telemon bristled with rage, his great chest heaving massively as he told of the outrage.

He and Orton, who had spoken together briefly during the last few days, had both been regularly followed by security guards, who had not even bothered to hide their suspicions.

On several occasions the day before, both had been stopped for questioning, and now Orton had been arrested and was being held at one of the small security stations that were to be found in each quarter of the city.

Furthermore, as Orfeo had found as soon as he emerged on the street that morning, the great city gates had been ordered closed for an indefinite period, and there were ominous rumors from all sides.

Apparently thousands of troops were pouring into Kalamatta from the surrounding countryside, and more Theran vessels had arrived during the night.

A great chain had been drawn across the harbor, and trading vessels from far away were being turned back with the message that no landing would be permitted until further notice.

Zurga at first could not be found, and Telemon had cursed the treachery of the Wanderer in leading them into this trap, but soon he managed to control his frustration and began to lay out a course of action.

From his point of view, they need not even consider leaving the city until Orton was rescued, despite his hatred of walls.

Zurga, however, was more cautious.

"The gate cannot stay closed for long," he said, "as the people must eat, and commerce must go on.

But I think it means that the invasion of Pylos is about to occur, and the Therans do not wish news of their fleet's departure to alert their victims.

That means, among other things, that Herron also sails, assuming he is on one of their ships, and our business here will soon be concluded."

"Not until Orton is free," Telemon added.

"A soldier does not desert his comrades, and he would not leave me to languish behind stone walls."

"I'm afraid that we will all languish behind these walls if we stay in the city much longer," Zurga added.

"And I have no doubt that spies are already suspicious that there is something strange about you and perhaps even myself.

When the Therans have the city completely organized, which I assure you will not be long, then there will be no chance.

We cannot remain here."

But there was nothing to be done that moment, and Orfeo decided to return to the docks in search of word about Herron.

He still had some cheap baubles to sell, and at least his guise as a peddler gave him a reason to be there.

The crowd was smaller today, as if a general torpor had descended about the city, but those who remained at the docks seemed busier than ever and disinclined to deal with itinerant peddlers of second rate merchandise.

He had gone for over an hour without making a sale, desperately looking for some access to the Theran compound, where he knew there was a chance that Herron could be held as a galley slave.

Surely the fruit sellers or the purveyors of salted meat should be loading the ships with their merchandise, but now it was past noon and still no deliveries.

Then he saw a group of wagons belonging to the city's bakers.

They were all arriving at once, and hopefully they would need help. He gathered his baubles into a pack and ran to meet them, thinking he should look hungry and in need of a quick job.

"We've no need of such as you," the first baker said.

"And we've been told to take only our most reliable men."

"Just some bread," pleaded Orfeo, who was ignored by the first, but rescued by the second heavily laden baker.

"Half a loaf to unload this cart and carry it out to the fleet."

The offer was immediately accepted, and Orfeo found himself trudging along with the others down the long walkways to the Theran compound.

They were counted as they entered and counted as they returned for other loads.

Orfeo waited until his third load before he lingered to look at the men around him.

He could see hundreds of slaves now permitted up on the decks with their chains.

He saw men from the far reaches of Africa and Asia, and he saw some who could be Achians.

The next trip he got lucky and saw Grakus, one of Herron's companions who had been taken at the same time.

He gave a quick nod of the head as he passed, and he thought Grakus had seen him.

The second time he passed he heard Grakus call out to him in the Achian dialect, "Get me away from here."

But he made no answer, and no one paid any attention.

Grakus looked like a caged animal, but he had not lost weight and seemed aptly suited to his new life with an oar.

One the third trip, and one Orfeo knew would be his last, he called out in the same Achian dialect to no one in particular.

"Where is the Herron we seek?"

He knew that if he got no answer from Grakus this time, there would be none.

He dropped the bag of loaves by the plank leading onto the ship and stopped to rest as though weary from his labor.

He glanced toward Grakus, who was not where he had been, but he answered from another part of the ship as though singing.

"Herron you will never see again, as he has been taken as a slave to Thera."

The man standing by the plank turned in anger and stepped toward Grakus as if to give him a lash for breaking the silence, but Orfeo, as if he had heard nothing of interest, simply wandered back toward the bread wagons for his payment.

There the baker was waiting for him with a loaf.

"You worked hard, my lad," he began.

"There's much more work to be done if you wish it at the shop of Simon the baker."

"I'll find it," said Orfeo, profusely thanking his benefactor.

And now it was back to the others with the news, which was ominous in tone, but still seemed better than knowing nothing.

A rescue now seemed all but impossible, although Orfeo realized that his companions would not let this deter them.

The king had chosen well for this task.

When Orfeo reached Zurga's lodging, Telemon had returned and was still complaining about Orton's confinement.

Orfeo delivered the news that Grakus, one of Herron's companions when he was seized, had said that Herron had been taken to Thera as a slave.

The news was duly registered, but did nothing to direct Telemon away from his rage about Orton's capture.

"Is there not a chance that he will be released when the gates are opened?" asked Orfeo.

"That's what we must hope," answered Zurga.

"But now that we know Herron is not here, there is no reason, except for Orton, for us to linger another hour in this city."

Zurga sounded resolute.

"That and the closed gate," retorted Orfeo.

"So now we have only two tasks, getting Orton released and escaping with our lives." the Wanderer seemed to ponder the choices.

"Surely it will take more than fighting our way free, as the Therans command here and are organized."

"My sword is eager for some fresh Theran blood," trumpeted Telemon, as he pulled aside his cloak to reveal that he wore battle armor beneath.

Zurga backed away with a sour look of disapproval, and the two engaged in a heated discussion as to whether this could jeopardize their entire undertaking. Finally Telemon agreed to risk going forth in the city unarmed, and it was agreed that Orfeo should be the one to visit the guardhouse where Orton was held.

As the two had arrived in the same caravan and stayed at the same inn, this would appear least suspicious.

By mid-afternoon, Orfeo presented himself in the narrow room with thick stone walls by a structure that looked like a partially dismantled city gate from a time when Kalamatta covered much less territory.

There a surly corporal confirmed to Orfeo that a person of that description lingered within the dungeon.

Allegedly he was suspected of being a spy, and he was to be questioned by the captain. He suggested with a wry grin that perhaps Orfeo should seek the captain within and ask personally.

The corporal nodded to the guard at the inner door, who stepped aside.

Immediately Orfeo suspected that he had made a mistake, as he entered a corridor with narrow slits along the walls.

Obviously it was part of an old system of fortifications, and armed men could intercept intruders at any point.

He walked past the openings with a shiver, feeling his skin react to the dampness and stale air, and then a new atmosphere invaded his senses. He was aware of a strange pungent smell, a mixture of dampness and spice, a peculiar musky emanation of caves and swamps and crawling things that made him think instinctively of snakes and salamanders.

There he was in a dimly lighted room with about a dozen tables and scribes busily covering rolls of parchment and smaller scraps of Egyptian papyrus with their peculiar symbols.

"What do you seek here, boy?"

The haughty voice emanated from the Theran who sat against the wall, a few paces to the rear.

Orfeo could now see a number of the creatures dressed in green placed throughout the room, obviously supervising the work of their underlings.

Somehow the darkness and damp seemed a more fitting place for them, as the Kalamattans dripped with perspiration.

In the midst of explaining his mission, Orfeo inspected the chamber as best he could, looking for some shred of information that at a future time might prove useful. He noticed, for example, that names of all the prisoners were kept in several large parchment books, and each had a number of symbols he could not decipher.

Apparently Theran letters were used here.

Finally the false name Orton had used was located, and a Kalamattan who identified himself as a lieutenant of the guard, scowled suspiciously, beginning to question Orfeo as to his connection with the prisoner.

Orfeo too found himself perspiring, wishing he had never ventured into this evil place, aware that no trace of the sun or fresh air ever penetrated here and that the Therans wished it so.

Orton was captive of a great slimy octopus, and now its tentacles reached even toward Orfeo.

Ultimately, however, the official seemed bored and merely added that Orton was being held in a nearby cistern, which was temporarily used to detain suspicious characters.

As to what was to happen, he smiled and shrugged with unconcern.

Perhaps he would be hanged or perhaps released the next day. As Orfeo gently pressed the point, the lieutenant still indicated that it would be decided tomorrow.

There was little reason to return to the inn with so little solace, and Orfeo shielded his eyes as he returned to the sunlight.

Quickly he scratched several figures with his small knife on the stonework of the courtyard.

There were four symbols after Orton's name in the book, and likely these represented numbers.

As this was all he had to go on, along with the strange fact that a cistern was being used as a holding cell, Orfeo was intent upon deriving maximum benefit from this shred.

His task was to translate from Theran to the common script of the Great Sea. Then at least he would know Orton's number.

The first symbol was the easiest, as a detachment of Theran soldiers arrived outside the station as he stood there.

Of the five men, the one obviously in command had a sign like an inverted heart sewn onto his sleeve. Was this the number five?

Orfeo stood undecided as to the next step when another detachment of Kalamattans marched from the station down the alleyway to the east.

They had two prisoners, both obviously outlanders.

Were they headed for the cistern?

He followed at a safe distance, watching while the men entered a narrow passageway off another courtyard about five hundred paces from the station.

Possibly it was an entrance to the jail.

Orfeo inspected the area with the idea in mind of locating the old cistern, and he followed with his eyes the drainage system that was both ancient and still in use.

Everything sloped toward an area adjacent to the corridor entered by the soldiers.

He approached toward the entryway only to see that it was guarded by armed men, and now there was a metal grill over the walkway.

Orfeo walked to the opposite side of the courtyard, purchased some fruit from a vendor, and unobtrusively engaged the man in conversation about the comings and goings from this place.

The necessary information slipped idly forth, along with observations that just today over fifty victims had arrived and a number had been hanged.

For whatever it was worth, Orfeo decided next to find out about the symbols, and he made his way to the docks where he began asking acquaintances among the Lakonian merchants if they could help.

Here no further information was forthcoming, although they were aware that the Therans kept accounts by another system.

Finally Orfeo found himself approaching the Theran navel compound, and here the prospects improved.

Each piece of Theran property had a number carved in its side.

When he finally came within view of the ships, the Theran passion for order showed itself most completely.

On the prow of each ship, which Orfeo could see in a line in front of him, were the symbols necessary to decipher Orton's number.

The fifth in line bore the inverted heart, while the tenth was a figure in two digits, with an X obviously signifying a zero.

For whatever it meant, Orton was listed as prisoner 2530, held in an old underground cistern to the east of the guard station, and more prisoners were arriving at a rapid rate, some of whom were to be executed.

With this Orfeo returned to Zurga, who received the news gloomily, indicating that he could well have read the numbers and that Orfeo had wasted his time by going to the docks again.

Then he began to plan a means of using the data to secure Orton's release.

By this time Telemon had returned, still tense from his confinement within the walls, joking grimly about spending his life as a prisoner here.

Several times during the day he had been stopped by prowling bands of security guards and only narrowly escaped a fate similar to Orton's.

Clearly their days at liberty in the city were numbered, and if only the gates would again open they would escape.

Still Orton lingered in captivity, and a complex plan evolved, dependent primarily upon opportunity of the moment.

About dusk troops had again began entering the city from the countryside, and as a high tide was due in the early morning hours, there was at least a possibility the great armada would then sail.

Security would no longer be so necessary in the city, and there would also likely be confusion in the midst of the military movements.

If Orfeo were to arrive at the jail first thing in the morning, complete with a request for the release of prisoner 2530, signed in Theran characters on parchment, perhaps there was a chance.

If Telemon would agree to inactivity, the risk would be lessened, and if the city gates were about to be opened at the same time, there was a remote possibility that they could all safely slip away to freedom.

There were so many variables, of course, as to make the plan a flimsy foundation for expectations, but they had little choice.

Zurga drew up an official looking document, not bothering to explain his knowledge of Theran writing, but the implications were not lost on Orfeo, who tossed with teeming fantasies during the night.

Tomorrow might spell doom for them all, and only a faint ray of hope shone for Orton.

Fortunately their guess about the invasion proved correct, and on Orfeo's first appearance in the street the next morning the rumor was everywhere that the ships had departed, and perhaps now the gates would open again.

As anticipated, there was also turmoil throughout the city, with soldiers and messengers almost tripping over each other in their haste to accomplish various obscure tasks.

Orfeo stood waiting at the iron grillwork for a guard, to whom he handed the parchment.

The man frowned, disappeared within obviously to have it read, and then opened the gate, indicating that Orfeo would wait while the prisoner was fetched.

Was the plan working?

Orton appeared a few minutes later, matted with dirt and covered with welts from the lash, but his eyes were as defiant as ever.

The guard studied the parchment, while another soldier escorted two prisoners outside, leaving the gate again open.

"There's no seal on this," he said.

"I can't let this man go without a seal," he growled angrily.

"They told me this would secure his release," Orfeo insisted, his heart beginning to race.

"There'll be trouble of he's not released."

"Who are you?

What identification do you have?"

Now the soldier was suspicious.

"Maybe I should send a messenger to check."

"Can't you read the message," Orfeo was relying on the guard's ignorance, but now he was joined by another, who appeared to find the scheme most unusual, and a third figure approached with a mark of rank upon his sleeve.

Orton was so close, and yet his freedom seemed slowly to be slipping away.

"Who sent you here?" asked the sergeant.

"I was sent from the guard station.

The chief scribe of the inner room gave me the number and told me to present this slip to you."

The sergeant studied the scrap with a puzzled expression, obviously unable to read it entirely.

"Maybe we had better hold you until we send a messenger."

He absent-mindedly signaled for the gates to open, admitting yet another prisoner with a giant guard.

Orfeo felt like running, but there was no escape, and the gate again swung closed.

The key never turned, however, as the large newcomer moved quickly into action.

The sword of Telemon cut quickly into the sergeant's neck, while the prisoner swung into action with a small knife that felled the first guard.

Within seconds Orton and Telemon had crossed the courtyard and disappeared into one of the numerous side corridors, while the new prisoner had grabbed Orfeo's hand and pulled him up a narrow flight of stairs so that they overlooked the scene below, observing the arrival of perhaps a dozen armed men from the depths of the prison.

"We're safe if we can get to the roof."

It was Clarice, who gave all the appearance of being and old and battered man until she flung back her cloak and revealed the long golden hair.

As the scurried up another crumbling flight of stairs, she handed him a set of garments, and when they crouched beneath the eaves of a neighboring building, she gave him a wig of long hair, while her fingers deftly applied lampblack and a reddish pigment to portions of his face.

Satisfied with her work, she laughed, poked him playfully in the ribs, and assumed a delicate, feminine demeanor after they had slid down a rope into a deserted alleyway.

"Nadahr and I have decided to leave the city if they open the gates," she said.

"Then will come the big test of your disguise."

Orfeo felt a warm surge of confidence and relief at the girl's appearance, and her confidence helped overcome the fear from his close brush with captivity.

Zurga obviously had nurtured plans of his own, but had given Orfeo the opportunity to play his own role to the maximum without the knowledge that another level lurked beneath.

Not that this was itself objectionable, but it was another fact to file away for future reference.

Detachments of Kalamattan and even Theran soldiers hurried through the streets, apparently headed for the site of the escape, but the two girls left the area without exciting the faintest interest, despite the fact that one of them looked like an unusually tall African girl.

Streets were being blocked off, and the clamor was growing, but the efforts appeared to be too late, if only Telemon and Orton had moved quickly enough. Clarice explained how Zurga and Nadahr had already taken up positions near the gate, and if the escape were not considered a major event, then it must indeed be open.

The city had not been prepared for siege, and even the market places had run short of food.

Merchants would have to be allowed to come and go.

The streets were unusually crowded this day, and as they approached the gate, they found that movement was almost impossible.

Thousands of people had jammed the approaches from all sides, hoping that today they would be permitted to leave, but at the moment only a few people at a time were being let through the gate after careful screening.

It was after Clarice brought her next change of appearance that whispers of a more liberal policy from the gate filtered back along the line.

Apparently no one dared shout, as life here had taken on a peculiarly somber tone.

The latest production, which again returned Orfeo to his male status, despite the addition of longer hair, was a bridal costume for Clarice and the appropriate trappings for a young bridegroom.

Garlanded with flowers and streamers, Orfeo and Clarice sought to detract particular attention from themselves onto their festive occasion, which was certain to bring crude jests from the gatekeepers and provoke enough mirth to keep their passes from being checked too closely. Still, as they approached the checkpoint, it was clear that each person was being subjected to a thorough search and questioning.

Word filtered along about a jail escape and house-to-house searches throughout the city.

The culprits were described as foreigners, which made anyone leaving doubly suspicious.

Then they were at the gate, and a coarse guffaw greeted them from behind.

“Trying to escape are you?”

The bystanders turned in wonderment.

A lame ruffian dressed gaudily in festive clothes was throwing colored pebbles, as was the custom at weddings.

"They wanted to sneak off into the country to have a little time alone," he made a semi-obscene gesture, and the response was immediate laughter, even from the guards.

"I've found them," he shouted toward the rear of the column.

A decrepit priest lumbered up and said that he must waste no more time making of his niece an honest woman, and he began to recite the words of a marriage ceremony in front of an amused crowd.

Orfeo answered that he accepted, and Clarice then answered that she agreed.

They kissed, and were in turn kissed by their four companions, which included the priest and someone dressed as the bride's mother.

By calling most attention to themselves, a motley party of four men, one woman, and one man dressed as a woman, was allowed to pass the gates virtually unobserved from an official point of view.

Orfeo was never even asked for a pass, although he was questioned coarsely about the attributes of his new bride.

The lame ruffian with a large pouch of colored pebbles was even brandishing his sword in semi-drunkenness, or so it would appear, and the stooped old woman, whose shawl covered her features, had also apparently indulged too much in the wine.

They cackled and shricked and embarrassed even the bride's father, who was garlanded with flowers and weeping.

Just off the road leading from the city, again a transformation took place, this time with six determined figures emerging and purchasing sleek, healthy horses.

While there was as yet no pursuit, there was no need to risk a delay.

By nightfall a comfortable distance intervened between the travelers and the city, but Orfeo still remembered all the checkpoints on the road, and they were far from safe.

# Chapter Seventeen

Before daybreak on the second day, Zurga had long been preparing a complex potion in a small bronze pot he had somehow acquired.

As the others feasted on bread and fruit, he built a small fire and watched the brew until it began to give off a heady, sweet aroma in billowing clouds that were rapidly dispersed by the wind.

Soon a peculiar phenomenon occurred, as great birds began to circle overhead, apparently drawn by the smell, and lower and lower came their passes.

Dozens now swarmed about the smoke, and suddenly they alighted, as if the travelers were no more than stones.

While the others remained motionless, Zurga went from one to the next, affixing to their necks small packets on which messages had apparently been affixed.

With a great stroke of his swirling mace they were dismissed, again circling high overhead and then dispersing in various directions, calling in shrill cries to each other and the wind.

"Pylos has been warned, just as others will receive the warning," he said. "Particularly I have instructed them not to engage their ships with the Therans, but to maintain their defensive positions.

At least the city will not fall by surprise, and perhaps we will manage to get there in time to join the fighting, although I cannot say that anything will change the ultimate outcome."

"My blade is again hungry for Theran blood," muttered Telemon.

"Once having tasted that rare delicacy, it wishes for more."

"You'll wade through many a Kalamattan before you find their masters," said Zurga.

"Therans well know the way of using slaves to absorb an enemy's wrath."

Soon the travelers were again on their way, passing a border customs house during the morning, and approaching the land beyond Kalamattan control.

Nadahr and Clarice had decided they would be safer traveling with the great warriors, as they too were bound back in the direction of Pylos, although no decision had yet been made as to whether they would return to the city they had abandoned in haste.

Later in the morning they approached the last customs house under Kalamattan control, which should have posed no challenge, but their flight was not to be so uneventful, as the vast but newly emerging machine of the Therans had at last combined information from a number of sources.

At some level the four criminals who had slain Therans in the debacle at Pylos were now suspected as being the same spies, disguised as merchants, who had recently escaped from Kalamatta.

Word had come to the gate too late to capture the one who had escaped, but now there was word that four riders, perhaps with two more, hastened toward the border.

By Theran means of transmission the messages flew forward faster than a man could ride, and by the last customs house before the wild land, word had arrived perhaps an hour before the travelers.

The Theran centurion had rallied together a troop of Therans and all the Kalamattan horsemen he could muster, which amounted to nearly a hundred.

The roads were no longer so well patrolled as they had been, although the Therans were even now recruiting more among the peasantry to correct this lack..

The Theran in command, a particularly strong and lithe warrior named Meeka, had stationed his men in a cluster of trees about five hundred paces from the stone buildings of the customs house, maintaining only a few soldiers to delay the riders and cause them to dismount.

The plan involved a surprise charge, with detachments approaching from all directions, surrounding the four and cutting off all means of escape.

The pursuers would have fresh horses, against the tired mounts of the fugitives, and a chase would be unlikely.

Still Meeka did not underestimate the men who had reputedly killed over a dozen of his countrymen and twice that number of Kalamattan guards.

He would take no chances.

The intended victims were, however, not so unaware as the plotters had hoped, as both Zurga and Telemon, by a series of widely differing observations, reached the same conclusion, and Nadahr, by yet other means, agreed.

One noticed signs of activity while another saw evidence of excessive grazing by the side of the road, indicating that there were more horses here than were visible.

Later Clarice said she noticed a different noise level from the birds, and perhaps the horses gave subliminal signals that they recognized others of their kin lying in wait.

Even Orfeo sensed a strangeness about the stone buildings of the customs house as they approached.

No business was being transacted, and no one labored to bring water from the stream or feed animals or cook lunch.

No sign of any human animal life stirred, and, indeed, no horses were tethered by the outbuildings.

What was not seen alerted Orfeo, and then, as he glanced first at Telemon and then Zurga, he knew they too were suspicious.

Even Orton had gently lifted his sword from its scabbard and then allowed it to slip back.

He wanted to make certain it would spring to his hand when needed.

"They're probably waiting in the woods," said Zurga.

"We've already been seen, and they likely have an idea who we are."

"There could hardly be fifty of them," said Telemon.

"If we could protect two sides, we might take them five by five."

He was, of course, not counting Clarice as a combatant.

"The horses are too tired to make a run for it," Zurga clenched his teeth as they continued to ride, slowing so that all could listen.

They approached showing no signs of suspicion, with two lazy soldiers asking that they dismount.

One side of the narrow yard was bordered by the remains of an old stone fortress, and at the top flags waved in the breeze.

A young soldier was just attaching a small red and white banner and preparing to run it up a pole.

Zurga let fly with a missile from a sling he pulled from his sleeve, while Telemon and Orton dispatched the soldiers in the courtyard.

Orfeo entered the stone building, caught a scribe with his sword before the other could avail himself of a knife, and ascended the stairs to the roof before another guard could signal.

"At least they won't immediately know what's happening," he shouted to Zurga, pushing both bodies from the narrow walkway that surveyed the yard.

By this time his companions had brought their horses inside through the narrow door, and Orton joined him on top.

"We're better off here than in the open," he said.

"There's no way they can get behind us, and they'll have to come single file through the doorway."

"They were probably told to take us alive," came Zurga's voice from inside.

"That gives us the advantage."

The grim nature of this advantage was not lost on Orfeo, who had a vivid picture of the fate in store for those who raised a hand against the Theran advance.

Better to die here than suffer the torments of slow Theran revenge.

He watched stealthily over the clearing beyond the customs house as a horseman appeared and then another, tentative as to how they should approach since there had been no signal.

Then came a decisive gesture from Meeka and a charge across the short distance from the woods.

But there was nothing to meet their fury, as they found a deserted courtyard.

"Search the buildings," Meeka directed his men, who dismounted and began to charge blindly within.

Telemon allowed perhaps half a dozen to enter before he struck, and then it was the twin terror of his sword and the vicious mace that Zurga now wielded, only the weighted, spiked end was illuminated by the same flickering fire he had wielded against the bandits.

Kalamattans fell over each other and effectively blocked the door, as Meeka now directed the assault toward the roof.

There Orton and Orfeo slashed wildly as various of the assailants grasped for a handhold at the top, but the time required to scale the wall was enough to allow the defenders to cut them down.

Clarice, surprisingly, held her own with a sword she must have carried with her, although there had previously been no evidence of it.

She swung it deftly, and caught several Kalamattans as they came near the top of the stairs.

Within minutes the fight had shifted from the expected overwhelming of six tired travelers into a slaughter of relatively helpless and poorly led soldiers, commanded to attack positions in which they were greatly disadvantaged.

Nadahr had stationed himself opposite Zurga and had produced from his pack a shortened mace on a stationary handle that burned with the same kind of fire, and all traces of age seemed to have vanished from the old Wanderer.

Clarice moved behind him, momentarily suggesting she was fearful for her life, but again she surprised two more Kalamattans.

Her victims were caught unaware that she could present a danger.

“Fall back.

We’ll burn them out.” Meeka shouted enraged.

“You devils, fall back.”

The command needed no seconding, but just behind the invaders the defenders burst forth from the building, seizing horses left unmounted by the attackers, again turning the attack into a route.

In the vanguard was Telemon, slashing with a furious abandon, cutting recklessly on all sides until Meeka called his remaining men back again and in the next breath called a retreat.

And then began the procession across the field.

The Kalamattans were never allowed to regroup, as they were caught either individually or in small clusters and cut down by their more determined pursuers.

Orton had ridden in an arc toward the trees, and his presence alone turned the retreating forms toward the road, where Orfeo and now the mounted Nadahr and Clarice provided an appearance of numbers, forming the other horn of a great claw.

Zurga smote fire and destruction, while the tireless Telemon rent bowels and brain with equal unconcern.

At last only Meeka rode before them, all the imperiousness of his mastery drained away by relentless terror.

Now it was a game, and at every turn at least one of the pursuers gained a few strides until they were all nearly within reach, now laughing and chiding, filling the air with unspeakable blasphemies as to the nature of Therans, and then he was unhorsed.

Zurga had clouted him on the temple, but the wound was minor.

He stood with drawn sword, trembling violently, awaiting disgrace and death.

“You’ll all be hunted down and die in shame and lingering pain.”

He shouted hoarsely, as hatred filled his eyes.

“Send more Therans, and we’ll kill more,” said Telemon,.

Orton, who was now closest to the Theran, moved forward for a final blow.

"Hold," said Telemon.

"This scum may yet play a role in our game."

He addressed the quivering Theran.

"If we spare your life, how will you repay us?"

"I would not rest until I had attained command of a special force aimed at your capture and destruction," he spat the words.

"Only next time I would know who I face."

"I think we should let him live," said Telemon.

"With this bungler directing the search for us, we need have no worry."

"What's one Theran more or less?" said Orton.

"You'll find out someday soon what one Theran means," Meeka sneered.

"Life for your world will be different."

"I recommend he be killed," said Zurga diplomatically.

"Even an inept Theran is a danger."

"He must die," seconded Nadahr.

"And we should be gone from here before worse arrives."

"I want him to confirm to the others that Therans are not invincible," continued Telemon, who seemed determined to spare this man consumed by hatred of them all.

"Strip off your clothes and stuff them in a saddle bag.

We'll take your horse, and you can save yourself any way you wish."

Telemon sounded scornful.

"Remove your boots too."

He now sounded bored.

"While you search for us, you might find instead that we are searching for you, and next time I will not be so generous with your life."

"You'll beg for us to kill you, son of a pig.

I'll have your guts wound onto a sizzling sword." Meeka cried out.

"Big talk for a naked man," said Orton. "Now run before we change our minds."

They watched him hobble away barefooted.

"I'm never comfortable sparing a sworn enemy," said Nadahr.

"He will dedicate his life to finding us."

"You can be sure they'll now redouble their efforts to punish our outrages."

Zurga glowered after the pitiful form of the running Theran.

"If they try to capture us, I would just as soon see their commander trembling with rage.

It might undermine his judgment, and he is more likely to make a mistake.

And yet it would be comforting to kill the only Theran who could actually identify us on sight."

"Indeed, he will be the one chosen to pursue us," said Nadahr.

"But we must save Theran armor, as one day we may need it for a ruse."

Telemon and Orton had taken on a look suggesting they knew it had been unwise to leave Meeka alive, but they would not now go back on what they had insisted was right.

They drove their companions hard for the rest of the day, passing out of Kalamattan lands and into the untamed wilderness ruled between sleepy towns only by bandits, and yet the term had various gradations of meaning.

To the men of Pylos, the Achians were little better and sometimes no better than bandits.

The difference between taking one's property by stealth and force or by a state sanctioned invasions could seem invisible to the victims.

Now the travelers felt safer, as a group of six looked harder to take than a group of four, and the bandits were known for an ability to appraise risks versus rewards.

Now, however, the companions rode with a new purpose, as they spoke around the campfire that night about uniting the brigands into an army that could help repel the Theran invasions to come.

Likely the brigands had already, at least indirectly, felt the new presence, and they may even have suspected that the Therans intended ultimately to enslave them as well as the city dwellers.

Perhaps they could recognize that defense of the cities was part of defending their lands.

The problem now was that one could not find bandits at will, if only for a conference.

With no visible wealth to attract attention the travelers were being ignored.

The most likely way of making contact lay in one of the small trading towns along the coast, where clearly the bandits had to sell their booty, buy necessary goods, and learn information as to the contents of caravans.

The bazaar would be a likely place, doubtless full of stolen goods with new pedigrees.

Zurga knew a wine merchant, who had obviously grown prosperous and now lived in a villa overlooking a small, rocky harbor.

During a quickly planned visit, this businessman, while pretending innocence, repeated, as alleged gossip, that representatives of the bandits lived in several smaller villages in the nearby mountains.

Tureg, the bandit chieftain, whose name was whispered along the coast from Pylos to Kalamatta, still lived, and the villagers of this coast would know how he might be found.

That night the travelers took a large room in the town's only inn, and Orfeo made his bed on the floor next to Clarice, who had a way of receding into the background as the men conversed.

Clearly she missed little of the conversation, but she always pretended to have her mind elsewhere.

"Your master and my companions seem to be drifting away from our original mission," Orfeo spoke softly to her.

"I wish Nadahr would take us back to the cities of the east," she whispered.

"I see nothing we can do here, and it is more dangerous every day.

The Therans will kill us if they catch us."

"And how did you become a Wanderer's apprentice?"

"He knew my mother, and I've even thought he may be my father, but Wanderers do not speak of such things."

"And what happens to you when he is no longer among the living?"

"Perhaps I will be a Wanderer."

She sounded uncertain as to what life held for her.

"Are there women Wanderers?"

"I've met two, and both are remarkable women," she said.

"They are welcomed in the cities of the east, and they bring wise counsel of what transpires in the world.

It is the Wanderers who know more than a single land, as they have no home.

They have their place in the great scheme of things, and they are respected and protected."

"Not by the Therans," Orfeo watched her face take on a serious tone.

“I like it not when we have no plan, and yet I see none.

We are searching for a role to play in great events, and yet we may be consumed in the process.”

“I have a plan,” Orfeo whispered.

“Is it Zurga’s plan?”

“No, but it concerns our mission to rescue my brother from slavery.”

“Is it a plan for just you, or docs it involve the rest of us?”

“I don’t know yet.

I’ll tell you when the time comes.”

# CHAPTER EIGHTEEN

At dawn the travelers rode to the village to seek Tureg. The matter involved little subtlety, as they were surrounded by armed and sullen men as soon as they arrived.

Clearly what transpired here required some degree of protection, although Zurga did his best to allay suspicions. Telemon seemed more subdued than usual, as though he realized that a boisterous attitude on his part could bring trouble for them all.

In the end Zurga alone was allowed to journey to see the bandit chieftain, accompanied by four stalwart mountaineers.

His safety was not guaranteed, but it was clear that Zurga's words the night before had already reached these men and that they were worried enough about the Therans to confer.

Zurga returned around noon with a look on his face that told nothing about what had transpired between him and the bandit chieftain, but he had with him cheese, fruit and bread for the journey.

Orfeo assumed that all had gone well, and yet Zurga was in no mood to linger, as though he did not want to trust his luck among the chieftain's underlings.

Again they set out for Pylos, a destination that carried a threat of another sort.

Most ominous was the idea that the Theran invasion had been aimed at this city, which held a high degree of probability, but there were several possible scenarios.

They could have caught the city's defenses unaware and overcome it, this time not as influential visitors with Theran escorts, but as conquerors.

In that case it was best for the travelers to learn of this before their arrival and not come within its territory before.

If that were the case they would be entirely without a plan for seeking out Herron and returning him to his place among the Achians.

The second possibility was that the Therans with their Kalamattan allies had invaded another city and were currently no immediate threat.

That presumably would mean that the travelers would not necessarily be unwelcomed, although they had left in haste after their first visit and had intervened before the king in a manner that had led to the killing of Kalamattans and Therans.

The result had been the withdrawal of these oppressive powers, but it was unlikely that the perpetrators of this crime would be greeted as conquering heroes.

They might still be taken into custody or denied admission to the city.

Orfeo, from his perspective, was dubious about a return visit.

The information they obtained from the villages along the way, particularly after they had entered territory of Pylos, was at first disturbing, as they heard that the Theran fleet had appeared suddenly one morning before the harbor of Pylos, but it was as if the attack had been expected, and a defensive perimeter had been established.

What happened after that was unclear, but villagers still spoke of Pylos standing as it had, with no Theran overlords.

By the time they were within a day's journey of the city the accounts were even more favorable.

The Theran fleet, seeing that it was expected, had turned aside and had disappeared to the west.

"The Therans are powerful but cautious warriors," Zurga explained. "They like to begin a battle with total surprise and with overwhelming numbers, leaving nothing to chance.

The tactics of Meeka were typical of Therans, as he had better than a ten to one numerical advantage over us, but still wished to take us by stealth."

"Lot of good that did him," said Telemon.

"It might have been different if we had truly been surprised," countered Nadahr.

When they arrived at the gates of Pylos, they had obviously been expected, and they passed the first hurdle with no signs of trouble.

They were referred directly to the palace, where they were given lodgings and told that they were expected in council with King Linaeus in little over an hour.

Even Telemon arranged his clothing more formally for the occasion, and it was decided to allow Orfeo to be with them.

After some discussion it was also determined that Nadahr should be present, and, lest Clarice be left alone, Orfeo suggested that as one of the survivors of a perilous journey she also be allowed to be present at whatever the king had in store for them.

"The gods are indeed generous, as days ago I had abandoned hope of ever seeing the six dangerous fugitives we had heard about, and now I see the other two and feel fortunate to have assembled such wise counsel at a most ominous time."

The king seemed ten years younger and in far better spirits than when they had last seem him on the day Isocles had rashly challenged the Kalamattans and Therans.

"I suppose you realize that as a group you have now achieved legendary proportions as the Six of Kalamatta."

"Our escape from Kalamatta was a matter of delicate timing," said Zurga, "but I hope my warning birds reached you with news of the planned invasion."

"I have missed your attendance here at court, my old friend Zurga, and when I was inattentive to you on your last visit, you must realize that I was close to being a total captive of the enemy.

It was the outburst of your companions that at first threatened our very survival, but soon emptied our city of these vermin.

But yes, to answer your question, it was your warning that prepared us for the invasion, and our preparedness seems to have discouraged it."

"For the time being," said Zurga.

"We all realize it is only a matter of time before we must encounter them, but for the moment we hear they have taken Sardis and are busy enslaving another people, no doubt becoming stronger in the process and becoming eventually an even greater threat."

"We have come to confer about threats and defenses," said Zurga.

"I have with me some remarkable people."

He turned to the travelers, none of whom had broken silence.

"I recognize your fellow Wanderer Nadahr, whom I have not seen in many years.

I assume the beautiful young woman with him is his daughter."

The king was obviously in a gracious mood.

"I would feel fortunate to have such a daughter," answered Nadahr, "but she is my apprentice who will follow in my footsteps when I no longer wander the cities of mankind."

So that was her role, thought Orfeo, who was also surprised to hear her described by the king as beautiful.

As he looked more closely, he saw that today she had taken special care with her appearance, arranging her golden hair to one side and showing herself as feminine, although he could well recall the boyish appearance she had shown in Kalamatta.

"I had also realized that the Theran-killing warrior with you was none other than the great Telemon, whose Achian sword is a legend even among us here."

Telemon rose and bowed, showing a diplomatic skill Orfeo had never expected, and then Orton was given his due.

"That leaves only one of your company unaccounted for, and yet there is something about him I find very familiar."

Orfeo rose with the usual thumping of his heart, but took a deep breath and willed himself to show composure.

"I am the Achian Orfeo, who was once a resident here in the palace and who had the good fortune to be taught by the master Isocles at the same time Prince Nestor was a pupil.

I return to Pylos as my second home and offer thanks for the hospitality I received during my stay here."

"Ahhhh, you are indeed a pupil of Isocles," the king flashed a sly smile as he spoke.

"As I recall you left rather unexpectedly, without telling the cook there would be one less for dinner.

Your departure was especially regretted by our dear Isocles, whom I miss."

"I pray that the king will forgive my lapse of manners and welcome me back among his subjects."

"Of course all is forgiven, and it warms my heart to see that you have grown so that you are nearly as tall as Telemon, and I expect you have not seen the end of your growing."

The king was obviously pleased.

"It should also please you to learn that in spite of your more manly appearance, there were others at court who recognized you after your second speedy departure.

I believe everyone in the room realized that Isocles recognized you, almost in the instant of his death.

It was a moment that will not soon be forgotten here."

"It is a tragic moment I will never forget," said Orfeo.

"But your presence again reminds me that when you and your friends were here the first time, you were seeking an Achian who had been seized by a Tyrian merchant ship, and you were concerned that he might have been brought here for sale as a slave."

"That was one purpose of our visit," Orfeo answered.

"Considering that the flower of Achian manhood was chosen for this errand, a prince and two great warriors, and the crafty Zurga came to lend his assistance, I assume this missing person must have been very important to your king."

Orfeo looked toward Zurga, whose face betrayed nothing, and made his own decision as to what to reveal.

"We were of course reluctant to let this grave matter be known to all, but to you I have no hesitation in saying that among the several Achians taken in a raid that day was my brother Herron, my father's heir."

"I suspected as much," said the king.

"And it does you credit that you place your trust in me, but surely you know yourself to be the next in line for the throne with your brother gone. Is it not strange that your king decided to send his second son into a dangerous world."

"I am placing even more trust in you by saying that there is one reason that I am not seen as a suitable replacement for my brother."

"I cannot imagine why, as you seem fine figure of a young man with a quick wit."

"Perhaps, my king, you and your court did your work too well while I was a guest here, as I am perceived by my people to be more a man of Pylos than an Achian."

The king laughed and beamed with an almost parental pride.

"We did appreciate you here, and we are pleased to think we did our work well, however inconvenient that may prove to you in the future."

"I am what I have become," said Orfeo.

"There is no turning back."

"And you will sing for us this evening after dinner.

Even now people speak of your marvelous voice and the way you could make them feel.

Can you still sing, or has your voice changed?"

"There is little need for song in an Achian camp," he answered, "but tonight I will do my best."

"So we have here a splendid group of people with whom to discuss the state of the world and the dangers we face."

He turned now to Zurga.

"If you teach all your skills to young Orfeo and he combines them with what he learned here, then we will truly have force to contend with."

"It was I who advised the king to send him with us."

"So what counsel do you have for us?" the king now lapsed into a harder-edged business mode. We are in danger and need all the wisdom we can find."

"When the Therans and their allies return, and we know that they will, have you thought of seeking help from the inland towns and villages that face as much loss of independence as you?"

"They have never been of much help to us in the past," said the king.

"You have never faced such a dire threat in the past," Zurga replied, and he went on to describe how even those so-called bandits - whom indeed, only lived upon the resources open to them - could be melded into a major fighting force. The discussion continued mostly between the king and Zurga, although Nadahr and Telemon made their contributions.

"Assuming for a moment that I take your suggestion, just how would I go about organizing such help, and how would I get them to go away in the event that we were successful?"

The king seemed reluctant to accept help from a group that had always been a thorn in his side, although they had never threatened the safety of the city.

"You send Orton and Telemon with one of your trusted aides whose name would be known to the bandits, and you instruct them to negotiate a treaty of mutual help.

After all, they would surely be enslaved should Pylos fall, and they know it."

"What makes you think they know it?"

The king sounded skeptical.

"I had a conference with their leader Tureg three mornings ago.

He keeps better track than you can imagine, and he is perceptive enough to see that the threat is to him as well as Pylos."

"How could he possibly know?"

"From my conversation with him, I had the clear impression that he has sources of information from your docks and from those who send your caravans inland.

You must be aware that some are unmolested while others are robbed, and that means that some know the right places to pay tribute." Zurga took on a delicate voice in suggesting to the king that there was business in his realm of which he knew nothing.

"Such payments of course are illegal, but I had always suspected that they were being made."

"Do you think Tureg wants to kill the cow from which he makes his cheese?"

"So what you are suggesting helps prevent the Therans from landing a force to attack my city from the land side, but what is to keep them from demolishing our fleet and moving into the harbor?"

Again there was a long discussion of tactics that came down to simple advice from Zurga.

"Their catapult could demolish your ships in a head to head battle in an hour, but they cannot sink them if they cannot get close enough."

Zurga sounded confident.

"But they can move faster than my ships, with their great banks of oars.

They can chase us down and then use the catapult to sink us with stones."

The king had obviously given the matter a great deal of thought.

"Why do you think the attack last week was not ordered?"

"Because we were prepared."

"And did you have your ships safely behind your sea wall, or were they spread across the harbor?"

"Our ships were all behind the sea wall."

The king appeared to be getting Zurga's point.

"And what would have happened if they had been out beyond the wall?"

The king was a quick witted man, and he seemed to ponder the situation.

"But to inflict any damage upon them, we must engage them at sea,"

"I have no easy answer, but will help you work out some kind of defense in which the great Theran ships will become vulnerable to missiles from the harbor, and as they present such large targets. I believe they can be sunk by the same kinds of machines that throw boulders against city walls."

Zurga looked satisfied.

"And I have taught several kings how to make such devices."

"How long would that take?"

"Within three weeks we could have the first example working, but for a real defense we would need two or three months to completely protect the harbor."

And so they all joined the discussion, as the king seemed gradually to lean in the direction of helping Zurga and of sending Telemon and Orton into the countryside to confer with Tureg.

They could help organize his band into a military organization that could stand against the Kalamattans, who would no doubt do most of the fighting on land for the Therans.

Nadahr also had some expertise in siege warfare, and he explained how he could help with the construction of yet another kind of machine that could hurl barrels of flaming pitch to great distances with enough accuracy to hit boats.

"The catapults the Therans use are devastating at close range, but if they are kept at a distance the ships are helpless against missiles," he again repeated the thesis.

Finally all had been said, perhaps all had been repeated several times, and the king ended the conference at dusk, inviting all to attend a great banquet he had arranged in the main room of the palace.

"There are people who wish to see you," he called to Orfeo, motioning for all to follow him into a great hall piled with the ingredients of a lavish feast at which the wine had already begun to flow. There was a cheer for Orfeo as he entered the room, and Nestor approached with a boisterousness that faded slightly when he realized that Orfeo was now the taller of the two.

"It has been too long."

Nestor embraced him and grasped his shoulders to demonstrate how sturdy Orfeo had become.

"It feels like a homecoming," Orfeo said truthfully, and the two old comrades spoke solemnly about their loss of Isocles and their long separation.

"We all wondered whether you had been kidnapped, and then some of us realized that you had probably felt drawn to your ancestral lands."

"I felt a duty," said Orfeo, "but I knew from my first hour after returning to my old home that I no longer belonged there and that I had made a terrible mistake that could not be corrected.

I could not crawl back and say I wished to be a hostage again."

"After the first few months you were here, we all saw you as more a part of the family than a hostage.

There was no thought of trying to force you back, but there were those who expressed puzzlement."

Nestor's sister joined them, and she had changed from an awkward twelve year old into a beautiful young woman.

They drank wine and helped themselves to the lavish assortment of food, and they were joined by others, making a grand reunion that almost, but not quite, erased those years in which he had not lived in Pylos.

The music created a languorous tone, and everyone seemed to wish Orfeo welcome until the king finally interrupted.

"Although we have six special guests with us tonight, only one of them has a tradition of having entertained us with his wonderful voice and his sublime poetry." The king seemed to radiate happiness.

"Bring the lyre and let us give silence for our returning minstrel and a member of our family we had thought lost forever."

Amidst the tide of warm greeting for Orfeo were cheers and toasts.

He stood before them not knowing whether he could remember the words of his poems or whether he could make his voice rise with the tide of his feelings.

It had been so long, and except for the brief song he had sung to his mother when he departed, he had not really sung in years.

The Achian camp was not, after all, the place for tender feelings.

He felt the lyre in his hands and plucked a few strings, and then he launched into the song he had sung so often but which had scarcely crossed his mind since his departure from Pylos.

He sang of the fields rich with wild flowers and the smell of the trees and the caress of the breezes, and the awakening of wondrous feelings of happiness on a spring day, and he knew he had at last returned, not merely to Pylos but to some part of himself that had felt chained since his escape.

As he held the last note the audience seemed so rapt that the applause started slowly, after a pause, and then grew to a great sound of welcome.

He was back among his people, at least one of the people to whom he belonged, and he was happy, and he began his next song of joy with a heart bounding with a sense of love for the world and for youth and life itself.

He sang until his voice began to tire, and he continued to sing, and when he was done his friends crowded around him with the love they felt for a boy who had touched them all, then and now.

And was he still a boy, or had he become a man?

It did not seem to matter.

He danced and talked and occasionally caught glances of his companions who seemed puzzled but pleased.

The hours passed in a delirious haze until the sounds finally began to fade, and the great trays of food were diminished and scarcely noticed by the guests who by now were satiated with wine.

Orfeo had surprised himself and those who had heard his voice before, but he had grown weary and walked slowly toward his quarters.

There sleeping on a bench in the hallway was Clarice, who was obviously waiting for him and sprang instantly awake as he approached.

"Clarice, I looked for you moments ago and could not find you," he said.

"Because I had known you would wish to say good night before you slept, and I saved you the trouble of finding me."

As usual, she seemed verbally, at least, to be seeking the upper hand.

They entered the room he had been assigned..

"Tonight you were both a powerful man and a charming boy," she said.

"You occupied the best of both worlds, and I realized suddenly that you will be a great man, that is if we live through this.

And I knew that I could be a help to you, and I wanted you to be aware that you need only call in the hour of need, and I will do all I can."

During the evening Orfeo had been approached by a number of women, both young and those old enough to be his mother, and he felt from some a sense of attraction toward him that could lead to various kinds of entanglements.

He had felt that from Sala, Nestor's sister, who had been only twelve when he had left Pylos, but who now had touched Orfeo whenever she could with her hands or by brushing close to him. But from Clarice there was no suggestion of her wanting to touch him or be touched by him.

She was simply pledging a special kind of allegiance that was so much more important, and he could recognize that she was someone who would stand beside him in the midst of terrible dangers.

"I will need your help and appreciate it," he said.

"But I am still not certain of how to move forward.

"You will tell me when you are ready," Clarice rose and slipped so quietly from the room that he hardly knew how it had happened so quickly.

The evening had left Orfeo strangely troubled in a state that verged between dreams and wakefulness, and reality maintained just enough hold so that he could not succumb completely to fantasy. He pondered over his mission to save Herron, yet try as he might to maintain the straight path he always seemed to stray toward another goal that at first he could not recognize.

He knew that the focus of the four travelers had now turned away from recovering Herron, and this Orfeo felt was a profound wrong, although he understood that from a Wanderer's point of view, the threat posed by the Therans was of greater significance to their world. Yet he had accepted a duty in spite of so many conflicting impulses.

At times he caught stray glimpses of the Theran princess in her consummate beauty, and at times the quest for Herron merged with this enchanting figure of feminine charm, each related and intertwined.

Seemingly at random various other figures stood in his path, and first, his old teacher Isocles, standing like a sphinx and asking endless unsolvable questions.

Then Telemon extended his own sword to the young warrior and bade him untie a knot with steel, while Nestor lurked in the background, perhaps not so benign as he had seemed this evening.

Above all and returning with a persistence that threatened to rend him into warring pieces was the presence of the Theran princess.

Could this vision undermine his determination to fight the awesome power she represented?

Orfeo awoke the next morning with a throbbing headache and a troubled heart.

He forced himself into activity, thrusting deep into his mind the awareness that he was yet but a twig afloat in a great ocean.

He had much to learn and experience.

# Chapter Nineteen

So he must make his decision this morning, and it would probably be the most painful choice in a life already full of painful choices. Zurga had arranged for the six of them to meet in the large room he had enjoyed alone, and there was a great tray of fruit and cheese so that they could breakfast leisurely and talk about their plans. After they had all settled in, Zurga began to make assignments, as he had since their departure from the Achian camp.

He had slowly, by force of personality, been assuming command.

"Some must organize and train the army of the villages," he began and then pointed toward Telemon and Orton.

"Are you two willing to deal with Tureg and, with one of Linaeus's counselors, arranging terms of their alliance with Pylos against the Therans."

Telemon glanced at Orton as if seeking his reaction, which was passed silently, and then he accepted.

"We should probably leave as soon as possible."

"I would like Nadahr and Clarice to travel east to where they are known in the cities of Tyre, Biblos, and Ebla.

We need someone there to first assess the degree of Theran penetration and try to enlist their aid in a war that will soon come to their doorstep if the Therans manage to overrun Pylos." He looked intently in their direction. "Do you accept?"

"It is the task for which I am best suited," said Nadahr.

"I will plead eloquently for an alliance."

"As for me," continued Zurga, "I will first assist the men of Pylos in building the great missile throwers they need to sink the Theran ships, and then I will take the dangerous task of visiting Minos, where I believe the Therans have long ruled a populace that hates them.

I will arrive by stealth and see whether there is any element willing to rise up against their Theran masters.

This could drain their energy in attempting to put down dissension from within what they see as their empire."

The others nodded.

"Orfeo, I would welcome your assistance on Minos, but I believe your major lessons are to be of a military nature, and I ask you to accompany Telemon and Orton so that you can hone your abilities as a swordsman and learn to command men in conflict.

It is part of your heritage, and you must learn it to assume your rightful place among the Achians."

He looked toward the young man as if he expected immediate assent.

"Respectfully, my teacher, I must explain why I will take another task."

The familiar feelings of restlessness accompanied the thumping of his heart as he rose to deliver what he had rehearsed silently all morning.

"The task I was sent to accomplish was to rescue my brother, and I swore to my father and mother that I would do my best.

So far nothing that has happened has relieved me of this oath, and I have received reliable word that my brother is now a slave in Thera.

I have no choice but to follow my original task and do what I can to rescue him."

This brought silence and discomfort upon every face.

"If you go, I must also live up to my oath," said Telemon.

"And you too," he pointed at Zurga.

"No, I think it is best that I travel alone," said Orfeo.

"But you need a grown man to make decisions," said Orton.

"I need to make my own decisions, as I have noticed that the decisions made thus far in our journey have not always been best calculated to achieve our goal."

"What do you mean by that?"

Zurga answered with a rare show of annoyance.

"I mean from our first move we have charged blindly ahead as we did when we boarded a ship while a storm was brewing and when we set out to reach Pylos by traveling inland, where we were beset by bandits, rather than await a ship in a few days.

And our experience in Kalamatta was nearly fatal, not to mention the decision to spare the life of a man who will spend the rest of it trying to track us down.

It is not the way I must travel to give me the best chance of rescuing my brother."

"But you have no chance to penetrate Thera alone.

You are still not skillful with weapons, and you would become enslaved yourself."

Telemon had not taken the criticism angrily but was now obviously concerned for the boy's welfare.

"You must come with us," pleaded Orton.

"Just how do you plan to get to Thera?" asked Zurga.

"I will return to Kalamatta looking more like myself than I did when I was there before.

I am not likely to be recognized when not in the company of great warriors and wanderers, as I am the least visible of us all."

"This is madness," said Telemon.

"And how would that get you closer to Herron?"

"While I was on the docks at Kalamatta, I heard the Therans recruiting craftsmen to come to Thera to work.

I saw them recruit a baker and a weaver, and I listened as they made a good offer of employment to a troop of dancers.

I will offer myself as a singer and hope for the best.

I am unknown, unmarked, and even Meeka would not recognize me since I have washed the blackness from my hair and removed the small growth of beard I had in Kalamatta.

I will find a way to get to Thera, and I will find Herron."

"Your chances of success are tiny?"

Zurga seemed less certain now.

"And yet I admire your courage and your plan."

"Are your chances here in fighting the Theran invasion any better?"

"Only the gods know that," he answered, and the group fell silent with a troubled demeanor.

"I will go with Orfeo."

Clarice suddenly stood and spoke with a resolute voice the others had never heard from her.

"I can sing as well as he, and I am a dancer.

My master, Nadahr, has made certain that I acquired skills in juggling and simple magic, and I can help Orfeo achieve his goal."

This brought an immediate movement from Nadahr, but at first he said nothing.

Then he spoke in a soft voice.

"It is a mission that you are well trained to assume," he then turned to Orfeo.

"Would you do all you can to insure the safety of my apprentice?"

"I would welcome her help and defend her as I defend myself."

"Then you have my permission," he spoke, gracefully allowing that which had been offered without his foreknowledge.

"So I planned our council down the last detail, and I am the one to be surprised," said Zurga, now shifting to a smiling mode.

"You are not as predictable as most Achians, but you have your ways of dealing with obstacles the gods place in your path.

And, who knows, you might even succeed, provided that Herron is still alive."

And thus the great council ended, or at least the business part of it did.

There were plans of a tactical nature and advice passed from one to another, but they all knew that soon after noon some of the group would leave the city.

When the others had gone to prepare for their journeys, Zurga motioned for Orfeo to remain behind.

"I must stop treating you like the child you were short months ago," he said.

"If you are not ready for the tasks you have set yourself, you will at least learn day by day, but I must tell you that you can assume the Therans will investigate everything about you before they decide to take you to their homeland.

They will be suspicious of anyone from Kalamatta at this point, and you should probably try to enter their service from Tyre, where they have long done business and where they still have the rank of traders rather than oppressors.

You should be in Type a matter of weeks before you seek their service, and you should be able to show that you arrived there from someplace other than Pylos.

Perhaps you should set out from some port to the west of here and be able to prove that you came straight to Tyre."

"Good advice which I will take." Orfeo answered.

"You must also realize that there are spies in every port working for the Therans, and you should learn to identify them by the questions they ask, however innocent they may sound.

Then when you believe you have identified the Theran spies, you must remind yourself that there are probably twice as many.

It is still probably good to give spies the feeling that they know you and that you are hiding nothing from them.

To that end, it should be understood that you are an Achian, as they will tell that from your appearance and speech.

Never tell a lie too far from the truth, and never expect to deceive people as to your origin.

You can talk with Clarice about the story she will use about her background, but you must both know everything you can about the fictions you create about yourselves.

Since she looks like you, she could well pass as your sister, but you must train her to speak as you do.

It will be easier because women are not so closely scrutinized."

"Tell me what you can about Thera."

"Alas, I have never been there, and I have had good reason to avoid the place, as I have given various of their minions grief in several parts of our world."

"Clarice and I should probably leave as soon as possible, but I do not want to appear publicly in Pylos by the docks, and I would like for someone else to make arrangements for me.

Then she and I will board ship in the opposite direction with a different look than we will have when we return to the east."

"Do you understand why I have, for the present, abandoned the search for Herron?"

Around this issue the Wanderer looked uncomfortable.

"You see the chances of our ever finding and rescuing him as very remote, and you see the Theran threat as a greater problem for the whole region, among which the Achians are a poor lot of rabble living not by trade but by the sheep they raise.

You realize our true importance in the whole scheme of things, and you will not sacrifice the rest of our world for such a small part of it."

"It is even deeper, and I want you to consider this well," Zurga took on a conspiratorial tone.

"Your brother is at best a mediocrity, and his capture by the Tyrian slavers was just another example of his carelessness.

He would be a willful and capricious king if he should succeed your father, and it would be best for all concerned if he stayed lost."

Orfeo looked in wonderment and had the sense of many of his own observations being validated.

"You would be a much better king than Herron, and your family and your people will slowly come to realize that you have qualities far stronger than his.

You will have allies from your mother's family, and should I survive the coming conflict, I will find ways of convincing them."

He paused as if organizing his final words of advice.

"If you sail to Thera searching for him, it will be known to Telemon, Orton, and myself, and you must realize how their respect for you has already grown.

They have seen how you handled yourself in the court of Pylos, and they know you are undertaking a dangerous journey.

Even if you come back with reports of Herron's death or perpetual slavery, you will be seen as a man who has risked much.

"I will bring him back," said Orfeo.

"Not likely, but I'm sure you will try."

"Have you no magic for me, oh mighty one?"

Orfeo smiled.

"As you have no doubt guessed, there is no such thing as magic.

It is a cheap explanation for that which is not understood.

I have many times been credited with performing magic, and yet I have never done anything that could not be explained by the laws of nature."

Zurga gave Orfeo a shockingly liberal sum of the money from what the Achian king had given him to finance the search, and he turned with no visible sentiment away from a young man he knew he might never see again.

He was such a promising leader, and yet he was intent upon taking risks that would make Telemon quake.

Next Orfeo found the room occupied by Nadahr and Clarice, where he was admitted in the midst of what must have been an uncomfortable moment for the two of them, as they were at first silent and only slowly began to sound welcoming.

Her offer to accompany Orfeo to Thera had taken the old Wanderer by surprise, and it appeared as though he had felt that her behavior involved a certain disrespect or lack of loyalty.

Nadahr soon left, closing the door loudly as he did so, leaving the impression that even Wanderers are capable of pettiness, but there was too much at stake now to let it intrude.

"Will you be ready to leave in an hour?"

He asked, and then he explained to her the strategy he had discussed with Zurga and how it actually seemed like a good idea to spend the better part of a month preparing the way to Thera rather than to rush into danger by a return to Kalamatta.

She seemed to understand but expressed no more feeling until he turned to her as he was preparing to leave.

"I will be eternally grateful for your decision to come with me."

The words sounded dry, like some formal retirement tribute to an old warrior.

"I know you are a thoughtful woman of judgment." Still he could not express the warmth he felt that she had believed in him enough to take a great risk of her life and freedom.

"You are the only one I would have wished to come along."

He softened his voice.

"We will learn to trust and rely upon each other."

"After all," she smiled playfully, referring to their escape from Kalamatta.

"I am your wife."

It would all work out well, and when Zurga returned from the harbor before noon with news that they were to sail westward, away from Tyre, in two hours, they enjoyed assuming the kinds of disguises even their companions would not recognize.

"Would your mother know you now?" asked Orfeo.

"I never knew my mother," said Clarice.

"But I doubt whether yours would know you."

"I believe my mother has not known me well since I was sent to Pylos as a hostage," he said, this time without rancor.

"And here are two motherless waifs who are attempting to rescue my mother's favorite son."

They laughed, left the palace unobtrusively like casual visitors, and carried their meager possessions to the harbor.

Their ship, the Adamantine, was captained by a man from the western port of Syracuse, across a stretch of sea south of Italy.

Orfeo had been there twice before during his time of wandering after his escape from Pylos, as he had not then known how to reach his homeland, which he passed several times in his search for it.

He had always been fearful of identifying himself as an Achian.

Once in Syracuse he and Clarice would establish an identity as entertainers and then work their way back toward Tyre and then to Thera.

Clarice thought the plan their best option, and once underway they discussed endlessly various strategies, although always careful not to be overheard.

The captain himself was almost certainly someone's spy, if not necessarily of the Therans, but it was certain there would be a Theran spy on board.

At the same time they were not likely to be particular objects of suspicion.

They had been assigned a small place for sleeping below deck and found a way to arrange a curtain around them for a modicum of privacy.

There were perhaps another two dozen travelers of both sexes in the same cramped quarters, but Orfeo and Clarice became strangely unsocial, limiting their world to themselves alone and in the process coming to know one another.

Clarice, who said she was fourteen, quickly came to depend upon her older companion, but in a chaste girlish manner that seemed to suit Orfeo, who as a hostage in Pylos and as a returned exile back at the Achian camp, had known young women only superficially.

Clarice suddenly found herself in the role of the sister he never had.

She told of her childhood among the Dorae, a tribe related to the Achians but even farther north.

There she had been rescued by Nadahr after a massacre of most of the tribe by the voracious Hannae, who spoke a different language and who claimed to have ruled the land before Achians and Dorae had arrived from the north several centuries before.

Nadahr had fed, clothed, and trained her to be an entertainer, with the idea that she would ultimately replace him among the ranks of Wanderers.

While he had been kindly and had always protected her, however, there had been no affection. He did not confide in her, and praise seemed to spring unnaturally from his mouth.

He had never communicated a sense that he had loved her as a parent would, nor had any genuine warmth arisen between them, although she was an infant who could barely walk when he had taken her.

At that time he traveled with another women, Roona, who had cared for the young girl until about three years ago, when she had met a villager she suddenly decided to marry.

Clarice thought that she had similarly felt no affection toward Nadahr, although he had never failed to be kind to her.

The issue of whether Orfeo and Clarice were going to travel as brother and sister or young husband and young wife was resolved when they determined that try as she might, Clarice would not speak in the manner of the Achians, and thus they could not be relatives.

Since they were obviously young, they thought it reasonable to pretend that they had met by accident when their respective tribes had occupied adjacent pastures, and they had decided to run away together and make their way in the world as entertainers.

On ship, however, they barely showed themselves, maintaining appearances they both thought of as disguises.

They did not wish to be traced from Pylos after they arrived in Syracuse, which would be the starting place of their journey to Thera.

They felt they were beneath notice of the captain, and without incident the days passed with good winds and fair weather until they reached the port, a bustling commercial hub that seemed less polished in its manners than Pylos, although the people were more sophisticated than the Achians.

They walked through the section of town near the docks where travelers stayed, and Orfeo found an inn that offered a rough kind of entertainment in the evening.

Usually such shows to entertain the guests and other travelers involved dancers, often of women in revealing dress, or men singing bawdy songs.

Orfeo had been there on the travels, and he hoped he could talk the owner into letting them perform for their lodgings, although he had enough money to cover the cost.

“So what makes you think you two can please my crowd?”

A smiling but obviously skeptical red haired man, built like a miniature Telemon, seemed willing to be convinced, although he did not expect this transformation to occur.

“All we need as payment is a room in your inn, and the only security we need is day to day.

Give us a chance before you agree to anything, and if we don’t make it tonight, I’ll pay for our room and move on tomorrow.”

“You’ll pay in advance,” the owner said.

“And no begging from my customers.

If they throw money at you, which I consider unlikely, you can pick it up, but I get half.

It's money that would otherwise be spent here.

I don't like my entertainers to drink wine, as you've got to stay on your toes here.

If there's a fight, just get out of the way.

If some of these seamen get too friendly with the lady, keep your temper and ignore it unless it gets too insistent, and then I'll make a move."

"Does that mean we're hired?"

"It means you get a trial run tonight, and if I don't like what I see, it's out you go."

All this was not so much unfriendly as a simple setting of the ground rules, and it was agreed that they could come on after a trained dog act, which itself was not first on the program.

"We've got five hours to buy what we need in the bazaar and get back here for a quick rehearsal," Clarice said.

"I have some ideas about how we should relate on stage."

They stayed together in the bazaar, with Clarice helping Orfeo choose a costume that made him look like a minstrel, while he helped her buy dozens of items whose purpose he did not understand.

She told him that it would be best if he were surprised and showed it.

In the meantime Orfeo explained to her the kinds of songs he expected to sing, and she seemed enthusiastic about some and doubtful about the ballades of young romantic love.

For some reason this did not seem like the crowd to appreciate tender feelings, at least not without the proper preparation, but she suggested a few bawdy songs of the sea and the men who ventured out under sail.

He was dubious, but said he would give it a try.

He did not know any such songs and quickly began rewriting the words for many of the tunes he had long used.

The most difficult item to find was a suitable lyre, as few dealers in the bazaar dealt with musical instruments, but when Orfeo finally found what he wanted, she purchased a small drum from the same man.

"Trust me," she said.

"I know what to do with this."

He was beginning to wonder whether their great debut on the provincial stage at Syracuse would be a disaster, but he had too much to worry about in finding just the right combination of features that would appeal to a crowd of hard-drinking, rowdy, and frequently violent men, although the owner had said there would also be some women in the audience.

Back in their room Clarice tried various combinations of veils and fabrics for her costume, and she made preparations Orfeo could not explain. In the meantime he tried to sing some of the songs he was preparing, but nothing seemed to go right.

The sun had set outside, and he knew that soon he and Clarice must appear below, but the lyre would not stay in tune, and she was absolutely no help, as she kept playing with a small medallion as if it were a coin.

Perhaps they should simply give up and find another inn.

Then they were downstairs, and they watched a silly act in which a man would tell his dog to do various tricks, and the dog would slavishly obey.

He would jump up when told to do so, lie down on command, and bark a certain number of times when told to do so.

Indeed, the dog could apparently do simple arithmetic and find a morsel of food his master put in a pouch at his waist.

"What if I were to play a dog, and you were to tell me what to do?"

"How would that amuse our audience?" he said.

"And how could you look like a dog?"

"Just try it and see what happens."

She gave him a smile that he would later learn to recognize as hiding more than it revealed.

Then he was before the audience, with almost no introduction from the owner, who had a skeptical look on his face.

Orfeo felt the usual tension in standing before an audience, but he focused on the task at hand rather than a mental accounting of all that could go wrong.

He took a deep breath and launched into a ballad about a seaman who arrived a week early at port only to reach his home and find his wife with another man.

It was not played for tragedy, but for the comic possibilities, and Clarice mimed the facial expressions of the guilty wife, caught in the act, pleading for an opportunity to make it all up to him.

The voice rang out clear and true, as it had in Pylos, but he had no sense of connecting with the audience.

They watched him, and there was a general silence throughout the large hall, but they had not yet made a commitment to like or dislike.

As he finished the song there were several raucous, but not unfriendly, comments, and then suddenly he saw Clarice appear, on all fours, with a piece of leather strapped to her face like a dog's muzzle.

She bounded toward him like a dog, and he responded by holding up his hand like the dog's master in the previous act and commanding that she jump up.

Instead she rolled over and pretended to go to sleep.

Step by step with the previous act, they began to go through the actions that the dog had made to its master's commands, only now the dog did the exact opposite. When silenced, Clarice barked loudly, and when asked to bark, she licked his hand.

The performance was not one of great depth or subtlety, but it began to strike the audience as hilariously funny, and soon everyone was laughing.

It was then that Orfeo launched into his second song about a man and his true love, who turned out to be not a woman but his dog.

More laughter and more affection flowing from audience to performers.

The new team was liked. They had been accepted, and when Clarice appeared with her magic act, pulling a seemingly endless rope from Orfeo's nose, and picking a large coin from behind the ear of the owner - who became part of the act when he demanded it back - there was a stamping of feet and cheers.

Finally, after songs and changes of pace, Orfeo began his serious song of heroism on the field of battle, and he thought as he sang of Telemon.

Clarice accompanied with militant rolls of the drum and an undercurrent of rhythm that gave the whole production a sense of momentum.

Then they were standing on the stage, raised less than a foot above the floor of the hall, and they were acclaimed with good spirits.

Even without rehearsals they had succeeded, and the owner said that they had earned their keep for the night.

He did not refund their money, but he said he would apply it to the next night, and then he applied it to the next and the next.

"You're a marvel," he hugged her warmly as they ascended the stairs to their room, and he could feel her excitement.

They both felt triumphant in that it had all turned out so much better than they feared, and they both understood that tomorrow would bring a better performance.

And day by day they improved rapidly.

The man with the dog act that had preceded them was at first angry, as though he was being held up to ridicule, but by the second night he was cooperating, becoming part of the act by making his routine even easier to parody.

Obviously the performance, which varied from night to night as it became more accomplished, was popular, and there were more people in the audience on the second night and then the third.

And although the crowds remained rowdy, the performers earned their respect, and they began to be greeted as they walked around the town.

By the end of the week the inn's owner agreed to begin paying them money in addition to their free room and board, and Clarice continued to find baubles and clothes and eventually even a few live animals for her magic act, which was growing in complexity.

Orfeo's repertoire of songs also improved from night to night, and soon they found stray visitors in the audience from Prince Rego's court.

Word spread that there was a new and lively act in town that could be both funny and moving when the handsome young man began to sing a sad song.

"Are you glad you came with me?"

Orfeo asked after a performance that had been their best yet.

"I have never been happier," she said.

"Although Nadahr had trained me to entertain, he had never really let me show the part of myself that is silly or even funny.

He always wanted me to be an actress rather than someone the men at an inn would applaud."

"Every night you amaze me with the quickness of your mind," he said.

"I am learning better to follow your lead even when we have not rehearsed."

"And I am loving the sound of your voice and your poet's way with feeling."

And then came the invitation they were truly not expecting.

Frakin, the inn's owner found them in the bazaar one afternoon and, looking none too happy about it, informed them that they had been invited to Prince Rego's palace that evening and that they were to arrive soon after dark. Of course he must release them, and they must perform.

But clearly the program tonight must not be the same as they presented to the rowdy guests at the inn.

And yet they had no idea what the tenor of the court might be.

Were they sentimental or pretentious or merely looking for a pleasant diversion?

Orfeo began to ask in the bazaar about performances in the palace and the preferences of the prince, and everyone had some opinion to give.

The prince was fair, but easily angered.

He was a tyrant who occasionally allowed himself to lapse into good behavior.

He had no sense of humor.

He was always looking at the humorous side of any occasion, even a hanging.

He was lecherous, excessively religious, tightfisted, and generous.

He was, so Orfeo and Clarice came to understand, unpredictable, and again they would have to play it all by ear, extemporizing based upon the feedback they received.

By this time Clarice had gathered together so many props for her act that Frakin had to send along one of his workers to help them carry it all to the palace and to show them the servant's entrance.

They were expected and taken to the Master of the Hunt, who was also obviously master of the king's other entertainments as well.

"You will follow a bear dancer, and you will be allotted a quarter of an hour unless the prince shows special favor, and then you will be allowed to remain on stage for another quarter hour or until he tires of you.

The prince laughs at coarse humor, but he can also be offended by immorality.

He responds to skillful singing, and he is something of a sentimentalist.

If you do not please him, it is likely this will be your last visit to the palace."

He then instructed them how to get to the servant's kitchen, where they would be fed.

So again Orfeo and Clarice had to make tentative plans for their program, hoping they could read the audience well enough to make adjustments as they went along.

They were kept behind a large curtain awaiting their entrance, and they were able to see the bear dancer manipulate his animal much as the trainer had done with his dog at the inn.

But the audience had obviously seen it before, and they shouted words of encouragement as the act moved forward.

Then they walked forward, approached the main platform, and bowed confidently before the prince.

They were so much better than they had been just days ago when they had arrived at the docks, but were they good enough for the local ruler?

Orfeo began with his lyre, accompanied by Clarice, who now had three different types of drums.

He sang of a wanderer whose life had been sad but who was fortunately enough to find himself in the port of Syracuse.

The melody provided a haunting refrain referring to the wanderer's loneliness, but the final resolution with its happiness at being in Syracuse stirred with a drumbeat that gave it an air of fulfillment.

The audience had begun by liking the two young performers.

And then they began to pretend to be the bear and his master, this time with Orfeo playing the bear in a dark shaggy coat and Clarice running him through his tricks, although he proved to be the most bumbling bear anyone had every seen.

He fell over himself, misunderstood commands, and brought laughter to a crowd that had only minutes before felt the melancholy and eventual triumph of his song, and then he was back again singing, this time in a duet with Clarice in which he was an ardent suitor and she a recalcitrant maiden.

It was sad and then funny, and suddenly it came to a happy ending.

The audience applauded, and Clarice started with her tricks, including the pulling of a live pigeon from her hat.

Obviously it was not an old trick in Syracuse, as everyone seemed astonished and then pleased.

The prince himself stood and told them to continue, and now Orfeo lapsed into a sad ballad of heartbreak and loss.

He felt the emotion pour forth in his voice, and he knew he held the attention of his audience.

He was singing better than ever before, and he spotted a familiar green color among the guests sitting next to the prince.

What could a Theran be doing among the audience?

He thought Clarice had not seen, but after her short acrobatic dance, just as they were to start on his final song of triumph, she whispered that she also had noticed.

There was obviously nothing to do but hope that it was not one of the few Therans who had a chance of recognizing them, but that was only a remote possibility. The song went well, and they were invited to face the price personally.

He was younger than they expected, and he had a casual manner about him.

"I understand that you have become popular at our finest inn, and I was advised that I should see your show."

"We sincerely hope we have brought pleasure and lightened the spirits of all who have seen us. We are grateful to have been asked to perform here."

Orfeo went through his usual gracious praise of the audience, particularly the prince, and then they were told to await the appearance of the Master of the Hunt at the end of the night's festivities.

They returned to the room where they had first been instructed and waited with the bear and his master, and others came in as they finished their acts. Finally the master returned, and he instructed several of the performers to come back the next night or next week, and he paid the bear dancer, who was apparently itinerant.

Orfeo thought they had failed to make enough of an impression when the master indicated that they should follow him for a special meeting with someone who had liked their performance.

They were led into a small darkened room and there at a table sat the Theran they had seen from the stage.

His face showed no emotion.

# CHAPTER TWENTY

AT FIRST ORFEO IMAGINED that the Therans had caught up with two fugitives from the Kalamattan escape and had come to arrest them, but this image was quickly dispelled by the man's facial expression, which showed little emotion - as was Theran custom - but still communicated an impression of satisfaction. He had liked their performance, and for some reason he wanted to tell them so.

"Have you two been performing together long?"

He asked in a rather flat voice.

"We have known each other and sung together, but mostly just for friends," said Orfeo.

"Someone told us there was an inn here in Syracuse that had entertainment, and we decided to come here to see if we could get some experience.

We had thought about an act for years, but this was our big chance, and everything seemed to come together."

Was that what he should have said?

He knew he had seemed enthusiastic as he blurted out the prepared story, and it probably sounded plausible.

"The two of you work well together, and both the music and the humor would be agreeable to Therans."

"Your comments make me happy, your highness, and I appreciate that you took the time to tell us.

I feel in your debt for those kind comments."

Orfeo covered his uncertainty with awkwardness.

"Are you ambitious to travel to the great cities and perform in front of crowds of important people?"

"That is our fondest dream, your highness, but I know that we need much more practice and time to develop more variety in our acts."

He still recognized the pleased countenance of the Theran. "But each night we become better, and eventually we hope to work hard enough to become truly accomplished performers."

"Where are you from, singer?"

"I am an Achian from the tribe of Kiros, and I...." He paused as if he did not want to admit that he had not fit in well with the others.

"You must not have fit very well with that crude people," the Theran retorted with a smile.

"As I understand it, the Achians take pleasure from their sheep."

"I left home when I met my wife," he gestured with his eyes toward Clarice, who bowed demurely."

"So you ran away from home, and you don't want to go back."

Now the Theran was enjoying the story and sounded sympathetic.

"I mean no disrespect to my parents, your highness, but I knew I would never be happy among them, nor could I fulfill my obligations toward them. My parents have other sons to tend the sheep."

"I think you and your wife have great promise as entertainers, and I also have the idea you would be appreciated on Thera?"

He let the thread drop at that point.

Orfeo and Clarice looked blankly at one another, concealing both their misgivings and their hope that what had promised to be a long, arduous task could have been accomplished so quickly.

"We know almost nothing about Thera," said Orfeo.

"We have heard that it is a rich and powerful nation, but we know nothing more.

Are you a Theran?"

"Most people immediately recognize Therans," he smiled knowingly, "but I can understand that your people from Achia know little of the world, and Thera has not spread her influence this far west.

But I assure you our city is clean, safe, and prosperous.

We take good care of our guests, and I have come here to recruit stone cutters to help us enlarge many of our public buildings.

We have no trouble recruiting skilled craftsmen because we pay well."

"You make Thera sound like a wonderful place, but how could we get there?"

"We furnish transportation to Thera and back to the mainland when the job is done.

We have a reputation for being strict, but we are fair.

You could leave with me day after tomorrow and be entertaining in our villas within two weeks.

You would be under contract to me, which means that we would split what you are paid by those who hire your services, but you would feel that it comes out fairly.

You would live a better life and leave Thera with gold and silver."

Orfeo turned to Clarice, who had a pleased look, and to make the matter clearer she nodded in the affirmative.

"We will gladly do as you suggest," Orfeo said.

"And thank your highness for his kindness and his words of encouragement."

They were told that they should perform at court the next night, and then on the next morning they were to sail on a Theran ship.

Could it be so easy?

Was it possible that they were falling into a trap?

In a sense they recognized that as performers they were more talented than the others they had seen at either the inn or the palace, but they realized that they lacked polish and needed much work to bring their act up to the level they wanted.

But they were heading toward Thera a month or more before they could have imagined, and the sooner they arrived, the sooner they would have an opportunity to find out about Herron.

They returned to their room in the inn that night but continued talking hour after hour.

"Are you sure you want to come?"

He wanted to give her a chance to back out.

"So long as you want me to come."

"You know I want you with me, but I don't want to put you at risk."

"So long as we simply entertain, then we will have done nothing to rouse the ire of the Therans.

It is only if you find Herron that we have a problem, and that may not be so serious.

After all, we have more money now, with our payment from Frankin, than when we started.

We can ransom him, buy his freedom."

"If he is on a Theran warship that is probably another matter," said Orfeo.

"Zurga has the idea that there are secrets on these ships that would keep them from allowing anyone to leave after once having been aboard."

"Do you believe him?"

"It's plausible, but we must find Herron first before any of this has meaning."

The second night of performing at the palace was even more successful, and they were again complimented by the Theran envoy.

They were at the docks early, complete with many bags of luggage, which the ship's captain at first did not wish to let aboard, but the envoy, who identified himself as Counselor Draik, insisted that it was all necessary.

After a careful search of the contents the captain agreed, and they sailed with the tide on what proved to be the largest ship either had ever seen, with hundreds of passengers, including a large group of stonecutters.

At this point there seemed nothing either threatening or unusual about the dreaded island, and Draik himself seemed in no way threatening.

There were other Therans tending to the needs of the ship, but apparently none of them had left the boat and mixed with the town's population.

On the third day of the voyage Draik invited them into his cabin, and there he began to tell them about Theran customs.

The advice seemed intended to help them make their performances confirm to Theran ideals, which sounded logical, although there was always a provision for punishment in case of an infraction.

These punishments also seemed particularly severe, and the death penalty was applied to cases that would require only a flogging among the Achians, and minor infractions which would merit a small loss of goods in Achia involved severe beatings.

The concept of treason was complex and covered virtually anything that could be interpreted as inimical to the nation, and punishment for this was swift, sure, and possibly could also involve friends and relatives.

"What are your concepts of heroism?" asked Orfeo, many of whose songs spoke of heroic deeds and sacrifice for virtuous causes.

"Your songs of heroic deeds are what finally convinced me to bring you to Thera," Draik answered.

"A Theran must always be prepared to sacrifice his life, if necessary, for the defense of our nation and its glory.

Whatever else we are doing at the time, we must be prepared to make the ultimate sacrifice.

Even at my age, and not being in the prime of my fighting condition, I could be called to duty and would gladly go."

"Does everyone feel that way?"

"Do the Achians not feel that way.?"

Orfeo smiled and inwardly assembled an answer that he hoped would satisfy the Theran.

"The Achians are of mixed qualities, and some are very forthright, hard working people, but many contribute little to the success of their families, and some live only by the efforts of others.

If they were to fight to defend their land, they would be very fierce at first, but if the efforts became too great, and many were killed, they would soon grow dispirited.

They are not a people who could maintain a long struggle, and the will to sacrifice would wane among them."

Draik appeared to consider this answer carefully and nodded in agreement.

"That has always been my impression of those people we refer to as hill tribes," he said.

"But does the description you gave also apply to you?"

"I think my wife and I are made of firmer fiber, as neither of us were satisfied among our peoples because there was not the kind of bond between us that would make the sacrifice of a life seem worthwhile.

We were disappointed again and again and left seeking a life with more meaning.

Neither of us had ever fit in with those around us, and we felt free as soon as we began to see more of the world and recognized that despite its sordid side, there was more of a life for us in civilized society.

I hope you can understand, without condemning us as being unfaithful to our traditional life."

Draik looked pleased and nodded acceptance.

"What if you were to find a place where the people were all dedicated to civic virtue and were willing to work and sacrifice for the common good?

If you lived in and were supported by a society of strong, thoughtful, dedicated men and women, could you imagine giving it your loyalty, even if it meant sacrifice?"

Orfeo felt an upsurge of genuine enthusiasm for such a place, imagining himself in a virtuous society taking part as a free citizen, and yet all he had heard of Thera denied Draik's description.

"If I were to become part of such a society, I would be grateful and would give of myself whatever was necessary.

I would admire that behavior in others, and I would do no less myself."

"Singer of songs, I have high hopes for you in Thera, and I think you will find a home.

You and your wife lack only a Theran pedigree, but you are people of personal beauty, intelligence, and the skill to entertain.

We will see what comes of this venture."

Later in the part of the ship where they slept among perhaps fifty stone cutters and a few of their women, they whispered their impressions.

Could it be that Thera was actually a better place than they had imagined?

The whole concept was difficult to accept, although Draik seemed like an unusually forthright and honest man.

Those who were heading toward Thera to work as stone cutters also showed no particular fear of the Therans.

As Orfeo and Clarice learned as they began to talk with their traveling companions, a number of the stone cutters had been there before and were returning for a second two-year term.

They described the Therans as hard taskmasters, whose commands must be followed to the letter, but they had the impression that the punishments for infractions were fair, even if severe. They uniformly felt that only the guilty were punished and that the Therans were willing to expend great energy in determining who was right in a dispute.

"It's good food, a clean safe place to sleep, and good money," one of the stone cutters said.

As for the ambitions of the Therans to dominate the world of Kalamatta, Pylos, and Tyre, Orfeo would not ask.

He felt confident there were spies among the men, and he did not wish to appear too curious. But Thera as described by the ship's passengers - by many people who had been there and were voluntarily returning - sounded surprisingly benign.

If the Therans were spawn of the devil, as many on the mainland claimed, then they concealed it well from a number of people who worked there.

Much of the trip involved little activity, and the sea did not provide intriguing scenery.

Orfeo and Clarice worked over and over on parts of their act and found a few Therans - mostly Draik's functionaries - who were willing to tell them what Therans liked in entertainment.

Repeatedly the concept of heroic deeds was discussed, but what about a heroic death?

Was it something to be portrayed or lamented or ignored?

Apparently, at least from what they were told by the Therans, it was a subject of celebration only if it resulted in a victory over enemies. The heroic self-sacrifice in a losing cause seemed like abject failure.

If one could not win the day, then death was a fitting reward.

The most heroic activities involved triumph against overwhelming odds.

There was also a kind of heroism associated with reporting one's closest relatives, even one's parents or children, to the authorities in case there was reason to believe they were not sufficiently zealous in pursuit of the king's objectives.

Another one of the passengers who had been an entertainer in his youth had much to say about what Therans found humorous.

They had no qualms about making fun of the blind or the lame, but they cherished loyalty.

They liked entertainments that showed enormous precision, with a number of people dancing in unison or singing as if in one voice.

The day before their arrival in port, there was an accident on board ship that seemed to show something about Theran sensibilities.

One of the sailors was working on the high mast when his feet became entangled in ropes, and he came crashing to the deck with a noise that brought Orfeo and Clarice rushing to see what had happened.

There the seaman lay with part of his thighbone protruding through his skin.

It was a horrible fracture of the sort that would probably leave him permanently crippled if he survived, and Orfeo's first impulse was to rush forward and try at least to position the leg so that the man would be in less pain.

The other seamen, however, ridiculed their comrade, as though he was no longer part of their community.

First they laughed, and then they pointed out how it was all his own fault.

When the captain arrived, he was furious that the man had precluded his further service to the ship when his labor was needed.

Instead of giving sympathy, the captain abused him as a fool and a danger to all the others with his ineptitude.

"For your mistake you will pay," he threatened.

"When we return you will stand trial for undermining the mission of the ship."

Orfeo and Clarice whispered together much of the evening about how different this attitude seemed and whether it was to be condemned or merely accepted as different.

It was clear that certain aspects of Theran culture were at odds with what they had known, but they were unwilling to pass value judgments.

Yet there was something in their mode of discussion that had become intimate.

They were beginning to become accustomed to being always together, and it was pleasurable for both.

Orfeo had never in his life had a companion so close and so sympathetic, and in that strange way men and women have - as they begin to close the distance between them - they came to understand the thoughts and feelings of each other.

It helped their act, in that now they could almost read each others' minds, but it also made them a good team to dissemble to the world.

They were so much of the same mind about their task that they seldom argued as to how to approach a given problem, but seemed instinctively to know how the other would react.

They had started the journey as individuals rather than as a couple, although Zurga, Nadahr, and probably even the warriors could recognize that Clarice felt a longing for greater closeness with Orfeo.

This constituted most of the reason why Nadahr had been so agreeable in letting her go off with this strange boy she barely knew, but he had felt deserted, perhaps even hurt that she so readily dissolved her relationship with him.

It was not at all clear that such a bond once broken could ever be mended to its former firmness, and now he found himself without an "apprentice," as he had called her.

Zurga had also seen that the stirrings of an adult woman played across Clarice's consciousness as she looked upon Orfeo, who was - almost before their eyes - growing into a remarkably handsome man.

The company all recognized that in the short time they had traveled together Orfeo had undergone one of these spurts of growth that usually comes earlier to a maturing male, but which had just come within the last few months.

Standing back to back it was possible he was now as tall as Telemon, and he had taken on a more confident way of moving through the world.

And the performances even lent him a more confident demeanor, as part of standing before others and performing was the ability to project a confidence well beyond what was inwardly felt.

He could now walk around the stage as though he owned it, and Clarice's adoring gaze - probably perceived by all at some level - lent him even greater stature.

This woman loved him, and others could feel it in the air around them.

From Orfeo the mirror image of that feeling was a growing sense of protectiveness that enveloped her in a cloak of both belonging and safety.

With his persona projected around her she felt a security she had never known with Nadahr, who indeed had surrounded her with a more impersonal protectiveness.

"You are growing so confident," she said.

"Your singing is truly the most moving I have ever heard, and your movements in our act have all the women enthralled."

"It's only fair that the women watch me, as the men cannot keep their eyes off you," he answered. And truly she was also blossoming before his eyes.

By the time they arrived in Thera all traces of a disguise had vanished, and she appeared in her golden haired glory and he with a darker blond hair, as descendants of barbarian tribes from the north who had migrated toward the sunnier climes of the great inland sea.

# CHAPTER TWENTY-ONE

DRAIK STOOD ON DECK looking expectantly forward.

"So how does it look to you?"

He asked Orfeo and Clarice.

"I see nothing," said Orfeo.

"There is only the thick, dark fog."

"Ah, you see more than you know," Draik answered.

"It is smoke from our friend Vulcan, who lives in the great volcano at the heart of our empire.

It is from Vulcan that we receive hundreds of springs of hot water, that we are able to heat many of our houses during our short winter, and why our crops grow faster than they do elsewhere.

Thera is indeed most fortunate of all lands in the world to be nourished by the god himself, who provides for us metals for our hearths and the heat to work them with.

He provides sulfur for our weapons, and the smell of home that greets every nostril as one returns from a stay abroad.

Can you smell the fragrance of our god?"

Draik was so obviously enraptured by the prospect of returning to his native land that it was difficult to tell whether he actually found the odor to his liking, but this thick smoke combined a certain acrid quality with another component that was almost like honey.

Clearly there were a number of strains mixed within the smoke, and it was something one could no doubt learn to appreciate, although first exposure was none too pleasant.

"Is the island always enshrouded in this fog?" asked Clarice.

"Perhaps one day in the week, and often it is clear or with just the white fog.

The god bestows upon us what he wishes, and it is not up to any mortal to command or to criticize.

We take our due from our more direct relationship with one of the great Olympian gods, who is our patron.

He favors us before all others, and we dedicate everything of ours to his mortal manifestation, our king, Sargon."

Draik busied himself preparing for the unloading of goods he had brought back on this trading mission, although when they landed - with the day still darkened by smoke - he bade they follow him to his home, where they would lodge in quarters he reserved for his troop of entertainers.

In a sense they represented another imported item that he had acquired in Syracuse, and thus they were seen as something of an investment, but he genuinely appeared to have a benign attitude toward them.

As they were drawn through the streets in a cart that also included some serving help Draik had imported from Syracuse, they found the city strange and wondrous in its own curiously orderly manner.

There was nothing of the bustle and disorganization of other ports on the inland sea, but an absence of pointless noise along with clear evidence of a somber quality characterized by the lack of a raucous effort of petty peddlers to hawk their wares with loud calls and pleas. There were shops, but nothing like the riotous bazaars of other cities.

From watching the behavior of Therans in Pylos and Kalamatta it could almost have been predicted that they lived in a city without visible manifestations of either joy or misery.

There were no beggars, and no one seemed shabbily dressed.

Everyone looked like a citizen who was mindful of his obligation to society.

And yet the people seen walking on the streets did not look downtrodden or unhappy.

There seemed to be a pride among them, perhaps for the simple reason of their being Therans.

The description that Clarice murmured with a smile into Orfeo's ear was "self important, they all look as though they feel superior to everyone else in the world."

She had given a restrained laugh, as though she had already come to understand that in Thera one did not publicly throw about laughter or any other outburst of feeling.

They had expected Draik's mansion to be splendid, but they were unprepared by the great concentration of statues and stone friezes which made his residence comparable to the royal palace of Pylos, although perhaps smaller, but it was even more full of art that seemed to be from the entire realm of the inland sea.

There was black stone statuary from Egypt, wonderfully surreal sculptures from Cyprus, and murals that Clarice thought to be from Minos.

There were pipes bringing hot water to all parts of the house, and everything had about it the smell of cleanliness.

Of course the room assigned to Orfeo and Clarice was undecorated, but it was surprisingly spacious, with two comfortable beds and chairs covered with soft cushions. It did not take them long to realize that bringing entertainers from various parts of the world was part of Draik's business, as the two men living in the room next door were Cretan dancers, who immediately wished to establish their seniority and superior status.

"I am Thonos, and my friend is Athos, and we have long been the best part of Draik's troupe."

He seemed bored.

"I hope you're not singers," he continued.

"They usually don't last long around her, as there are too many of them, and they all use the same old tired material."

"The only thing more common than singers are the magic acts," Athos surveyed the newcomers with a mild disdain that was not entirely unfriendly, although clearly they were uncertain enough of their own tenure that they felt each newcomer to be a potential threat.

"Unfortunately I am mostly a singer, and my wife is drummer and dancer, but she also does magic tricks."

He watched the reaction of two people he wished to enlist as friends, as even on this short acquaintance he had the impression they could be damaging as enemies.

"But I would beg your advice about our act, as we are new in Thera today and know nothing of the kinds of people we will be performing before, and we know nothing of their likes and dislikes."

"You will be performing in the great houses owned by the nobility of Thera, and the audiences have seen everything and have grown quite hard to please.

Anywhere else a bad act is merely sent packing, but here they punish those who have offended or bored them," said Thonos.

"Oh my," said Clarice, as though suddenly frightened.

"What can I do for them that they have not already seen?"

She had caught Orfeo's drift and wished to enlist the aid of these rather bitchy characters rather than their enmity.

"They had a juggler beaten last weak for dropping the apples he had in the air.

He was told to return to Biblos, where he came from.

And don't imagine they will be entertained if you can balance things on your head."

Athos had already become more friendly, as if he was seldom taken seriously, even by Thonos, and these people were listening intently to every word.

So they talked through the afternoon and then they walked with the dancers to the dining room where the hired help were fed.

The food was surprisingly luxurious, and they found perhaps twenty more performers there with about an equal number of men and women.

Some would barely deign to nod in their direction, but Thonos and Athos supplied a steady commentary on what each of the performers did and how they seemed to be received by the audience.

"That short man is Neddo, and I believe he will be the next to go," said Thonos.

"He sings sad songs, and he still doesn't seem to understand that the Therans like only sad songs when the final verse resolves the feeling of loss."

He spoke softly so as not to be overheard.

"I've seen a Tyrian singer beaten for such songs, and Neddo will probably be gone within the week.

Draik is fair with us, but he knows that his business depends upon satisfied customers."

Draik sent one of his stewards to the entertainers' quarters early the next morning for a quick meeting with those who would be performing the next evening in the mansion of an important government official.

He gave them the order in which they were to appear and instructed the lead act and the concluding act as to how they should start and end the evening.

He directed not a word to Orfeo and Clarice, although he had mentioned when they were to appear.

Orfeo stopped the older man who was to precede them and tried to engage him in a conversation about his act.

At first he seemed suspicious, but eventually stopped long enough to tell them that he was a teller of stories, both funny and sad.

The implication was that other story tellers could only be expected to specialize in one type of story.

"What difference does it make what I tell?" said the man, who identified himself as the Egyptian Samwel.

"We want to avoid beginning our act with something that runs contrary to the mood of your act," said Clarice.

"We would like to blend with what comes before rather than interrupt the momentum."

"So you wish to profit from the mood I have set," Samwel shot back suspiciously.

"You'll just have to wait and see what I do and then I challenge you to match it"

Obviously he had no intention of cooperating, which left them without a plan, but Thonos had overheard the exchange, and he invited them to the room he shared with Athos.

"His act is exactly the same week in and week out, and everyone in town has heard every story he has to tell and everyone knows how they end."

"We just wanted to begin with something that doesn't break a mood that's already been established," said Clarice.

"His last story ends with the death of an innocent fair maiden, and the first several times one hears the story it's quite sad, but really, he's driven it into the ground.

He tells of finding a young girl drowned by the side of a lake, and he has an actual girl lie at his feet as he grieves.

Of course she's his one true love, and he soon goes off to spend the rest of his life in mourning, while the girl crawls off hoping not to be noticed."

Athos walked in as Thonos's account was ending.

"We've heard the same story at least fifty times, and now the audience yawns while he tells it."

Orfeo asked about the girl and her costume, and he and Clarice returned to their room for a final rehearsal and preparations for the show, which would take place in a mansion only about a ten minute walk away.

At dusk all the performers could be seen trudging slowly uphill to a house even grander than that occupied by Draik.

Most were carrying bags of costumes or props.

The show began with a small group of lively, kinetic dancers from Crete, who seemed both graceful and acrobatic.

Obviously these performers far outclassed those Orfeo and Clarice had seen in Syracuse.

They both had misgivings about what they planned to do, but when they went on stage they began as planned, each watching for audience reaction.

Samwel had ended with his hero standing by the side of what was supposed to represent a lake calling forlornly to his lost lover Chloe.

Orfeo began their own act looking very much like Samwel, with Clarice lying in the lake.

He called with a sad voice that now had descended into parody.

"Chloe, Chloe, where art thou my Chloe?"

Soon he slumped forlornly away just as Clarice pulled herself up out of the water with a disgusted grunt.

"Now where did that useless man go?"

She asked, eliciting almost a gasp from the audience. She wondered whether she should continue as planned, but launched herself into it.

"I call for help over and over again, but all he can do is look sad."

By now there were the first titters from the audience.

"You would think he would jump in and rescue me, but no.

He's afraid of ruining his best clothes."

More giggling, at times breaking into open laughter.

"So I manage to swim to shore, and I see him walking away feeling sorry for himself."

Now the laughter began to increase.

"Who needs him?"

She gestured rudely.

"I'll find myself a better man."

The noise of applause and laughter was now deafening.

At this point Orfeo appeared looking like a young hero.

He sang one of his tenderest love songs, and the two trotted off obviously intent upon becoming lovers. Their debut was successful, and the rest of their show was greeted warmly by an audience that had somehow heard an admirable chord struck by the newcomers. Don't stand around wailing, but live to enjoy another day.

Samwel was waiting for them when they returned, and, not surprisingly, he was furious.

"You ruined my act," he sputtered.

"It's unprofessional to satirize another performer.

I'll complain to Draik and have you thrown out."

"We asked for cooperation, and you refused," said Orfeo.

"But it's not too late.

Starting tomorrow we can work together with these old stories and all of us can profit from it."

The concept was alien to Samwel, but he seemed to think it over.

They talked long into the night and finally came up with other ways that could spice up his act with contributions by both Orfeo and Clarice, at times with her adding emphasis to his narrative with flourishes on the drums, and Orfeo could give him accompaniment on the lyre.

Samwel gradually warmed to the idea, and when they tried it the next night, all were satisfied.

They had performed the function of entertainers in that they truly entertained.

People laughed, and at times when there was real pathos, they were moved even to tears.

By their third show they had been changed to second from the last, a spot usually reserved for the best acts.

Draik seemed delighted.

"You've even given new life to that old bore Samwel," he said as he circulated among the performers prior to yet another show at another grand house.

And tonight, in their fifth appearance before Theran nobility, it was clear that word of their performances had circulated among those who cared about such things, and there was anticipation. Orfeo could feel it in the hush that preceded his last song, a paean to heroism and self-sacrifice that was identical to what he had sung before guests in Pylos, only here he knew that it meant something different - perhaps more profound - to those for whom self-sacrifice was an obligation. They liked the tribute the song paid to this part of their lives, and the ovation was the most enthusiastic they had yet received.

In her own right, Clarice had become known for her biting wit and irony.

She performed sleight of hand tricks and then told the audience they had not really seen what they thought they saw.

She formed a bantering give and take relationship with those who watched her, and she was becoming a crowd favorite.

As Clarice and Orfeo came to understand their role in elite Theran society, as entertainers for those who neither worked nor labored intensely at the task of governing, they were celebrities of a sort, and, according to Draik, everyone spoke of them with favor.

It was only a matter of time until the king himself requested their presence.

In the meantime Draik was as good as his word in paying them half of the money he collected from his clients, minus a few minor administrative costs.

Clearly Draik was wealthy and upwardly mobile, but Orfeo could sense that he was not actually a member of that class his players entertained.

If all went well his son and daughter, who were now eight and ten years old, would eventually become members of the true aristocracy of Thera.

And Theran society, despite several peculiar quirks, did not seem so evil to either Clarice of Orfeo.

Certainly it could be harsh on those who failed to carry out their tasks, but the two had seen nothing yet that would seem to justify Zurga's insistence that the Therans represented a threat to civilization itself.

The streets were safe and orderly.

When they went to the bazaar, they dealt with honest merchants.

There were no beggars, apparently no criminals, and nothing of the sense of tight security Zurga accused the Therans of imposing upon Kalamatta.

Of course in the heart of the empire itself there was no need for spies and the arrest of people on suspicion of being spies.

Walking down the street in Thera was much like walking around Pylos in the carefree days of Orfeo's life there as a hostage.

The difference was that Thera was more orderly, cleaner, with more beautiful public buildings.

Even the smells were more wholesome, except on days when the volcano emitted an oddly sulfurous aroma.

Other days there was no trace of Vulcan's hearth within, and the sky was clear and nourishing.

Of course there were the occasional rumblings of the earth - also thought to relate to Vulcan's toil in working metal - although at times it rattled the dishes and made the taller buildings sway.

Then before their next program at the home of a wealthy trader, there was a joyous announcement.

The Theran fleet had attacked the evil, traitorous city of Pylos, where peaceful Theran envoys had been slaughtered without warning.

The announcement was accompanied by what was an unquestioning assumption that a victory would soon follow.

It also reminded Orfeo that since he had taken part in this atrocity, his true identity had best not be exposed to the Therans, who were not known for their ability to forgive.

# CHAPTER TWENTY-TWO

For the next week there was no news of the war, which to Orfeo meant that perhaps Zurga's idea of mounting great catapults around the harbor had accomplished something.

But it could also be the result of the well known Theran habit of not committing to a military engagement until the odds were overwhelmingly in its favor.

The one item that suggested the possibility of a Theran reversal was that Draik quickly commissioned a ship he had been building.

Orfeo learned of this by accident, as he was conferring with his employer when the latter was interrupted by a messenger saying that the king required the warship being built with Draik's own resources must be made ready to sail by the next day, and it was expected to help the situation that had emerged in Pylos.

Perhaps a dozen sentences had been exchanged between Draik and the king's messenger, and most of it had been praise for Draik for his patriotic gesture of contributing a warship to the nation's effort.

Yet Draik was obviously unhappy about the visit, and he made an unguarded remark to Orfeo that he would not have ventured had he known it could be interpreted correctly.

"When success is not achieved, there always must be someone of lower rank to make an extra sacrifice."

He sounded less upbeat than usual, but then he smiled at one of the positive entries on his balance sheet.

There was no question that Orfeo was making him money, as the new act seemed to have had an invigorating effect on the whole, and Draik's players were in enormous demand.

Indeed, next week they would even be performing before the king and his court, many of whom had already seen Draik's entertainers at other private homes.

In the meantime it was one triumphant evening after another, and Orfeo knew that with the practice he was getting his voice was becoming ever stronger and smoother.

His way of injecting emotion into his sound, in addition to whatever message the lyrics carried, seemed not to have been common in Thera, but it quickly became popular.

During the daytime Clarice and Orfeo walked into the town and bought supplies at the bazaar.

For the most part this was a cover for a search Orfeo had instituted for Herron, and this part of his task appeared to be easier than he had imagined.

While the galley slaves were all kept chained to their ship when they were in foreign ports, there was much less need for security while the ships were in Thera.

After all, where could an escaping slave run?

He could have no friends among the Therans, who would make a concerted effort to catch anyone so rash.

The penalty for such a transgression would almost certainly be death, and thus one saw a number of slaves around town, running errands for their masters or even walking about when they had no duties as oarsmen.

Thus thousands of slaves passed before Orfeo's eyes, and every day he saw at least one who seemed to be an Achian, although there were no familiar faces, and he dared not risk approaching a slave who might report him for suspicious behavior.

Oddly enough some slaves seemed to be able to acquire enough money to buy small items in the bazaar.

Others spent time in the wine houses, where they were not allowed to beg, but at times seemed to have enough money to do moderate drinking.

As for getting closer to the boats, however, Orfeo decided that this would be a last resort only, as even here in their home port they were closely guarded.

There was also always a strong chance that if Herron were truly a galley slave he would even now be participating in the war against Pylos.

So while Orfeo's search was diligent and occupied part of every day, he had little hope that it would be successful.

In the meantime he was adding to the sum of money that Zurga had given him to use as ransom, although this also seemed problematic.

There was a legalistic strain among the Therans that seemed to insist that a slave became a slave because of something he had done - resulting from some guilt that was often poorly defined - and if the Theran belief system were to be defended, then it must rest upon the insistence that everyone enslaved had deserved it, and therefore it would be wrong to ransom a slave or to allow someone else to purchase his freedom.

One could sell a slave to someone who planned to use him as a slave, but presumably not to set him free.

Orfeo and Clarice obviously had no need of a slave and as non-citizens of Thera would not even be allowed to own someone who had already been identified as a slave of Thera.

The system was thus complex, but ultimately slanted against the idea of being able to legally rescue Herron.

And legality was the crux of Theran behavior.

The other issue revolved around how one could leave the island with a slave that had decided to escape.

While various wealthy Therans owned large ships, anything suitable for warfare theoretically could be requisitioned by the navy at any time.

During the war outgoing trading ships were carefully inspected to see that no slaves were escaping, and incoming boats were searched for stowaways, all of whom were assumed to be spies and executed on the spot.

Thus if Orfeo came across Herron in the bazaar and said that he had come to rescue him, just what could he have been expected to arrange.

He almost certainly would not be allowed to purchase him, and there would be no readily accessible means of getting to the mainland.

So he looked without much hope of success, but the effort at least gave him the impression that he was trying his best.

On the fifth week of their performances on Thera, Orfeo and Clarice were waiting for the show to begin at one of the grander houses when a representative of the king interrupted the festivities just after they had started with what he described as news from the battle front.

"Our ships and fighting men on land are achieving heroic victories and are teaching the treacherous men of Pylos that attacks on Therans have only one possible outcome.

They are punished by death of the perpetrators and enslavement of their families.

But in order to achieve an even more overwhelming victory, we are asking that yet greater efforts be made to organize battalions of older men who have already been through our rigorous military training.

While this may deplete some of your businesses of able-bodied help, it will in the long run help us all by bringing the war to a speedier conclusion."

The oration continued for perhaps another twenty minutes, but Orfeo understood - or at least thought he understood - that the battle against Pylos on both sea and land was not moving forward with quite the anticipated success.

Something was going wrong, and the citizenry was being asked to make sacrifices, a request they all seemed to take in stride.

There was mention of Draik's unselfish contribution to the effort in sending one of the largest Theran vessels ever built to crush the defense of Pylos.

The impresario appeared briefly and was cheered.

That night Orfeo and Clarice laced their act with a greater than usual content of patriotic songs and ballades of heroic deeds.

Samwel told a few war stories that no one seemed to have heard before.

Thonos and Athos danced a battle in which Therans mercilessly cut down the evil men of Pylos and the treacherous Lakonians.

The next day Orfeo recognized an Achian slave in the bazaar.

He was purchasing new sandals to replace some that had completely worn out, and he pretended to strike up a conversation about different types of sandals until they could walk together down one of the less busy streets.

"You look like an Achian and sound like one," Orfeo began.

"Now I am no more than a Theran slave," the other replied, obviously reluctant to say anything that might get him punished.

Orfeo recognized the man from before the time he was given up as a hostage, but he assumed the latter could not recognize him in his adult form.

"I am from Kiros's tribe," Orfeo added.

"And I've heard some strange rumors that Kiros's heir, Herron, was kidnapped, sold into slavery, and now mans the oars of a Theran warship."

He delivered the information as no more than idle gossip about which he had only a passing curiosity.

"And what interest is that to you?"

The man was still suspicious.

"No real interest, but I find it an amusing rumor."

He must deliver the next question cautiously. "Have you heard it?"

"I have heard it," the man answered after looking around to see whether they were being watched.

"Is it true?"

Orfeo had now committed himself.

"How would I know, as I'm not the kind to spread rumors, but I've heard he's at the oars of a boat fighting the navy of Pylos."

"Then he'll be back when we've achieved our victory," said Orfeo.

"The Therans will surely crush the men of Pylos."

They each headed in separate directions, aware that they had exchanged information in a manner the Theran authorities would consider an offense against the public good, but they had probably not been observed.

Clarice and Orfeo always exchanged their confidences in whispers after the lights were extinguished at night, and he informed her of what he had learned.

"When we first came here, I felt that what Nadahr and Zurga had said about the Therans was wrong and that they had placed everything in the worst possible light, but now I am becoming fearful again," Clarice said. "They are treating us very well and paying us more than we would earn any other place in the world, but I have the impression that with the first slip, we could instantly be ordered to death.

It is as if they value their society, but no individual human life."

"Evil takes many forms, and sometimes it masquerades under the guise of the law.

I am beginning to feel less safe."

"You must take no chances," she cautioned.

"Without your protection I would be helpless."

After two days of no performances, they were again performing their patriotic numbers to great applause.

Again a messenger from the king stood before the crowd and announced great victories.

"The armies we command on land, which include some troops of our allies of Kalamatta, have inflicted a stunning defeat on a pathetic army raised by the Lakonians.

This army consisted of little more than bandits who had been impressed into Lakonian service to aid their allies the evil men of Pylos, killers of our diplomats. At sea our invincible ships have crushed virtually all the navy of Pylos, with the loss of life of over ten thousand of their sailors.

The victorious forces of Thera march on to greater glories."

After that the songs had made specific reference to the victories, but at the end of the performance Draik seemed disconsolate, reacting as though he had suddenly heard grave tiding with reference to himself.

Clarice, who had always found him warm and supportive, tried to cheer him up, but he seemed worried as they walked back toward his mansion.

"The war may go well for the others," he said.

"But for me it is not so fortunate."

He seemed to hesitate, lest he say something that could be interpreted as disloyal, thus deepening his trouble. "The great quadruple tiered warship I financed and had built to the most up-to-date specifications has ...

" He hesitated as if not even wishing to think about what had happened.

"In an effort to break through the harbor of Pylos, it led a charge and within minutes was hit by an enormous stone hurled by their catapults.

It must have been only a lucky shot, but the boat sank within minutes, and less than half of the crew was saved.

It was a disaster, and I fear there will be punishments."

"But who could they punish?" Clarice asked.

"Surely you were doing your patriotic duty in sending the ship, but perhaps they could hold the captain responsible."

"The captain was my younger brother, and he was killed." Draik seemed suffused with dread. "They could see me as a harbinger of ill luck."

He looked at them apparently aware that they were concerned for his welfare.

"Don't worry, if something happens to me, you will always have a place in Thera.

You're probably the most popular act in town at the moment."

By the next evening he seemed to have recovered from his pessimism, and they performed at the home of the king's chief minister.

As usual before the first act there was an announcement, this time by the minister himself, that all was moving forward as planned in the great mainland war.

He took time to point out that the conflict had been brought about by Pylos and its allies, as they had been preparing an invasion of Thera.

"Those evil men have for years coveted our prosperity, and they knew there was only one way to achieve it.

They planned craftily to steal it all from us, and so we must all understand that our war is one of self defense.

It is absolutely necessary that we triumph to preserve our homeland and our way of life.

We must also use this period of national renewal to seek out those among us who have brought us ill fortune.

We must return to the worship of our god Vulcan, and we must walk forward with strength and virtue."

Of course everyone greeted such an announcement as though it actually entailed wisdom and piety. But within those words was an implicit threat against those who were somehow responsible for a campaign that had so far been described as a triumph, but which now was beginning to sound like a looming disaster.

The performance that night lacked a certain sparkle, although Orfeo compensated by adding more patriotic songs.

His voice seemed more clarion pure than ever, and the audience now greeted him like a beloved institution.

"Orfeo, I'm afraid."

That night she clung to him with an unusual outburst of worry.

"It sounds as though the war goes badly for them, which is what I strongly hope, but if they lose, I suspect there will be bloody times here.

It's the kind of time when a people turns against foreigners and blames them for anything that has gone wrong."

"We must find a way to leave," he said.

"I too fear what is happening, and it seems that Herron - if he still lives - is not in Thera.

The next day Orfeo drifted among the ships moored at the docks and wondered how he could get passage for himself and Clarice.

He was aware that commerce with other parts of the inland sea was still a reality, as various foodstuffs and luxury goods remained in demand.

Foreign workers were still coming to Thera, and every day ships left for distant ports.

But from what Orfeo could tell the boarding of these ships was carefully controlled and seemed to require passes provided by local authorities.

For all Orfeo knew he could simply purchase passage, as they were then earning more money than they had ever imagined from their act.

But then again an attempt to leave could well result in the arrest of both himself and Clarice.

# Chapter Twenty-Three

The next day something happened that seemed to freeze everything in place.

Early in the morning, before anyone in the household was out of bed, a platoon of the king's soldiers had arrested Draik and had taken him off to the palace dungeon.

There was, of course, nothing to be done about it.

One did not argue with the king's guards, nor was there any appeal from his justice.

The players, all lodged in the basement level of the mansion, could nevertheless hear the wailing of the women upstairs, and clearly they were anticipating the worst.

Thonos and Athos were both agitated, and neither seemed able to maintain a coherent train of thought.

"They'll execute him and then come for us," Athos said.

"But they don't destroy valuable possessions of those who they find to be bringers of bad fortune," Thonos answered with an effort to keep his voice from showing complete panic.

"Remember, my dear friend, that we are valuable."

He turned to Clarice and Orfeo, who were standing in the hallway in front of their rooms.

"You are also valuable, and you will not be destroyed."

He seemed not entirely convinced.

None of the performers stirred much that day, and Draik's steward, who acted as Master of Entertainers, appeared after the noon meal.

"No performance tonight," he said, and then he tried to slip back upstairs without giving any more of an explanation as to what was happening, but one of the larger dancers had already blocked the stairs.

"We need to know what will happen to us." Thonos had taken on a demanding tone.

The Master turned angrily upon those who sought to impede his exit.

"Worry more about what is happening to Counselor Draik, as your fate depends upon his.

If he is found guilty as charged, then all of his possessions, including his contracts for your services, will be divided up among the royal family."

"But will they continue to pay us as Draik did?"

"That depends upon who ends up with your contracts," said the Master.

"You could continue your employment on its current basis, you could be sent back to your lands of origin, or you could be reduced to the rank of slaves.

It is all up to the magistrates today, and they will hear the case in the forum two hours after mid-day."

He would say no more, and a clamor arose from the performers.

There was talk about going to the forum to hear what was transpiring, and this seemed like a reasonable move, although Orfeo thought it best to dress as closely as possible like citizens of Thera - with covered hair and their best clothes - and go separately from the other performers.

"It's what I've been fearing," said Clarice.

"I now understand the evil of this place, which is all beneath the surface and is more inhuman than even Zurga and Nadahr understand.

They make themselves look so much like the rest of us on the surface, and yet their ways allow for no loyalty between citizens, but only to the king."

"I wish the best for Draik," Orfeo said.

"He's been fair to us and I believe he is a good man, but he is a part of a corrupt system."

As the streets became more crowded the closer they came to the forum, they grew silent, not wishing to be overheard.

It appeared as though a large portion of the city had turned out for the public hearing, although the nature of their interest was not immediately apparent.

Finally they got to a place where they could both see the priests standing before the temple that overlooked the great square.

The figure in chains stood a platform beneath them.

"They're not going to release him, are they," said Clarice.

"This isn't a trial, it's an announcement."

At about that time the chief among the priests, dressed in robes of a brighter green than those worn by envoys traveling abroad, began to speak.

His voice was full of contempt, and he gestured toward Draik as he would to an animal.

"We have inflicted great pain and loss upon our enemies on the northern shore of the inland sea.

But they have been saved at times from total annihilation by some intervention of the gods, and it was not difficult to see that the reason came from right here in Thera.

In our midst we had a doubter and a traitor who sought to curry favor with the king by building at his expense a great quadreme that he boasted would overcome the enemy's resistance.

But you all know what happened."

There was a shout from the crowd suggesting that at least they had a good idea that something about Draik had brought disaster to the ship.

"Our protector, Vulcan, gave us a signal that our citizen Draik was not a virtuous and devout man.

Our protector personally sank the ship that Draik had sent to war, giving an unambiguous signal that he was the fatal flaw in our plans, the ingredient that has so far stood in the way of the success we know will come.

But we have a responsibility to thank the god for his warning and to appease his wrath by punishing this rotten, cowardly, unbelieving traitor among us.

The only remedy for the ill fortune that has so far befallen our invading forces is death to the traitor."

Again the crowd erupted in a great outpouring of venom aimed at the cowering figure in chains. There could be no doubt they wanted his blood."

"Do we know the manner of this death?"

The priest roared confidently, aware that he held the will of the crowd in his hands.

"In Vulcan's hearth," the crowd roared as if with one voice.

And they repeated the chant over and over.

"That must mean he'll be thrown into the volcano," whispered Orfeo.

"Do you have anything to say for yourself, you miserable traitor.

Are there any last words before the priests lead you up the mountain and throw you into the hearth."

The crowd was slow to become quiet enough to hear the reply, but Draik finally shouted his answer for all to hear.

Instead of the outraged defiance Orfeo hoped to hear, he began with a plea for forgiveness.

"I was led astray by my ambitions," he shouted. "And all the guilt rests with me alone.

I have been served loyally by many good Therans, who know nothing of my treachery and insolence toward Vulcan's will.

I ask that my wife and family forgive my lack of piety, and I ask that the people of Thera see them as blameless.

I also request the favor of being able to throw myself into the fiery hearth to save these good priests the need to touch my miserable body.

I deserve nothing more than a painful, lingering death."

The crowd seemed doubtful for a moment, but cries arose suggesting that it was only fitting that he jump of his own accord to better expiate his sin.

The priests responded with acceptance, reminding all the assembled citizens that Draik had taken the entire guilt of the slowness of the Theran victory upon himself.

"We will take him to the holy place on the mountain and allow him to take his own life," the chief priest sounded satisfied and just slightly forgiving of Draik's sins, so long as they would quickly be washed away by fire.

The priests disappeared with their captive and called for the citizens to witness.

"He's a good man," Clarice whispered.

"He's done for us what he said and more."

"This is an evil place," said Orfeo.

"He is being made the scapegoat for failure, and he has confessed all in the hope that he can save his family and retainers from carrying some of the guilt themselves."

"I don't want to see the execution," she said, turning back toward the mansion where they had now lived for nearly two months.

"We can only return there and await word of what will happen to us," he said.

"Draik's contract for our services must be worth something when the king and priests divide up his possessions."

And so disconsolately and disillusioned they trudged back up the hill and awaited further word.

It was then that Orfeo most regretted that he had not yet found an escape route, and Draik's death would probably make the task all the more difficult.

The next morning no word had yet come, although Clarice and Orfeo listened to an account from the entertainers who had followed the crowd to the great volcano that lay no more than a several hour walk from the city.

They described Draik's dramatic leap into a cauldron that seemed to emit great clouds of foul-smelling smoke as he ended his life, which the priests described as Vulcan's acceptance of the sacrifice but his distaste at having such a wretch thrown into his hearth.

"So what about us?"

Samwel moaned.

"I fear we'll meet the same fate when the priests realize we were favored by Draik."

Of course that was the real concern of the group, and neither Orfeo not Clarice heard a single word spoken in praise of the man who had treated them well and enriched several of them.

It was as if he had never existed.

Later that night, after having heard nothing more, the performers drifted off to the rooms before a series of rumblings troubled the sleep of many that night.

It was not the noise so much as the shaking or the lurching of the earth, as some described it later.

For some reason the volcano was unusually active that night, and in the morning several described it as a sign from Vulcan that the sacrifice had been accepted and that Draik's death had appeased him.

Yet the shaking continued throughout the day and actually became worse in the afternoon.

Earthquakes were not unusual on the island, and the Therans had turned a positive light on it.

Of course they built their houses to withstand moderate rumblings, but no real damage - in the memory of the inhabitants - had ever resulted in injury or death.

The quaking was thus seen as something benevolent, as if it gave them a special closeness and an intimate relationship with their god, who was surely greatest in the pantheon.

He had, indeed, taught them metallurgy, a skill that had made them masters of much of the mainland and would eventually make them masters of the earth.

As many Therans had a profound belief in their destiny, they knew that no harm could come from the volcano, providing they live lives free of blasphemy and sin.

Just after one of the worst outbreaks of rumbling, a representative of the king arrived with Draik's Master of Entertainers, and he seemed to bear no ill will toward any of them.

"I congratulate you and welcome you to the service of the king," he began.

"The council has decided that the household of your former master will be absorbed by the king's household, and all of his possessions will now belong to the king.

The contracts he holds with you as entertainers will be honored, but the master here will now report directly to the royal chamberlain.

You will continue to live here, as members of the king's family will move into the house, and the family of the former owner will move to the palace."

No one said anything until after he left, and the old Master of Entertainers assured them all that he had been allowed to keep his job and would manage them in the same way as before.

Their next performance would be on the very next evening in the royal palace, where they would be assessed as to value and told whether they would be reassigned elsewhere.

"What has happened to the Counselor Draik's wife," one of the dancers asked.

It was an impertinent question, but the master answered with more than a twinkle in his eye.

"She has graciously consented to be one of the king's wives," he said.

"I thought a cat always landed on its feet rather than its back," one of the storytellers said softly, although everyone heard it.

"It has yet to be determined how many of us will stay on our feet," the master said as if warning one and all not to become complacent.

"The king is not known to tolerate insolence or ineptitude, and some of us may be demoted to more menial tasks."

Was it a hint that their status had changed so dramatically that they could be seen now as slaves of the king.

"I like it not," whispered Orfeo to Clarice.

"The more we know of Thera, the more its evil is obvious." she answered.

"I must make a final search for Herron and then find a way to get us to safety.

We have already done all that is humanly possible to find him."

He walked down into the bazaar as it opened again from its mid-afternoon break, and he bought several fine woolen scarves for Clarice.

Once past the last stalls of the market he turned toward the docks, where he saw several merchant ships that had recently arrived, but they all were guarded by king's soldiers.

Security was tightening perhaps for the very purpose of preventing escapes, but the people of Thera truly had no place to go.

They would be welcomed no place on the mainland where Theran armies fought and the navy blockaded the ports.

He heard rumors that injured galley slaves had been brought back to Thera for treatment of their wounds, but he had no way to find them.

Back at Draik's old palace he and Clarice planned how they would perform before the royal court, which involved no real changes, as they knew that those connected with the court had attended many of their performances in the great houses of the city.

Still it was obvious that the other performers were edgier than usual and played a more conservative kind of program, with no risque humor and even more restrained costumes.

Again Orfeo and Clarice had been held for next to last, and tonight things came together from their very first appearance on stage.

They were warmly greeted as though already well known, and each of their numbers seemed to strike just the right chord.

The patriotic songs were received better than ever before, and Orfeo's final lament for a lost love found him at his most vocally resplendent.

His voice carried pathos and the pain of heartbreak.

He had never done better, and as his gaze rose from his final bow, he started directly into the eyes of Princess Zaide, whom, fortunately, he had not noticed sitting several places away from the king.

How fortunate that he had finished the performance, as he felt his knees suddenly weaken and his heart begin to race.

She was more stunningly beautiful than ever, and she was looking appreciatively at him.

Her eyes seemed to find their way to the far corners of his soul, and she moved not a muscle in applause but seemed to transmit a sense that she was aware of him and liked what she saw.

Then it was over as he ran off the stage to be replaced by the dancers.

The contact had lasted five seconds at the most, but he felt as though he would never be the same. If she had asked him that moment if he would stay in Thera forever, he would have agreed.

He did not wish to fantasize on what else he would have agreed to.

# Chapter Twenty-Four

Orfeo knew that thoughts of Princess Zaide would only undermine his effectiveness at his real task of getting himself and Clarice to safety more than it did rescuing Herron, which was probably an impossibility even if he were still alive.

Yet he thought about the princess during the day, and Clarice, who almost certainly had not noticed Zaide any more than she had focused upon anyone in the audience, mentioned that he seemed preoccupied.

She asked him what he was so concerned about, but he could not think of a way to answer that would not bring her pain, and so he evaded her questions.

By now Orfeo fully recognized that Clarice had developed special feelings for him, and although he had never stopped to clarify his own feelings while they were both in so much danger, he sensed that the strong reaction the princess brought forth would bring pain to Clarice. In the afternoon he decided it was best to make another trip to the bazaar rather than sit uselessly in their room and feel confused.

Perhaps he would finally find Herron, and they would have an excuse to focus all their attention on leaving.

He was walking through the bazaar toward the docks when he nearly tripped over an old man who quietly asked him for a spare coin to purchase a cup of ale at the nearby tavern.

Since begging was forbidden by law, he was taking a chance, but it happened that Orfeo had not carried coins with him, and he told the poorly dressed creature that he could not help.

"Then I'll buy you a cup of ale, young Achian, and I'll bet I can guess your name and your father's name."

There was something familiar in the voice, although the appearance was like no one he knew. Then he realized that it was none other than Zurga, who should not have been on the island at all.

Orfeo - fearful that they had already come to the attention of spies - agreed to take the ale, and the two went through the motions of exchanging names and getting acquainted. It was probably better to meet in public rather than in some secretive way, although a gathering as large as the fifty-odd people in the tavern would almost certainly include several who would pass on anything suspicious to the security monitors.

Until the barmaid brought their cups, they spoke only in generalities, but as the noise level rose in the establishment, Zurga began in a soft voice to bring him up to date on what was happening in Pylos and surrounding territories.

"The war has not yet produced a victory for either side," he said.

"My great catapults on the sea wall have kept the larger Theran ships from entering the harbor, but they maintain a steady blockade.

King Linaeus has not ventured out with any of his weaker warships, which are being held in reserve for a surprise attack."

"There have been all kinds of victory claims here, but they are growing less boastful.

They know the outcome is not assured."

"Any word of Herron?" Zurga asked.

"I'm about to give up and head back to the mainland.

I've learned for certain that he's been kept as a galley slave, but he's either in one of the ships blockading Pylos or dead.

And we cannot allow ourselves to feel too secure here."

"I understand you're a great favorite with the ladies, both young and old.

Your fame as a singer has spread throughout the island in a short time."

"The only one I worry about is Clarice, for whose safety I am responsible."

"If Herron is truly lost, it is best that your father have one heir rather than none."

Zurga spoke even more softly.

"You had best leave while you can."

"You know I can never be king of people who see me as an outsider."

"You may have noticed by now that life takes many strange turns."

"What are you doing here?"

Orfeo wished to change the subject.

"Nadahr and I both signed on as healers to care for the wounded.

The Therans were recruiting in Kalamatta, and we just happened to be there, but we have other plans that are not related to healing so much as destruction."

He glanced around.

"Best not even to hint at what might happen."

"Do you have a way back?"

"If we are successful there will be no way back for us," he said.

"But I've lived a long and useful life.

I've walked this earth for nearly ninety summers, and I fear my time is coming to an end."

"So you'll leave without ever training me in the wisdom you may have.

Or perhaps the wisdom is only an illusion."

"Tell the Theran sailors who died under my catapults that it is only an illusion."

"I have only your word about the catapults," said Orfeo.

"It's that spark of humor that gives me hope for you," said Zurga.

"You've been doubting my wisdom since the first evening we met, but I know you respect my judgment and my ability to slightly shift the world's direction."

He drained the last of his ale and seemed to be preparing himself to leave.

"You have learned much from me already - which you will only recognize after I am gone - and I have much I can still teach you.

But we have never had the time.

We have been on the run since we left the Achian camp."

"Don't let go of your life until you've taught me more," Orfeo said.

"Selfish as ever," said Zurga. "I can't promise survival, but I won't sell my life cheap."

He walked away as though there had been no more than casual conversation between them, and Orfeo remained another few moments before he left and began walking along the docks and focusing his attention on how he and Clarice could escape.

He noticed that there was a great Theran warship moored where there had been none yesterday, and he realized that it had been torn dreadfully asunder at the bow so that it was barely seaworthy.

Perhaps one of Zurga's great catapults had struck, necessitating the ship's return to port for repairs.

Was it possible that Herron was on board?

He walked past as near as he could get several times, but there was no way he could tell who was still chained below to the oars, and he knew that he would arouse suspicion should he linger longer. When he got back to the palace that had formerly belonged to Draik, he was greeted by Thonos and Athos, who were full of news about the palace's new owners.

"It now is inhabited by the king's brother, who will be in charge of entertainments, and we are under his direction, but officially our contracts belong to the king."

Thonos seemed worried, but covered it with ceaseless chatter.

"And we must perform tonight right here for our new masters," groaned Athos, as though he expected an ordeal they could not survive.

Could this be the brother who was father to Princess Zaide? Orfeo inwardly knew that it must be, but he could not tell whether such news would be favorable or fatal to him.

Part of him wished that Zaide would be living in this very palace, and yet he knew that it could place dangerous temptations within his path and that he would more likely be harmed than helped by it.

He did not even know for certain whether he would be able to talk with her.

He found Clarice in their room doing stretching exercises, and she had already heard about their new masters.

"Everyone believes that Murgon is even more of a tyrant than his brother, King Sargon," she said. "Perhaps it is already too late to leave."

"We must find a way," Orfeo answered, and he whispered to her about his meeting with Zurga and the latter's agreement that they must leave.

"We'll get some idea of where we stand tonight," she said.

And, indeed, all went unexpectedly well for most of the performers that evening.

Again most of them emphasized patriotism and the great gift of an advanced civilization that Thera had given to the world.

Apparently Therans were never bored by praise, and by the time Orfeo and Clarice appeared, this time scheduled last on the program, the audience was obviously in a good mood.

Orfeo strode forward with his usual appearance of confidence, but when he saw Princess Zaide sitting beside her father on a raised platform, he felt his knees weaken.

She was radiant, even more striking than when he had seen her during those memorable seconds in Kalamatta.

And he felt her eyes upon him.

He knew it was not his imagination.

So he began with the patriotic ballades, surprised that his voice was still rich and secure despite his anxiety.

The show progressed to Clarice's comic magic tricks, which she had now learned to turn humorously upon herself.

While she announced that she would pull a pigeon from beneath her cloak, she ended up with a dog so large that it seemed impossible to have been concealed. She was greeted with great outbursts of laughter.

The same happened when she flew suspended from a wire that was invisible to the audience, but her path became tangled, and she ended up suspended upside down.

Orfeo, in the meantime interrupted each humorous debacle with a short song about the magician's great skill.

But the crowd was hushed when he began his final romantic ballad about a young man who has seen a beautiful goddess from afar and fallen under her spell so completely that he brings himself to an unhappy end for wanting the unwinnable.

It was not, of course, an original concept, but he brought it off with the performance of a lifetime, which Clarice subtly accented with her drum and various other percussion instruments she had come to master.

By the final bars he was prostrate on the floor, dying of a broken heart, but drawing tears even from hard-hearted Therans, who took pride in their ability to withstand a sad story unmoved.

Walking back to their quarters with the other performers they were congratulated by several of the others, who knew they had been well received.

They all gathered in the area where they were served their meals for a review of events and to share observations of their new masters.

There was a general optimism, probably based on the enthusiastic applause.

"They loved us," gushed Thonos.

Many others voiced optimism before the old Master of Entertainments appeared with a foreboding look.

He began by calling several names and then announcing that their services would no longer be needed.

"But what are we to do?" asked Samwel, who was one of the players whose contract had been terminated.

"Report to the king's labor pool for reassignment," said the master.

"They'll probably just send you back to your original home in Biblos," he said.

There were also those who were specifically told their contracts had been accepted. At last he turned to Orfeo and indicated that he was to follow him back upstairs for a conference.

Had he been recognized?

Were they suspicious?

Would he ever return?

He was so worried that it never occurred to him that the call from above might be positive, or at least have more pleasant implications.

There, waiting for him in a spacious, dimly-lit room with the sound of water running into a pool, sat Princess Zaide, more glorious than ever with her slender but voluptuous body and glistening black hair.

Her eyes seemed enormous, and her lips appeared disembodied as she spoke, as though they moved only from one enticing position to another.

"You please me, barbarian," she said, as if immediately emphasizing the social difference between them.

"You bring to consciousness a deep longing that I seldom experience.

You are the only singer I have ever heard who could arouse strong feelings within."

Her words were still phrased in a manner as to suggest a vast gulf between them.

"How is it you have learned to make even a stony hearted princess weep?"

"Your majesty, I cannot but suspect that comparison to a stone falls far short of an accurate description.

I have always believed that among those who hear my music only those with the soul of a poet truly experience the feeling I hope to create."

Had he been too forward or not slavish enough?

He watched a succession of impulses flicker across her face.

"I have seen you before, have I not?" she asked after a long silence between them.

"I saw you last at the king's palace," he said.

"No, she answered firmly.

"It was before that, on the mainland.

Our eyes met."

"Yes," he began, not knowing where this would lead.

If he admitted to having seen her in Kalamatta could that not identify him as one of the six fugitives who had escaped.

"I saw you once in Kalamatta, but I cannot imagine you noticed me. I was merely a face in the crowd."

She smiled and nodded her head as if, indeed, she had seen and remembered those brief seconds.

"You looked in my direction when the others averted their eyes as they were told to do."

He knelt in front of her, not knowing whether he was now in serious trouble or had been singled out for special favor.

"I beg your forgiveness," he said.

"But it was a moment that has come back to my mind every day since then." He wondered how much he dared.

"I could describe every garment you wore that day."

Her laughter was like the silver bells of heaven, and she covered the lower part of her face with a small fan, as if to conceal a look she wished to hide.

"You are priceless," she said.

"I'm glad you're here, and I think we'll see more of each other."

She turned to leave and then faced him again.. "I wonder what was there about that short moment that we both remember?" she asked.

"Perhaps we may find out."

And then she was gone.

He had a difficult time finding his way back downstairs, and when he was there he encountered the other players still mulling over their change in status.

Some were disconsolate, and the question about their fates remained.

Was being asked to report to the king's labor pool essentially an assignment to slavery?

Samwel was obviously distraught, and others had begun to fret.

Orfeo found Clarice in their room, but she had not been able to sleep.

He told her that he had merely met with a member of the royal household, who had praised their act.

"We must leave here as soon as we can," she said.

"Now that we have a better understanding of Thera, we know that anything can happen even to innocent people."

She seemed to shudder.

"I've never been so frightened even when we faced death at the hands of all those Kalamattan soldiers."

Sleep came slowly that night, as the volcano rumbled incessantly.

Whether the Therans still thought that the increase in Vulcan's activity was a good sign was unclear, but it had become so frequent and was so ominous that it seemed constantly to intrude upon one's thoughts.

Indeed, could it be a signal of something worse?

But could Orfeo leave now that romantic fantasies had begun to form around a woman who had up to then seemed an impossible dream?

Was it possible that she had similar feelings toward him?

# CHAPTER TWENTY-FIVE

PERFORMANCES FOR THE NEXT TWO EVENINGS were at other mansions of other government officials, and Orfeo was disappointed each time he noticed that Princess Zaide was not there.

At times he wondered whether he had dreamed the whole encounter, and at other times his imagination carried him into flights of fantasy, constructing scenarios in which she felt an undying love for him.

He knew it was implausible, but he let his mind dwell on it.

He seemed preoccupied to Clarice, but she assumed it was related to his desire to find some way off the island, and on this issue they received some frightening news.

Samwel, the storyteller whose presence was no longer needed among the performers, had been reassigned to the king's labor pool, and apparently he had been told that he could not leave the island. As an able-bodied man in his forties he was thought to be able to work, and he had been assigned to a repair crew for one of the boats that had returned to port damaged by Zurga's great catapults, which had so far been able to keep the massive Theran ships from using their shorter range catapults that had sunk the navy of Kalamatta.

The fact that they could not enter the harbor of Pylos had kept them from winning the victory they were expecting.

A number of ships had been sunk, while others were forced to return to Thera for repairs.

But Samwel had interpreted his new assignment as a prelude to his being declared a simple slave, and apparently he had panicked.

Possibly he was right in his fear, but he had appeared at the docks and tried to bribe his way onto a merchant ship.

He was apprehended and - probably to set an example lest others try the same thing - he was beheaded on the spot.

Word spread quickly among the entertainers, none of whom had particularly liked Samwel, but all of whom consequently felt they had a greater burden of worry to carry around.

The Master of Entertainment announced that the next evening would be free, and Orfeo and Clarice took the opportunity again to visit the bazaar, which was usually a prelude to looking along the docks where the warships were being repaired and trying to find some trace of Herron.

At the same time they continued to search for a means of escape.

This time it was Clarice who was found by Zurga, as he did not wish to be seen twice within a short time talking to Orfeo.

"How can we leave?" she asked, after he had explained that he was working on an important project that could cause a great disruption on Thera.

"The harbor guards are checking everyone who boards a ship, as they suspect that spies from the mainland are here and will want to return to bring information to Pylos."

"But there must be a way, even if in a small fishing boat that could slip away at night."

"Nadahr and I have been looking for just such an opportunity and have found nothing promising.

Even the fishing boats are carefully monitored.

The Therans are thorough, and as their campaign hovers on the brink of failure, they are becoming more suspicious of outsiders, which makes it all the more imperative that you leave."

She asked about Nadahr and wondered whether she could see him, but Zurga only indicated that he was working night and day to prepare some powder made of bird droppings and sulfur, and he could not be disturbed.

"Tell him that I wish him well and am thankful for everything he did for me."

"Nadahr is a good man, but you made a good choice when you decided to accompany Orfeo," Zurga said just before he turned to disappear into the crowd.

But the afternoon and evening produced nothing that promised to help either in finding Herron or in getting off the island.

The next day Orfeo walked toward the volcano - which rumbled all night, although it had now stopped smoking - and then turned toward a small harbor to the west of the main Theran port where he hoped to find fishermen who might be able to help them leave the island, but he immediately saw that there were guards set up around the dock area and other men who were no doubt told to look for deserters, as they were now called.

Orfeo did not allow himself to be seen and hurried back the way he had come.

There would be no easy escape through the fishing fleet.

At one point on the way back to the port, Orfeo was nearly knocked to the ground by the earth's violent shaking, but it soon subsided, and yet he felt tense when he returned.

They had another performance that night, again in the mansion in which they lived, and he expected the princess to be there.

He had mixed feelings about seeing her again, as he realized that she had the power of life and death over him and at the same time held him emotionally in her spell.

Again he was tense as their act began, but they were still placed last on the program, which meant that they had delivered last time. He and Clarice had talked about making the act entirely different this time. They began with a new set of patriotic songs, now feeling secure enough to mention the men of Pylos by name along with slurs as to their parentage and moral character.

The better their reception was, the freer they felt in making the show into a paean to Theran superiority, which they could do with flawless technique as they were not hampered by feelings that any of it was true.

Such a deception fed upon itself.

But the finale of their performance always focused upon Orfeo's ballades of heart broken lovers, and much to his pleasure and chagrin, he noticed that princess Zaide had moved from her father's side and now sat as close to the performer's area as she could.

Her eyes were focused solely on him, and he felt a certain heat from her gaze, as if she owned part of his soul and could bring him pleasure or pain at will.

And yet the sensation filled him with a new kind of pleasure.

He had never felt more vulnerable, but had also never experienced such total euphoria.

The sensation brought a new understanding of his ballades, which in the past had been based more on theory than experience, although they had never ceased to communicate something of his soul.

And then it was over, and as he bowed, she threw him a single rose.

As he bent to pick it up, he was again nearly knocked from his feet as the earth moved, but he hardly noticed. Yet others in the audience looked worried, as a cascade of dust and powdered plaster rained down from the ceiling.

Was the instability of the earth becoming so serious that one should worry?

Was it a bad or good omen that since Draik's gruesome death, the hearth of Vulcan had become more active than anyone could recall from the past.

Yet he thought little of it as he saw the master waiting for him as they began to descend the stairs.

He signaled that Orfeo was to follow, and he indicated to Clarice that he would be back in their room soon.

He again followed, but instead of stopping by the pond, they walked to one of the far wings of the house, where a woman Orfeo had not seen before ushered him into a bath chamber that overlooked a lavishly decorated sleeping room.

He had been told to wait, and although he expected the princess to appear soon, he was still overwhelmed when she walked slowly into the room in a diaphanous dress that barely covered her torso and left her legs exposed in a manner that was particularly unusual for Thera.

"I can't believe how deeply your songs move me," she began as though discussing the weather. "And it occurred to me that maybe there has been something in your barbarian's life that is more exciting than what we civilized people here know as love."

She now stood close enough to reach out and touch him, and yet he did not move away.

"It is you who inspire me," he said.

"When you have been in the audience I have given the performances of my life because reality is a better inspiration than imagination."

He had learned the rhetoric of Isocles well, but never imagined that he would fall back upon it under such circumstances.

"You don't really sound like a barbarian," she said.

"But I'm told that the Achians are a people who don't even stay in cities and live from the textiles they make from wool."

She took his hands in hers.

"And yet your hands are soft, and your face is not weather beaten, and you look like a young god rather than a shepherd."

"Never have I been more flattered than to be compared to a god by a goddess," he answered, beginning to feel that he was losing all control, floating on an ever yielding bed of rose petals and lotus blossoms.

Could it be real?

Was she toying with him?

"I want you to spend the night here with me, and I want to wake up in sight of you in the morning."

She placed one arm around his neck and pulled his face toward hers.

"Do the Achians know how to kiss, or to they have some other way of showing affection.?"

He was guided by her touch, which he would not have resisted if he could, and the next minutes seemed to vanish in a blur of pleasure beyond even his imaginings.

"If I made you love me," she whispered with her lips close to his ear, "would you sing sad songs about your broken heart if I were to send you away."

"I could never sing again," he answered, perhaps even believing it at the time.

"And if I kept you with me from this day on."

"Then I would sing like a contented nightingale," he said.

"I would sing to break the hearts of lovers everyplace."

"Would you break my heart?"

"My own heart is yours to command."

"Would you become a Theran to stay with me?" she asked coyly.

"Can one who is not born a Theran ever truly become one?

"The king can do anything he wishes, and if I were to tell him that you would be a loyal subject, he would give the command and you would be a Theran."

"Then I would be eternally grateful to the king and would have a new homeland that would fit me better than the one of my birth."

"Could you stop being an Achian?"

"I stopped being one the moment I saw you," he said.

"That was odd," she said.

"I remember you clearly, and that's never happened to me before.

You looked directly into my eyes, and we seemed to say to each other that we would meet again under other circumstances."

Again the palace shook as it had earlier as his performance ended.

The stones from which the building was constructed seemed to scrape together and sing an agonized refrain.

"Does this happen often?" he asked.

"It's never happened before," she said.

"It's probably related to my passion and will cease when we are more accustomed to each other."

He watched for the trace of a smile.

"But what if it becomes stronger?"

"Let's find out," she answered demurely.

And the rumbling continued throughout the night, seemingly worse from hour to hour.

But he could not find the energy to worry about it.

He slept on a small bed arranged crosswise at the foot of her bed.

# CHAPTER TWENTY-SIX

ORFEO AWAKENED WITH A START, unaware of where he was and believing momentarily that he lay back in the entertainers' quarters on the bed next to Clarice.

Then the new realities flooded in upon him with a mixture of delight and pain.

He appreciated the wonderful creature who had enchanted his evening.

She was real, and he could see her sleeping form on the bed across the room; and yet she was the stuff of dreams.

But what of the loyal and loving Clarice, and what of his mission to rescue his brother?

What of Zurga and his announcement that he was intent upon destroying this island and, presumably, the princess along with it?

He knew he could not share with her any of his concerns, but this did not undermine his euphoria. He had found the most beautiful woman in the world, and she seemed to appreciate his finest qualities.

She stirred on her bed and faced him with a look of sheer delight on her face..

"Wake me with a song," she said with a kittenish purr, and he complied.

"I would like you to move your clothes here today," she said after he had finished.

"But what would your father think?

He would think you have taken up with a barbarian."

"He cares little how I amuse myself," she answered, as though that would explain it all.

"I told him that I would try to persuade you to keep me company, and he said I could have you."

There was something a trifle disconcerting about the remark, although she clearly did not intend to arouse his anxieties.

"You knew I would come?"

"I was hoping I could lure you into my web," she lowered her voice.

"I'm caught.

Do what you will."

"Don't worry, I'll make you the happiest man on Thera."

"But sometime today I should rehearse with my partner for our next entertainment," he said, wondering how he would explain to Clarice why he would not be staying in their room.

"Don't worry about her," the princess answered.

"You won't need to perform any more, except for me privately, and I already gave orders last night for the Master of Entertainments to send her to the king's labor pool.

I hope you don't mind.

She's probably already gone."

The palace lurched again in the way that had grown familiar during the last week, but the sensation seemed internal rather than related to the volcano, suddenly awakening some part of Orfeo that had been expertly lulled to sleep.

He must not allow Clarice to become a slave, and the very thought of it put everything Zaide had done into another light. The Therans were evil, he saw with a sudden blinding insight, and Zaide was one of them.

She had the power to dispose of Clarice, and therefore she had done so.

He could not remain here, and now it was more important than ever to escape.

His thoughts had abruptly returned to earth, and he could see again that whether his life was long or short, it would be with Clarice rather than this consummately selfish and heedless young woman.

But Orfeo knew this was a delicate situation in which he must pretend that nothing had happened.

He must take his time in returning to his room for his possessions, and then he must find the labor pool as quickly as possible.

He must rescue Clarice, and they must find a way to leave the island, but he now carefully arranged his departure so it would not appear that he was in a hurry.

"Is there a place where I can put my costumes and other parts of the act?"

"Tell the master to store them for you, and I will in the meantime have you dressed in greater luxury."

She looked pleased with herself, and no doubt she would always be pleased when every whim was satisfied.

"I'll be back soon," he embraced her warmly as he left and looked back appraisingly as if to fix the image in his mind.

He first went to his room and was not surprised to hear that Clarice had been taken away just after the performance.

He calmly went through the business of packing clothing to be taken upstairs and instructing the Master which of the costumes and props should be stored. Then he walked toward the stairs as if ready again to ascend to the upper levels, but instead he slipped out the side door and walked briskly down the hill toward the forum where he expected to find the king's labor pool.

Rumblings of the earth were even greater this morning, and he could see that some buildings had suffered damage, and several statues in the forum had fallen over and were already being righted.

Whatever the volcano was doing should have worried everyone, as there was even a red glow, but it seemed to be part of a patriotic Theran's duty to ignore the wrath of their god.

Not surprisingly, the people managing the labor pool seemed worried as he went indoors.

Some bricks on one wall had begun to crumble, but the net effect seemed to be to encourage them to focus upon something else.

To his surprise, Orfeo was able to learn where Clarice had been sent, and he hurried to a building near the harbor with no clear intention as to what he would do when he found her.

There were no guards in front of the building where he was told she was working, and he slipped inside a large room with several hundred wounded men lying on the floor.

Clarice was immediately visible, and she stood out from the others because she was still dressed as she had been the night before..

"I've come from the labor pool to question that woman," he spoke to a young man in uniform.

"And who sent you?"

The man appeared uncertain as to whether he should forbid it, but Orfeo assumed his most imperious scowl.

"I've been sent by the king's brother," he answered.

"And I will not be detained."

He started across the room toward Clarice, who appeared immensely relieved to see him.

She ran toward him and grasped his hands.

"We were too late," she said.

"I've been assigned here until the war's over, and even then I don't think they'll ever give me my freedom."

"We're leaving now," He looked around the room to see that he had attracted the attention of the only three armed men, who were all young and typically short Therans.

"But your brother is here," she whispered.

"I recognized him immediately, as he's a smaller version of you.

He has a broken arm."

She quickly led to a cot where Herron lay, greeting his brother with a sour look.

"So that's why it took so long," he said bitterly.

"They sent a boy to do a man's job."

Orfeo looked upon the smug countenance of a brother he had never loved.

Herron had always radiated an arrogance that seemed inspired by an inner awareness that he was far less a man than his father and lacked the intelligence of his insignificant younger brother.

"Is there a ship in the harbor ready to sail?"

Orfeo snapped impatiently.

"There are three ships nearly repaired," said Herron insolently.

"And what's it to you?"

"Are the oarsmen in place?"

"They're probably all in place, except for those like myself who were injured."

"How heavily guarded are they?"

"Four or five men," Herron spat the words.

"You're not thinking of anything crazy, I hope."

"Come along and help or die here," said Orfeo.

"Clarice and I have no time to waste."

Orfeo walked quietly across the room toward the only door and approached the guard with a smile.

Keeping in mind all the lessons and advice from Telemon, he disarmed and killed the first man with a deft move.

The other two came running and were dispatched with no more difficulty.

There was little outcry from the wounded men, as though they had barely noticed or perhaps were frightened even to be witnesses to something that should not have happened, could not have happened.

Orfeo walked resolutely down the street with Clarice, who had one of the weapons secreted in her dress.

Herron limped along, complaining, but also concealing one of the guards' swords, which he said he could use.

"If we must die, we should board the boat on which I was chained," he said.

"We have no chance at all to escape, but I know the men on that ship hate the Therans so much they will do anything to leave here."

They continued to walk, now noticing that smoke was again pouring from the volcano for the first time in several weeks.

The paving stones seemed to dance beneath their feet.

They reached the boat and were immediately challenged by the single harbor guard on duty.

"No one boards this ship without authorization," he seemed confident that his word alone would stop them, as he had not unsheathed his sword.

Orfeo cut him down with a quick thrust.

They were soon on the ship, as Orfeo cut down two guards on the deck and Clarice took another from behind.

Herron looked frightened.

Orfeo cut the two lines fastening the ship to the dock and pushed it free.

He then stepped down into the hold to see more than a hundred pairs of eyes staring back at him.

"I am Orfeo of the Achians," he spoke resolutely with little trace of his usual fear. There was no time for it, nor time for any hesitation.

"I am escaping from Thera, and I intend to sail this ship to the mainland and free all on board.

If we are caught, we will be killed, but the prospects for our survival are better if we run."

He raised his voice to a rousing exhortation.

"Death to the Therans," he called out. "Are you with me, or must I board another ship and kill more guards."

Herron looked stunned and was unable at first to say anything, but soon added his words of encouragement.

Within a few minutes they were underway, although someone had warned that they had no provisions for a major voyage but only enough for a few days.

"Remove the chains and throw them overboard," Orfeo instructed Herron, who found the keys above deck and was soon working to free his former shipmates.

Surprisingly, they cleared the harbor before there was any recognition by the Theran port officers that something was amiss, and it would take some time before other ships could be launched in pursuit.

The men had begun to chant as they seemed to put maximum effort into a journey that promised escape.

No one left the bench, and one of the lead men began directing, shouting commands to his cohorts as though they had suddenly coalesced into a team.

Herron limped onto the deck with his usual angry visage, obviously offended by his recognition that the detested younger brother had taken control.

"You always did resent me," Herron spoke with a bitter tone.

"All the Achians resented me, and my capture was no accident.

Men who could have saved me did not, and help could have been sent earlier." He made a disgusted sound and spat over the side of the vessel.

"And then they sent you," he laughed bitterly.

"The king sent Telemon, Orton, Zurga and me, because I knew the ways of Pylos.

When we found that you had been taken to Thera, we determined that I had a better chance of finding you alone.

And you might remind yourself that if I had not come along you would still be under guard with the other injured galley slaves."

The tone was unapologetic.

"You never wanted to rescue me."

Herron continued his angry attack.

"You just wanted to be king."

In looking back toward the island, Orfeo now saw that the smoke had increased, and the sounds were now immense.

Fire seemed to shoot from the top of the volcano, and even the sea had become rougher, as though the shaking was not confined only to the land.

There was still no sign of pursuit, although Orfeo expected that the fastest ships would be sent, and the commanders would be inspiring the oarsmen to greater efforts by the expedient of beating chained men.

Clarice had checked the provisions and began to distribute bread to the men, as one bank of oarsmen at a time ceased their work while the others continued.

They would have enough for the rest of the day and tomorrow, but the day after would be sparse with both food and water.

As the sky began to darken they had moved beyond sight of Thera, but now they could steer by the stars.

Orfeo had never navigated before, but knew that by going north and veering slightly to the left they would eventually hit the mainland, if only they could avoid the Theran boats blockading the harbor of Pylos.

"You don't know where you're going, do you?" said Herron with hatred in his voice.

In the last light of day Orfeo looked closely at his brother and began to wonder about the forces that had so darkened Herron's life.

His brother was now physically smaller, unfavored with a face that had become twisted in his bitterness, and now, after months in the galleys of a Theran ship, he was marked by the lash even on his brow. There was a large scar across his forehead, which seemed to be of recent vintage, and his hands were calloused like a laborer.

"Do you most hate me or yourself?" Orfeo asked.

Herron turned with barely suppressed rage.

"I should have strangled you when you were a babe in arms," he said.

"There were many times I could have done it, and I always wanted to do it."

He said.

"Then, when you were sent as a hostage, I thought we were rid of you, but our mother never looked at me the same again, as if it was my fault you were gone.

I know they would rather have sent me, but the council decided that it must be the younger son."

"Have you ever imagined what it meant to me to be torn from my family and taken to a strange land where I had a status little better than a slave?

Do you think I was the lucky one?"

"But you came back, didn't you.

And the king and our mother took you in, even though many on the council advised against it."

"Much happened that was neither my fault nor yours," Orfeo answered.

"But now we must work together to survive.

Now we must forget past wrongs and reach the northern shore before we are caught."

"When I'm king there will be no place for you among the Achians," muttered Herron.

"You have been the curse of my life, and I no longer need pretend that there is love between us.

For all I know you planned my kidnapping with the others who did not lift a hand to help me.

When this is all over, we will have a score to settle."

As he walked to the front of the ship, leaving Orfeo at the back to steer. Clarice stood behind him with her arms around him.

"I knew you would rescue me," she said.

"I was frightened, but I had placed all my faith in you, and there you were."

She said no more but leaned against him and made soft noises almost like a cat.

Behind them, although the island was no longer visible, the red glow of the volcano flickered and seemed to become ever brighter.

The rumbling continued.

# Chapter Twenty-Seven

At first light the brightness on the southern horizon had increased, but as daylight stole upon them sails were spotted against the red glow.

It seemed impossible that the pursuers had steered a course that was bringing them ever closer, but the stimulus of pursuit brought about greater efforts from the oarsmen, and Orfeo worked with several of the rowers who claimed to know how to set sails. Surely the oarsmen in the pursuing ships were being driven to their maximum capacity, but men desiring freedom had more incentive.

While the pursuers pulled closer during the morning, the rate of their advance was slowed.

Whether or not they were caught depended upon where they would strike land or rather in what lands the Theran armies were in control.

By afternoon the ships were obviously coming closer.

There was a rotation in which part of the crew took time out for a quick meal, but they were running out of food as well as energy.

How much longer could the Theran pursuers continue their relentless pace?

Could they have brought extra oarsmen aboard to relieve those who had been worn to uselessness?

"You still think you're the great rescuer?"

A full day of freedom had obviously done nothing to improve Herron's disposition, and now he seemed to blame his entire dilemma upon Orfeo.

"You tried to displace me as the future king, and now you've lured me into a futile attempt to escape.

I would have been better staying in Thera."

"If you were more concerned about escaping our pursuers, you could go into the hold and help the oarsmen stay together.

You could make yourself useful." Orfeo said.

"At least I would have stayed alive if I had remained behind."

"How long do you think you would have lived as a galley slave?

Do you think someone else would have come for you?"

"Telemon could have rescued me."

There was no use arguing with an embittered man who had never developed either the philosophy to accept his lot in life or the determination to change it.

He would have been an unsuccessful king, and his people would have suffered.

With none of the steady wisdom of Kiros or the military skills of Telemon, Herron would have failed to provide prosperity and safety for his people.

He was probably right that those with him when the slave raiders came probably did not risk too much to save him.

And all these years Orfeo had been perceived by him as an evil schemer.

It seemed ironic.

Orfeo went below to talk with the men, who were reaching the point of exhaustion.

He left Clarice at the wheel, as he did not trust Herron, and she knew how to keep the red glow in the sky immediately behind them as well as anyone.

They were rationing the water, as little remained, but there was hope for rain.

"The Theran ships pursuing us have gained slightly during the day, but we will be able to maintain a safe distance, and I believe they cannot drive their oarsmen any harder.

We are getting some help from the sails, as there is a steady tail wind that helps our pursuers as well.

As you know, we will be painfully executed if we are caught, but I believe we can reach land first."

The oarsmen cheered, but Orfeo was uncertain whether they believed him.

The problem was that they had no one aboard who could steer a safe course through the islands that lay between Thera and the mainland.

Paros, Naxos, Sifnos, and other smaller islands would seem to have provided safety for them except that they had long been dominated by Thera, and as soon as the ship landed they could be detained.

The problem was that they had to steer past the islands when they saw them, but so far even though they had presumably traveled far enough north, they had seen no land.

Orfeo questioned some of the more experienced oarsmen who had been seafarers before they had been captured by or sold to the Therans, but they were of little help.

There was no one aboard who could tell them just where they were or how far they had to go to reach safety.

If they had sailed westerly, however, they were likely first to reach the Peloponnese, large parts of which were ruled by Thera.

Pylos was yet farther to the west.

By the next morning the glow from Thera seemed to be fading, but the Theran ships were closer now and seemed to be steadily gaining.

Everyone aboard was hungry and thirsty.

Some of the oarsmen had come on deck to rest momentarily and take their last water ration when someone noticed that the distant glow of Thera had increased and continued to grow brighter.

Within a few moments a great thunderous sound seemed to buffet the sides of the ship, as now smoke began to fill the southern sky.

Had the volcano finally released its energy in a sudden violent explosion?

The other boat did not slow, and nothing seemed changed in their status even if horrifying things had happened on Thera.

"We left just in time," said Clarice.

"I fear those left behind are all dead."

"It was not our land," said Orfeo, "and the world will be better without its evil."

He had not slept more than a few minutes for two nights, and as he stood by the wheel it was becoming increasingly difficult to focus his thoughts.

He momentarily let his imagination stray to Princess Zaide, and somehow the thought of her leaving the world of the living did not trouble his thoughts.

When he had recognized the extent of her selfishness - just three morning ago - it had as much as extinguished any warmth he felt toward her.

When he had seen Clarice across the great room where the wounded were being treated for their injuries, he had known that he never again wished to live separately from her.

He had found something more meaningful to him than his people or any concept of loyalty to a city or a king or a master.

He knew that for the rest of their lives - short or long - they were bound together not by obligation but by choice.

The sky seemed to darken from the great plume of volcanic smoke, which seemed almost to be following and then overtaking them, blown by the wind.

“Are they still gaining on us?”

Clarice peered toward their pursuers and seemed puzzled. “I can’t see them.”

Orfeo looked back and could see only a whiteness, but no trace of the ships.

Then he looked again and realized what was wrong.

They were rapidly being overtaken by a great tidal wave that threatened to overwhelm them and smash the ship to kindling with its force.

Orfeo ran to the hold and shouted.

“Tidal wave.

Prepare to abandon ship.

Take the oars and cling to something.”

The men moved slowly, as if they could hardly believe in their danger.

Orfeo attached himself to Clarice with a rope and made certain she had her flotation belt as he began to inflate his.

The first part of the wave was now beginning to push the ship, but that could last only for seconds.

Everything seemed frozen in time as the boat first dipped lower into the water and then rose precipitously and for a moment seemed safe, but then it turned crossways to the wave and descended with the sound of shattering timbers and screaming men.

They were in the water and struggling to find the light.

The rope attaching them was perhaps eight feet long, and Orfeo caught sight of Clarice also struggling toward the light.

They broke the surface amidst scattered debris and slowly the bodies of men became visible, some unmoving, some trying to grasp pieces of the shattered vessel on which to cling.

Clarice seemed uninjured, but some of the oarsmen appeared to have broken bodies.

Behind the great tidal wave there were other smaller ones, with a period of unnatural calm between, as if the normal pattern of waves had been entirely disrupted by the great explosion and its reaction upon the surrounding sea.

Orfeo had caught the largest piece of a broken oar, and he and Clarice clung to it to lift their heads higher about the water.

"Gather round," Orfeo stuttered.

"There's safety in clinging together."

A group of other survivors, all grasping something floatable, began to form a crude circle.

"No ship could have survived that wave, and there will be no rescue," one of them shouted.

"I'll not give up while there's still life," replied Orfeo.

"None of us know what the gods have in store for us."

Others sounded a more hopeful message.

The fishermen will be out from the islands tomorrow," said one.

"They can't afford to stay in port when there are fish to catch.

The survivors were now clustered closer, and Orfeo could count nearly thirty, with three of them having lashed themselves to what was left of the main mast.

"Has anyone seen your former shipmate Herron, the one who came on board with me yesterday?"

Orfeo had found no trace of him and hoped for his safety despite his brother's bitterness.

But he did not appear.

With only one arm with which to swim, he may have remained submerged after the ship's destruction. Yet there was nothing to do now except to continue to look for other scattered survivors.

Each time he was born up by a swell, Orfeo continued to scan the surrounding sea, but of Herron no trace was ever found.

As darkness descended the survivors clustered ever closer together.

Some men expressed optimism and others bemoaned their doom, but all seemed to carry enough hope to cling to whatever support they had managed to grasp.

Orfeo and Clarice brought their torsos together for comfort and a feeling of security.

"We must survive," he said.

"I intend to make you my wife."

"So be it and so it has been," she said.

"Did you not know?"

"I had wanted it to happen when we were safe," he said.

"But as we left Kalamatta we were married by Nadahr," she said.

"You may have thought it was just pretense to make the guards let us go, but he and Zurga knew we were destined for each other. I knew it from your first word to me, maybe even before.

I think I knew it as I followed you through the streets that first evening."

"But why didn't you tell me?

Why did you wait until we were both facing a damp death?"

"Nadahr said you would know when the time came.

He said you still had to find your true self before we became one."

He kissed her and held her as best he could amidst the swells.

He did not know exactly where to address his prayers, as the Achians had identified themselves with the god of thunder and the men of Pylos with Aphrodite, but he hoped that someone would hear, and then he had nothing more to say.

"Do you think Zurga and Nadahr had a chance of escaping?" she asked.

"It's probably unwise to bet against Zurga," he said, "but he did not think they would leave the island alive."

"So you'll never be king of the Achians, and I won't be your queen."

She laughed.

"And the world must get by without Nadahr and Zurga to help guide them along the correct path."

"Poor world," said Orfeo, and he began to sing.

# Chapter Twenty-Eight

As dawn broke it was clear that the number of survivors had diminished during the night. Now there were a dozen men left and one woman, and they were all feeling weakened.

How many would still be alive at dusk no one would have been willing to speculate.

"I was once a fisherman," said one of the men.

"If I could only fashion a net I would try to catch us a fish."

"But how would we cook it?" asked another.

"I won't eat a fish unless it is properly cooked."

"You think the Therans were all cooked when their precious god destroyed their home?"

And so the desultory conversation went, as if they were all trying to stay awake.

Finally one of the men said, as if in jest, "I see a small boat.

Should I call out to it?"

Everyone looked around and, to their surprise, also saw a small boat approaching from the east. It must have set out after the tidal wave.

Soon they found themselves inspected by a grizzled captain of a small fishing craft.

"Do we have room for thirteen men?" he asked no one in particular.

"Might it be bad luck?"

"One of us is a woman," Clarice shouted.

"Ah, that makes it better.

We'll take the woman and leave the rest," he laughed.

"But first I must know whether you be for or against the Therans?"

"Most were galley slaves on a Theran ship," said Orfeo.

"We all want to reach the mainland and return to our people."

"If I bring you on board, I expect to be compensated," the captain said. "But I won't sell you to the Therans, who I reckon are not feeling so generous now."

The crew had already begun helping the shipwreck victims aboard.

Those who had now been in the water about a day and a quarter could barely stand and collapsed on the deck in weakness and gratitude.

"Get them something hot to eat and drink," the captain said.

When they were all on deck, Orfeo began to assess their situation.

"Where are you bound?

The great battle is coming up, and we want to take part,"

Captain Kithnos said.

"We're all men of Milos, and we've been slaves of the Therans ourselves, although they never called us slaves.

As the war went badly for them, some of our men decided to revolt, and one of the Wanderers was there to help."

"Was it Zurga or Nadahr?" Orfeo asked.

"Zurga, it was, and he told us the days of the Therans were coming to an end.

I think it was he who must have destroyed most of their island and the capital and Theran court as well," he smiled. "We've known Zurga these many years."

"I spoke with him on Thera," said Orfeo.

"He was doubtful about his own survival."

"Oh, he'll find a way.

He always does."

So they were safe, at least for now, heading toward landfall where the armies of Pylos and Lakonia were gathering together all the men they could to withstand the Therans and their allies.

It was not surprising to hear that Telemon was the leader of this army, and Orton still stood among his captains.

They too had survived the time of separation.

"Perhaps he'll have room for me someplace in his army," said Orfeo.

"I know why you must go," Clarice said, "but I hope it is the last time.

I want us to have all the time together we can."

"And when it's over, should we still be alive and free of Therans?" asked Orfeo.

"How will we live, where shall we go?

What have our experiences taught us to do better than anyone?"

"We could always be itinerant performers," she said.

"At least until you grow so old that the ladies no longer swoon when you sing romantic ballades."

Two days later they reached the small port of Lakonia, which was not being blockaded, but, according to Captain Kithnos, its overland communications with Pylos were blocked by enemy armies.

They were told that the headquarters of Telemon was about half a day's ride inland, and they traveled with Kithnos and his crew, who were determined to stand and be counted against the people who had kept them in slavery for three generations.

The other former galley slaves who were also rescued were asked to come along and fight Therans in compensation for being rescued.

It seemed a fair bargain to all.

"Do you actually know this warrior Telemon?"

Asked Kithnos.

"Is he really as much of a champion as his reputation would have it?"

"He's a man with much more subtlety than he is credited," said Orfeo, "but he will not hesitate to draw his sword and smite.

He is rash, but generally his judgment is good."

When they finally reached the tent of the great warrior, they could hear him bellowing orders.

When Orfeo the Achian and Clarice were announced, there was a great cry of delight.

"Welcome to the only living man who's ever bested me in combat," he burst from the tent and embraced Orfeo.

"My boy, you're quite as tall or even taller than I am now, but not so well muscled or as cunning."

Orfeo introduced his companions and the sea captain who had rescued him.

The sailors were assigned to companies of men, and Orfeo and Clarice were brought into the tent.

"We have heard from spies that the two of you actually reached Thera and had become popular entertainers, but how is it that you were able to escape?"

Orfeo told the story and described how they had rescued the wounded Herron, but that he had died in the shipwreck caused by the tidal wave.

"Did he die like an Achian?"

"His death was honorable."

Orfeo knew that there are times when the truth does not serve as well as a gentle untruth.

"And word of the Wanderers?

I heard reports that Zurga and Nadahr were stirring up trouble everyplace."

Telemon looked saddened.

"Zurga would probably not believe this, but I would miss him if he were no longer among the living."

Orton arrived in the midst of the stories, and he too was gladdened to see the two who had returned from the land of no return.

"There is yet another old foe on the field," Orton said.

"Do you recall the short Theran who tried to ambush us as we left Kalamatta?"

"Captain Meeka," said Clarice.

"He vowed to kill us all painfully."

"I have seen him once and came close enough for him to hiss the same threats," said Orton.

"That means he will be commanding a special brigade aimed at you and Telemon," said Orfeo.

"And perhaps he remembers even me."

"The stories of the Four of Pylos and the Six of Kalamatta have become legends," said Orton. "We have all become famous, or infamous, depending on the side you have taken."

"What role would you like to play in our army?" asked Telemon.

"Since Meeka will be less concerned about winning the battle than killing the men who humiliated him, then I must command a brigade to meet whatever treachery he puts forth."

"Well considered," said Telemon.

"I can't complain about having you defending my back.

In an hour we will have a council here and I will introduce you to the rest of our command," He looked at Clarice, who made no move to abandon her place by Orfeo.

"Are we going to have words about a woman accompanying her husband into a battle?" asked Orfeo.

"I know she is the inheritor of Nadahr's wisdom, and Nadahr and Zurga were from the same line.

We must have a place for her."

"If you remember, my lord Telemon, I was one of the Six of Kalamatta when Meeka promised our painful deaths, and I feel I have a right to stand against his revenge."

"But how can you be among the warriors?" asked Telemon.

"If you were there Orfeo would be more concerned about defending you than defending me."

He accompanied this with a laugh, but at the same time managed to look serious.

"But I know the secret of the Wanderer's fire, and I can fashion tubes that can be carried on horseback into battle.

I also know how to wait until the last minute to turn back warriors who have just begun to taste victory.

I must have help, but I can fashion a defense around you and my husband that will take the Therans by surprise."

"Although we six are now down to four again, I believe we are just as strong," Orton said.

"You will be the only woman on the field."

When the great council began, Orfeo sat on one side of Telemon and Orton the other.

The bandit chieftains arrived first, and they made their demands that if the Therans were beaten that they be allowed to occupy lands by which they could live without brigandage.

"When Praxis and Linaeus of Pylos arrive, we will make a settlement," said Telemon, and Praxis, the next king to walk into the tent, immediately agreed, mentioning a fertile valley in which the former brigands would be allowed to farm.

Linaeus was less willing, but Orton, who had been persuasive in urging the bandits to join with the army, supported their cause and urged concessions.

"When we have such powerful enemies, can we afford to maintain age old grudges?

If we cannot present a united front, the Therans will enslave us all and have us fighting their future wars of conquest just as they have turned the Kalamattans to their purposes."

As the other kings of hill tribes arrived, all had some concession to ask, and within reason it was granted.

Some asked to fight on a particular wing of the army, but on that score Telemon was reluctant to agree until he knew just where the armies would be arrayed against each other.

Scouts sent to chart the path of the invading army were in disagreement as to where the armies would meet, but on one question they were unanimous.

The Therans and Kalamattans had brought massive additions to their forces from the east, and they would outnumber the defenders at least two to one, probably much more.

Not one of the scouts seemed to have a clear estimate of the opposing forces, as each had seen different components.

The Achian King Kiros arrived with a group of his northern warriors, all of whom seemed to be dressed in imitation of their hero Telemon.

He was greeted and given a place in the circle, but not before he rose again and with a stricken face asked.

"The man sitting to your left, my lord Telemon.

He looks very much like my youngest son."

He looked with unbelieving eyes.

"And well you might be proud of him, my king, as he has fought more than once at my side and has earned his place here."

There was a silence that was unbroken until someone spoke out as the tension became unbearable.

"Orfeo is one of the Six of Kalamatta."

Clearly the legend had already traveled far about that day's adventures.

"He killed Therans under Meeka's command," said another.

"Father, I greet you warmly but with bad news," Orfeo rose and approached the old man who rose and embraced him with apparent misgivings.

"And have you found your brother?"

The old man spoke in a gruff voice.

"My wife and I traveled to Thera four months ago and finally, just before we left, we found Herron, where he had been placed in a hospital so that his wounds could heal.

He had been abused by the Therans as a galley slave, and we were able to commandeer a Theran ship and escape.

But before we reached land, we were overtaken by the great tidal wave.

Of two hundred on the ship only thirteen survived, including my wife and I."

"You have married without my permission," said the king, still not accepting of the news he had just heard.

"And when will you do me the honor of introducing your wife?" he asked caustically.

"May I present the Lady Clarice of the Wanderers."

Orfeo gestured to where she had sat silently and hooded, although he had noticed that she had been unobtrusively rearranging her hair and covertly applying the various unguents that changed her appearance.

When she arose and approached Kiros, she carried with her the radiance of a dream, the mystery of a long summer evening and a beauty that far outshone the Princess Zaide. It was as if Orfeo were also seeing her for the first time as his father beheld her.

She was unusually tall for a woman, and she carried herself with the grace of a lady born to the most sophisticated royal court.

"I will be on the field when we meet the Therans at your son's back protecting him, just as he will be protecting Telemon.

I was also one of the Six whom the Therans have vowed to kill, but we will prevail."

The old man stepped back as though struck, but it did not take him long to smile.

He approached her with an embrace and welcomed her to the family.

It was over quickly, and Telemon punctuated the scene with a great laugh.

"Your little son came to us as a raw lad, and now he is taller than his father and has become something of a combination between a warrior and a Wanderer and a diplomat of Pylos. We don't know exactly what to make of him except to call him Orfeo and feel happy that he is among us."

The tension was gone, and although he had just absorbed news that his eldest son was dead, Kiros seemed satisfied with the state of the world.

Battle plans were laid in theory, considering that no one as yet knew where the encounter would come.

But just before they were to break up, a scout arrived with news that a force of at least ten thousand men had been landed between Telemon's army and the sea .

This now began to seem like they could be hit from all four sides.

Perhaps the battle would occur tomorrow, and in such case they had better prepare quickly.

The scouts that had already reported were roused from their slumber and sent out again to bring up-to-the-minute word of where the various contingents of the enemy happened to be at the moment.

"Surprise attack is a trademark of the Therans," Linaeus of Pylos spoke.

"It has been our experience that they do not attack unless they can do it in stealth."

On the table in front of Telemon one of the commanders had drawn a map in chalk of their present position, and he had drawn squares showing the disposition on their own army versus components of the Therans.

Adding the recently landed group from the south would seem to have increased the Theran's numerical advantage and also made retreat to the sea impossible.

Two hours later, with only a few of the leaders remaining in Telemon's tent, other scouts arrived on exhausted horses with news that the Therans had moved closer and were even now on the march.

Other scouts did not return, which suggested they had been intercepted.

Telemon had often boasted that he never made a camp that he could not defend, but he seemed to think better of his disposition.

Ordering that the main body of the army leave their campfires burning, they were to occupy a nearby hill with a rounded top.

The Achians and other hill tribes were to be held in readiness to cut off the soldiers advancing from the south, while the brigands were to seek defensive positions in their own hills, which one large contingent of the Theran army would be forced to cross before they could fall on the men of Pylos they hoped to find sleeping.

As for the bulk of Telemon's cavalry, which had not yet been assigned a position, there were questions as to how it should be deployed.

"We will take no position," he said.

"We're riding east until we find the advancing body of their army, and then we'll attack them before they can devise a new plan."

# Chapter Twenty-Nine

THERE HAD BEEN LITTLE TIME for Clarice to prepare her surprise, but Telemon assigned to her a group of women who had accompanied their brigand men to the battle.

She would work on preparing the necessary powder and would remain as close as possible to Telemon's troop, in which Orfeo was the member focusing specifically upon Meeka's brigade.

They were all prepared to leave when a horseman appeared at a sedate pace.

As he was the only rider that night who had not been flying in great haste, the men of Telemon's troop looked up curiously.

"I suppose you don't need me to tell you that they'll be trying to surprise you well before dawn."

It was Zurga, looking grayer and perhaps frailer, but unmistakably alive.

To the various questions, he replied that rumors of his death merely represented the wishful thinking of some.

But he confirmed that Nadahr had, indeed, perished in their attempt to escape the island.

He also took some of the credit for the volcano's explosion, which, he confirmed, had completely destroyed the city and had resulted in the death of the country's king and nobility.

"If we defeat their armies here, they will not again in the next century, perhaps never, pose such a threat to us, and either the army about to attack you does not fully understand the disaster at home, or it is being kept from them by their leaders."

It was the same old Zurga, dispensing wisdom that was, as usual, right in its basic message. "But make no mistake, if they win they will have absolute control over this area, and they may be able to dominate without their home island. The battle is crucial for your freedom."

This was hardly news, and there was always the reassurance of something familiar in his voice and pronouncements.

He consulted briefly with Telemon and Orton, but he had no real advice, as he did not know the disposition of the troops on either side, nor did he know the numbers of the Theran troops.

He then took Orfeo aside for a personal conference.

"With Herron gone, you must be the next king of the Achians when your father dies."

"And just how does that fit in with your plans?" Orfeo asked.

"It means the northern tribes that are often thought by the rulers of the great seaports to be barbarians, will come under the sway of a man who knows the sophistication of the world.

Your experiences, particularly in Pylos and Thera, have given you a unique viewpoint for a hill tribesman, and your people need to become more a part of the civilization that is now turning our world into a richer and more humane place."

"What about the fact that the typical Achian tribesman considers me as little better than a traitor to his traditions?

And what about the wishes of my father?"

"You will acquit yourself well in the battle today and will probably survive.

But even if the battle is lost, the Achians will continue to exist, and they will need a king when your father is gone."

"Let us speak of realities when the battle is done and we know whether we must become slaves or continue as free men."

Zurga smiled as though he had carried his point, but there was much to transpire before he would know.

In the meantime the army's vanguard now set out, led by Telemon and Orton, and they intended to ride for the hour or two or three necessary to close with the advancing main force of the Therans before daybreak.

Hopefully it would be a total surprise, but if they were at too great a distance Telemon's force would be exhausted on spent horses by the time they arrived.

And if the Therans learned of their coming, even ten minutes before their arrival, they could prepare a reception from fixed positions.

Whatever happened would be a close call, and each rider knew that he could either cut into an oblivious Theran mass or meet a well prepared, confident enemy.

They rode for an hour with no sign of the invaders, and by the end of the second hour they had slowed and were beginning to wonder whether their intelligence had been correct.

There were no Therans here, and Orfeo was beginning to wonder whether they had somehow missed the Theran advance.

But just after they reached the top of a small hill, the Therans were there, caught entirely by surprise, moving forward more slowly and not arrayed in any kind of formation.

The only factor that made a contest of the engagement was that they were far more numerous than anyone had imagined.

Telemon, not taking precautions with his own safety even though he was the leader, charged into a mass of Theran officers who were leading the column, but who would surely have gravitated toward the rear in the combat they imagined.

Instead they were cut down like stalks of wheat before the scythe, helpless in the face of a foe they could see but could not stand against.

Across a widening front the Therans could do nothing to establish a line, even when they had minutes warning before actually encountering a soldier of Pylos or an Achian.

But the very success of the venture became a liability.

Telemon's forces could not kill half of this army and then return to the original site of their camp - where the main battle would probably take place - leaving even half of this force in their rear.

It could then surely be reorganized by some effective officer, who could bring it into the battle later in the day.

There was no choice but to take this force so close to extermination that the survivors could only straggle off into the hills and hope to escape the general conflagration.

And so they remained not just to defeat this part of the enemy hydra, but to crush it past any hope of revival.

And this took valuable time while there would no doubt soon be fighting at the camp.

It was when the job of destroying the first wave of Therans was accomplished that Telemon had to urge his tired men to greet the daybreak with a determined trek back the way they had come.

They had won the first part of the battle, but now they faced the bulk of the Theran army, tired and with nearly spent horses.

And so they rode back, not as quickly as they had ventured forth, but they could hear battle ahead as they neared the scene, and Telemon ordered the column to move westward so that they would hopefully strike the Therans in the rear.

At least they could enjoy the element of surprise for the second time that morning.

Obviously the Therans had fallen for the bait and attacked the campfires that had been left burning, thus showing their location and strength without achieving the least element of surprise.

Yet the force that attacked them was slowly being overwhelmed by sheer numbers.

The tide of battle briefly turned as Telemon and his warriors cut a great path through the Theran rear, but the enemy numbers were so great that even this massive blow was eventually absorbed, and Telemon's army became engulfed on all sides by forces that outnumbered them perhaps five to one.

And it was here that Meeka's special brigade of assassins - all wearing the traditional red hats of Theran death squads - began to seek their prey with a deadly efficiency that could not be deflected onto lesser targets.

Orfeo's sword had worked hard during the first engagement, but now he began a relentless trajectory of his own directly toward Meeka, who so far had focused only upon Telemon.

It was a difficult path, as the battle raged fiercely with both mounted and unmounted troops, but Orfeo maintained his mount, losing a foot of distance for every two he advanced.

And Meeka's ruthless assassins had already begun to cut into the group of men around Telemon.

Orfeo spurred on his own mount and exhorted his troops to push harder, but they were meeting the resistance of men inflamed by the hope of conquest and honor and riches.

Yet the Theran allies fought as hard as the Therans, believing that their status just above slavery demanded that they sacrifice all for the Theran standard.

At one point Telemon turned on the red-hatted attackers and felled those closest to him, and this gave Orfeo the opportunity to come closer and interpose himself with his closest troops.

The leader had pulled again toward a safer route, cleaving his way through the ordinary rank and file who broke before him with little resistance.

Linaeus himself had joined the battle with his son Nestor, who engaged and finally stopped the advance of the western wing of the Theran army Troops that landed the night before from the south had finally arrived, adding yet more bulk to the assault, but Zurga and Kiros led a group of hill tribesmen in cutting them down nearly as fast as they could reach the field of battle. The Theran plan had obviously included both surprise and massive numerical superiority.

They would not have begun the battle unless they considered the odds to be overwhelmingly in their favor.

Again Telemon seemed threatened by the red hats, who were aided by a maneuver of their own troop to form a corridor into which the red-hats could charge toward the great Achian champion.

In response Orfeo led his band, now drained of numbers, and again he managed to interpose himself between the enemy and Telemon's own guard.

But the assassin troop pressed so hard that it seemed they must break through.

At this point Orfeo took off his helmet and shouted to Meeka, who was now less than twenty feet away.

"Naked Meeka, bootless little man," he bellowed over the commotion.

"I am one of the Six, and I've come again to take your boots."

At this the enraged Theran turned his wrath toward Orfeo, who charged headlong at him.

Although he was unable to land a blow on Meeka, he disabled his horse, while the latter's men clustered around to allow him to change mounts.

But they paid dearly for the rescue, as Orfeo clove the nearest and was again threatening Meeka before too many other red-hats crowded into his path.

But Telemon continued to plow through the opposition, whose numbers slowed him down and would ultimately tire him so that he would eventually lose the strength to keep lifting his sword and smiting.

And then another brigade of men suddenly placed red plumes upon their helmets and joined Meeka's assassins.

It had been a trick, but one which worked well enough, and now even Telemon had to turn from the business in front of him and defend his back.

Orfeo was there striking right and left at the charging assassins, now bent only on taking out the leader of the Six and any others of that legendary group of heroes who had beaten the Therans once in their very stronghold of Kalamatta.

Now vengeance was at hand.

And it appeared to be succeeding, as even the terrifying devastation of Telemon's sword was not enough, as he continued to back away, but there was no easy route to take through the enemy army now behind him.

Orfeo continued to slash as he saw the mighty Orton go down, now beneath the horses, one arm limp and couched to his side.

Telemon smote the man who had struck his companion, but even in doing so had to back up where there was no space to retreat.

The noose was tightening.

"The Six shall perish in this hour," shouted Meeka.

"Theran honor shall be avenged, and we will kick their heads across the field in a game."

Orfeo was now nearly close enough to smite him, but the leader of the red hats kept lurching forward toward Telemon until more than a dozen stood on all sides of the great champion, trying to break his defense.

Orfeo defended his back, but Orton, whether dead or alive, had been left behind, while Telemon was taking blows to the legs and arms.

These would not kill him, but they weakened him, and at times he seemed to totter.

Orfeo was now unhorsed as was Telemon, but the press of bodies around them kept any men still mounted from coming closer.

And then an armored man with a red hat carrying a small tree trunk charged into the crowd.

It looked bleak, as the weapon seemed aimed at Telemon, but suddenly it turned and exploded in a great outpouring of fire from the other end.

Meeka fell, instantly incinerated.

The others drew back in indecision as another great flame shot toward them.

The odor of burning flesh seemed to dishearten the attackers.

The rider who wore a red hat was neither a Theran nor a man, as Clarice had joined the fight with a weapon that seemed suddenly to take the resolve from an army that still outnumbered those fighting with Telemon.

From this point on the slaughter began, and Orfeo shouted an order that suddenly turned members of the enemy against each other.

"Kill every Theran, but spare any Kalamattan who throws down his weapon and leaves." He shouted it again, and the cry was then taken up by others.

It seemed to make every man of Kalamatta on the field stop to consider.

If he could merely walk away while his slavemasters were killed, did he really want to give his life for a cause that was not his?

Did it really look as though the Therans would win now that the red hats had been vanquished?

From that moment the Kalamattans on the field began to fade away, and some even slew the Therans who came after them, either to escape themselves or to urge the Kalamattans back.

The massive army that moments before had seemed on the brink of a great victory now seemed to waver and begin to give way.

First a few men began to run away, and then more stragglers.

As Theran officers would ride up to order them back, the officers suddenly came under attack from men who had just moments before been under their command.

The battle was not won while there were still so many Therans on the field, but the change of direction accelerated.

The last Theran reserves were committed before noon, and a significant number of them - perhaps all the Kalamattans - never reached the line of battle, but found ways to disappear.

A battle thus became a slaughter, made all the more bloody by the proverbial unwillingness of the Therans ever to surrender.

They continued to fight when it was hopeless, when they were surrounded even by countless enemies from whom escape would be impossible.

They fought until the only Therans remaining were those too injured to raise a sword against their enemies, and even then the survivors muttered curses and threats.

And so the clamor of battle quieted, and the field was held by Telemon and his army.

All the Therans had been committed to the battle, and - as Zurga had suggested - they had no way to recover their numbers after the massive loss of life with the destruction of most of their island.

Orfeo found Orton among the fallen and recognized that although unconscious he still clung to life.

He and Clarice carried him to the command tent, where the physicians were called, but it was Clarice - who had learned healing from Nadahr - tended him non-stop, muttering that one of the fabled Six had died on Thera, but it was too soon for another soul to depart.

Telemon had taken heavy wounds, but he retained his ability to eat and sleep, and after the battle he simply retreated to his bed until the next morning, when he awoke in time to call a council before the various components of his army began to drift away toward their native lands.

Murray Lee Eiland Jr.

# CHAPTER THIRTY

As the great council began to gather, Telemon walked wearily to his place at the head of the table and began with an announcement. "My dear friend and companion Orton will live," he said, "but I fear that his wounds are so severe that he will never fight again."

"Orton will fight even if he is left with one leg and a single arm," a voice from the back of the tent spoke with warmth.

"He was a mighty machine of war yesterday."

"We all have much to be proud of, but what we learned about ourselves is even more important." Telemon began a message that was to be repeated among his people long after he was gone. "What we learned is that we are a single people, even though some of us speak with a slightly different sound.

Even though we live in different cities and in different tribes, we are still one.

And together we showed that we could not be beaten."

Orfeo marveled at the diplomacy that had at times lain hidden within this mighty warrior, but now he knew there was a message beyond what could be delivered with his sword.

"We must remember the lesson of this day and remind ourselves that when the call to convene came, there is not one of our leaders who refused.

Every tribe, every city, town, and each village responded, and with the help of all we were able to survive."

"I move that we have a council every year at this time to reaffirm our commitment to each other and to settle grievances that have arisen."

Surprisingly the speaker was King Kiros of the Achians, who had traditionally felt least connected to the larger group.

Today, he was not the aloof, angry man of years gone by, but a true believer.

The others eagerly gave their assent, but Kiros remained standing as if he had further business.

"Two days ago I learned what I had feared for a long time that my eldest son Herron no longer lived.

Yesterday I witnessed that my youngest son has grown to a manhood that does credit to his family and his people."

"I fear I would not be here today were it not for young Orfeo and his beautiful wife," Telemon added.

"Between them they destroyed the red hats and helped turn the tide of battle."

"I bring this up not to boast of my son's exploits, but first to welcome Clarice as the wife of my son and as my daughter as well," Kiros continued.

Clarice rose, again radiantly beautiful with a mane of golden hair that seemed to move even when she stood still.

"I would also like to affirm that Orfeo is my true and only heir and will become king of the Achians upon my death."

This seemed to surprise everyone, most of all Orfeo, who rose to respond, but Zurga was first to speak.

"It seems only yesterday that I found young Orfeo as a young man with no apparent status among his tribesmen, but the search for Herron has brought out qualities that I always suspected he had.

I believe he would make a strong and just king."

Orfeo then began to speak in an almost imploring voice.

"Dearest father, I thank you for welcoming my wife, whose exploits on the field yesterday and, hopefully, in the years to come, will bring great pride to you.

But I have another suggestion for the kingship, and this I say in all sincerity.

While those of the Achian warriors who fought beside us yesterday may welcome your decision, I know that most of the tribe see me as more of a city dweller than a tribesman, and there would be some dissension should you make this announcement closer to home."

He paused to give his words time to sink in.

"While I am grateful for your confidence in me, may I suggest that our kinsman Telemon, who has become such a skilled and unifying diplomat, would help unite rather than divide the tribe if he were your successor.

Then, should I outlive the great warrior, who is thirty years my senior, the matter could be reconsidered by the council."

"But what about now?"

Kiros said.

"Will you be with us?"

"For better or for worse, Clarice and I have already become Wanderers, and it is now the life we are suited for.

But that means you will see us in times of need.

We will always be there, just as you always seemed able to find Zurga."

"Orfeo will also be welcomed in the court of Lakonia," Praxis spoke with evident warmth.

"And he will always have his own apartment in the palace of Pylos, where he and Clarice can give both counsel and entertainment."

Linaeus spoke in tones of both respect and affection.

Three hours later the council ended with a universal agreement to the terms set out by Telemon at the very beginning.

Telemon returned to the Achians with Kiros, and Orfeo and Clarice accompanied them on their journey.

Yet they soon were called to Kalamatta to help with the reorganization of that city, whose prospects had risen since the Theran yoke had been thrown off.

Following the council, all the Theran ships that had been abandoned on the beach after they had unloaded their troops were seized and sailed to Pylos, where they were converted from ships of war into ships of trade, in which they moved by sail rather than by galley slaves.

Indeed, Pylos prospered, and when Linaeus's heir Nestor decided to become a priest, Orfeo became the heir and eventually was King of Pylos, ruling with his radiant, golden haired queen Clarice, formerly of the Wanderers.

They were followed by a long line of descendants.

# An Historical Note

During the early phases of preparing this book for publication, the question arose as to just how much of the story had survived over the centuries and how much of it might be a work of more recent fiction, or is the story based upon actual events, and did the personages described here actually exist?

While one might expect a clear affirmative or negative answer, the matter is not nearly so simple.

The one thing we know with absolutely certainty is that Thera exploded in a violent volcanic eruption that destroyed much of the island and sent a great tsunami that devastated low lying areas of other islands in the eastern Mediterranean.

Thera, in greatly reduced form, still exists, although it is now known by the name Santorini and its shape – with a great crater now mostly covered by the sea – gives a clear outline of the island's original contour.

It is not so clear, however, just when this happened, and various dates, most around the mid-fifteenth century, B.C., have been given as estimates, usually based upon questionable records from neighboring areas.

No undisputed historic evidence has survived, however, suggesting that the inhabitants of Thera constituted a threat to their neighbors, and if it had not been for the chance archaeological discovery in the hills behind ancient Pylos of an elaborate, undisturbed fifteenth century B.C. tomb, then all awareness of the importance of this event in the historical record would have vanished.

But the manuscript found in the tomb is also problematic.

It appears as hundreds of large pages of Egyptian papyrus, only a small fraction of which have currently been translated, and this story occupies only slightly more than 5% of the surviving pages.

But problems were present from the very beginning of the manuscript's assessment.

First of all, Papyrus is not as durable as stone or clay tablets, and no other Papyrus manuscript has been found in what is now modern Greece from that early time period, although smaller papyrus documents survive from Egypt.

Because of this several noted scholars have suggested that the manuscript is a late forgery.

The other problem, perhaps even greater, relates to the language.

There are two scripts, or forms of writing, that appear in the Aegean region at about the time from which this great manuscript is thought to have originated.

Linear A and Linear B, while related to the forms of writing that later developed into our modern Greek and Roman alphabets, have introduced many questions around translation.

Linear B is now known to have been used by the Mycenaean Greeks, and a number of inscriptions in this alphabet have been translated.

Unfortunately, Linear A has not been translated so that everyone agrees on just what sounds the letters represent.

Consequently, there are those who believe it was used for a Semitic language and others who believe that it – like Linear B - relates to an early Greek dialect.

My own contribution to this controversy is the translation of the first part of this great papyrus manuscript into an early form of Greek and subsequently into English.

Thus the saga of Orfeo re-emerges.

But this has presented problems from the very beginning of my efforts.

While I am preparing publication of a volume dealing only with the language, which I hope will settle the controversy, I have been so fascinated with the manuscript that I have devoted most of my efforts to telling the story, leaving aside the technicalities until later.

Yet I may have introduced another complication by making changes in the manuscript itself.

What one might notice most prominently about the original is that there are so many references to the intervention of gods in the development of the story that I have arbitrarily made the editorial decision to leave out most of this material.

The narrative, which I see as an inspiring coming-of-age saga of a most remarkable young man, would only have been crippled by frequent interjections of the several dozen gods and goddesses who are described as taking an interest – both positive and negative – in Orfeo's adventures.

Particularly when the gods argue among themselves for page after page as to how he should behave, it seems appropriate for the modern reader to have much of this material expunged.

Later, when the scholarly version of this book goes to press, all the material will be included, but here it would only interfere with the enjoyment of those who should find most interest in the story.

So what I can say to help the reader place this story in context is that it takes place in the early world of Greece well before the classic period.

It can be dated as occurring at the same time as the eruption of Thera, although that date is not know for certain by historians.

On a map I have arranged the places described together, as best I could from the text, although parts of it – particularly in the interior of the Peloponnese – are speculative.

It is useful to recall that in the 15th century B.C. the Greek cities of Athens and Sparta, which became prominent later, are not so important, and many of the cities that were powerful when this story occurs – such as Pylos – later became far less important.

Several of my colleagues have suggested that the events described here may possibly have inspired the story of Orfeo and Euridice, in which the hero attempts to rescue his beloved from the underworld, but I consider this highly unlikely.